Conversations with…

THE

FRIEND

Conversations with…
The Friend

Pearl Olsen

Prós Publishing

ISBN 978-1-917049-00-9

First Published by Prós Publishing 2024

Website: prospublishing.com
Email: connect@prospublishing.com

Poem *Almost Valentine's Day Again*
© Brian Docherty

Email: hello@briandochertypoet.com

Front cover photo © Pearl Olsen

Back cover photo and cover art design (front and back)
© Design WAV

Website: designwav.com

Dedication

This book is dedicated to my Friend. He who knows me best
and is the reason why I wrote it.

Acknowledgements

Creative writing for me personally is a strange way to spend time — it involves constant learning, hard work and frequent failure. So why do it at all? Well, I believe everyone has a voice, even if it remains silent much of the time. Sometimes it has a need to shout out loudly to the world. For me, creativity is part of being a human; as is a desire to entertain and occasionally provoke.

This book is fictional — it does not describe real people or true events. Any resemblance to reality is purely coincidental. It arose out of a Pandemic Lockdown challenge set by some writing friends, Edel McGrath and Nettie Bowie based in County Wexford, The Republic of Ireland. We had done a basic Creative Writing course together which had catapulted me into the writing world. I must thank one of our tutors in particular, the writer S.A Dunphy, who provided me with early mentoring on some other projects. The next important person to join the journey of this novel was Michael Freeman from Three Sisters Press, a Wexford based independent publishing company. He read the original draft of *Conversations with…The Friend* and was so encouraging, I persevered with honing it further.

Another publishing professional who contributed to the assessment process was Lana Hughes, and she urged me to tell more. And if you can cross paths with someone eminently qualified to have a look too, then that is great. That person was Bishop Laurie Green who pushed me to get the book out there. The poet, Doctor Brian Docherty (briandochertypoet.com) furnished the poem *Almost Valentine's Day Again*© to use in the story, and also kindly proofread the final manuscript.

Lastly, my thanks to the person who has stood steadfastly alongside me; encouraged and pieced me back together when the weight of it all crushed me; whose belief in me has never wavered — my daughter, Eilís.

In short, all were human angels to whom I will always be grateful.

Chapter 1

Booted footsteps echoed down the hall and her stomach danced, keeping in time with the rhythm. Feeling lightheaded with anticipation, she felt something else too. A small stirring within her chest, like a trapped and anxious butterfly. She knew it signified something important. Struggling to understand, she realised it alluded to a split in her existence. A separation that yearned to be bridged. It was a longing for.…

The dream is snatched away by the insistent sensation of running perspiration. A slippery layer has formed between her skin and the synthetic fabric M&S pyjamas she wears. Imperceptibly sliding her forefinger, she feels reassured that by pressing the orange wine gum button resting on the light blue cotton hospital blanket, a nurse will be summoned.

Torn between the comfort of feeling clean and what that would endure, she lacks the strength to have the bedclothes stripped from her limp body and undergo another mauling. Where she will shiver despite the tropical temperature in the room. A sudsy sponge rasp her flesh and no rinsed cloth offered to wipe away the soap because of time constraints, leaving her in a cloud of sour vapour from its residues. Just let the sweat dry, she tells herself. Reeking of body odour is the least of her problems.

The jabbing dagger had broken through her reverie. Perhaps it had been that which had stolen her sleep story and shoved her back into the real world. Predicting what will transpire if she ignores it, she finds the impetus to move her other hand, reach the machine pump and depress the trigger. The process of engaging her lumpen body initiated, she shifts her tired skeleton into a different position, one that relieves the pressure a little. The pain will subside if she waits patiently and accepts the bodily processes she is prisoner to. She has learnt that the hard way.

Unnoticed, her Friend looking relaxed in the armchair next to the bed, speaks, 'darling, did you ever imagine yourself being in this position? I mean, considering how relatively young you are?'

The implications of that simply worded enquiry catches her off guard. A rapid video of scenes, complete with different characters whirrs through her head and uncomfortable emotions stampede across her heart.

A different voice takes her attention, 'Ruth, how are you this morning?' Senior nurse Sonia has opened the door and nursing assistant, Mary O, to differentiate her from all the other Marys working on the ward, follows behind with a blood pressure monitor. The two women take no notice of her Friend as though he is invisible. 'We'll just help you sit up a small bit — that's it — how's the pain? Let me see, you took a shot half an hour ago — that's good. Now remember — take a shot for the pain before the pain takes you. We'll come back later to give you a good wash. I'm sure you'll feel so much better after that.'

Her Friend silently observes the nurses as they depart pulling the monitor with them and he addresses her again. 'Do you remember Maura Mahoney?'

Maura Mahoney?

She has not given that woman a single thought for years. Maura, God Bless her, was someone who drove her to distraction. Whenever the older woman entered the shop, her heart would sink. A widow with children who had escaped long before, Maura had a daily round collecting an item or two from each of the shops, and would gossip with staff and customers for as long as she could get away with. If she could get to Maura first, she would dispatch her in a businesslike, or professional manner she would rather think and steer her to the door. If she was occupied with another customer or a company rep, Lisa or one of the assistants could be monopolised for a good half hour.

But worst of all was when Paudie heard Maura's voice. He would fly from behind the glazed dispensary like a flapping wood pigeon and give Maura all the time she wanted.

On the face of it, Maura was one of hundreds and it perturbed her to have such antipathy towards a customer, particularly as she considered herself a caring woman. When Maura eventually succumbed to a real illness, a long drawn out one where everyone was regaled with updates on symptoms, procedures and treatments, she had to fight back her impatience and irritation even more. At Maura's funeral Mass, she silently begged forgiveness for her lack of empathy and common kindness.

'You're wondering why I ask about Maura. And you're trying to work out why she got to you,' her Friend slides the chair closer. 'To you, she seemed a silly, attention seeking woman who loved to talk about the failings in others.' Leaning forwards a little, 'but think about it, Ruth. Deep down, you knew she only did that because it made her feel better about herself — that is — be of a higher moral standard than other people because there was precious little else in her life to make her feel good.' Warming to his argument, 'like most women of her generation, especially in this area, scant regard was given to Maura's education. Nor to any possible career. The expectation was that she should marry and raise a family. And that would largely have been the extent of her achievements.' Sitting back, tugging and stroking his beard in thought, 'when she lost her husband, she not only lost her companion, regardless of whether the marriage was good or not, she also lost status. Then to compound her loneliness and lack of purpose, all her children decided to move away to find better opportunities.' Watching her face closely, 'but you understand all of that, Ruth, don't you? You've witnessed it so often, haven't you?'

A bang on the door heralds Tilly pushing in the breakfast trolley. Oblivious to the visitor in the room, 'hello, gorgeous! Whoops — sorry,' Tilly giggling. 'We've just been told by

Management to only call patients by their name — sorry, Ruth,' laughing some more. Then in a tender tone, 'will you have some porridge? Or Weetabix softened in warm milk? Is your mouth sore, sweetheart? Sorry, Ruth? Mary will come help you to eat it. I'd help you myself, but I've to finish the rest of the ward.' Tilly manoeuvres her bulk backwards through the doorway, pulling the trolley.

While they wait for assistance, her Friend resumes talking. 'I'd put it to you, Ruth, that Maura troubled you because she highlighted painful issues for you.' Settling back in the chair, and crossing his legs. 'Let me explain what I mean. Firstly, she was a local and knew everyone, and everyone knew her. She was accepted as one of the town's own, although she wasn't particularly likeable. You were only a "blow-in", as they say. Just a stranger and you would always be considered as such. You suspected that no matter how much you tried to win people over, or gain their admiration — or even just their respect — they would withhold something of themselves from you. It didn't matter how hard you worked — whatever selfless service you offered — if calamity was to strike, you never fully trusted the townspeople to support you. When Maura criticised others, you imagined that's what you would get from the community too, if you fell from your pedestal.' Shrugging his shoulders, 'but that's normal behaviour in small societies, that is, to look after their own. In order of priority,' counting down with his fingers. 'First support themselves and their own families.' Hooking his middle finger, 'then other community members.' Tapping his ring finger, 'and then, if there's anything left over — then the outsiders. It's how to survive harsh conditions where the production of food in particular, is dependant on uncontrollable factors such as poor land, erratic weather or pestilence. Poverty and subsistence farming have been the history of your adopted home, you know that. Up until relatively recently, it's been a rural area with poor transport connections, far from the big cities and insular in attitudes with few new arrivals to bring in different perspectives —'

Mary O enters interrupting her Friend in mid flow. Seeing no-one other than Ruth, she deftly takes a handful of paper towels from the dispenser near the sink and strides over to the bed while offering a greeting. Spreading the towels to protect the bed covers, Mary picks up the porridge and scoops a small spoonful. Making conversation, 'will those lovely girls be in to see you today, do you think, Ruth? And have you heard from Daithí?'

Speaking slowly between painful mouthfuls, 'I don't know — they're so busy — they have their own lives — I don't want them feeling obliged.'

'Ah now, Ruth, I'm sure they don't begrudge time with you. You've been a great Mam to them. I'm sure the least they'll want to do is help you now. Let them know you want to see them. It'll be as important for them as it is for you.'

Silently wondering how Mary could know what kind of mother she has been, but responding politely, 'Deidre maybe — I'm sure she'll call in — after school — But Sophie has exams — and work — and she's renovating — her new house.'

'Here, have this soft wipe for your mouth. Can you manage? Or will I do it for you? I'll be back as soon as we're able — you know, to help Nurse Sonia with your wash. Talk to you later, Ruth.'

Sensing that Mary is committed to her patients, she also recognises that the woman is under pressure to complete multiple care tasks during a busy shift. She does not like to ask for too much as other patients are probably more dependent than her.

The figure in the chair begins again, 'as I was saying, back to Maura. Another issue was time. Maura had lots of it. And it needed filling. Whereas you never had enough of it, as you well know.'

She knows everything he has said is true. Every point that her Friend brought up is completely valid and she knows she cannot deny it, either to him or to herself, even if she had the energy to protest. There is little to be gained from doing so as it is all in the past and of little relevance now. She begins to ponder why he has thought to raise it at all when to her dismay, she hears the boom of a familiar voice in the corridor.

The door is pushed back swiftly on its hinges and in pours the Consultant, Dr Mulhall, followed by a larger than normal team of medics with Nurse Sonia at the rear.

'Mrs O'Sullivan, good morning, how are you? May I sit down?' repositioning her Friend's chair before she can accede.

The team move in formation around the bed and peer down at her. Some have curiosity on their faces as though she is an interesting laboratory specimen; others have indifferent expressions.

'Dr Geraghty, would you care to take over please?' The Consultant sits back and claws his hands over the arm ends of the chair reminding her of a Sphinx. Noticing a gold signet ring on his little finger, she finds it coordinates with equally expensive looking cufflinks that restrain crisp white cotton, long at the wrists. A matching tiepin adorns his soberly striped silk tie. An expensively suited prig, dotted with incongruent flashy gold is her assessment. He is like some car showroom salesman, she decides.

A young woman about the same age as Deidre, she guesses, performs elaborate hand washing rituals at the sink. Gliding over with a smooth smile, she seeks permission for a body examination. The Formation agog observes Dr Geraghty's performance closely. Wondering why, she thinks maybe they want to catch Dr Confident out. Or perhaps they predict an individual interrogation from The Leader later. Sensing an uneasy tension, she cogitates about that too. Is it competitiveness between ambitious high flyers, or is it fear? There is a nuance she cannot quite identify.

'Excellent — thank you, Dr Geraghty.' Turning his attention to her, 'Mrs O'Sullivan, I would like to talk to you about an opportunity that has just come to my attention. How would you feel about becoming involved in testing out a new type of treatment? One that is currently being developed and….'

At last, just as her concentration completely lapses, The Leader and his Formation hasten out with an outlier pulling the door shut behind them. The doctor's probing has unsheathed the dagger and the stabbing is back. Drained by all the talking, she presses the trigger and sinks back into the rustling, plastic protected pillows.

Her Friend regains the chair and reaches over to take her hand in his, 'my love, your hand's cold despite the heat in this room. Please request another blanket when they make your bed. Now back to Maura — when the girls in the shop, particularly Lisa, were happy to indulge her, this unsettled you. Partly it was because you didn't want them distracted from work — you were paying them, after all. But it was more than that, wasn't it?' peering at her face intently. 'Was it because they showed an easy warmth towards her? You couldn't understand why they would enjoy her company when she spoke such boring trivia and had a tendency to repeat herself which often made you want to explode with impatience.' Pulling the cover over her exposed hands, 'but that was only one facet. What you longed for was friendship, especially with Lisa. You admired Lisa with her charming personality — her flair, her young carefree lifestyle — her apparent contentment with life. But you felt she never liked you, however much you tried to gain influence with her. And you really tried, didn't you? You gave her special privileges — greater responsibility — argued with Paudie to give her a more generous wage — and you let her know that you had interceded for her. But it didn't make any difference, did it?'

Her Friend is interrupted by the door being edged open by a rattling trolley pushed by Tilly. Once inside, she puts the brake on with her foot, 'it's tea for you, isn't it, darling?'

'Yes, please,' croaking. 'Just a drop of milk.'

Tilly launches into song, 'tea for two, and two for tea — just me for you and you for me — traa, la, la.' Slopping copious slugs from the plastic milk bottle and placing a cup of opal coloured liquid onto the bedside locker. Continuing to sing her way out of the door, she turns around with a friendly grin before pulling it closed.

Her Friend looks at the cup, 'go on, drink it, unpalatable as it is — you must keep your fluid intake up, Ruth. It's very important with all the medication you are on and to avoid urinary infections. If you get dehydrated, you'll feel a lot worse than you already do.'

Ensuring she takes a sip, he notes her wincing, 'dreadful is it? Back to Maura — perhaps the most difficult thing for you was Paudie's reaction to her. The way he'd pay attention to her while the scripts piled up at the back. Knowing that people would be coming in to collect their medication, you took on responsibility for dealing with them with all the inherent risks. That was stressful as you weren't qualified — what if you'd got it wrong? The consequences were unbearable to think about and what alarmed you most, was that Paudie didn't seem to consider or acknowledge them. You felt obliged to keep the business running efficiently so protecting Paudie's reputation and his livelihood at the same time. Is that how you'd expected your life to be?'

A squeaky wheeled trolley out in the corridor approaches the room and her Friend gets up to leave. The ward staff entering do not acknowledge him passing by them.

'Ruth, can we bathe you now, please?' Nurse Sonia walking over to the locker making it clear it is more a command than a request.

Mary O wheels the trolley topped with a large stainless steel bowl alongside the bed and collects a bath towel drying on the radiator. Sonia retrieves a floral wash bag and a fresh set of nightwear from the bedside unit.

'Will these PJs suit, Ruth? They're just fabulous and the fabric is so soft.'

Mary joining in, 'and that bag! Beautiful! Is it from your shop?'

Sonia takes the opportunity to clarify, 'now, Ruth, did you understand everything Dr Mulhall was saying this morning about going on the drug trial? It's completely your own decision, you know that, don't you? Don't feel you have to take any personal risks just to promote research. And don't feel bullied into it by the medics — it's entirely up to you. Talk to Paudie. The doctors will probably discuss it with him anyway. They'll talk to him on a different level on account of his background, you know that yourself. And look, if you have any questions just ask me — is that clear?'

The intermittent squeaks recede down the corridor and she remembers too late about asking for another blanket.

Preoccupied with the indignity of having others empty her urine bag and attend to her ablutions, it was low on her list of needs. Always being self conscious about her body with a full audit of its flaws, she does not want strangers seeing it, let alone handle it, however respectful they are. In addition, she finds their remarks patronising at times. To them she is just a patient. They do not see a successful business woman who has standing in the Town Festival Committee. Someone who takes great care with her personal grooming and social manners. Every time a hospital worker comes into her room, they leave her with a lingering feeling of degradation. Somehow less of the person she really is.

Her Friend returns and sits in the chair, 'this is a huge trial for you, my love,' reading her thoughts. 'Come now, let's go back in time, please. Remember that day at the Pollock Holes, the one you spent with Paudie.'

Wow, that was a long time ago.

Her memory hurtles in reverse and she recalls a wonderful, carefree existence. And as her Friend suggests, one day in particular.

For a change, a mini heatwave that summer meant she did not need to prevaricate about what to wear as a hot, dry day could be relied upon. She slipped on a favourite Laura Ashley sundress bought on a trip to London, in a tiny floral print with mother-of-pearl buttons down the front. And retrieved a pair of Scholl clogs from under the bed. There was no need to find a matching cardigan and there was definitely no need for a coat.

Clattering doors downstairs signalled Paudie had let himself in and was rummaging for something to put on his sandwiches. Probably his usual baked ham as he loved meat of all kinds. For her it would be Heinz Sandwich Spread acquired when she had last gone home, it being an unheard of exotic in the local shops.

Setting off in Paudie's old Citroen, he showed off the new cassette machine he had just installed. With only the one tape bought, it was The Eagles played on loop. She had not minded as it was great to have in-car music and with the glorious weather, she could have been in California with Glenn Frey.

And she was in love for the first time, apart from crushes. Realising that earlier puppy love had never been the real thing, she was certain that this romance was what all the magazines and novels had been going on about.

Parking up on the grass verge, they climbed down on to the ocean sculpted rocks. Laying out an old table cloth in place of the beach towel she could not afford to buy, she stripped to a daring bikini put on under her dress. Flattered by the admiring, lustful gaze in Paudie's eyes, she playfully gave a teasing wiggle of her hips while seeking footholds down into the salt water. Initially gasping at the temperature of the sea, she laughed as the floating strands of seaweed tickled her legs and abdomen. In no time, Paudie appeared beside her, reaching out as she swam away from him. Undeterred, he caught up with her, wrapping his arms around her slim waist. Pulling her close, she felt his penis hardening as her body heat countered the cold Atlantic waters. Aware of interested stares from other sunbathers, she felt embarrassed and tittering to soften her rejection, pushed away from him to climb out onto the baking hot slabs of ancient rock....

Her reverie is broken by a clanging noise outside the room. Pushing the lunch trolley ahead of him, in comes a porter she recognises from a free trip down to the CT scanner.

'You've to put up with me now, em —' picking up his sheet, 'Ruth. Tilly's flat out — yer Soft, aren't ya?' Moving a bed table up to her lap, he carefully adjusts the height to a comfortable level for eating. Collecting a serving of soup, a main course and dessert bowl from the trolley, the porter places them in order of eating across the table. Then taking the plastic glass from her locker, he fills it from the water jug. 'A few minerals wouldn't go astray, in that, hun, I mean — um — Ruth. Have ya any? No? Tell the folks to bring some in for ya.' Grabbing the trolley handle, he speeds out of the room.

Recovered a little from her lavage, she studies the dishes. Thick, off-white stoneware marked with grey scratches from multiple usage. She misses her fine porcelain — fragile looking, but nonetheless, robust. Inexorably, her mind wanders back in time.

Shopping had been a reliable joy; a passion she had to work hard at reigning in. Something that had to be hidden from Paudie and his inherent parsimony. There had been many satisfying times purchasing sale bargains of Wedgwood, Royal Doulton and Spode from Shaws Department Store using her Christmas vouchers. One voucher was always a tax deductible "gift" from O'Sullivan's Pharmacy and Paudie would usually match it with one from himself. He had given up on buying her personal presents years previously, probably dispirited by her poorly concealed disappointment when he bought lingerie in the wrong size. At the time, she would tut to herself wondering why he had not used some gumption and looked in her underwear drawers for the correct sizes. Or he would have bought gold jewellery that she considered trashy when she only ever wore the silver or platinum that suited her skin tone. Or the supersize box of Cadbury's Milktray when she had moved onto more sophisticated Belgian brands.

Looking back, she acknowledges that she must have seemed hard to please and feels a twinge of sympathy for him. But then again, hardening her stance, she has reason to expect more effort from him. She has certainly made it with him over the years.

The soup is pale green and she surmises it is made from the previous day's leftover vegetables. As a student in Dublin, she had worked part-time in a nursing home and recognises the shortcuts and money saving techniques used in commercial cooking. On the dinner plate are two ice-cream scoops of mashed potato; an orange coloured ball that she thinks is probably a blend of turnip and carrot and a blob of pureed brown stuff that looks savoury, perhaps stewed beef in gravy. Dessert is some pink goo with lime green jelly. She knows her mouth ulcers will scream when she takes the first few mouthfuls, but then either they, or her, will toughen up if she persists. When nobody comes to help feed her, she decides to try a few spoonfuls.

Her Friend leans against the wall by the window and waits patiently until she has eaten all she can. Looking out, 'the butcher shop in the parade opposite has a new sign in the window. It looks like it's been taken over by someone else. Oh, someone is putting up another one offering special introductory deals. Turning to face her, 'Ruth, do you remember how you used to take such a pride in cooking?'

Indeed, she does.

Every woman while she was growing up had cooked and baked. It was what women did back then. Sure, there were male chefs on the telly and in restaurants, but in Ireland every man expected his mother, grandmother and subsequent wife to cook for him. Bachelors went to eat in the pub where other women fed them.

As a child, she learned the basics from hanging around the kitchen as there was little else to do. By observing her mother and maternal grandmother, the essentials were absorbed in some osmosis-like process. When older in Home Economics class at school, she learned more challenging techniques like making puff and choux pastry. Never clever enough to keep up with the more academic subjects, she had been put in the lower streams for those. Creativity however, was her area of excellence. Along with cookery and dressmaking, all the disciplines of art were her favourite and most successful subjects. She brought home countless drawings, paintings and pieces of pottery that were always 'oohed and ahed' at indulgently by her parents. And her sisters and father would fall like a pack of wolves on the baking she brought home in an old Rover biscuit tin.

When she married, it seemed quite natural to take charge of the kitchen. Not that there had been any choice. Paudie had not a clue, or so he demonstrated. She learnt in time that this is a clever deception men frequently use to avoid any chore they do not care for. Apart from that, there were Nora's expectations to contend with, although that woman was a fine one to comment, probably never lifting a wooden spoon in her life.

In the early days of their relationship, Paudie's single friends soon realised a good meal could be found at their place and as each fellow got snapped up by his own homemaker, the cheapest form of entertainment was the round of informal supper parties their circle of friends developed. Most of them were hard up with poor incomes on the lowest rungs of their fledgling careers and either had mortgages with exorbitant interest rates or inflated rents.

Being reared in the middle of a family of girls, she had a well developed competitive streak and regarded menu planning as a challenge to be risen to. Priding herself on being "with it", she would always be the first to try out the latest idea. Dishes such as chilli-con-carne or Black Forest gateau. Or cheese soufflé, a concoction that sometimes worked out. Buying coloured card, she wrote up the menus practising different scripts from her set of calligraphy nibs. Then she would glue flowers onto the corners that had been dried in a flower press her Granny had provided for her 12th birthday. The blossoms were from Granny's country style garden which was rich with colourful annuals despite being in Inchicore, inner Dublin City.

Her greatest difficulty was sourcing more unusual ingredients. Soon after moving over to the West, she quickly learned that the grocery shops in Balnarath did not stock anything other than the basic, traditional foodstuffs. Fortunately, she visited home in Dublin regularly and could pick up unusual spices like black pepper, or foreign vegetables like mushrooms. As demanding babies arrived, the dinner party circuit eventually died away….

Her Friend breaking into her thoughts, 'so what went wrong?'

That does not need much analysis.

Fatigue, disillusionment and resentment — all of them were what went wrong. The daily grind of providing three meals a day and a constant supply of snacks. Having to take on the full responsibility of menu planning, shopping and squashing food away into the fridge and freezer; the incessant meal preparation after a full day in the shop. She reckons, she must have prepared a mountain of spuds the size of Croagh Patrick during her lifetime. The inconsideration when one of the children, or himself, complained about what was on offer even though it was cooked perfectly. Mealtimes not being suitable for "whoever", who had to do "whatever", at "such a such a time". And a complete lack of gratitude although she knew she was partly to blame for not instilling better manners into the children from an early age. Her invisibility in the kitchen, but the automatic assumption that she would be ever present annoyed her intensely.

Thanks to a growing awareness of feminist issues, although steadfastly resisted by almost everyone, male or female, that she knew. Or perhaps with a growing maturity, she began to rebel. Coming to the conclusion that nobody in the family was actually going to die if they had a takeaway once in a while. And the discovery that cook-chill meals could be tasty led to many diversions via the Foodhall in M&S on the way home from Dublin.

A failed history of steering Paudie towards the stove meant she gave up on him, but she certainly got the girls to help out more as they got older. She has to admit though, matters in that area were a bit more lax in respect of Daithí. Ingrained gender socialisation over millennia was not going to be overturned singlehandedly by her. Inevitably, sports practice and music lessons; exam years; an endless list of essential other activities, all meant her efforts at an egalitarian society at River House failed. Eventually she tired of trying and gave up. But the unfairness of it burned like a small pilot light of anger inside her. And that pilot light quickly ignited a burning blast of rage if given enough fuel….

Whistling comes into earshot and the trolley enters first, piled high with dirty dishes and a slop bowl, ably pushed by the porter from behind. The odour of food scraps drifts over and she feels a familiar nausea rising. Grasping at a tissue from the box on her table, she holds the crumpled paper to her mouth and nostrils in protection.

Surveying the table, the porter declares, 'now, oh good woman, yerself, managing a small bit of dinner. Leave me wipe that table for you, hun. And find something to keep yerself entertained this afternoon, if yer feel up to it.' Scooping up the crockery, a knife clangs onto the floor leaving a dollop of gravy on the linoleum. Jimmy, she remembers his name, looks on the lower shelf of the trolley to find a damp cloth to clean the table as promised.

Finishing his tasks he goes to the door and addresses her, 'Finishing up in a few, hon, someone else will drop down the tea. I'll talk to ya tomorrow, bye now — em — Olive.'

A wave of fatigue washes over her. She immerses herself into it, aware that her Friend is watching over her.

Chapter 2

The tinkling of a teaspoon against a cup rouses her. 'Sorry, Ruth, I hope, I didn't disturb you.'

Unable to lift her heavy eyelids, 'no — you're fine,' her voice crackling.

'Let me settle that pillow — it's almost out of the bed — there, that's done now.'

Feeling the draught of the unseen figure, she hears the door click shut. As ever when woken, the pain wakes with her. Prising open her swollen eyelids, she moves her hand to depress the trigger.

Her Friend's gentle voice drifts over to her, 'try to relax, my sweet — relax into it — until it subsides. Now — is that better?' He gives her some time. Then asks, 'thinking about it, Ruth, how was your life supposed to be? What hopes did you have for the future?'

Well, not being stuck in a hospital bed, that's for sure.

Paudie and her built up a good bit of financial wealth over the decades. For all his faults, Paudie was never feckless and always prioritised the business and the acquisition of investments that would generate even more income. He was neither a gambler, nor a substance misuser, and rarely spent their hard earned money on frivolities. Their accountant, Liam Walsh, and he spoke the same language. Any surplus cash was shifted into buying properties that were promptly rented out. Other financial investments were made and financial products purchased that provided dividends and bonuses. She did not know all the details, but she was able to ascertain that a very comfortable retirement was provided for them both. This incentivised her, somewhat, whenever she felt overwhelmed by the demands of the shop. Paudie's overly careful approach to money, to the point of tightfistedness, did have its positive aspects, she has to admit.

It is in her own nature to work hard too, and she can be wealth focused at times. Yet despite this, she also feels strongly that they should live beyond the confines of their business. They should enjoy some of that wealth whilst young and healthy enough to do so. How bittersweet that seems and that irony burns like a red hot branding iron.

Looking back, she can recognise a recurring pattern. Burgeoning fatigue caused by overwork and stress would evolve to barely suppressed and volatile resentment. Over time this would intensify to an almost screaming intolerance. Paudie, for his own sake, learned to read the signs and would usually intervene with some kind of amelioration. He would suggest an afternoon off to go clothes shopping, thrusting a wad of banknotes into her hand. Or encourage her to go out for dinner with a friend, allowing her to leave work early to miss the rush hour traffic, and have adequate time to get dressed up. Or he would approach Lisa to take some admin task from her. Then the near despair would subside just enough until the next cycle began again.

Certain that this was "burnout" from articles she has read since, she experienced it mostly after the busy times of Christmas and the New Year sales. And then again, during the various festivals held in the town throughout the year. Afterwards, when there was a lull in the shop, she would plead with Paudie for a break away. She would even call into Maeve Cullen, the travel agent, to discuss bespoke holidays since money was not an issue. Paudie has never had any interest in travel or holidays throughout their marriage, citing difficulties in getting reliable locum cover. He promises to go to all the places she wants to when they retire, but cannot countenance it before.

Unable to argue against his logic, one way to manage her disappointment was to go home to Dublin for a few days. After work on selected Saturdays, she would stay a night or two with her parents, finding some solace in their relaxed approach and good humour. Sleeping in her old childhood bed was soothing, and reminded her of her once youthful optimism. In more recent years since her parents died, she would book a spa day at The Manor Hotel, a destination resort a few miles out of town, occasionally staying overnight to partake of their sumptuous breakfast….

Nurse Nóirín, Sonia's counterpart, enters the room wheeling a blood pressure monitor . 'Hello, Ruth, time for your obs,' moving deftly to complete a list of tasks. Clicking a ballpoint and scribbling on a chart taken from a rail at the bottom of the bed, 'your urine looks very dark in this bag. Have you been drinking plenty of water? What time did you last take medication from your machine? Have you opened your bowels today? No? I will get the SHO to sign you up for Lactulose. I think you need extra assistance. Any new pains anywhere? Let me take that clip off your finger — I need to put this thermometer in your ear. I'll come back later with the Lactulose.' The door swishes to a close.

Her Friend stands looking out of the window. 'The Bolgers are coming into the building. They are probably due to start their shift in the hospital shop. They've taken up volunteering since they both retired. Were you looking forward to retirement, Ruth? Was Paudie looking forward to it as well, do you think? Had you agreed upon a date for it?'

She does not have to think about that too hard. Personally, it could not have come a day too soon.

When they first set up the business in their twenties, the State retirement age had been 60 years for women, and 65 for men. When they discussed their long term plans, Dr O'Sullivan, Paudie's father, recommended his financial advisor. That man implored them to start a pension plan as soon as possible even if they could only afford a small monthly premium. Explaining that every pound, the currency back then, put into the pension pot from an early stage would be far more valuable than one put in later, he urged them to prioritise this.

When she visited home next, she raised the issue with her father, Billy, and he confirmed it. Billy was a trade union shop steward at CIE, the state bus company. He had been afforded training on legal and personal finance matters so that he could give impartial advice to union members. A straightforward, working class man, he disliked subterfuge and the endemic corruption he observed through all echelons of Irish society. A man of principle, he baulked at being manipulated or being deceived. She could always rely on her father to be instinctively suspicious about anyone doing her wrong. He gave her all the assurance she needed. With Paudie four years older than her, they agreed that she should continue working alongside him until she was 61. Then they could retire at the same time, and sell the business as a going concern which would make it more lucrative. A combination of their own business acumen, and an improving Irish economy from EU investment ensured that the practice flourished. Liam kept advising them to add hefty sums to the pension plan as a tax efficient way of managing profit.

Once she passed through the horrors of the peri-menopause, and the children finished their education, she distinctly remembers being 52. It was when she undertook a life review, partly because she had the emotional and practical space to do it, but also the energy to do so. Friends had tended to do it at the 'big' birthdays ending in a 0, but when she had turned 50, she had resisted the idea. Better to keep her head down and hope for the best was her thinking back then. However, a year or so later, she felt an urge to focus on where her life was going. Maybe she had just been bored with it all. A favourite fantasy at the time was to imagine the wonderful day she would walk out of the shop as the owner, and only ever return as a customer. The longed for sense of freedom felt almost palpable, an almost unbelievable goal.

Her Friend interjecting, 'but why particularly at the age of 52? Did something important happen then?'

Presumably it had.

One morning coming up her 51st birthday celebrations, she woke up feeling every bit of her age. Unable to pull herself up out of bed, she reflected on how tired she felt physically at that moment, but also on how weary she was with life in general. Lying there with every muscle immobilised, she wondered if it was normal to feel like that at her age. Then another thought struck her. She had to mind herself as no-one else ever did. And it was also her responsibility to deal with any dissatisfaction in her life. It was a moment of maturation.

A prime concern was her body. Inexplicably, it had been morphing from a sort of hourglass shape in her younger years to its current formless blob with a much wider middle. Always proud of her slim waist, she was now the dreaded apple shape. In the shop, she talked to countless customers about the dangers of belly fat; flicking a tape measure at them like Miss Whiplash, and weighing their gluttony on the medical grade scales in the corner. To her horror, she had amassed a barrel load of her own. Appalled by her general level of fitness where even a single flight of stairs seemed mountainous, and in a panic, she sought out a personal trainer. This was the latest "must have" amongst people who could afford it. After assessing her, he prescribed aerobic, muscle building and stretch training; or else, in a most alarmist way, he predicted that the bottom would fall out of her world. Her immediate thought was that her own bottom had already beaten it to it. An exercise programme was drawn up comprising a yoga class for stretching movements one evening a week. Resistance training at the gym scheduled for three lunchtimes a week was to be supervised rigorously by the trainer. And an early morning swim at the Manor House Hotel was prescribed twice weekly. He encouraged her to walk instead of drive whenever possible, and to fit in a recreational walk on fine evenings.

Once she set her mind on it; and got into a regular routine where the trainer refused to accept any excuse for not doing a session, she grudgingly acknowledged feeling better in herself. Her energy levels rose which seemed counter-intuitive; she expected to be worn out by all the extra activity. Most importantly, she began to feel pleased with her more shapely appearance. The two together made her question how she perceived herself with regards her age, and stage of life. For a long time, she had described herself as an older woman, and considered herself frumpy and sexless. But the time spent on self-improvement was rejuvenating. People commented on how well she looked; and a different hairstyle helped. There were other consequences to re-embracing her female self, but there is no need to think about that now. Like any bad habit that needs breaking, and new habit needing to be instituted, she pushed on through the first painful weeks, persevering until the new way of life became part of her.

A year later whilst diligently breaststroking up and down an unusually empty pool, she contemplated her forthcoming 52nd birthday due the following Saturday. Saturdays were like any other day of the week, just extra busy with city visitors on weekend breaks. She had booked a dinner table for them all at the Manor House because she knew nobody else would get around to doing it. It had crossed her mind briefly to book a room for the night, but had quickly dismissed it, predicting what would happen.

She knew from previous experience that Paudie would take the opportunity to drink more than normal. In an effort to cope with the tediousness of his drunkenness, she would drink more than she would like herself. They would fall untidily into bed with little sex on offer as Paudie would fail to get an erection. After kneading her breasts in an attempt at foreplay, he would begin snoring before his hands traveled any further.

The next morning she would prod him repeatedly to shift him out of the bed. Giving up when the dead weight failed to move, she would go down to the Breakfast Room alone. Unable to enjoy the delicious food because of dyspepsia and a thumping head, she would disappointedly wonder why she had bothered at all. After a lot of cajoling, she would get Paudie out of the room by checkout time; drive him home as he would still be over the legal limit, and watch him drag himself up the stairs to their bedroom for the remainder of the day. At some point in the early evening, he would surface looking for some dinner, and generally rally around. Then, declaring what a fine evening it was for a pint, he would go down to the pub to meet with the usual gang of male characters. After putting the Government to rights, he would stagger home around 1am.

Turning at the end of the pool, she swam back towards a mural of an ancient Hellenic idyll on the far wall, and conceded that a meal with the children would probably be nice, but not guaranteed to be entirely tension free. It would depend largely upon Sophie's mood.

Thinking about Sophie usually set her emotional regulator into minus mode. Reaching the watercolour Grecian cornucopia, a shocking realisation hit her. Was this how the rest of her life was going to be? A relentless daily grind of hard labour, six days a week in the shop? A few hours carved out of a hard block for essential personal maintenance? A marriage that seemed to offer precisely, what? Nothing? Retirement spent with a man she no longer liked? And tip-toeing around a family who seemed to bring more angst than joy?

There was little she could do to fix her marriage; she had learned that by trying to, and failing. And her adult children had to be accepted for who they were. But her career? Could anything have been done about that? In reality, very little; her current wealth and future earnings were tied up in the business. If she left Paudie, or changed job, she could not extricate a fair share for herself without crashing the mini empire. The Irish legal system was not designed to assist unhappy women gain their freedom. The men had made sure of that….

'Mammy, Mammy, how are you?' A high pitched voice in the doorway breaks her thoughts. Her daughter, Deidre, enters effusing and hugging a large bunch of roses under one arm, and clutching a Supervalu shopping bag in the other hand. 'I brought your clean washing. I'll get the dirty stuff out from the locker in a minute. And look, here's some Lucozade and some Butler's chocolates — they're from me — and that's the Johnson's Baby Wash you asked for — don't you use soap anymore?' waving a plastic bottle. 'Oh, and the flowers are from Daithí. He transferred some money over. I hope you like them — are they the right colour? They don't seem to have any perfume. But they've come in their own container of water — isn't that so smart?'

'You are both — very good to me — you shouldn't have — either of you,' finding the strength to straighten up a little and smile back.

'I had a word with Nurse Nóirín on the way in and she told me about the drug trial — that's AMAZING news, Mammy! When are they going to start?'

'I don't know yet — I haven't decided — not even thought about it —'

'But Mammy, there's nothing to think about! You just have to do it! There's nothing to lose, is there? — only gain.'

'I'll have to talk —to your father — see what he thinks — find out about side effects —'

'Don't be silly, Mammy! Of COURSE Daddy's going to agree. And the side effects will be worth it — if it's as successful as they're making out.'

'Maybe —' losing the energy to debate. 'Tell me about you, pet — how's the inspection going?'

'OH MY GOD! Don't even get me started me on that one — you'll never guess what happened…?'

After Deidre leaves to go to her small town house, and do the day's copy book marking, she ruminates on how Deidre can lift her spirits even when describing some crisis, or having a moan. But with other people, although the interaction can seem innocuous, they leave her feeling emotionally flat, or drained in some way; unsettled even, although the words seemed inconsequential at the time. Nora had been like that. And even though she hates to admit it, her daughter Sophie, Nora's granddaughter, has that effect on her too.

Her Friend takes over the empty chair, 'tell me, what did you do after that moment of realisation in the swimming pool?'

Much contemplation was needed to consider the implications.

Being such major stuff, she did not know where to start. But she had to do something; anything. Time alone undistracted, with the opportunity to think was needed. Adjusting her routine, she began preparing the evening meal and serving it promptly before being sidetracked into emptying the washing machine, or opening the household post. After clearing the evening meal away, she would invite Paudie to join her for a walk knowing full well he would decline. Donning walking shoes, she would opt for the path on the other side of the river because most of her neighbours frequented the one nearest the house where the dog waste bins were positioned. Familiar to most people, she did not want to have to make polite small talk. For the first few minutes, she would review her day. Then she would assess whether it had helped towards her long term objectives, or not. And what had they been?

The most pressing was to get through the next nine years without going insane. An annual cycle of events in the shop had been established. The year was punctuated by religious celebrations like Christmas and Easter, and secular ones like Valentine's, Paddy's and Mother's Day; and these were all good earners. Dressing the front windows with different themes was a task she enjoyed as it gave her an excuse to exercise her artistry.

She was instrumental in setting up a Town Festival Committee to promote such events in the town. There was a general consensus that this would attract visitors, and most importantly, their cash. The Traditional Music and Irish Dancing Fleadh Cheoil was popular with them being located in the West. For erudite types, there was a Literary week. Chess Championships were organised for the intelligentsia; and different sorts of foodie and drinking festivals suiting a wide range of folk were inaugurated. Also there was a local Ploughing Match Competition and Agricultural Show which had occurred for as long as anyone could remember. Finally, a frivolous Matchmaking event was organised in the late autumn when things could get a bit slow. As Committee Secretary, she was charged with getting things actioned, penning the necessary letters to the Town and County Councils, and legitimately exerting pressure on committee members to keep up with their allocated tasks. The shop was decked out according to the week, and she initiated competitions for the best decorated windows — commercial and residential — to be judged by The Mayor….

The door is walloped with a jangling trolley and flies open. Tilly enters with a light evening meal, 'Ruthie girl, would you be able for a sandwich? No, that wouldn't do — too hard. How about a cup of soup? And a strawberry yogurt? And a cup of tea? How about I give you a slice of brown soda bread and you dip it in the soup to soften? Would that do for ya?' Tilly's large hands set everything on the high table and she hurriedly exits.

Leaning towards the pump, she releases a dose and waits for the pain to subside. The discomfort eased, she breaks the bread into small pieces, and drops it into a familiar pale green liquid. Exhausted by the effort, she pauses and looks over towards her Friend standing by the window.

He is peering out and remarks, 'a woman is putting some acrylic transfers on the window of the fancy goods shop opposite. Preparing it for Easter, it looks like. Yes, I'm right. Up goes a large bunny. And now some yellow chicks.' Turning and walking over to the chair, 'did being on the Festival Committee help you, at all?'

Indeed it did.

It was another responsibility with more tasks to fit in, but it brought benefits too. Townspeople got to know her better and perceived another side to her; not just as Paudie's wife; or local shopkeeper; or mother to Daithí, Deidre and Sophie. She mingled with local politicians and civil servants, gaining some influence over their decision making. Other interesting relationships with festival organisers from around the country developed. Even some from overseas which were particularly stimulating. Many became friends especially if they returned to the town regularly during town-twinning collaborations. There were return invitations, but to her regret, only other committee members could take them up. Paudie disallowed her going, claiming his need for her in the shop; arguing her case was always futile.

Securing regular visits back home to Dublin had been enough of a battle. They were skirmishes hard fought, and hard won early in the marriage. These visits could only begin after Saturday night Mass, and continue until early Monday morning at the latest. Bank holidays had been a Godsend up until it became acceptable, and then the norm, for shops to open on those days too. Paudie would have opened Sundays if it had been economically viable. He often raised the issue and then, thankfully, talked himself out of it again. Instead he went into the dispensary alone to make up emergency prescriptions.

To have been able to visit festival colleagues abroad would have been a dream come true. It became a poignant reminder of her thwarted ambitions to travel….

The food beckons her attention and she knows it is important to eat. The soup is almost cold having traveled a long way from the hospital kitchens in the basement. She eats some of the soggy bread; and the cool Greek style, gelatinous yogurt feels soothing on her mouth ulcers.

Tilly returns looking for the dishes, 'are you finished up, hon? If you have, I can go home. See you tomorrow, hon; sorry, I mean, Ruth — it's been a long day!' laughing at her poor memory as she leaves the room.

Her Friend has returned to the window. 'That shop looks most attractive now it's finished. They've even put a cross on a small green hill in one of the lower corners. You don't always find religious symbols nowadays,' sighing wistfully. 'Tell me please, what else did you do to get through those years at work?'

Good question — looking back, just how had she managed to cope?

At one point, a small office created for her in the shop had helped. Paudie instigated it as the last thing he wanted was for her to be away from him working on paperwork at home. Being party to inside knowledge on the forthcoming Festivals, during the first week of January, she drew up a large planner and put in on the office wall for everyone to consult. After inserting the Festival dates, she added staff holidays as the girls booked leave with her. A page-a-day diary was used to block out time each week for the different admin tasks she had to do such as ordering stock, or completing statutory paperwork for Paudie to sign off. Then getting the drug company and supplier reps to understand that she would only deal with them by prior appointment; with all of this, she effected some kind of time management….

The pain interrupts her thoughts and she searches for the pump. She breathes deeply until she can think of something other than the agony. Helpfully her mind drifts. Recollections of yet more annoyances stomp in.

Every single day customers called in to talk to the "Physik", if they were a farmer, or the "Chemist", if they were elderly. Younger people and outsiders looked for the "Pharmacist" and Gearóid Hanley, a local poet and dramatist, would ask to speak to the "Apothecary". Out from his loft Paudie would fly, taking his client by the elbow for a personal consultation to a quiet corner set up behind some rotating display stands holding hair accessories and costume jewellery. The word physik always amused her because Paudie was neither a physicist nor a physician. Predicting a lengthy discussion about health issues; and anything else, ranging from the price of cattle fodder to last Sunday's hurling match, that happened to be on the customer's mind would ensue, she would relocate to Paudie's glass eyrie to take over preparing the prescriptions. This was probably the most frustrating aspect of her job. Having her pressured time hijacked.

Her Friend returns to the bedside chair, 'it seems like you tried to bring some predictability to the working day. Was that to manage stress? In turn, did that reduce the chronic fatigue you felt?'

Exactly.
It helped make work more tolerable. The dread of going in on a Monday ruined her Sunday nights for years. When she finished cleaning the house, or during her drive back from Crumlin, she started ruminating on what she had to achieve the following week. This mental planning continued as she tried to sleep; her mind whizzing in an endless loop over the same details. When she did eventually fall asleep, it was fitful and non-refreshing. The next morning, dragging herself out of bed with the help of a screaming alarm clock, her head was a fog of drowsiness and low mood. With effort, she pulled herself together, and arrived at the shop with a professional facade fully erected. But she could never describe herself as happy in her work.

Whenever she tried to talk to Paudie about it, he argued that he had no choice but to make himself available to the customers on demand. It was his duty as a pharmacist to ensure that the symptoms and medications prescribed were a good match; and that people relied on him, and trusted him with their health issues. He had the reputation of being as good as a GP amongst many of them, and importantly, his advice was free. Many an expensive trip to the doctors' surgeries was avoided that way. And people had appreciated that.

Unable to challenge any of it, she simply asked him to keep the chats more brief and to the point. This would work for a while, but Paudie gained too much personally from these interactions to be motivated to change for her benefit. He enjoyed any opportunity to have a break, and a good gossip too much….

A knock followed by the slow opening of the door signals Paudie's arrival. Involved with community hospitals and nursing homes long enough to understand the protocols of patient confidentiality and privacy — and Health and Safety issues around staff — he is cautious around closed doors. 'Hello, Ruth, my love — how are you?' coming over to kiss her gently on the forehead and on both cheeks. Pulling the now empty armchair nearer to sit down, he then takes both her hands and lightly lands butterfly kisses on each knuckle.

Looking at the thick silver hair on his bowed head, she remembers how indignant he was noticing his first grey hair aged around 30. It had been so black up until then, with almost a blueness to it. Like a magpie's feather, she always thought. But the creeping grey-fox look only enhances his handsome appearance now. His full mop was always the envy of the thin topped fellows at the Polo Club. Playing polo on Sundays had been Paudie's passion. Due to circumstances, he has retired his polo ponies, but he visits them at the stables as often as he can. She knows he would love to be back involved and care for his own ponies by exercising and training them instead of paying for full livery. But that was his choice and of his own making.

Paudie searches her eyes and speaks softly, 'how are you feeling, my love? How has your day been? Are you keeping the pain under control? Let me look at the pump for a minute, please, darling.'

'Don't fuss, Paudie — please,' impatiently. 'I'm fine — as well as can be expected.' Then deflecting his attention away from herself, 'how's the shop? — how's everyone getting on?'

'Hey, woman, don't be fretting about any of that. That's none of your concern. Just concentrate on getting well, please.'

Recognising a mixture of love and humour in his eyes, she quickly averts her own. Not wanting to think about what they are trying to convey, she needs to change the subject to one that pulls him out of his heart, and back into his head. The trick is to get his intellect working. 'Dr Mulhall came to see me today.'

'I know, pet. That's why I'm late visiting — he wanted to see me before he left for the evening. He called my mobile this afternoon to check I'd be visiting, like I wouldn't be,' chuckling while rolling his eyes. 'Seriously though, I had a very interesting conversation with him about these new immunotherapy trials. I hadn't realised they were so close to putting them out for general testing. It's fantastic news really. Absolutely game changing. We've got to go for it. The only down side is if you end up being in the Control Group, and none of us, including Mulhall, will be told that by the drug company. But it's well worth a shot. We've got to go for it….'

Chapter 3

'It'll take about an hour for the infusion. During that time as the lead researcher acting on behalf the Company — I don't mean I'm employed by them — I'm still a HSE doctor. It's just I'm going to be the doctor here in the hospital assisting the research. Am I making sense?' Dr Geraghty positioning a plastic bag of turquoise coloured fluid on a stand, and fixing the end of a long tube leading from it into the port inserted below her patient's neck. 'Sorry, Ruth, as I was saying, during the time the infusion's going in, I'll need to check your obs every 5 minutes just to make sure you don't have a reaction. I'll stay with you and check your blood pressure, temperature, heart rate etc.on the monitor and record them on this form. I'll be quite busy, so would you mind if we don't talk? I'll ask you every 15 minutes if you are experiencing any strange symptoms. If you wave like this,' demonstrating with a smaller than average hand, like a child's, 'that'll tell me you're feeling normal. Is that okay? But if you do feel anything odd, please tell me straight away. I'll be keeping an eye on you anyway.'

A cool rush into her chest, one she has experienced many times before, heralds the new treatment. Maybe this time it will work; maybe it will not. Feeling detached from the final outcome, she feels neither hope nor despair. Emotions are irrelevant. She has learnt that they make no difference and simply wear her out in the process. The consent form had been signed with a feeble scrawl not for her sake, but for all the rest of them. Unable to deal with their continual encouragement and positivity until she agreed; nor the desperate disappointment if she had refused, she empathises with prisoners who confess to crimes they have not committed.

'So you're not doing this for yourself, Ruth?' her Friend queries whilst standing behind Dr Geraghty as she sorts through a sheaf of papers.

Is there any part of her that is doing this for herself?

If she is completely honest, and she may as well be because she instinctively trusts her Friend, she does have a small spark of hope. But she is not going to feed it. She wants to see some results first. Studying Dr Geraghty, she notes her fingers are ring free. Her long hair is shiny clean; her figure trim and she has a finely boned blemish-free face apart from a few freckles. An attractive and obviously bright woman, she is curious about any love interest. Or is the doctor purely focused on her career? As a Senior House Officer, she guesses Dr Geraghty has a long way to climb and wonders if she will be impeded by the competitive males around her. During her previous stays in hospital, she often noticed a masculinity in the ethos amongst doctors although nearly half of them would be female. With the other disciplines such as nursing, physiotherapy or dietetics, she felt more feminine vibes; a more supportive atmosphere between colleagues although she did detect friction at times.

'Are you feeling okay? Any different symptoms or strange feelings? — No? — That's excellent,' the doctor lifts her head momentarily before continuing with her notes.

Her Friend catches her attention, 'do you sense that Dr Geraghty might be troubled?'

Strangely enough, yes — so you've picked that up too? There is an indescribable vibration in the interaction between Dr Geraghty and her boss, Dr Mulhall. An impression she recognises from something she has personally experienced in the past. It is a sexual frisson, but with an extra added tension that does not feel quite right. Is it unrequited love? Or forbidden love — is he married? Or an even darker, inappropriate love that pressures and coerces? The more she thinks about it, the more convinced she is that there is an issue causing discomfort for Dr Geraghty. A surge of sympathy wells up into her throat and tears prickle her closed eyelids.

The doctor stands up, 'the bag's completely empty now. Tell me, Ruth, do you feel any different?'

'No worse than normal, doctor.'

'Good — that's excellent — your obs have remained stable throughout which is good too.' Moving to disconnect the equipment, 'now, as I've already explained, I'll be back to you around the same time tomorrow to repeat the procedure.' Wheeling the stand away from the bed, 'and that'll be repeated for 5 days in a row. Then it'll drop to twice a week for 6 weeks and then weekly. At present, I'm thinking of Mondays and Thursdays for the twice weekly doses.' Sitting back down to talk some more, 'the drug company will arrange for you to have a PET scan at the 7 week mark, if they can get you booked in, that is. There's fierce pressure for those machines, I'm afraid. That'll indicate if the treatment is having any effect at all.' Standing again with an intention to leave, 'is that all clear, Ruth? Do you have any questions you want to ask me?'

Sensing an element of relaxation in the medic, 'Doctor? — You're happy — with how it went?'

Dr Geraghty smiling, 'yes, very happy — it's always a worry trying out something new like this especially on someone who is — um —'

'As frail as me?' wanting to rescue the doctor. 'Would you do something — for me, please — Doctor — before you go? — in my locker — the box of chocolates.'

The doctor squats and retrieves the box of Butlers, 'will I put them on top, or do you want to eat them now?'

'No, neither — thank you — I want you — to have them, Doctor — don't refuse —I'll be offended — if you refuse — I won't let you finish the trial,' exhaling a hoarse laugh.

Dr Geraghty pauses and looks intensely at her face as if deciding what she should do. Ruth stares back and the doctor's face reddens as she turns away bashfully. 'Thank you very much, Ruth. You shouldn't have,' walking towards the doorway. 'If you feel anything unusual over the course of the day, call the nurse and I will come down to you. Otherwise, I will see you with the next infusion tomorrow,' the doctor closes the door gently behind her.

Her Friend comes into her eye line as he sits down, 'that was a thoughtful thing you did then, Ruth. There's something I've been wanting to ask you. Please tell me about your and Paudie's love story, starting with how you met?'

Are you that interested? Okay, sure.

Retrieving the memory reels for the late 1970s, early 80s, she re-enters an era when she was a student living away from home for the first time. Commuting to Art College from Crumlin was easily possible, but she had wanted to get away from the cramped, crowded house she shared with her family. She yearned to feel more grown up and experience life without restriction — and in her own way. Although she largely got on with her family, unlike some of her friends, they all had the propensity to express their views loudly. Comments were made with the best of intentions, but she did not want to be controlled any longer by their uninvited opinions on what she should do, wear and eat / when she should go to bed, get up and study / who she should date, give out to or avoid.

Her rented accommodation was a house-share in Stoneybatter with a new friend, Bríd, enjoying what she always envisioned student life to be. Bríd was full of enthusiasm and drive, and was her kind of woman. How she still misses her even after all these years. They remain friends despite living on different sides of the World. The last time she saw Bríd was watching her hare through the Departures Gate at Shannon Airport. It had felt like one of the loneliest times in her life. As normal, Bríd tried to cram in too many tasks into her last morning. If it had not been for Paudie's driving, Bríd would have missed her flight altogether, and it left no time for farewells at the airport.

Bríd had moved up from the country to go to university, and had been like a cork let fly from a bottle — an extremely fizzy vintage, at that. Although she had lived in Dublin all her life, Bríd made her look at the city in a completely novel way. Bríd was like one of the emerald eyed jackdaws that hopped around The Phoenix Park, picking up on things that she had never noticed before, or even heard about.

One example was the All Ireland Polo Club. She had walked around that vast city parkland hundreds of times, but neither her, nor her parents, had ever paid any attention to the white railed arena and pavilion. Perhaps it was because it had always been there as background scenery whilst her attention would have been on an anticipated visit to the nearby zoo. Or more likely, she would have been messing with her sisters while her parents tried corralling them without losing one. Bríd had been brought up with horses, and with an almost comical inability to manage her allowance, rarely had the fare to go back home to see them. And she complained loudly and frequently about the fact. Veterinary Science was Bríd's chosen career so when she learned that horses were to be found locally, there was no stopping her trying to see them.

One sunny Sunday afternoon, Bríd and her walked through the terraced streets and entered the park gates near the An Garda Síochána Headquarters. It was a long trek, but neither of them was a car driver so they were used to walking everywhere, and it saved on fares. She remembers wearing her favourite denim flares, and a new buttercup yellow blouse with puffed sleeves and a large collar, the dye from which made her armpits itchy and red. On her feet, she had donned platform sandals, but not so high as to be impractical, unlike the towering ones she wore for discos.

When they reached the Polo Grounds, Bríd, with her usual confidence marched them over to the clubhouse where they were greeted by an older man whose warmth of welcome surprised her. Without introduction, he urged them to go into the bar, order a drink and take it up onto the viewing terrace at the top of the building. He said to be quick because the first chukka, whatever that was, would be starting soon. Grabbing bottles of Coke as they were unable to afford alcohol, they legged it up the outside stairway, and found a couple of empty seats in the front row. The players were positioning their ponies, and Bríd immediately started cooing, extolling the beauty of the animals. Bríd kept nudging her to look at this horse or that one, making what sounded like knowledgable observations. She, however, was far more interested in a different kind of beast altogether. On top of a magnificently gleaming chestnut was an equally magnificent-looking young man. Attired in pale cream jodhpurs, and a dazzlingly white short-sleeved shirt, the man kept perfect control of his waiting mount. From that distance, she felt safe to stare as intently as she liked, and kept her eyes fully trained on him. Assessing him to be tall from the length of his thighs, she regarded him as more muscular than the male students at college, but not as hefty as the lads on the building sites. His hair extended below the helmet to his collar, and was so black she wondered if he was Irish at all. But when she looked at the darker skins on some of the other riders in comparison, she decided he had to be....

Nurse Nóirín enters with the drugs trolley, and picks up the chart. 'Ruth, Dr Geraghty has been issued with some oral medication for you to take as part of the trial.'

'What is it? — Does it say?' laying motionless.

'Prednisolone — it's a steroid. We'll build the dose up over a few days because it can take time for the body to adjust to it. And there may be some side effects. Usually increased appetite, but you could do with eating more to build your weight up. Disturbed sleep, but we'll try to keep the doses early in the day to avoid that. And possibly some irritability or emotional lability, you know, tearfulness. But as you're a quiet person, that probably won't be an issue for you.' The nurse keeps her eyes fixed on the note taking. 'Apparently there's some evidence from earlier trials that it might work well in conjunction with the new therapy. Some patients will be issued with it, and some won't — to see if it helps or not.'

Quiet person? If only that nurse knew. Then audibly, 'will some patients be given blanks as a control?'

Nóirín looks up, her eyebrows raised, 'that's a good question, Ruth. All the drugs being used on the trial are coming directly from the company, none from the hospital pharmacy. Yes, these could be blanks, as you call them. None of us will know until after the trial ends — to prevent bias you understand.'

Although the little paper cup is filled with tablets, they are small, and she can swallow them with the stale, lukewarm water from the bedside jug.

With Nóirín gone, her Friend returns to the earlier conversation, 'back to the polo game, please, Ruth — it sounds most intriguing.'

Yes, thinking about it does bring back some nice memories.

As she watched the match, she got caught up in the action, finding it more interesting and exciting than she had anticipated. Although she knew very little about horses, and even less about polo, she appreciated what appeared to be impressive skills from each rider and pony as they had worked together in unison. The animals understood the game as much as the players and displayed competitiveness around the field. It was like watching an elegant, courtly dance. Mesmerised, she sought out the pale, dark haired man trying her best to work out the rules by matching action with points coming up on the score board. She had never felt so interested in a sport in all her life and felt compelled to learn the intricacies. Each round was called a chukka by the people around them, and she was surprised to see the riders come out with fresh horses each time. Her man alternated between the chestnut and a black pony with a white star on its forehead which made her think of the novel *Black Beauty,* one she had read and reread as a child.

Bríd had no problem articulating loud whoops, and the other spectators looked over approvingly. At various intervals, the older man came to check that they were enjoying themselves. Towards the end of the tournament, he let them know there would be a roast hog downstairs, and that they must join them all for the BBQ.

Receiving the invitation, Bríd and her looked at each other. With unspoken communication, they simultaneously remembered the fridge back at the house containing in total a small piece of cheddar with green furry patches, some stale bread and a pan of greying, left over boiled spuds from the night before.

Bríd responds for them both, 'hey, that'd be great! Where do we go for that, then? I mean — sorry, my apologies — thank you very much, sir — that's very good of you. But are you sure we're allowed?'

'Of course, I'm sure,' smiling genially. 'I'm the Manager and I'm inviting you both. I'm George Phillips, by the way,' shaking hands with them both. 'And you are?'

After extracting information about where they came from, their history of the sport and knowledge of equine matters, they seemed to pass the test, although she had to put their success all down to Bríd who clearly understood what the right replies should be.

'Maybe I could interest you both in joining our club? We're always looking for new members especially ones as pretty as you two,' George chortling at his own charm. Horse sense did not seem that important to George after all. His bristly moustache twitching like a rabbit's nose, 'come, come with me and I'll introduce you to some of the players on the home team,' gesturing for them to vacate their seats.

This was getting even better, she thought to herself, and was mighty glad to have given into Bríd's pestering. Down on the field, George led them over to one side where the various players and grooms were attending to the ponies close to parked horse boxes and equine lorries.

'Ramón! Paudie! Please allow me to introduce you to some new members, Bríd and Ruth. Could I prevail upon you young fellows to escort these ladies over to supper when you're finished? My apologies, I can hear someone calling my name, I'd better go!'….

The door flies open with the trolley leading the way, and Tilly steering from the rear. 'Ruthie, baby, have I got a treat for you today? Cook's gone crazy — homemade tomato soup made by herself, no less — no packet rubbish. Fish in parsley sauce, mashed for you, of course, and guess what? Something new for dessert — tiramisu! How fancy is that? You're all spoilt,' guffawing. 'All of ye — spoilt rotten.' Still laughing and whooshing the door shut on her way out. The door re-opens immediately, and with her head poking around, Tilly proclaims 'hey, you're looking good, girl — I meant to say. You've some colour there in your cheeks.'

Colour in her cheeks? Oh, she certainly had some colour in her cheeks the first evening she met Paudie.

Her Friend holds his hand up in a "stop" gesture, 'eat your dinner first please, Ruth. Then you can carry on with your story.'

Tasting the soup, the acidity stings her mouth, but she persists. Consuming what she can manage from the main course, she goes on to clear her dessert plate. Putting the spoon in the dish, she nestles back into her crackly pillow, and thinks back to that most important day in her life.

Bríd wasted no time asking questions about the ponies, and Ramón responded with warm enthusiasm. The pair of them chatted while Bríd ran her hands over the three ponies he had ridden, stroking and talking soothingly to each one in turn. Ramón warned her to be careful, but soon relaxed when he saw the animals behaving docile as lambs.

She, however, was feeling decidedly awkward. It was always the same when she was around someone she liked the look of. If it was a lad she considered ordinary, or just a friend, she would feel as she did with any of her female friends. But with Paudie, she felt overawed, gauche and stupid. Knowing she could not ask sensible questions, nor make competent observations about the match, she felt stymied.

Paudie did not help her at all. Regarding her for a long, cool moment, he excused himself to attend to his two horses. For a while she stood watching him in lonely discomfort. She considered joining Bríd, but did not want to spoil her chances with Ramón. At the precise moment she resolved to kill time by excusing herself to find the Ladies' toilet, Paudie found some chivalry. Either that, or he had taken pity on her. He suggested she remain where she was until he was finished, assuring her he would not be much longer.

During the interim, she assessed the situation. Being so good looking, she decided that he was probably used to a gang of women crawling all over him like groupies. Or alternatively, he had a girlfriend. Or more likely, he found her unattractive, and certainly not good enough for him.

'That shirt — that blouse — whatever you call it — it's very loud,' Paudie announces without removing his eyes from the brush smoothing the horse's flank.

She remains silent, wondering whether to respond to this somewhat rude remark.

'I mean — you couldn't really miss it — could you?'
Paudie digs the hole some more. 'I mean — on the terrace —
you stood out a mile,' the hole deepening.

Oh fuck, she thinks in a panic, he noticed me. Had he seen
her goggling at him? The mortification makes her want to
leave there and then. But Bríd has disappeared; leading horses
with Ramón into a lorry. 'Yeh — well — umm — its very
important that I live my art, you know.' Thinking on her feet,
'Mondrian said, "The colour you wear, is the life that you'll
lead",' waving her hand airily for effect. This is utter made up
bullshit, but she has to say something that does not make her
seem like a complete thick .

'Oh — really? So bright yellow means — what exactly?'
Paudie looks up from a horse leg with one eyebrow cocked
quizzically.

Oh lord, think quickly, girl. 'Umm — yes — yellow is the
colour of the soul!' Developing her theme, vaguely
remembering a conversation she once had with a hippy friend.
'People think it means frivolity. But it actually means
spirituality, you know — as in Far Eastern monks — their
robes are saffron. Valuable pigments are used to demonstrate
their state of holiness — set them aside from the rest of the
community.' Beginning to enjoy herself, 'when they take up
their robes during the rites of ordination, they are accepting the
vows of obedience, poverty and chastity — to further their
quest for spiritual enlightenment.'

Not having a notion as to what she is talking about really,
only having half understood what the hippy had gone on about,
she thinks, at the very least, it sounds distracting.

'Wow! — I see — that explains everything,' Paudie
grabbing the mare's lead rope. 'Would you be ready to eat
now? I'm famished, myself,' beckoning her to follow him.
'We'll put herself into the box. Then we'll walk over to the
Pavilion. Would you care to sit with me for the meal?'

On the way over to the building feeling rather smug that
she had extricated herself from that little disaster, she holds her
head high, and straightens her back. Sashaying as model-like
as she can muster across the lumpy grass, Paudie queries the
reference to "her art". She explains being a fresher on a degree

in Fine Art, and he discloses that he too is a student doing his final year of Pharmacology. Circling around the perimeter of the grounds to avoid the greenskeeper patching up the pitch, they wade through some rougher grass. Whilst looking up into Paudie's face, she stumbles into a hillock, and her foot slips sideways out of her platformed shoe, ricking it painfully in the process. As she falls, Paudie with the quick reflexes his sport has conditioned him to, hooks his arm around her waist before she hits the ground. Keeping his arm around her, and holding her firmly to his side, he insists on supporting her as she limps over to the clubhouse. Feeling even more embarrassed, she considers herself ungainly and idiotic. On the plus side though, it feels nice being held securely in a strong male arm. The scent of his armpit is quite attractive too. Brut deodorant, she reckons — not like the stale, sweaty pong that wafts from her male friends most of the time.

After seating her at an empty table, Paudie gallantly enquires what she would like from the buffet to avoid her having to stand in the queue. Bríd and Ramón join them shortly after and the four of them chat away easily. Ramón is from Argentina and opted to further his Equine Studies in Ireland. He is studying for a Masters Degree at Kildalton College in Piltown, South Kilkenny, and has been living and working part time at a stud near the college where he can keep his polo ponies as part of his wages. As Paudie is enrolled in Trinity College, Dublin, but comes from Balnarath, he liveries his two ponies at some stables near Lucan. After the meal, Ramón is keen to drive back down to Kilkenny to get the ponies settled for the night. Bríd asks if she can walk over with him to have one last look, and say goodbye to them.

Meanwhile under the table, her foot has ballooned, and she has no idea how Bríd and her are going to walk home. She rises teetering to find a telephone, and Paudie watching with alarm on his face, asks her the same question. In response, she enquires if the clubhouse has a phone to call for a taxi cab, whilst imagining the number of meals she will have to forgo to finance it. Paudie instantly offers a lift, and when Bríd comes back with a most satisfied look on her face, they depart with Paudie propping her up, and Bríd carrying her shoulder bag.

On the way out, George bounds over fussing, hoping the accident had not put the young ladies off from returning.

Paudie replies for them, 'absolutely not, George — they'll be coming back. Soon!'

Not daring to look at Bríd, she knows that there will be a full de-briefing later….

Pulled back to the present by the slowly opening door, her heart dips as a young woman enters. 'Sophie —how nice to see you — Thank you for coming,' Ruth smiles weakly at her tall and slim daughter.

Sophie kisses her on the cheek and sits on the armchair rearranged against the wall by a cleaner. She sits upright on the front edge as though planning to not stay long.

'Bring the chair closer, Sophie — it'll be easier to talk.'

Sophie pulls the chair a little, less than halfway between the wall and the bed, 'I'll leave a gap so the nurses can get to you, Mam.'

'How are you, darling? — How's the job? — How's the studying going? — Where are you with the house?'

'One question at a time please, Mammy,' Sophie gives a small smile. 'Work is fine. I got my latest assignment in on time. Downstairs is finished and I'm starting upstairs tomorrow after work.'

'That's good — do you have another piece — for your course yet? — Or do you get a break? — And how's Seánie?'

'Seánie's fine. He said to send you his regards. I can start the next assignment whenever I want as long as I have all of them submitted by the end of May. I've told you that before, Mammy. But I'll do it now to get it over with.'

'Be careful, my love — Don't overdo things — Take your time — There's no rush.'

'Don't fret, Mammy, I'll be fine. I hear you've started some new treatment,' Sophie pausing.

'Yes — did they explain it to you? — I don't really understand all of it.'

'Yes — Daddy and Dee Dee filled me in,' Sophie falling silent.

'That's good,' then she falls silent too.

Sophie soon makes excuses to leave, and after her daughter's exit, Ruth slumps deeper into the clinical white cotton. Staring up at the greying ceiling, she watches a string of dusty gossamer missed by the cleaner waft around in the convecting heat of the room. Moving her gaze towards the floor, she notices the damp mop has failed to fully remove the hardened gravy deposit.

She spies her Friend out the corner of her eye as he walks over to fill the vacant seat. 'How do you feel after Sophie's visit, sweet one?'

Like she always does.

Letting out an involuntary sigh, she considers how she feels. Interactions with her daughter are rarely pleasant. She never feels warm or satisfied afterwards, assured that she has a mutually supportive relationship with her youngest offspring. Instead, she is left with unease. Describing it in more detail, she would say it is a mixture of feelings. A sense of failure as a parent combined with disappointment that it is not the same as it is with Daithí and Deidre. And guilt. Somehow in trying to keep all the plates spinning during Sophie's childhood, she neglected to truly connect with her. Unable to understand Sophie's complex needs, and through misunderstanding them, has failed in her duty as a parent to meet them. In her opinion Sophie, the adult, is at face value a success at everything she chooses to do. But underneath a tough outer veneer, there is a core of needy sadness. And she does not know how to break through that hard shell; reach into the little lost girl inside and bring comfort to her. No longer having the prospect of being a supportive grandmother to Sophie's future children, there is little chance of connecting with Sophie in that way. It would have been an opportunity for the young woman to gain insight into the challenges of parenthood. And those realisations could illuminate aspects of Sophie's own childhood. She recalls when she had Daithí, and later the girls, how much better she understood her own parents, finally empathising with the "how?" and the "why?"; the reasons why they had been the way they were during her childhood. Now she feels there is no time left to build a bridge, not even a temporary, wobbly rope one between her and Sophie.

Her Friend nods with sympathy, and understanding glows from his eyes, 'tell me some more, Ruth. More about your experiences as Sophie's mother.'

Thinking back over her childbearing history, she acknowledges that Sophie came in quick succession after the older two. And that would inevitably have been challenging for any working mother. Daithí was just turned three and Deidre nearly two. Unlike the previous ones, that third pregnancy had not been part of her original plan. She always wanted a family of two children, and after settling with Paudie while so young, she also accepted having children at an earlier age than she originally envisaged. Probably too early, now that she recognises a marriage needs attention to develop it, particularly in the initial years when couples are getting to understand each other. When her first pregnancy was confirmed by the doctor, she had an urgent need to talk with her mother, Vera.

Visiting Vera's kitchen, they sit at a square table covered with a floral oilskin cloth. As usual, her mother is pouring mugs of tea, and pushes plates of scones and sandwiches towards her until she relents, and stuffs her face. Morning sickness has not kicked in yet.

'Look-it, Ruth, it's not a bad thing at all, really. The older you get, the harder pregnancy is. You get tired more easily,' checking to see if the mugs need refilling. 'When I had you five girls it was a lot easier having your oldest sister, Rachel, than Samantha, your baby sis,' passing over the milk jug. 'Besides which, once the baby grows up, you and Paudie will still be young. You'll be able to do all the things you've always wanted to do — and be fit enough to enjoy them. Try one of those fruit scones. I added chopped apricots for a change. See what you think to them,' pointing to the plate. 'Later on, you'll be a young granny like me, and it's a lot more fun being able to run round the park with them than being stuck in a chair just watching,' referring to her own mother-in-law. 'Look-it, you might even go back to studying. I've seen more and more women going back to school once the children are off their hands. They're nice aren't they?' nodding towards the baking. 'And, your lovely artwork. You'll be able to go back to that too; all in good time.'

Wailing in protest, 'but Mum, I don't know if I'm ready for children yet. I don't even know what to do with a baby!'

Her mother throws her head back in laughter, 'you'll soon learn, girl; you soon will, I promise!'

When morning sickness arrived, she found it a tough endurance test, and complained to Paudie that "morning" was a complete misnomer. It was more like "all day sickness" for her. He was sympathetic, but added quickly that he did not want to prescribe her anything for it. She found that unusual as normally he would provide painkillers, ointments and medical appliances at the merest hint of a complaint. He was always a zealot of modern pharmaceuticals. She lived off porridge and tinned Heinz spaghetti on toast as these were all she could face until she was about sixteen weeks into her term. Once that phase passed, she had a strange craving for tinned fish, and sought out tins of pilchards in tomato sauce. Acquiring some renewed energy, she became increasingly excited about the baby's arrival. In the local library, she found books on pregnancy and childbirth, and the community midwife put her touch with the local La Lêche League group. They both attended the meetings regularly, where she soaked up information about her changing body, and the growing baby inside her. Discovering what to expect during labour, she thought about a birth plan. Deciding to forego pain relief, she was determined to do it as naturally as possible. Looking back, how naive she was. There was tuition about baby care, particularly about feeding options. Despite breastfeeding being unfashionable, and sales of powdered milk soaring in the shop, she wanted to feed the baby in a more instinctive way.

Since moving to the West, she had developed an affinity with nature, and most of her paintings during that period were outdoor scenes. Local landscapes, and images of flowers and farm animals dominated her work. Although reared a "townie", and loving to visit home, she fully embraced rural life. And everything it had to offer, seeing inspiration everywhere.

Putting it into perspective, her pregnancy and labour were straightforward, and Daithí a dream baby, although it did not always feel like it at the time. Her youth meant her energy levels rose quickly after rare sleepless nights. Daithí was completely "portable", and by getting Paudie to order a baby sling from a UK supplier, she carried him against her chest everywhere, regardless of Nora's assertions that it was not good for him. Nora opined that he should be left to sleep in his pram outside as she had done with her own children. Daithí was a springtime baby, and she recalls carrying him across the fields down to the sea, or over to the clifftops. Setting up a day camp, she would pull out a travel set of watercolour paints, and depict coastal scenes. This was her happy occupation throughout that summer — her baby and her art together. When Daithí grew bigger requiring a pram, she then had the means to bring larger canvasses and different paints. On wet days, she had a studio set up in an out-house. Billy, her father, suspended a baby bouncer from a rafter to amuse Daithí and erected a playpen over to one side. Mother and baby could happily watch each other all day. Ensuring to arrive back in the kitchen in time to cook, she settled into a routine that met everyone's needs, including her own.

But while she blossomed, she noticed Paudie wilting. When they first reopened the pharmacy originally belonging to Nora's father, Paudie had been a young contender to Tóibín's, the main pharmacy in town. People were suspicious of a newly qualified young fellow, priding themselves on their loyalty to providers they were used to. They set up in opposition with enthusiastic optimism. Paudie had a modern approach, and she used her design skills to fit out the shop. They utilised money Nora had given them most effectively. Newcomers to the area, and the growing number of tourists, or "visitors" as they respectfully called them, made up most of their customer profile in the early months. As the townspeople's stances yielded; when they remembered how good a chemist old Mr Walsh, Nora's father, had been; they agreed amongst themselves that his grandson would not have "fallen far from the tree". A trickle of them started to defect from Tóibín's which gradually increased to a steady flow.

Initially Paudie found it easy to manage the shop and dispense on his own. But with increasing customer numbers, he struggled. Looking at the turnover figures, he said they were not in a position to pay staff wages so asked if she could give him a hand.

Nora agreed to minding Daithí in the mornings which were Paudie's busiest times for customers coming in after the GPs' clinics. He promised to look for a student to come in on Saturdays, but none ever impressed him. Paudie could not run the business on his own. She had no income, and she recognised that if they were going to manage financially, she would have to help. There was no choice but for her to agree.

Chapter 4

'That's the third infusion finished now,' Dr Geraghty declares with satisfaction while closing the valve. Winding the trailing tubing onto a hook, 'I'll get this out of your way, Ruth. Have you any questions? Anything I can help you with?'

'Yes, doctor — can you have Mary O get me a bedpan, please.'

'Do you feel okay? Has this come on suddenly? Do you need to open your bowels urgently?' with concern.

'No, no, it's okay. I just think the Lactulose's finally working.'

Later as Mary efficiently wipes her clean, 'Mary, can I ask you a personal question? Did you enjoy having all your babies?'

'Yes, I did, Ruth. I have to say they were God's good gifts to me, all eight of them. And now I have twenty grandchildren and I love them all to bits. I can't wait to see them on my days off. And my husband, Syl, is as taken with them too,' removing her gloves and dropping them into the medical waste bin.

'Ruth, I'm thinking we could remove your catheter seeing how you used the bedpan so successfully. I'll talk to Sonia. I'll see you later for your obs.'

Her Friend reappears at the foot of the bed and seems keen to talk again. 'The other day when Sophie visited, I asked about her arrival in the family. Tell me how was it for you when she came along.'

It was not a particularly good time in her life, but as he has asked, she will face it again.

It needs putting into perspective, though; some explanation as to how it all transpired; what led to Sophie's arrival.

Paudie and her decided that as they had got into such a good routine with Daithí, they would try for a second child quickly. Paudie was one of four children and wanted that many for himself. She heard his words, but did not necessarily agree with them. The political idea to preserve the planet and its finite resources by curbing population growth was more her philosophy. To have two children to replace Paudie and herself seemed responsible on a societal level, and on a personal one, more practical to manage. Whenever she raised these arguments, Paudie brushed them aside saying it would be great to have their own team.

Her second pregnancy with Deidre was a different experience to the first. Experience over the years has taught her that all pregnancies are unique even with the same set of parents. Despite being less nervous with knowing what to expect, that pregnancy was more troublesome. The fatigue was overwhelming at times, and the midwife reassured her that this was normal in second pregnancies. It would take time for her body to recover from the first, and she was not fully over it with the pregnancies being so close together. And there was a toddler in the family, and everyone knows what demands that involves. Plus she was working full-time outside of the home.

There were also additional health issues not evident in her first gestation. As the foetus grew, her body expanded more quickly as though the muscles remembered what to do. With the rapidly increasing bulge, she developed lower back pain as her spine contorted with the extra weight carried at the front. Towards the end of the pregnancy, it worsened to sciatic pain extending down her left leg. Lifting Daithí antagonised it and she lay awake at night unable to get comfortable. Morning sickness was quickly replaced by chronic heartburn and she feared ever enjoying a meal again. Towards the end, she struggled to get in and out of the car, and became increasingly breathless simply moving around. Paudie told her to stop coming into the shop a couple of weeks before her due date because she could no longer fit the seat belt around herself. Being at home was no holiday as she caught a cold that developed into a chest infection. The midwife voiced concern over her being able to cope with a normal delivery on account of her breathing difficulties. In the event, as often happens with second pregnancies, her labour was thankfully short with Deidre arriving quickly, and with minimal medical intervention. She did not even need stitches. Once her early cracked nipples healed, she had got into a satisfying routine of feeding Deidre. Daithí was so sweet climbing up on to the chair alongside them for a cuddle. Those times were wonderful; the three of them snuggled together, all cosy.

Paudie's grey, strained face in the evenings told her that this bliss had a short life span. As soon as was practical, she had to hand Deidre over to Nora, and go back to the shop.

I'm feeling tired now, it's so exhausting thinking about all this stuff — that's enough for now, my Friend.

Apart from some local soreness, she cannot believe the sense of relief in her lower abdomen now the catheter is out. Smoothing the sheet, and turning it over the top of the blanket, she thinks about ordering a magazine from the hospital shop. Nothing too taxing, maybe one on home decor with some nice photos, and not too much text to have to take in.

A gentle rap on the door sounds a prior warning, and Paudie puts his head around with a stupid grin on his face.

Without smiling back, she beckons him in.

On autopilot, he says, 'hello, beautiful.' Then with eyes opening wide, 'hey! You're looking so much better, Ruth. Do you feel it?'

Thinking sardonically, he's come in expecting one thing and has found something quite different, she pats the side of her bed, 'look — look down here — No bag.'

'Thanks be to God! That's incredible!'

Pulling herself higher in the bed, she remains silent.

'Here, let me help you,' Paudie moving swiftly to lift her scrawny body, then lays it tenderly against the propped pillows. 'Well, now, girl, it IS good to see you.'

'Is it, Paudie?'

His face turning serious, 'Yes, Ruth, it IS.'

'Even though I'm the state I am — I must look a real witch — my hair, my body, my nails — this disease has been such a horror —'

He interrupts the flow of her self-critique, 'yes, despite everything — you're still beautiful — the same beautiful person inside — the mother of my children, my best friend. The very BEST thing that ever happened to me was meeting you, and then you agreeing to be my wife —'

Turning her head away from him and looking towards the door, 'go to the nurses' station, and have them bring me a bedpan, Paudie. They take too long answering the bell.' She does not want to hear any more guff and needs to steer him away from dangerous territory.

The atmosphere in the room feels too still, and with a lack of physical distraction, she feels a little lonely. Startled, she realises that this is a new. Normally in pain, or exhausted, or in a low mood, the company of others is tolerated at best, but usually endured rather than enjoyed. Debating internally whether this is a good development or not, her Friend attracts her attention from the armchair.

'I know it's not pleasant thinking about painful memories, so let's go back to something altogether more agreeable — that time you first met Paudie. What happened after you sprained your ankle at the polo match?'

Yes, she has to admit, that was a truly lovely and romantic episode.

With her being unable to walk to college, Paudie kindly offered lifts. The swelling went down considerably after a week, but because of persistent yellowish bruising, he said she should not put excessive weight on it, and insisted on chauffeuring her for another week. By the following weekend, she was back to normal. But he recommended another week of car journeys because of the possibility of inflammation and not wanting chronic problems to develop in the ankle.

After three weeks of meeting daily, the habit of seeing each other was not going to be broken easily. Throughout that time, Paudie had acted the complete gentleman, not even attempting to kiss her. For her however, there were stirrings in her vagina that intensified the more she got to know him. By the time he left the house in the evenings, her knickers would be damp. Later in bed, she would finger herself to a climax imagining what they would do to each other if she ever had the opportunity. Out of increasing impatience, she decided to create that opportunity.

One evening, Bríd and her are lolling around the sparsely furnished sitting room with neither of them in the mood for study. 'Bríd, now listen up. I've been saving a bit of money, you know, with not going out as much with the foot and all. I was thinking, how about I give you the fare to go down home this weekend and see those terrible nags of yours?'.

'Weeell, if you were to give me a few pound more so I could get the train further, to say Kilkenny City, then you'd have a deal partner — no hang on, I think I have the extra in my bag because I haven't been spending either on account of your ankle.'

'Kilkenny? Why Kilkenny? — Hey, you little chancer — you're planning on visiting Ramón aren't you?' laughing loudly.

Bríd's eyes twinkling back, 'and you want the house to yourself. Now, why would that be? — hmm? — nothing at all to do with having a certain visitor over, now would it be? Don't move for a minute,' Bríd leaping out of the chair and disappearing out of the room. Crashing up the wooden stairs then thumping back down again, Bríd re-enters the room and thrusts something into her hand. 'Ramón gave me that for if I was ever "in an emergency". I think you'd better have it.'

Looking into her palm and then at Bríd's face for clarification, 'but what about you?'

'Ramón can get them anytime from the Embassy,' shrugging her shoulders in dismissal. 'You know, from his Argentinian friends. I think they get them from The States. Go on, take it. I can always get more from him. Honestly, I mean it, take it. You'll need it,' giving her an exaggerated wink.

Turning the package over carefully, something she had never seen before, she notes what a packet of Durex looks like in real life. Then grinning at her mate, she puts it in the large patch pocket of her dungarees, 'thanks, Bríd, girl. I owe you one,' punching her playfully on the arm.

The following Saturday queuing in the butchers, she eyes the various meats on the marble counter, comparing prices and calculating what else she needs to buy. In her purse is cash her parents have given her for art materials. But this is by far a worthier cause.

'Can I have three quarters of a pound of that fillet beef steak, please?' pointing to the stainless steel tray in the centre of the display.

'In two pieces, missus? One for you and one for the auld fella?'

'No, one piece will be fine, thank you — Yes, that's enough. Now, can you put it through the mincer, please?'

'Whaa?! Mince it, did you say? Holy Mother of God! Why would you want me to be doing that to the finest meat in the shop? Look-it, I've a heap of the best mince there. Good quality, and it'll cost you a fraction of this.' The fillet dangling from his hand passively awaiting its fate.

Beaming at him until he gives in.

Muttering, 'Jaysus, missus,' putting the package wrapped in white paper on the counter.

'And can I have a quarter of that pork fillet over there, please?'

'And I expect you want that minced too, ha, ha,' howling with laughter. Looking at her face, 'oh for fuck's sake, you do! Hmm — sorry, missus. But why, for God's sake?' throwing his hands up in mock horror. Shaking his head and walking along the counter muttering, 'no, no — don't tell me. I don't want to know.'

At her favourite Italian delicatessen, she collected more foodstuffs including tomato puree, dried oregano and basil. Over in Moore Street she bought Bramley cooking apples, carrots, onions and a garlic bulb from the stall her mother always frequented. And mushrooms; a good pound and a half of those.

Back at the house, she surveyed the empty kitchen and sighed with contentment. Not as well equipped as the one at home, she was still fairly confident that she could make do. For the mushroom soup starter, she intended to chop the fungi as finely as possible, and when cooked, pound them into a puree through a battered flour sieve she had located at the bottom of the blue coloured kitchen larder cabinet. Her mother had recently talked Billy into buying a blender, and had been making batches of different soup until, as Billy had put it, it was coming out of their ears.

The apples were peeled, sliced and baked in a pastry tart which she decorated with "apples" and "leaves" fashioned from the pastry trimmings. The recipe was one of her Granny's comprising a half and half mix of pig lard and real butter, not margarine. She was unable to justify beating a whole egg to glue the decorations on, so substituted it with milk, glazing the top and sprinkling sugar on to sweeten.

In the second biggest aluminium saucepan she could find under the sink, she browned the beef and pork mince along with chopped onion, crushed garlic and grated carrot. When satisfied with the colour, she added tinned tomatoes and the tomato puree leaving the mixture to simmer for as long as she could, which she calculated to be about three hours. The herbs would be added towards the end. For good measure, she decided to crumble in an Oxo cube to ensure it salty enough to counter the sweetness of the tomato and vegetables. The largest saucepan was given a good scrub with a Brillo pad as it looked decidedly grimy to her. Once rinsed thoroughly, she considered it good enough for boiling the water she would need later.

During her shopping trip, she had collected a bale of briquettes. The next job was to prepare a fire ready for lighting in the open grate in the front sitting room. Using scrunched up newspaper and a few old sticks found in the empty coal house — any solid fuel had long been used up by previous tenants — she expertly laid the incendiaries. The briquettes, although not as hot as coal, were lighter to carry and had to do.

A small dining room was situated between the front parlour and the back scullery kitchen. It had a yellow Formica table patterned with thin black squiggles. She scraped it clean of ancient, dried spillages set like cement. Whilst collecting the kindling, she had found some orange marigolds and multicoloured snapdragons growing in the cracks of the concreted backyard. They were refugee seedlings escaping from neighbouring dogs and cats, and had resisted the pernicious pecking of wood pigeons. Delighted to discover them, she had picked and arranged some in a jam jar, placing it in the middle the table. Attempting to find matching place settings of cutlery from the random discards in the drawer, and failing, she selected one of everything needed for each course. To one side of the flowers, she put a saucer of peanuts and on the other, a dish of green olives. Opening the tin, she tasted one for the first time, and had not been entirely sure she liked it. Nonetheless, she considered it the height of sophistication to offer them.

Paudie was due to arrive at 6 o'clock. His punctuality thus far had been impressive, not what she was used to at all. She made sure to be ready. For the occasion, she decided to wear an A line skirt that she was keeping for interviews. It was chocolate brown with diagonal pinstripes in a camel colour, and had large, black plastic buttons down the front. She opted for knee length boots because her only pair of tights had a ladder in them. As a finishing touch, around a beige turtle necked skinny rib top, she draped strings of tiny multicoloured love beads. She had bought them from an early pioneering Punk rocker selling jewellery at a concert held in the Student Union. From the hippy friend that she discussed metaphysics with, she acquired a tiny bottle of Patchouli oil, and that was dabbed behind her ears, on her wrists and for added effect, between her breasts.

Paudie duly arrives on time as predicted, bearing a strange shape hidden in white tissue paper. Unwrapped, a bottle of Mateus Rosé is revealed. Along with it, is a box of Black Magic chocolates. Delving around the kitchen, he locates a single wine glass which he rinses and polishes with a tea cloth. He fills it with wine for her, but makes do with a badly scratched Duralex hotel bathroom glass for himself.

Standing opposite each other in the tiny dining room, she finds her manners, 'thank you for bringing the wine, Paudie,' clinking his glass.

'No, thank YOU, Ruth, for inviting me to dinner,' looking directly into her eyes.

'No, thank YOU, Paudie, for giving me the lifts while I was banjaxed,' gazing back into his.

Putting his glass down on the table, 'thank YOU, Ruth, for accepting them,' stepping closer to take hers.

'Thank,YOU, Paudie, for the chocolates.'

'Thank,YOU, Ruth,' yanking her towards him, 'for coming into my life,' leaning down to kiss her. Receptively, she wraps her arms around his neck and moulds herself into his body.

With firm insistence, he presses his slightly open mouth against hers, and separates her lips. As they kiss and kiss, she enjoys electrifying sensations in her body; responding to the stimulation of that exquisitely sensitive part. She reciprocates, nervously quivering her lips around his. Emboldened by her compliance, he uses his tongue to prise her mouth wider and seek out hers. His competence tells her he is no novice in the world of lovemaking which she finds both strangely reassuring, and worrying. But before going any further, she wants to feed him the efforts of her labours. Pushing him away with an enigmatic smile to keep relations friendly, she invites him to sit down at the table. Pausing for a moment or two as if to decide which of his needs to give into first, he opts for his stomach. There will be plenty of time for the other.

The soup bowl on Paudie's side of the table is emptied before she gets halfway through her own. She leaps up and refills it, giving the large simmering pan a stir while out in the kitchen. The main course turns out well. Paudie would go on for years afterwards about her version being the best Spag Bol in the world, including Italy. Not that he ever went. And he has a third helping of the apple tart with Bird's custard.

Stacking the dirty dishes, 'I've a fire laid ready in the parlour, Paudie. Do you want to go light it for me?'

'Let me carry those into the kitchen for you first — they look heavy.'

'I'll fill the kettle for tea,' going ahead. 'I've some cake, too.'

Paudie puts the plates onto a wooden draining board then comes up behind her, nuzzling into the skin above her neckline and below her ear, 'hmm, you smell good.' Then turning her around, away from the humming kettle, he reaches over to turn the gas ring off.

Feeling anxious about his intentions, 'will you not have some tea, Paudie?' she squeaks.

Recommencing where he left off, he softly kisses her, running his tongue around the inner line of her lips. Rubbing his hands up and down her back, he moves them lower to grasp and knead her rounded buttocks.

She battles with an inner conflict. Her upbringing warns of disapproval and disappointment from her deeply respected father. The teachings of the church prohibiting fornication shout in her ear. Warnings from older female relatives of the wicked ways of young men, revolve around her head. The bad experiences of girlfriends flare up in her mind. The fear of pregnancy hits her solar plexus. They all scream of terrible danger ahead.

Her responding body has other ideas. It yells back forcefully, ignore all that old fashioned stuff — let's go for it, girl! You fancy the pants off him — you know you want it! This is the twentieth century, for God's sake! Haven't you heard of free love?

Ultimately her heart acts as adjudicator, and gives the final verdict. Paudie is to be bestowed her best prizes: her virginity, and more importantly, her devoted love. She lets him take the lead. He knows what to do with her body that now trembles uncontrollably as he escorts her to the bedroom. Permitted to enter her sanctuary, she lets him remove her clothing, piece by piece. Allows him see, and touch, and smell her hidden places. Probe, and lick, and taste her with his flickering tongue. Pierce and pull aside membrane curtains to visit the unexplored with his engorged penis. Knowing he is the first to explore this hidden territory, he wants to generously teach her pleasures she has not fully experienced before.

She trusts him, and believes him to be a decent fellow. There could be a happy, secure future with him, however vague that concept is. He will look after her, she feels certain.

Looking back now, was that all she wanted and expected from a permanent relationship? And was Paudie the right man to provide it in reality? Or was he just a cinema screen to project her hopes and desires upon?

Chapter 5

'That's the end of the first phase, Ruth. I'll be back on Monday to start Phase 2. Any questions?' Dr Geraghty gathers her notes together.

Feeling better groomed having pulled a comb through her hair earlier, but aware how lank it is, 'yes, there is something I want to ask you, Doctor. Can I be unplugged from this machine easily? I mean, can I be detached from it temporarily to go have a shower? If I felt up to it?'

'Certainly, but how often are you using it? Let me look at the readings.' Doctor Geraghty walking around to the other side of the bed. 'Ruth, your use has dropped markedly. Let me talk to Dr Mulhall about putting you on patches instead — they are like sticking plasters filled with liquid pain relief that's absorbed across the skin.'

'Yes, Doctor, I know about them from the pharmacy. I'm not sure I'm ready to come off the machine completely, though — the pain's still bad at times.'

'Yes, I can imagine that would be the case. But don't worry, the pump can easily be set up again if the patches are not enough. It's just — it'd be better for you if you changed your pain relief protocol. This is such an excellent improvement. I'll come back to you as soon as I have spoken with Dr Mulhall.'

She watches Dr Geraghty almost skipping out the door, and believes she has made someone's day at least.

Her Friend leans against the wash basin, arms and ankles crossed. 'Do you think you often make a person's day, Ruth?' looking at her quizzically.

She tries her best, but suspects she fails most of the time.

It is not that she is not empathetic enough to pick up on other people's feelings. On the contrary, she often considers herself too sensitive at times. It is just she knows she can lose patience quickly, and get irritated easily. Not knowing where this bad humour comes from most of the time, she always feels bad afterwards, and worries that she has offended someone.

Her Friend walks over to the chair, 'really, Ruth? Are you sure you don't know why you feel like that? Tell me about Nora.'

Nora? My God, she was some woman; and what a challenge.

Nora was Paudie's mother. She did not meet her for over a year after they became an item. This was partly due to geographical distance, and the roads being under developed and slow going back then. Because of studying commitments and playing polo, Paudie opted to stay in Dublin at the weekends. During longer college holidays, he couch surfed at friends' places, or went home with them to their families. She wondered why he had been reluctant to go home, but when he fudged an answer, she assumed he was like herself and most of her friends: that he just wanted freedom from parental nagging.

When he proposed to her, meeting with his family became imperative. A weekend visit was arranged, and he booked her into a conveniently sited Bed and Breakfast in Balnarath town centre. The introductory meeting with his parents was planned for Saturday lunchtime at the family home. Dropping her off at the guesthouse the night before, he reiterated the need to arrive punctually the next day, knowing she was a tad lackadaisical.

Waking the next morning, she was surprised at how well she had slept in a strange bed. Then remembering the purpose of the visit, a surge of anxiety rose up into her throat. Dressed in her best brown skirt, she went down to the dining room, but only managed half the porridge presented to her, and a bite or two from the Full Irish breakfast. Deciding that a brisk walk might calm her nerves, the landlady directed her to a path alongside the river which culminated in a large town park. Making a note of the time, she worked out how long she could amble before turning around again. The path was thankfully dry so her only footwear stayed clean. She took deep, calming breaths as she wended her way under willow stands and alder trees, purposefully admiring upright tufts of furry pussy willow to distract herself. The dangling alder catkins in golds and purples would make lovely fringing on curtains, she thought. Turning heel at the allotted time, she made her way back to the town centre. Part way down the Main Street, she happened across a florist shop.

'…I have these perfect yellow chrysanthemums here. I could mix in a few of the white and the brown for you, too. You're not from around here. Are you new in town?' the florist stands arms akimbo and dressed in a pink nylon overall.

'No, I don't live here,' knowing her heavy Dublin accent is a clear a giveaway. 'Hmm — I'm not really a fan of chrysanthemums.'

'How about roses, then? I've different varieties, there, there and there,' the woman points to various galvanised buckets. 'So, are you visiting or just passing through?'

'A short visit. I wasn't thinking of roses really,' circling the buckets.

'Well, how about some Alstroemeria? They're very new — the latest thing. They're in some perfectly gorgeous shades of orange. Visiting, so you are? So, where would you be staying now? Hanrahan's Hotel, is it?'

'No — at Mrs Mooney's,' she picks a path through the display vases.

'Ahh, at Gloria's — she keeps a clean and tidy place, I heard tell. I could put in a few sprays of white Gypsophila — that would set the orange off perfectly. So, your husband is waiting for you back there, then?'

'No, I'm staying on my own. Hmm — I'm not sure about orange,' tapping her chin in contemplation.

'"Not sure about orange", so. Now, let me see —how about blue, then? Those irises are a perfect shade of blue. Really? All on your own? We're a bit out of the way here, so tell me why would —?'

Interrupting, 'no, I never choose irises.'

She had history with an Iris. Iris was a girl at National School who bullied her. Iris was from a poor family, and had decided that she was posh and spoilt, and therefore would automatically look down on anyone who had a father on the dole. This was completely untrue, but Iris remained unfriendly, bordering on aggressive. One day, Iris decided she wanted her new colouring pencils, but she stood her ground, and refused to hand them over. Iris forced the issue by trying to snatch them. There was no way anyone was going to get her drawing materials, so they pushed and shoved each other until they ended up rolling around on the ground in a tussle. Used to fighting with her sisters, she knew how to handle herself. Iris eventually scrambled up off the playground floor, and retreated, vowing to get her back at a later date. At home that evening, Vera went mad seeing the state of her torn school uniform until she explained what had happened. Rachel, her fearless oldest sister overheard the whole conversation from the front sitting room, and told Ronnie, the next sister down, who had a gentler disposition. Both agreed that anyone threatening to even breathe in the direction of their younger sister was going to be toast — and fairly rapidly — led to a major showdown with Iris the next day. Afterwards there was a wary distance between them and Iris, and the girl was always held up in family history as an example of unpleasant behaviour. The beautiful flowers sharing the same name became forever tainted.

'How about Carnations then? Those lads over there,' the proprietor walks towards a container at the other side. 'They're in perfect shades of red and pink. So, what brought you to our small town?'

'I was thinking something more impressive — you know — something luxurious?' carefully ignoring the last question.

'Luxurious — you say?' The woman's face is a picture of amazement, and unable to contain her curiosity any further, 'and what would the special occasion be? It must be for someone very special —'

Another deflection, 'those big white flowers there! I like the look of those.'

'The lilies? Yes, they're perfectly beautiful. And they're heavily scented. And luxurious, as you say.'

Hearing "lilies" brings another word to mind — peace. She is certain she has heard of peace lilies. Visiting the O'Sullivans with the intention of peace, she thinks them ideal.

The florist looks her up and down, 'now, they'd be the most expensive flowers I have, mind.'

'They'll do!'

'Well, if that's what you want,' sniffily. Then warming to a prospective sale, 'I could do you a best price — say — 6 stems for the price of 5 — would that be agreeable?'

'Yes, indeed — that would be perfect.'

The woman gathering the flowers into a bouquet is not prepared to yield just yet, 'so, will we be seeing you again, miss?'

'Maybe — who knows?' Then feeling guilty for not playing the game while handing over the money, 'thank you for making such a beautiful gift. You're very good,' smiling sweetly at the woman, and exiting the shop without delay .

Following Paudie's hand sketched map, she turned into what had to be the swankiest street in town. At the end of a tree lined avenue, the O'Sullivans' house stood in prominent position. It was a large detached, double fronted villa flanked by smaller, yet equally grand period houses acting as bridesmaids to the all important bride.

The cast iron gate was well maintained with no rust spots, and swung open on well oiled hinges. Miniature clipped box hedging, bordered terracotta clay rope edging, that ran alongside a black and white chequered, encaustic tiled path. The heavy brass door knocker gleamed, and the paint work around was faded, probably by frequent applications of Brasso. Equally shiny was a brass plate set in the brick wall engraved, "Dr Brendan O'Sullivan", with a list of letters after the name that meant nothing to her. Inscribed in gold leaf on a glass fanlight above the door was the name "Rath House".

Looking for an electric doorbell, all she finds is an upside down metal handle attached to a rod. Hoping for the best, she gives it a tug. After a few minutes the door opens, and an older woman wearing an apron smiles out at her.

Offering her hand politely, 'Mrs O'Sullivan, how nice to meet you.'

'No, no, I'm not Mrs O'Sullivan, my dear,' warmly. 'I'm Carmel, the housekeeper. Come in, won't you, please.' The woman shoos her in with welcome, 'you must be Ruth Wilton. They're expecting you. Follow me, please, and I'll show you in.'

Out from a glazed vestibule, she is brought into a wide hallway with doors either side, and a staircase with mahogany handrails going up the middle. The first door on the left has a sign lettered "Waiting Room", but she is ushered into the first door on the right labelled "Private".

Inside the room, to her excited relief, is Paudie standing with an older man, whom she thinks has to be his father. An older woman, his mother presumably, sits in a dark blue velvet winged arm chair with curved Queen Anne legs.

Paudie rushes over to her grinning and kisses her chastely on the cheek. Cupping her elbow, he guides her across the room, 'Dad, please meet, Ruth Wilton.' The man peers over half rimmed glasses and nods a friendly greeting while extending his hand. Then Paudie propels her towards the velvet chair. 'And Mother, may I introduce my fiancée, Ruth Wilton?' with pride in his voice.

She detects a slight edge of defiance in his tone, but has no time to process that idea fully. At the mention of the word fiancée, the woman's close mouthed smile lets slip a fleeting wince. With all the tension in the room, she feels even more nervous and has to do something.

Thrusting the paper and cellophane wrapped bouquet at the woman, 'pleased to meet you, Mrs O'Sullivan. I brought these for you.'

Looking down into the floral cone, the doyenne instinctively shrinks back, pushing the flowers away with an outstretched arm as though they are radioactive. 'Oh, lilies! — Oh — oh—!' turning her grimacing face protectively away to one side.

Dr O'Sullivan moves agilely, whisking the bunch of blooms away and intervening, 'thank you very much, Ruth.

That is most thoughtful of you. I'll go and give them to Carmel to deal with. Can I get you a sherry on the way back?'

Later, Paudie explained that his mother had a morbid dread of lilies considering them to signify the imminent death of someone close. He apologised profusely for not warning her to never bring them to the house.

Over a lunch of roast chicken, she is subjected to a formal interview about her family of origin (working class), and where she has been brought up (in a Dublin Corporation housing estate). Her educational background (ordinary state schools), and chosen degree course ('airy fairy' Fine Art), all principally conducted by Nora O'Sullivan. Dr O'Sullivan jovially requests that Nora leaves the girl alone, but Nora is not shaken from her mission. Her defence is that this is her prospective daughter in-law, and in becoming part of the family, everyone, meaning herself, needs to get to know all about Ruth.

Nora nibbles small spoonfuls of trifle from a cut glass dessert bowl placed before her by Carmel. 'Which is your parish in Dublin, Ruth? Have your parents met with the priest to discuss possible dates for the wedding?'

Looking up from her food, 'we attend St. Mary's church in Crumlin, and yes, I spoke with Reverend Driver last Sunday about it.'

'Reverend?' Nora echos, her brows knotting; she places her spoon down carefully into the bowl. 'Are you a Protestant, by any chance, Ruth?' her eyebrows lifting slightly.

A loud clanging noise comes from the direction of the mahogany sideboard where Carmel has dropped the silver serving spoon into a large crystal fruit bowl.

'Your name —ah —of course,' Nora leans back in her chair with a thoughtful expression.

Looking over at Paudie, she is concerned about the impact of this information. He says nothing; just sits back, sighs and rolls his eyes upwards in resignation. She turns her attention towards Dr O'Sullivan whose own spoon remains in suspended animation somewhere level with the breast pocket of his Donegal tweed jacket. Answering brightly as if of no consequence, 'yes, I am, Mrs O'Sullivan — I'm Church of Ireland.' Except she knows it will be of great consequence, and is deceiving herself to think otherwise. It is going to be of such significant importance to Nora she could bet money on it.

All her life she had to deal with being a Protestant. There was name calling from other children at school, especially from Iris who was a catholic, despite her having a typically Protestant girl's name. She later learned that Iris had a Presbyterian grandfather who had asked for her to be named after his own mother, and was deeply embarrassed about it.

Over the years, when people found out, she endured anything ranging from mild suspicion to undisguised hostility. The discrimination had improved within her own life time as The Troubles in the North brought a lot of issues around religious prejudice out into the open. Since then, the exposure of scandals in the Catholic Church, plus a general societal move towards secularisation meant fewer people idealised the Roman Church in the way they once had. Politicians began to resist church interference, and the numbers of active church goers dwindled. People would profess that it was not an issue for them. But for Nora, and people of her generation, it had been a most contentious matter. For particularly devout followers such as Nora, it was a major one.

Sitting at the dining table with its pure white table linen dressed almost like an altar, she makes a mental note to keep her forked tail well hidden under her skirt. Ensure that her hooves do not mark the highly polished parquet flooring, and to keep her horns closely trimmed to her scalp at all times.

In due course to smooth the situation, she offered somewhat reluctantly to accommodate the O'Sullivans, and convert to the Roman Church. This seemed to resolve a difficult dilemma for the O'Sullivans. But it was not that simple for her family. Billy was most affronted, and the Rector had to be called in to discuss the issue several times before he resolved his feelings enough to attend the nuptials.

During the rest of the engagement, she attended Catholic Mass regularly, and enrolled in a Church marriage preparation course with the Parish Priest which seemed to satisfy Nora. It bemused her however, that a man who had taken up a life of celibacy could lecture her and Paudie on marital relations, sex and family life. At least Reverend Driver was married and had raised a family. Whenever the subject of future baptisms, First Holy Communions and Confirmations came up, she made sure to say the appropriate thing. Struggling at first, she did not fully understood the rituals of her new church. There had been no Book of Common Prayer to guide her like she was used to; she did not know the responses off by heart like the other churchgoers, and she had countless questions for Paudie. She missed singing hymns which had been one of her favourites things about church, making what could be a boring ordeal much more tolerable.

At the wedding itself, Paudie's side of the church lined up to receive the Eucharist, but her much smaller side remained in their seats. Glancing at her father as she returned from the altar rail, she recognised the tightly held anger on his face, and noticed her mother squeezing his hand in calming support. Vera was much more relaxed about the issue, understanding the difficult situation she was in. Vera declared them all Christians and that was what counted. Coming to the same conclusion herself, she observed the two traditions having much more in common than they differed….

Her reminisces are halted by Dr Geraghty putting her head around the door. The doctor hesitates briefly as though in two minds, but then seemingly satisfied, enters fully. Walking over to the bed, 'Dr Mulhall, and I, have had a discussion, Ruth.' The doctor halts, a troubled look crossing her face.

'Dr Geraghty?'

Refocusing her attention onto Ruth, 'we've decided to not change your medication this side of the weekend as we don't want to leave you at any risk of discomfort. But if you still want to try the patches on Monday, we'll take it from there. Is that ok?'

'Yes, I think that's for the best. I don't think I have the energy for a shower just yet. Thank you, Doctor. Is everything okay?'

'Yes, indeed — I'm delighted with the progress you are making.'

'No, not with me — with you? How are you, doctor?'

'Good — good — maybe a little tired. But that's no concern of yours, Ruth,' smiling with a forced brightness.

'Have you a nice weekend planned? Are you off duty? Will you get to do something nice for yourself?'

'No, no, I'm on call. But that's okay — I've studying to do between patients. That's if I get a chance. If other pressures don't make demands,' ruefully, then lapsing into frowning thought.

She waits for the doctor to speak. The doctor stares at the floor, her brow knotted.

Trying to be helpful, 'remember, Dr Geraghty, "All work and no play, makes Jill a dull girl",' feeling concern for the woman.

The medic lifts her head, 'good point, I'll try and remember that. Thanks, Ruth,' and slowly leaves the room. Her Friend quickly poses, 'and does, "all work and no play, makes Ruth a dull girl" — hmm?'

'Hello, Sophie! I wasn't expecting you. I thought you had camogie practice on Saturday mornings?' feeling startled and unprepared.

'I fell off the stepladder last night and landed awkwardly — I walloped my knee on the way down,' her daughter bends over to pull up a track suit bottom leg to display a swollen red and purple knee. Hobbling over to the armchair, she sits heavily with a thump.

Shuddering involuntarily, 'ouch! Be careful! That looks so sore, Sophie! And I can see you've stiffened up so much. That's not like you — you're so fit and supple. Did you put ice on it, and arnica? Have you shown it to your father? No, I agree, you couldn't possibly go to practice with that. That needs rest and plenty of it.'

Looking forlorn, 'Daddy dropped some things over to me. And a support bandage to wear for when I go back.'

'Hmm — accidents — they can be a sign. It might be an idea to slow down. I worry that you're doing too much. Accidents are often a warning that's happening.'

'You're a fine one to talk, Mammy. I get it from someone, you know,' defensively.

Switching into admonishing mode, 'yes, I know. But I had no choice. You, however, have chosen to take on all your commitments, Sophie. You could trim some of them — give yourself a break and not be so hard on yourself,'

'But I need to be busy — it stops me from thinking too much.'

'Need to be busy? Thinking too much? What do you mean, Sophie? Think about what?' a distant klaxon sounds in her head.

'Nothing, Mammy,' looking away, not wanting to engage with her mother's concern. 'It really doesn't matter.'

'Yes, it does. It matters to me,' feeling more alarm at her dismissal. 'You're my daughter,' a sense of responsibility mounting. 'And I love you very much,' nearing an emotional hair trigger. 'And I want you to be happy,' feeling panic. 'Tell me what you mean, please, Sophie!' beseeching.

'Don't Mammy, you're making me want to cry.'

'Tell me!' making clear this is an order, not an option.

Pulling a tissue out of her pocket, Sophie faltering, 'It's just — it's just — I don't think I can cope anymore.'

'Go on, I'm listening — cope with what?' feeling relief at Sophie's apparent cooperation.

'It's just — I'm trying hard to not think about you leaving us — you passing — I keep thinking I won't miss you — I managed to look after myself all these years — I don't really need — anyone. But then I keep thinking that I won't be able to manage when you've actually gone — It's like — at the moment — I know you're there, if I really needed you — but once you go…' tears pour down her face and sobs hinder further speech.

'Oh, Sophie,' beginning to cry herself.

Tilly barges through the door with the tea trolley, 'Hi, hon —' then surveying the scene, makes a quick assessment. Thrusting a tea cup at Ruth and asking Sophie, 'now will it be tea or coffee, you'll be having? Milk? Sugar? — Okay, white coffee,' shoving a cup and saucer at Sophie. 'Now, let me see,' bending to look on the lower shelf of the trolley and rummaging around in a plastic box. Procuring two bars of Cadbury's Dairy Milk chocolate and handing them over, 'here's one for each of you. Chocolate cures all ills known to man, I promise. Eat it up, I tell you,' then discreetly departs.

Amid snot filled snorts of tension releasing laughter, they sip at their drinks and suck on pieces of chocolate, both united for a rare moment.

Wanting to return to an important question, 'Sophie, what did you mean when you said you've learned to look after yourself over the years?'

'I just had to,' shrugging and resisting her mother's probing. Then relenting, 'you were always too busy trying to do everything and when you did sit down, you were too tired. I could see that. When I tried to talk to you about something, you always said, "later Sophie, I'm doing something." But "later" never happened. Then on Sundays when you didn't have to go to work, you never let me stay back with you when Daddy took the three of us to Polo. I didn't like Polo and I wasn't interested in hanging around the matches like the others did. I wanted to stay home with you and play.'

Gently countering, 'but you did stay home when you were older.'

'I know I did, but that was when I was much older — only after I caught Glandular Fever and was too ill to go.'

Confused, 'but you loved the stables and riding the ponies when your father gave up the polo.'

'Yes, I know I did. But it was always for too long. Daddy would get talking to people and we would end up being there all day. It felt like I never saw you, what with work, minding Granny and Grandad and everything else you had to do.'

Feeling stunned by this revelation, yet knowing to ameliorate, 'I'm so sorry, Sophie. I had no idea…,' trailing off, trying to think of some reasonable defence. 'But many mothers work. And I thought you liked spending time with your father.'

Beginning to cry again, 'I did. But I wanted to spend time with you too — at home — And help you with the housework, I knew you had no support — I wanted to make you feel better about things…,' tears beginning to choke her voice.

Ruth spluttering, 'God Bless you, Sophie! You poor —'

Interrupting her mother, 'And then, when THAT time happened —'

Deidre strides into the room talking loudly, 'Hello, Mammy! How are you? Hey! Sophs, what are you doing here? Are you okay?'

Sniffing loudly and straightening from a crumpled pose, Sophie answers without emotion, 'yes, I'm fine. Just a banjaxed knee, is all.'

'What? Now? Has it just happened? What did you do? Is that why you're crying?'

'No, yesterday — I have to go now. Seánie has a list of stuff he wants to get done today,' rising from the seat with difficulty. Limping over to kiss her mother's cheek; her sister standing, mouth open, lost for words. 'Bye, Mammy, I'll see you soon. Talk to you later, Dee.'

Sophie drags her leg to the door and pulls the door closed behind her, always protective of privacy.

Deidre thumbs towards the shut door, 'hey! What's up with her? Is it JUST her leg?'

'It's nothing, Pet — nothing you need worry about. Now tell me, what have you been up to? How's the rest of your week been?'

Settling back into her pillows, she knows Deidre's chattering on about inconsequential matters demanding her full attention, and requiring appropriate responses, will keep her from worrying about Sophie.

Chapter 6

The thud of boots came to a standstill and the bronze doorknob rattled. Pushing her chair back to arise, she felt her heart expanding in anticipation. Poised to glide over to him and enter his aura. Absorb his….

A noise wakes her. Keeping her eyelids closed, she hopes to enjoy a lovely long moment before real life elbows its way into her consciousness.

'Ruth? I have your medication here — I need to refill the pump,' Nurse Nóirín stands at the foot of the bed with the drugs trolley. 'You're to have extra tablets today bringing you up to the full dosage of Predisolone.'

Nóirín passes the paper cup of pills while she pours Lucozade into the plastic glass.

'I've heard some interesting things about you at the team meeting this morning,' Nóirín continuing. 'I understand you want to come off the pump next week and try morphine patches. And that you want to get up and do some self care — that's excellent news, Ruth. I think we'll leave you with bowls to wash yourself over the weekend — a "cat lick" if you like. And then we'll help you shower next week when more of us are on the ward.' Nóirín leaves the room, her practical crêpe soled shoes radiating efficiency with every step.

Her Friend moves from the corner where he has been standing and sits on the armchair. A slight frown, then a look of care on his face, 'what do you think about Sophie's revelations this morning, Ruth? How do you feel about them?'

Regrettably, she cannot deny any of them.

Painful as it was to hear, she knows Sophie was right and had every reason to say it. Guilt gnaws away in her gut from its basic truth. If she is completely honest, she had resented it whenever Sophie came looking for her. When the child wanted her attention; to listen to her, or for some help with a task. A sense of maternal responsibility led her to oblige — but with reluctance. She never enjoyed spending time with Sophie like she had the other two. She feared that whenever she gave of herself to Sophie, her daughter would always look for more. Sophie would never get on with things by herself, and free her up to get on with her own tasks. The girl would seem needy and greedy of her attention. There was never enough time, or energy to pander to her insatiability.

Nodding with understanding and acceptance, her Friend sits in an open posture, his arms resting lightly on the armrests with a look of unconditional love on his face. Pushing for more disclosure, 'when did it all start, darling? Or had it always been like that with Sophie?'

It was like it before Sophie was even born.

As far as she was concerned, her family was made complete with Dee Dee's birth. The cottage was tiny with only two bedrooms, but it had not mattered as Daithí and Dee Dee were small. It was a pretty place to live in, and was practical in that it was easy to clean and keep tidy. This left plenty of time to paint while the children played and napped. Cadging equipment from Vera and Carmel, she set up a functioning kitchen and prepared meals that Paudie savoured. On fine days, she would take the children outside into the fresh air where she created a cottage style garden with seeds bought at Cuddihy Builders Providers and donations from her Granny. Nora's gardener, Tom, taught her the basics of horticulture and offered advice. Painting, garden design and cooking satiated her creative yearnings; and her family of two children and Paudie, were enough to meet her emotional needs.

One looming cloud in her sunny world was the requirement to help with the business as soon as Deidre was weaned off the breast. Nora, after some hesitation, and with caveats about her and Carmel being allowed to care for the children as they saw fit, agreed to mind Deidre as well as Daithí. With all that arranged, she returned to the pharmacy.

Not at all comfortable with handing the children over to Nora as she had considered Nora dated in her views on childrearing, she felt powerless to challenge them. Thankfully, she knew that the children spent most of the time with Carmel in the kitchen. Daily women coming in to Rath House did the bulk of the house cleaning and laundry which freed Carmel up principally to order supplies and cook. In between meal preparation, Carmel was available to play with the children which she loved doing. With her warmth had come a natural kindness, and Carmel had been open enough to pick up on her more modern ideas on parenting.

It was orchestrated harmoniously with two small children; any more would prove difficult to accommodate. Whenever Paudie raised the subject of having another child, she declined. Because her arguments had been reasonable and practical, he usually conceded. Yet, he would always have to have the last word, proclaiming his longing for a larger family at the end of every discussion.

Going on the Pill was something she avoided, not wanting to incur regular doctor's fees. They continued using condoms which were cost price for them through the business. Her libido remained high once recovered from the hiatus of child birth, and she had enough youthful energy for them to indulge in their favourite pastime together. There had never been any opportunity, or time to develop other joint interests and hobbies. Paudie was a good, considerate lover, she reckoned, albeit with her limited experience of men. He encouraged her to try new things which she generally responded to with enthusiasm, although she often wondered where on earth he got his ideas from. A hidden stash of porn magazines discovered in a cupboard in Paudie's dispensary answered that question for her. She carefully replaced them, and after a chat with Vera to talk through her shock and dismay, she took her mother's advice to keep schtum, and accepted that it was what "normal" men did. As the children were placid by nature, there were few problems getting them to bed, and they would generally sleep through. The household would wake early, everyone refreshed and looking forward to the day ahead.

As is the pattern of life, she has come to learn, nothing ever stays the same. In her experience, it goes through phases, some of them good; but on the whole, most are challenging. Looking back, her life was idyllic up until Paudie came home one evening with a new brand of French wine called Le Piat D'or.

She had spent the afternoon post-work playing with the children, splashing about in a trickling stream near the cottage. The pair of them were so exhausted by all the fun, she cleaned and fed them without delay, and got them into bed early. Once Paudie had calculated the day's takings, they had the whole evening to themselves. Paudie put on a U2 cassette tape while she put out a lasagne with side salad and garlic bread. Afterwards, Paudie conjured up a Cadbury Starbar which he knew was her favourite, and she sat munching it on the sofa while he cleared the dirty dishes into the sink. He did not go as far as washing them, but with the wine, she felt relaxed enough to leave them to soak until morning.

Paudie takes the cassette player up to their room and puts on Led Zeppelin's 'Houses of the Holy'. As the rhythmic music plays, he presses her into acting out a new fantasy of his; for her to be his personal stripper. While he lies propped up on the bed watching, she gets into role, draping herself in various stages of undress across his body, teasingly undoing his garments as she goes along. Paudie takes the opportunity to alternately stroke, and slap her flesh as parts are revealed; he pays particular attention to her vulva, and homes in on her clitoris. Once his straining penis is freed from his jeans, she repeatedly licks its full length slowly up and down until eventually she takes the organ's tip into her mouth. She swirls her tongue around the weeping orifice, enjoying the groans of encouragement from Paudie. His increasingly urgent moans indicate the need to grab the pre-opened condom, and she rolls it over the end, fully down the shaft until it fits quite snugly. She climbs onto him, and straddles facing him. While she guides his erection up into her vagina, he holds the weight of her breasts in his hands, and tweaks and rubs her nipples with his forefingers and thumbs. After an enthusiastic riding which elicits several orgasms in her, he tells her to get into a doggie position. She knows it is a favourite of his as it gives him better traction, and a more forceful thrust. Her hormones are at screaming pitch, and after yet more climaxes, Paudie finally lets go of his self-control, and allows himself to ejaculate. He quickly withdraws from her, exhausted, and both of them flop onto the bed. Her knees are weak with physical effort, and vaginal contractions. She turns on to her side to cuddle up to her husband. Paudie, equally spent, lies on his back motionless. His flaccid penis reposes across his groin, naked and glistening. Mildly concerned about the whereabouts of the missing condom, she rolls on to her back, and draws her knees up to check. Putting her fingers inside, she feels something that shakes her post-coital reverie. Tugging on an alien object, she pulls out a pale pink, sticky rubber.

'Paudie! Paudie! Your johnny's come off!' shaking his shoulder.

'Hmm?' Paudie dozing.

'Your fucking johnny Paudie! It's not on you, you eejit. It's after coming off and was still inside me!'

'Hmm? Really?' turning onto his side, his back towards her in tired indifference.

With the mellowness of afterglow, she mutters in defeat, 'too late now…'

A few weeks later when she was unable to keep awake in the early evenings, followed by a late period, and the arrival of all too familiar vomiting, she guessed irreversible consequences were on the way. Paudie was delighted with the news. She was much more circumspect. Daithí's conception had provoked anxious excitement. Deidre's planned arrival had been welcomed with confidence. But this third pregnancy left her feeling, frankly, despondent. As she anticipated, hearty congratulations came from both extended families. The morning after the announcement when she took the two children over to the surgery, Nora cornered her.

Nora targeting the issue without preamble, 'as you will no doubt agree, Ruth, I have provided you with free childcare over these last few years. I have enjoyed it immensely, of course. BUT having THREE small children here in the surgery would not be feasible. I, and Carmel for that matter, are not getting any younger. I think the two children, and their new baby brother or sister, would benefit from some more formal preschool education, would you not agree? Such as Montessori classes.' Holding her in a piercing, hawklike gaze, 'now, if finance is an issue, Dr O'Sullivan and I would be more than happy to help out with fees. We would be delighted to contribute to the education of our grandchildren.' Looking down at her polished talons, 'I understand that there is an excellent Montessori school here in the town, and I can undertake further enquiries on your behalf. Brendan has many contacts in the relevant Authorities, and can obtain adequate references and assurances.'

Predicting that Nora's commitment to another child would be problematic was one of her reasons to limit the family size. Unable to afford childcare, the offer of fees helped somewhat in resolving the issue. In some ways, she acknowledged it would be for the best. The children were getting to an age when preschool would be good for their development. Another positive would be less disapproving interference from Nora. But a young baby going into a crèche with lots of children and few staff? She was not at all sure about that. If the O'Sullivans were willing to cough up some cash, she thought Paudie might agree to employing someone part-time to cover for her while she took some form of maternity leave; not that the concept really existed in family businesses. But Nora and Carmel's services were free anyway, so they would be no better off, and she was certain that Paudie would argue that point.

A different kind of concern also disturbed her. One that was to impact on her well beyond the preschool years. It was the issue of trust. A few years previously, an article about contraception had been in a copy of Cosmopolitan magazine that her sister, Susie, had passed on to her. She had read that modern condoms had strict quality control, and did not burst under normal use. The writer had gone on to say that care had to be taken to hold onto the condom securely while withdrawing when the erection subsidised post-climax. But she knew that Paudie understood all that, and it was not as though they had not practised the procedure hundreds of times before. He always removed the condom fastidiously, tied a knot in it and cleaned himself up with paper tissues or toilet roll kept next to the bed. So why had it come off inside her that time? Why had Paudie changed his habit of dealing with the thing himself? Why had he not noticed that it was not still on him? It did not make sense based on her previous experience, even after drink was taken. An awful suspicion developed in her mind. Had Paudie been culpable in some way? Had he been so determined to have his own way, have the larger family he wanted, that he had facilitated "an accident"? These were questions that had eaten away at her, but she never had the effrontery to openly raise with him. But Doubt looked for further evidence; joined forces with Disrespect, and later invited Resentment along. It was only a matter of time before Contempt showed up….

A new face appears through the door piquing her curiosity. A different young woman brings in the lunch. Slowly and carefully taking up position, the domestic assistant repositions the items on the trolley repeatedly until satisfied with some order seemingly important to her. Reminding her of someone setting up stall on Moore Street Market, but in a more pernickety way, she recalls traders priding themselves on the creation of perfect pyramids of even sized oranges and apples. She observes patiently.

Eventually she needs to break the silence, and wants to initiate some kind of relationship, 'hello, how are you? I haven't seen you before. My name's Ruth. What's for dinner today? I'm quite ready for it — truth be told, I'm starving.'

Enunciating slowly, 'I am Naomi. I have been away. You are Soft so you have soup. I think it is vegetable soup. Then, you have mince and mashed potatoes and mashed carrot and mashed turnip. Afterwards, you have strawberry fool.'

Disappointed with what is on offer, what she actually craves is lamb curry, preferably a Rogan Josh, with a generous serving of pilau rice, and a whole naan bread to herself. Followed by a rich chocolate brownie with mint ice-cream.

And thinking about mint, a starter of poppadoms with cucumber and mint in yogurt, with some vegetable samosas. That would be most welcome. Running a tongue around the inside of her mouth, she realises to her surprise that there are no sore patches — her ulcers have disappeared. She is determined to get onto the Ordinary list.

As she clears her plates clean of food, her Friend laughs, 'was that nice, Ruth? Did you enjoy that, darling? Speaking of enjoyment, were you able to enjoy your third pregnancy?'

No, unfortunately — not in the least.

In fact, it was an absolute trial from start to finish. The morning sickness was even more brutal than before, and that coupled with later indigestion meant she struggled to eat anything properly throughout her term. The smell of cooking alone was enough to make her retch. She had no choice but to prepare food for the children and Paudie. Forcing herself to eat because she felt entirely responsible for the healthy development of the foetus, food consumption was a necessary evil, and no longer a pleasure. The nausea did not abate until week 26 into the pregnancy and then transformed into raging heartburn. An earlier than usual onset of sciatica made caring for the two children painfully difficult. Paudie was helpful when he was at home, but that was only at bath time in the evenings and during Sundays. To be fair to him, he did forego polo which gave her chance to rest. When she had 6 weeks left to go, once she had dropped the children off at Nora's, Paudie would instruct her to gather up the paperwork and work from home for the rest of the day.

During antenatal appointments, the foetus was found to be in a breech position, but she was told that the baby would most likely turn and engage into the birth canal a few weeks prior to delivery. When her labour pains started three weeks early, she knew not to delay as Dee Dee had arrived quickly; and more importantly baby, had not turned around during her clinical review that week. Thankfully, it was a Sunday and Paudie was at home. They drove the children to his parents' with Carmel waiting on the pavement ready to gather them up as they did a speedy drive past on the way to the hospital.

After examining her, the obstetrician agreed that the cervix was enlarged; her waters already broken and the baby had not turned around. He had her prepared for an emergency Caesarian section. Paudie asked to go down to the theatre with her, and the doctor knowing who he was, welcomed him on the proviso he leave the room promptly if asked to. After Sophie was delivered safely, she began to bleed heavily and needed a blood transfusion. Afterwards, the surgeon who was a good Catholic, reassured them that he had saved her uterus so that she could have more children. But as far as she was concerned, THAT WAS NEVER GOING TO HAPPEN AGAIN! EVER!

Chapter 7

A knock on the door, then a pause, and no-one enters.

Ruth yells across the room, 'you can come in!'

'Hello, Ruth — thank you,' a softly spoken woman in her 40s walks over to the bed. 'Do you remember me?' She is wearing a plain, dark unbuttoned jacket, and a rose-pink shirt with a small piece of white clerical collar centred at the neck.

'Yes, I do,' replying in surprised wonder. 'You're the Rector at the small church in Clonlough, aren't you?'

The priest holds out her hand, smiles with delight and nods, 'yes, I'm Barbara Rothwell. How are you feeling? Would you like me to sit with you for a while? I have just been appointed to the Chaplaincy team here at the hospital, and I saw from the list that you're an Anglican — Church of Ireland.'

'Oh, please do — it would be nice to talk to someone different.'

At Barbara's behest, she explains her medical condition, and why she ended up in hospital. She tells her about the treatment trial and how she is noticing some improvements already. After offering The Eucharist from a small Communion travel set kept in a wheelie case, Barbara wipes a tiny chalice and silver plate with a cloth, and puts them away.

'I'll clean those in the ward kitchen before I make my next call. Is there anything else you would like to discuss with me, Ruth, while I'm here?'

'Um — well there is something — a matter I've been pondering about lately. Barbara, do you ever feel God close to you? I mean — you've chosen to be ordained — I know, but — I mean — do you ever have — um, conversations with — Him?'

Barbara remains still and watching Ruth's face closely, 'The Lord is available to EVERYONE who wants to talk to Him. And the amazing thing is, He listens every single time. But He chooses when to talk back, Ruth. Sometimes He will speak completely unexpectedly and other times He waits patiently for someone to work at their relationship with Him first. But be assured, He ALWAYS hears. As to myself, do I ever have conversations with Him? Yes, I do. Everyday I set time aside to sit quietly and pray. And anytime during the day, whenever I feel unsure or troubled, I will ask for His help.'

'That's most interesting, Reverend — I'll think about what you've said,' feeling embarrassed that she might have revealed too much about herself, she closes down the topic.

After Barbara leaves, she thinks back to the day she was admitted onto the ward. Nurse Sonia filled in her personal information sheets. When asked her religion, she spontaneously declared herself Church of Ireland. Paudie looked at her with one eyebrow cocked, an expression she had seen so many times. He used it with the children, the staff and with her whenever he doubted the veracity or wisdom of some declaration. Usually it was enough for the recipient to either amend, or qualify themselves. But on that occasion, it was her decision, and she was determined to stick with it.

Her Friend having withdrawn whilst Barbara was in the room reappears between her bed and the door. His pacing tells her that he is thinking how to phrase something. Stopping at the foot of her bed, 'what significance is it for you, the religion you observe, Ruth?'

What a strange question to ask. But it's no secret.

She was brought up an Anglican and only converted to Roman Catholicism to please Paudie's family so she could marry him. Now older and wiser, and having given some thought to faith recently, she has come to the conclusion that those reasons were not strong enough.

'Fair dues to you, Ruth — so when did this new contemplation about religion begin for you?' running his hands lightly along the top rail of the foot board.

Probably when she agreed to run some urgent stock over to a pharmacist in another town.

It was a business they mutually collaborated with and the local courier was not free to do the transportation. It was nearly lunchtime when she finished dropping the package off, so she picked up a sandwich from a local Centra shop, and planned to find a nice spot to eat it on her way back. Driving through a small hamlet she had always considered picturesque, but had never explored, she pulled over. It was a bright sunny day, and noticing a side road going downhill towards the sea, she had an inclination to walk. It felt good to be away from the shop and stretch her legs out in the fresh air. She passed neatly trimmed hedges that were bursting into leaf and listened to Spring songbirds calling out from them. The road ended near the shore and circled around a small stone built church. Recognising the distinctive architecture and the blue door, she had already surmised it to be a Church of Ireland chapel. Part of a union of churches from nearby villages and the town, the noticeboard also named The Rector as Rev. Canon Barbara Rothwell. A timetable listed a service of The Eucharist on the First Sunday of each month, and a service of Morning prayer on the Third Sunday, both at 10am. Walking around the neatly kept graveyard, she looked at headstones with dates so old they were illegible, to one more recent grave with fading flowers and a wooden cross awaiting a memorial stone. There was a cast iron bench set against the southern face of the church and she sat in the warm sun to eat her lunch. Climbing back up to the car, she felt more relaxed than she had felt in a long while.

One Sunday a few weeks later, having woken at her ingrained time of 6am, she knew Paudie would be off to the stables soon. Pondering what to do with her day off, an idea had formulated. Although she had attended Saturday Evening Mass the day before, she had an urge to attend the little church. Later that morning entering the vestibule, an elderly man dressed in a suit welcomed her, and presented her with a green prayer book, a red hymnal and a copy of that month's parish newsletter. In the nave, couples and single worshippers were sparsely scattered with the pews nearest the front completely vacant. Walking partway up the aisle, she slid on to an ancient patinated oak bench realising too late that she had neither curtsied nor genuflected towards the alter. She had slipped subconsciously into the traditions of her youth. While an older woman delivered the day's readings from the lectionary, she took the opportunity to study the parishioners. Comprising two couples, one elderly and one middle aged; a frail looking woman seated with a boy of about 10 years; a young woman, and another older woman some way apart, and two elderly men sitting alone. The smallness of the congregation saddened her. She felt pessimistic about the church's future wondering how long it could be sustained with so few members.

Reverend Barbara led the service and gave an interesting address about the weaknesses of Peter. Saying how she sympathised with him getting things so wrong with Jesus, and having to be admonished often, she went on to stress that Peter was ultimately forgiven despite everything that had transpired. At the door when leaving, Barbara greeted her, enquiring was she local or visiting, and thanked her warmly for attending.

Out on the gravel path, people gathered into small groups to chat, but no-one spoke to her. She was neither surprised nor offended knowing that Anglicans could be reserved. They often wait until a face becomes familiar before making conversation. Not wishing to appear either inquisitive or pushy, newcomers are viewed like timid deer needing to be gently coaxed into church at their own pace. Not realising she could have parked on the road by the church like everyone else, she walked back up to the village to her car.

Aware of someone behind her, a strong, clear voice had spoken, 'how do you feel now after receiving Holy Communion?'

Turning her head slightly and joking, 'it's my second time in two days. Having been so good, I now have a free pass to be really bad next week, haha.' Not wishing to seem entirely flippant, 'actually, I do feel a sense of peace, thank you. Here's my car.'

Spinning around to say goodbye, she found no-one there. Driving home, she thought some more about the encounter and the people who had been at church. She increasingly felt that whoever had addressed her, had not been a parishioner. Whilst keeping up her regular attendance at Roman Catholic Mass, she returned to the little church two or three times before her illness stopped her continuing.

In retrospect, it was significant to her on a number of levels. Part of it was a return to her roots and the comfort of childhood which for her had been a happy, nurturing experience. The more she learned about society, the more she felt gratitude for this. The simplicity of the liturgy and the stillness of the church felt soothing amidst the chaos of her life. Being allowed to sing loudly without worrying about the quality of her voice was uplifting and the familiar melodies brought a sense of connectivity. The time given over to pray for others, and herself, was an opportunity she rarely thought to take. She has to confess though, it was also an act of rebellion, particularly against Paudie....

She opts for a cheese and pickle sandwich, and a Danish pastry from the tea trolley.

Tilly looks at her, but makes no comment, 'can I give you a yogurt as well, girl?'

Nodding, then teasing, 'don't you have a home to go to, Tilly?'.

Tilly bantering back, 'no, girl, I can't seem to keep away from you. Couldn't leave ye all to suffer under poor Jimmy. He's a great man for the portering, and very thoughtful, but in fairness, it has to be said, he's useless when it comes to the domestics of life. But I love him to bits, all the same,' giggling. 'I'll see ya in the morning, God willing. Sleep well, hon,' trundling out.

Pushing the table away, she brushes away crumbs scattered across the sheets. The sun has set, and she turns on the bedside lamp as the room darkens rapidly. Leaning into the rustling pillows, she savours the remains of the Danish in her mouth. Thinking how she could eat more if she had the chance, she marvels at the return of her appetite. It is all down to the steroids, she knows. Patients in the shop told her stories about raiding their fridges in desperation for cheese, or being unable to contain themselves while eggs boiled for 5 minutes whilst on the same drug. She thinks about what can be brought in from home. Chocolate digestives, family sized bags of hand fried salt and vinegar crisps, some large bananas....

Her Friend comes out of a shadowy corner and stands illuminated by the white glow of the reading light, 'tell me, how does your faith relate to your religion, Ruth?'

Funnily enough, she has given that a lot of thought recently. Maybe because she feels closer to the end.

For her, they are not necessarily the same thing. In other words, faith and religion are not interchangeable terms. She is not convinced that all people who observe religious practises have a strong belief in God. This opinion has been compounded by hearing of the heinous acts that priests and members of the religious orders have committed over the years. Conversely, there are people she has come across who firmly believe in God, but choose not to attend church even during the traditional Christian Festivals of Christmas and Easter. Other people she has witnessed, have displayed Christian values like kindness, charity and forgiveness, but have said unequivocally they believe in neither religion nor in the existence of a Higher Power. In between these polarised extremes of unwavering belief and atheism, she has observed different combinations of faith and religious observance to varying degrees. So where does she fit in to all that? She thinks she believes. But is not sure all of the time. Opting to make the effort to attend church, she does get something out of it, if only to get away from the demands of life. Overall, she thinks she believes in God, even if she can no longer attend church....

Paudie's recognisable knock and slow opening of the door warns of his imminent arrival.

'Darling? How are you? No, I can see for myself, you don't need to tell me, you look SO much better!'

Ignoring his comments, 'How are you? How was the shop today? Did you see Sophie's knee...?'

She listens to general chit-chat about Paudie's day which largely involves his frustration with customers, staff and suppliers; the huge volume of scripts he had to process; the amount of paperwork this then generated, and how he has to

85

deal with it all after he leaves her that evening. The fact his car is due a NCT inspection, but he does not know how he will fit it in. And a chronic toothache that he must get seen to by their dentist. Half listening to stuff she has heard so many times before, she thinks exasperatedly about how some people — namely Paudie — come in and exhaust her with all their problems when she has no energy for it. She decides to take charge and stop his flow. She wants to bring up something that is on her mind, and she then recounts the earlier conversation with Sophie.

'…so, she was feeling very sorry for herself — hard done by — blaming me, and you, for dragging her off to polo against her will.'

Paudie looks crestfallen, 'I'll talk to her about it — she shouldn't be bringing this to you now. It's completely unfair on you with everything you're going through — very inappropriate. Leave it with me.'

She looks at him pointedly, is about to make a remark about people living in glass houses, but decides against it, 'Paudie, will you be coming back tomorrow?'

'Of course, I will!' looking taken aback.

'I didn't want to assume. You CAN have a day off, you know — do your own thing — go to polo or whatever. I wouldn't mind — I'd understand, you know.'

'Ruth, there's nothing else I'd rather be doing; or anyone else's company I'd rather have. I want to see you. Is that OK? Or are you trying to get rid of me?' laughing wryly, then stopping suddenly with a tinge of sadness on his face.

Flapping her hand dismissively, not wanting to talk about them and their relationship, 'when you do so, can you bring me in a piece of Brie de Meaux?…'

On their own again, her Friend asks, 'did you REALLY mean what you said about Sophie?'

Blushing at the thought of it, she knows she put an unfair slant on it. Not being entirely plain-spoken with Paudie is something she's had to develop with him over the years; to protect her real self from him as she doesn't want him getting too close. She mustn't let him see her flaws and weaknesses.

'And why's that, Ruth?', her Friend relaxing back in the chair, in a non-threatening way which encourages her to disclose more.

The less someone knows about you, the less they are able to hurt you. She does not want to give Paudie any ammunition to fire back at her, whenever it suits him; whenever he wants to win an argument, or get his own way. He WOULD do that, you know.

'So does Paudie ALWAYS get his own way?' her Friend persists.

Yes, he does. He always has. And he always will.

'So where does Sophie fit into that?', her Friend seeking clarification.

Paudie and Sophie have been as thick as thieves with each other as soon as the infant was pulled from her womb. To compound matters, Sophie is like her late grandmother, Nora.
It took her a long time to recover from the Caesarian Section. The midwife, and the Community Nurse who took over her care, both said that she would need time to get back to normal. A combination of losing blood and tissue repair meant her body needed a lot of healing. The nurses emphasised not underestimating the emotional effect of an emergency procedure and that it had been a traumatic experience. They advised her to rest as much as possible and relinquish all non-essential activities including work in the shop. But it was not as easy as that. There were three small children; a husband who had a demanding career and her family support network living on the other side of the country. Breastfeeding Sophie was difficult because the scar was agonising whilst holding her. It turned out that the wound was infected. She was put on antibiotics, but after commencing the first of several courses,

Sophie developed colic and could not settle. The poor creature screamed in pain most nights, waking the other children as well as Paudie and herself. Paudie came home armed with different breast pumps so that Sophie could be bottle fed by him, or propped up on a cushion. But she was never able to express milk artificially. Admitting defeat, she put Sophie on formula milk.

There was never the cuddling of Sophie during feeding like the other two, due to the scar. Sometimes she would look at Sophie in her baby rocker and wonder who that small creature was. To her shame, she likened her to some disruptive foundling come to ruin her contented world.

Based on life experience, she realises now that Sophie's normal need for security could have either made her clingy, or look to her father to have her emotional demands met. And Sophie chose the latter, probably because Paudie responded to her. Whenever Sophie hurt herself, or needed reassurance, she would go to Paudie for comfort. If the other children upset her, she would run to him to mete out justice. When she got to the questioning age, she would automatically seek out her father for the answer. If Sophie did ask her something, she would always double check the answer with her father, until in exasperation, she had told her to go directly to him and not waste her time….

She wakes with a start. The night time cacophony of activity out in the corridor is in full swing. The steroids are making getting back to sleep difficult. She resigns herself to lying awake and musing. In the dim light, she can discern her Friend propped up in the chair.

Reading her thoughts, he speaks out, 'yes, I'm awake too. Go on, I'm listening.'

Reflecting back on his earlier question, she ponders why she made Sophie out to be the villain. She knew it was wrong, and feels guilty about presenting it the way she did to Paudie. This is on top of the disgust she already feels about her daughter's assertion of emotional neglect. A tear runs down her temple and soaks into the pillow. She had pushed Sophie away, and at times, her brother and sister too. But those two always remained close to her and still were. Daithí and Deidre were very supportive when she got her original diagnosis and had been steadfast in addressing her needs throughout the illness, with all its ups and downs.

Sophie had brought up Sundays in particular. With working Monday to Saturday full time, Sunday was the only day available to do the bulk of the housework and she had to organise it with precision with the limited time available. Saturday evening Mass left Sunday free from religious obligation. Lunch hours in the week were taken up with food shopping and buying school items for the children. Paudie wanted to keep up his polo and she let him, partly because he deserved a break from work, and partly because she deserved a break from him. When the children were young, she went to mind them. But as soon as they were old enough to amuse themselves while he played, she opted to stay home and get a head start on the week's duties. Paudie soon discovered that it was in everyone's best interests to leave her uninterrupted to focus on the tasks she did not enjoy, but felt obliged to do. He claimed to not see the dust she did. Despite keeping his dispensary as pristine as a pathology lab, she wondered why he could not transfer some of that meticulousness to the kitchen counters at home. If she ever left him to prepare the simplest of meals, the kitchen looked like the Army Catering Corps had been in to feed a battalion. Utensils, mixing bowls and spillages covered every surface, and considering it only fair to help him, she cleared up his mess. She concluded that it was not worth letting him loose in the kitchen.

On the days when there were no tournaments, Paudie took the children to the stables to learn how to ride and care for horses. Then took them to the beach or woods afterwards, if there was time left. If one of the children was unwell, recognising the panic on her face, he provided comics and games to keep them occupied while she got on with her day.

Typically, Sunday dawned with the household rising early and her cooking a big fry for breakfast. Preparing a picnic for them while Paudie got the children ready, she multitasked emptying the dishwasher and reloading it with the greasy breakfast dishes. When the front door closed after them leaving, sighing with relief, she girded her loins and commenced the big clean.

First job was to strip all the beds, get the first load in to the washing machine and remake the beds with fresh linen. If the day was fine, she hung each load outside to dry; otherwise the tumble dryer was put into action. Paudie always complained about the size of the utility bills, and although she was fairly frugal herself, she would say to herself, what the Hell? Just use the fucking dryer and give yourself a break, woman. There was always satisfaction to be gained from doing something that annoyed Paudie.

Next she would tackle the three bathrooms, scrubbing the baths, shower trays, wash hand basins and toilet pans. The vacuum cleaner was hauled upstairs from the utility room and all the upstairs floors cleaned, putting the small head on the hose to do the seemingly endless flights of stairs. A mop, and pail of soapy water with a splash of Zoflora purchased from a small hardware shop in Dublin added for pleasantness was used for the tedious washing of bathroom floors, especially around the toilets. It never mattered how many times she mentioned it, the males in the household could never aim accurately, and by Tuesday there would be a strong whiff of stale urine.

Downstairs was similarly vacuumed and the hard floors mopped with fresh buckets of water. Flying around with a cloth and feather duster, surfaces were left shiny upstairs and down. All the radios in the house had to be switched on to ameliorate her boredom, and a mug of tea for fortification brought along with her. Lunch was forsaken as a waste of time and another reason to have a substantial breakfast.

After the house appeared sufficiently clean, she would pause momentarily. Then without further delay, the ironing board was set up and the iron plugged in. A mountain of crumpled clean laundry grew during the week from a daily wash load of clothes. Paudie's shirts and trousers for work; the children's school uniforms, and her own work blouses and skirts had to be all made fit for public inspection.

By about 6pm, her work would be completed, and now exhausted, she would lay a tray. Warming some home made soup and preparing a salad, she could enjoy a favourite meal in peace. The family, particularly Paudie, looked disappointed if she produced a salad meal. He half joked about enjoying the starter, wanting to know what the main course was going to be.

Pre-planning, she would have bought a selection of different types from the Salad Bar at Supervalu. From the back of the fridge, she retrieved the fresh cream cake bought from the bakery the day before, and hidden away from marauders. From the bottom of her sewing box, concealed under a tray of cotton reels, a box of Leonidas chocolates was revealed. Using immense willpower, she restricted herself to a selection of three. After carefully stashing the chocolates again, the tray and a big pot of tea was carried into the front sitting room. Settling down to a light hearted romantic film, or occasional thriller, she put her throbbing feet on a footstool, and placed a cushion into the small of her aching back. Now at last, she revelled in her favourite time of the week.

A few hours later, hearing voices at the front door, the key turn in the lock, and a noisy jumble of people, bags and equipment skid along the freshly cleaned hallway floor, her heart would plummet. Her precious "me time" was over for another seven days....

Enveloped in bliss the moment she heard him close the front door, the sound of his boots clattering down the bare floor boards made her heart soar....

'Ruth, here's some porridge for you — how are you feeling this morning?' her favourite nursing assistant comes into the room before sunrise.

'Good morning, Mary,' pulling herself up from a prone position. 'What was the weather like coming into work?'

'Frosty — I had to scrape the windscreen clear — but that's not unusual for this time of the year. Here, let me adjust your bed — I'll put the back rest up and rearrange those pillows, for you. How are the pain levels?'

'Not too bad — I don't remember using the pump at all in the night. A bit of a niggle now — but that could be how I slept — you know, on my back.'

'That's good to hear, Ruth — I'll make a note of that on your chart. The porridge, so?'

'Actually, Mary, do you have any boiled eggs on that trolley?'

After the breakfast dishes have been collected, she feels curiously ready to face the day. Such a rare feeling of optimism, she thinks, and wonders where it comes from.

Her Friend has something on his mind, 'what do you think that dream is about — you know — that recurring one you keep having?'

It's about HIM of course.

Over the years she has worked hard to forget. But nobody can control their dream life, can they? In a way, dreaming about seeing him is quite nice; it makes her feel happy for a few moments until she remembers. Maybe that is why she feels in better form his morning.

'Ding, ding-a-ling; ding, ding-a-ling; ding, ding-a —' she jumps at the noise. Scrabbling for the phone on the locker, she taps the screen, and Daithí's attractive face grins out at her. 'Hi Mom, you look great! How are you?'

'Daithí! What a lovely surprise!' then with concern, 'what time is it there? You must be up very early.'

'5am — Ben and I are going hiking up the redwood forests. We want to make the best of the day. Anyhow, that's how we were reared,' laughing. 'There was no shirking in the scratcher with you and Dad, Mom,' chuckling heartily. 'Tell me, how are you? How's this drug trial I've been hearing about, going?'

'Good Daithí — I feel a lot better already. I think there may be something in this immunotherapy theory. Either that, or it's the masses of steroids they've put me on,' reassuring him.

'Or maybe both, Mom — that's fantastic news!'

'What's with all the "mom"? Have you forgotten your roots? I'm Mammy, don't you know?' She decides to stop chastising, 'anyway, tell me, son, how are you? How's Ben? How's the filming going?'

'Everything is good, real good. Ben says to say, Hi, to you,' another good-looking man comes into view, and mouths 'Hi', waves maniacally, then disappears. 'Tell me again, Mom — Mam, I mean — you're feeling you're improving on the trial? Yeh? Is that right?'

'I do, Daithí, I do. In fact,' feeling a sob rising, 'I'm even feeling a little hopeful.' Starting to cry.

'Mammy! Mammy! Don't get upset! Hey! That's great news! Oh, Mammy, I SO want to come home and see you!' his own eyes welling up.

Forcing herself to stop so as to not upset him further, she croaks, 'absolutely not — I forbid it. Look-it, it's only the Prednisolone. I was warned it could make me emotional — a bit cranky. Listen, you're not to come back. Do you hear? Not yet — not until after the wedding, and you've sorted out your citizenship. Not until your re-entry status is secure. Imagine if you couldn't get back into the US again? What would you and poor Ben do then? And your career? You've worked so hard to get this far.'

'Mammy, it'd be worth the risk. Just to see you — you know —just in case.'

Voicing what Daithí struggles to say, 'in case I pass before you see me again — I know, I know. But you mustn't — under any circumstances — travel over. In fact if you do, I'll ban you from seeing me. I'll — I'll instruct the hospital security to not let you in — see — I mean it! But listen,' softening her tone. 'I promise I'll come over and visit you and Benjamin instead. As soon as I am strong enough to travel — I promise, I will.'

'Oh Mammy, I do love you so much.'

Chapter 8

Jimmy plonks down a bowl onto the table, 'I think that's — em — some soup, missus.' Next a plate, and lifting a yellowing plastic cover, presents two scoops of mash, the ubiquitous orange coloured ball and a beige puddle of baby food mush. 'And here's your dessert,' wedging a bowl of custard with pink juice seeping from under the yellow sauce against a small up-stand at the far side of the table.

'What's the rest of the world having, Jimmy?'

'Huh?'

'The others, on the ward — what are they getting to eat?'

'Huh? — oh, yeh — roast chicken, roast spuds, turnip, peas. All on account of it being Sunday. I'll bring yer tea in later, missus, I mean — em.'

'Ruth. Thank you, Jimmy. And say hello to Tilly for me, will you?' giving a theatrical wink.

Jimmy's jaw drops, he closes it again quickly and coughing, 'em, yeh — I will, of course,' flies out as fast as safety will allow.

Her request to come off the Soft list has evidently not trickled down to the kitchen. She scoops everything up with a spoon. The soup is tasty, but she considers her own far nicer. The rhubarb is refreshing, and she is surprised to find it on the Soft menu because a few weeks previously, the tartness would have stung her mouth. Yes, she has to acknowledge, she has made such unexpected progress. Entering the hospital she had said to herself, this is it girlo, you won't be coming out of here again except in a box. But now, what she had said to Daithí earlier was genuinely meant, and not to just placate him.

Her Friend challenges her, 'don't you always say how you are genuinely feeling — what your honest thoughts are, Ruth?'

No, she has to admit, not all the time.

In fact, when she thinks about it, rarely. How could she? She would fall out with people all the time. Even if she did, would they ever listen? Would they care about what she thinks and feels? Highly unlikely, she reckons. Take Nora, for example. Did she ever express a genuine opinion with her? She doubts it; it would have been far too dangerous.

From that first meeting over lunch when she sussed out the situation, she gave up even trying with Nora. Instantly, she knew that she would never be considered a good enough match for Paudie. Her father was a public services bus driver. Her mother had part-time office cleaning jobs, that would have made her lower in rank than Carmel. Her family were perfectly respectable, but did not own property; that came later with the 'right-to-buy', and instead rented a Corporation house in Crumlin, an area with a mixed reputation. None of her sisters were high flyers. They all went to local state schools, and out of the five of them, she was the only one to go on to Third Level education. Sammie, her youngest sister, got a degree in Education and trained as a national school teacher much later as a mature student. Her parents were immensely proud of her, and it was a cause for celebration when she was offered a place on her course. However, as an arts degree, she knew people did not take it seriously unless they were in the art world themselves.

In contrast, Paudie's older brother, two sisters and he were educated at private boarding schools, a concept she had little understanding of apart from reading Enid Blyton books. All four O'Sullivans became professionals. His brother, Vincent, and the youngest of the two older sisters, Theresa, were doctors. Vincent was a surgeon, and Theresa, a GP like their father. The other sister, Mairéad, took the long arduous route to becoming a barrister. Nora was smug with pride about her offspring, despite Paudie's "little difficulties".

The blame for some of the "difficulties" were pointed in her direction because some occurred after he met her, therefore must clearly have been her fault. Paudie failed two of his final papers, and needed to resit and pass them before he could get his degree, then apply for his license to practice. She knew that she was considered a distraction, and that none of it was to do with his preference for playing polo, frequenting the Student Union, and bedding her rather than studying. His mother also conveniently forgot that Paudie's original plan was to do medicine, but his Leaving Certificate results were not good enough. His parents had then steered him towards pharmacology like his maternal grandfather. They had paid for him to return to school for an extra year to work on his chemistry and resit his Leaving Cert.

Scraping just enough points that time, he sometimes hinted that his father with having contacts in Trinity, had by some means or other, arranged a prestigious place there, much to Nora's relief. Nora had made it clear that if he knuckled down, she would help him to pick up the threads of her late father's pharmacy business. His future career would be assured with few uncertainties or risks. He would never have to sit a job interview, or claw his way up the career ladder.

As for her career prospects, when they enquired over that first lunch what she intended to do with her degree, she felt flustered and mumbled nonsense, having no notion herself. All she had ever wanted to do was create art, and just being given the opportunity to do so for 3 years had been enough at the time. As it turned out, she never did finish her degree, and knew that it was always held against her. The fact that Paudie begged her to leave Dublin and join him as he could not bear her being away from him, did not seem to improve Nora's opinion of her. She suspected that Nora always considered her feckless; lacking in moral stamina; not clever nor talented enough to finish the course; prepare a portfolio of work; sit her finals and thus succeed in getting a degree.

Her Friend nods in understanding about her logic, but is not satisfied with her reasoning, 'was that Nora's perception of you? Or was that the perception you had of yourself, Ruth?'

Before she can think that suggestion through, the door swings open and in pours Deidre followed by Seánie then Marcus, Deidre's husband, and lastly Sophie hobbling with Paudie supporting her.

'Lads, you're supposed to knock first — what if your mother needed some privacy?', Paudie admonishes them.

A mixed chorus of 'hello, Ruth', 'how are you, Mammy?', 'God, it's stifling in here', 'yeh, are we allowed open a window?' and the crowd surrounds her bed.

Taking charge, Paudie announces, 'I'll go and gather up some chairs from somewhere.'

Marcus adds quickly, 'I'll come and help.'

Turning back around again, Paudie walks over to the foot of the bed and places a paper bag on the coverlet, 'I'd better leave that here. Pass it up to your Mother, please, someone.'

Opening it, she finds a box of Leonidas chocolates and a creamy wedge wrapped in clingfilm. Licking her lips, she picks at the plastic for a loose seam and unwraps the divine smelling, or so she considers, Brie.

Deidre looks aghast, 'I'll go get a plate and knife for that, Mammy — hold on a minute — why didn't Daddy think of that?' tutting.

Unable to resist, she bites into the "nose" and lets the cheese melt across her tongue, savouring its pungent flavour. Then she waves regally for Sophie and Seánie to carry on talking while she eats.

Later, Deidre interjects angrily, '…Mammy, stop changing the subject, answer my question please, do you think this new treatment is working, or not?'

Paudie comes to the rescue, 'Deidre, will you please leave your mother in peace — you can see she doesn't want to talk about it. Now, is there anything else you'd like to talk about instead?'

Deidre throws a dagger-like look at her father's head then turns her back on him, and faces her mother, 'I'm sorry, Mammy — Daddy does have a point, I suppose,' dropping her chin.

Shaking her head, she smiles at her daughter indulgently, 'there's no need to apologise, Deidre — I just need time to process it a bit, is all. A lot has happened this week.' Her eyes fill up and she reaches for a tissue. 'Sorry, guys, it's the steroids — they make me cry all the time.'

Deidre stands up and leans over to hug her mother, her own eyes glistening too.

Paudie exercises his seniority, 'now, has anyone anything nice to say? Some news worth sharing?'

Deirdre sits down and looks at her husband, 'Marcus?'

Marcus nods, 'go on then.'

'We weren't going to say just yet, wait a few weeks,' Deidre leans sideways to put her arm around her husband's waist, 'Mammy, Daddy, everyone, we're going to have a baby!…'

Paudie is last to leave the room. Bending over to kiss her goodbye, he grabs her around the shoulders and pulls her close to him. As usual, she feels her body stiffen and her jaw clench. But something about the warmth of his chest, the firm but yielding quality of the flesh on his arms, and his scent, make her want to be comforted. To be cuddled and feel safe again. Go back to a time when she never questioned their love for each other. Return to the optimism of a fruitful future together. Drop all her anger and resentment towards him. She involuntarily relaxes against him, and allows herself to enjoy his embrace. She wants to feel loved.

'Goodbye, my love,' he whispers through her hair, the heat of his breath caressing her ear.

Standing to leave, his eyes goggle, 'Ruth! You've eaten the whole of that cheese!'

Feeling unsettled about the revelations from the visit, not least her reaction to Paudie, she lies motionless while she gathers her thoughts. But they refuse to be collected up — like a group of giddy lambs. She stares vacantly at the ceiling. Eventually focusing, she notices the gossamer strand floating freely. Wishing she could drift like that — within a warm current, and be carried far away from life's tribulations.

Bored with her daydream, she notices her Friend sitting on one of the fold-up chairs brought in by the family. 'Come on, how DO you feel about the improvement in your health, Ruth?' stroking his silky beard with long fingers.

Contrary; she feels annoyingly contrary.

Anyone would hope to get better if they were in her position, would they not? But strangely, the prospect of being cured is not as welcome as she once imagined it would be. Maybe she has got used to the idea of not living for much longer and has accepted her death sentence as inevitable. There is a kind of relief knowing she will not have to struggle with the challenges of life; deal with difficult people; have to accept the disappointment of people letting her down; feel compelled to act in ways that suit everybody except herself. Should she be alarmed at her ambivalence, she wonders? But as she does not feel that concerned about it, why worry?

Deidre and Marcus' news had not filled her with the excitement she had always anticipated when hearing she would be a grandmother for the first time. What kind of mother is she, she asks herself? Being less self critical, maybe she is just tired. Tired of being ill, or tired of life? She does not know which. Or is it the prednisolone making her depressed?

'And what about Paudie, how do you feel about him, my love?'

You mean his sudden niceness? — suspicious, very suspicious about his motives. Why the sudden change?

Remembering back to the time when she first noticed some symptoms, particularly the spotting even though her periods had finished years previously. The swollen belly that would not respond to her exercise regime. And the resumption of fatigue even though she had less responsibilities. By that stage in the marriage, she rarely shared personal issues with Paudie, but she was sufficiently concerned to raise these with him because she did trust him on medical matters. He half listened, but that was normal for him. Closing down the conversation, he suggested she wait and if she was still anxious in a few weeks, make an appointment with their GP.

Irina noticed her being off peak and she confided in her. When referred for further investigations, it was Irina who shared that part of the cancer journey with her. Getting the phone call from the gynaecologist's secretary offering an early follow up appointment more quickly than expected; and the secretary suggesting she bring along her husband or some other close relative, Paudie started to pay attention and went with her. During the subsequent referral to oncology and her first appointment with Dr Mulhall, Paudie became fully engaged, publicly playing the role of dutiful partner. In the early days after being given a poor prognosis, she felt like a fully laden 40 ton lorry had hurtled through her life, tossing every aspect and person up in its wake. And leaving her flattened on the road behind. So much had to be considered. The treatment plan of chemo, surgery and radiotherapy, and all the gruelling implications of those. The children and their despair. The business and the changes needing to be managed. The realisation of a now limited future, and the repercussions of that, especially her disappointment over the longed for travel. And the sense of urgency where she felt pushed into actions before she could get prepared and accept them. Finally, she had to make end of life arrangements that prior to her illness would have seemed completely premature.

With a strong sense of personal responsibility, her first thoughts on practicalities were to get her finances and legal matters in order. Neither of them had drawn up wills, but it was imperative now considering their substantial assets. Wishing to be as helpful as possible, she did not want legal complications for everyone with her dying intestate. But Paudie would not hear of it, refusing to think of the worst possible scenario. He pressed her to think positively and focus on getting well, not on pessimistic time and energy consuming legal issues.

Initially her treatment seemed successful. However through its journey of procedures, she became increasingly more disappointed with Paudie. He demonstrated selfishness and impatience when she was no longer able to fulfil his needs. That disappointment turned into resentment; then resentment into anger. A year or so after her last treatment, she relapsed. To her dismay, instead of offering support and acknowledging her terror, Paudie's attitude worsened. As though he accepted that she was on her way out, he pushed her to make that appointment with the solicitor. In her reduced state, there were not many ways left to punish him. Making his life more difficult after she had gone was one of them. Realistically, she knew her belligerence would make little difference. Legally he would get half of everything she had worked so hard for, and the children the rest.

The thought of him having the comfortable, even premium retirement; that carrot he had used to keep her motivated, and she was now being denied, was hard to countenance.

Recognising a lava of bubbling anger inside, one that hisses and spits toxic sentiments towards Paudie, she knows it does not serve her well. But she does not know how to deal with it. How to move on to a more serene state of grace. Paudie suddenly being nice to her is not helping; if anything it is making it worse. Part of her knows she should be forgiving and understanding of his point of view. But the other part wants to hang on to that anger; it is familiar and feels acceptable. The dilemma just makes her feel guilty, and bad tempered….

 Jimmy comes into the room whistling a traditional ballad that she cannot quite place. He is in a cheerful humour setting up her evening meal.

'Jimmy, Tilly's a lovely woman, isn't she?'

Jimmy inhales sharply, and coughs from saliva entering his windpipe. 'Apologies, missus — sorry, er — Ruth,' coughing into his elbow between putting a sausage roll with flaky pastry, a bag of crisps and an apple on her table. Still coughing and waving goodbye, he scurries out as fast as his legs can carry him.

In his haste to escape, she realises Jimmy forgot his list and has given her normal food, 'Oh, good!'.

She cuts her apple into bite sized pieces with a blunt tea knife.

Her Friend strikes up conversation, 'you appear to have loved Paudie deeply early in your relationship. When did that start to change?'

Shortly after she had Sophie.

The months after Sophie's birth were challenging with having to recover from the C section and take care of three small children. Paudie managed without her in the shop for about 5 months, but then raised the spectre of her return. Feeling pressured, she visited the Montessori school suggested by Nora, and being sufficiently satisfied, she booked Daithí and Deidre in. To her relief, Sophie was too young and the school principal suggested an alternative: to use a woman she knew as a childminder. It was Irina, the mother of one of her staff members.

Irina was Polish and lived with her daughter, Ingrida, and son-in-law, Marius, in a new housing estate at the edge of town. When she first visited Irina to discuss the possibility of taking Sophie, she assumed that the woman opening the door was Ingrida as Irina seemed so young. Another initial impression was the orderliness of the house and the way it was so child centred. Irina took her to inspect a securely fenced garden used entirely as a play area. It was equipped with good quality toddler and standard sized swings; and a sunny yellow plastic slide descended from a quaint, raised playhouse adorned with large overhanging eaves and fretwork bargeboards making it look like an alpine chalet. Irina proudly declared that Marius had constructed it, boasting what a skilled and sought after carpenter he was. There was a paddling pool and a sand pit, both with protective plastic covers. Under a sheltered lean-to was a selection of pedal toys and different sized bikes. Around the edge of the garden, a pathway was laid out like a mini racetrack.

The kitchen/dining room had an additional child height table with small chairs, and a high chair was folded against the wall. The front sitting room had chests of toys, comfortable looking easy chairs and a bookcase full of colourful children's books fixed securely to the wall.

Irina had faltering English, but her vocabulary was good and there was no problem communicating with her. With twin grandchildren in primary school, childcare remained her preferred occupation. Her last minded child had just relocated with her family to Galway. Irina produced excellent written references from the child's parents and the mother's mobile number for further followup. Once Sophie was placed with her, she proved to be most capable, and it was soon arranged for her to collect Daithí and Deidre from preschool. While all three children were minded until the shop closed, they could play with Irina's grandchildren. Irina's people carrier car was equipped with children's car and booster seats, and she thought nothing of taking the small tribe of children off to exciting places like the beach on fine days, and the ball pool when it was wet. These arrangements continued successfully right through primary school, including the school holidays, and well into second level education.

She knew in her heart that Irina grew to love the children as much as she did. Irina was one of the true blessings in her life, particularly the support and affirmation she provided to her personally. Irina remarked how hard she worked and what a good mother she was; how impressed she was with the way she kept all 'the balls spinning' mixing her metaphors. And these compliments always felt genuine.

With regards Paudie, Irina never showed the same warmth. Whenever she attended the Pharmacy, she would decline a consultation with him, and request Ruth instead. When she did not know the answer, Irina insisted she act as go between and ask Paudie on her behalf. On the rare occasions that Paudie collected the children, she would asked for Ruth to call her later. When Paudie offered to take a message, or say he could deal with any matters arising, Irina turned truculent, insisting she must speak with the children's mother directly. He commented on Irina's frostiness saying he did not know how he had offended the woman. She thought privately that him just being him was enough. It secretly pleased her because it was irritating how Paudie was always seen as Mr Nice Guy. If she is honest, she never hid her anger from Irina. They never overtly acknowledged that they were co-conspirators, it was an implicit understanding between them about Paudie and his family. They would always meet each other's eyes when Paudie, or some other O'Sullivan did some annoying thing.

'I see, so you solved the issue of childcare satisfactorily which for working mothers is always an anxiety. You returned to work with good arrangements sorted out. Go on Ruth, what happened to sour your relationship with Paudie?'

Where they lived did not help.

The cottage became a source of friction between them. Although she adored living there in its semi rural setting, and paying an economical rent, it simply became too small. Whenever she raised the issue of the three children sharing a tiny bedroom, Paudie would acknowledge that something should be done, but that was as far as he went. Scouring the small ads in the free papers; looking on the noticeboards in the Post Office, and asking Maeve Cullen to let her know if she heard of anything, she would come across alternatives quite often. But Paudie would claim to be too busy to go to a viewing. Or he would declare it too expensive and not value for money. Or it would be in the wrong part of town. Coming to the conclusion that Paudie was too comfortable with the status quo, not being affected in any practical way, she gave up trying until some exasperating event happened. Such as trying to find space to store larger sized clothing for the children. Or Daithí screaming that Sophie had broken his newly built Lego model. Or one of the children vomiting in the night waking the other two. Then she was incentivised to work on Paudie again. It made little difference to him as they were out of the house most of the week. Nora had agreed, which meant Carmel, to have the children on Saturdays to give Irina time off. Then with polo on Sundays, only nights were spent there.

But the issue was significant for her in other ways. It demonstrated what was important to Paudie. And from her perspective, her needs were not high on his list. This made her question whether he truly loved her. Would not a man who loved his wife want her to be happy, she asked herself repeatedly? And the unsatisfactory answer she gave herself nibbled away at her self confidence.

Chapter 9

'That's the next stage started, Ruth,' Dr Geraghty disconnects the tubing from the port in her chest. 'I've a questionnaire about how you are feeling — any symptoms — any changes you've experienced during the first phase, that kind of thing. Do you mind if we go through it now.'

Dr Geraghty had looked tired and preoccupied when she first entered the room, but seems to brighten visibly as they fly through the questions that require little consideration from her, the answers being obvious and positive. No, she is not suffering any new symptoms, and yes, she would say her established symptoms are improving. She notices the medic's back straightening and her head lifting as though a weight has rolled away from the top of her head

Dr Geraghty emits undisguised delight. 'I have to say, in seven days, you've made remarkable progress, Ruth. Much more than I would have thought possible considering how you were when you were first admitted. Do you feel ready to remove the morphine pump and start with patches?'

Her arm aches where the cannula was inserted and she rubs at the sticky residue left by the dressing securing it in place. There was no solvent on the instrument tray collected from the nurses' station, but Dr Geraghty promised to request for someone to deal with it.

Absentmindedly pressing around the area to feel the extent of the tenderness, she becomes aware of the clock ticking on the wall. Strangely, she has never noticed it before. Now aware of it, she hopes she will not be annoyed by the noise when trying to sleep. It occurs to her that her other senses have been sharpening too. Food seems more flavoursome and she can enjoy it again. Conversely, her over-sensitivity to strong smells seems to have abated. And her eyesight; she is not so reliant on her reading spectacles; but what about distance vision? Her Friend standing at the far end of the room by the door appears much the same.

Noticing her peering at him, he takes the opportunity, 'can we talk again, Ruth? You don't mind, do you? Tell me, how was the housing problem eventually resolved?'

Now, that is a story.

One evening Paudie comes home much later than normal, explaining that he called into his parents. As he was invited to dine with them, she feels grumpy about cooking for him for no reason, this being a time before they signed up for mobile phones. She fed the children earlier, so dishes up her own meal and sits down at the cramped kitchen table in a hangry, sulky silence. Paudie is oblivious to her tetchy humour. He has important news about his parents that he is eager to impart: his father has suddenly announced he is going to retire imminently without any prior hints to Paudie or his siblings; not ones he knows about, anyway.

'Mother and he talked about his retirement plans — what he intends to do with his time — and more interestingly — what they plan to do with the surgery,' Paudie takes a slurp of tea and looks to her for a response to this major piece of information.

Swallowing a mouthful of food, 'hmm — yeh — and?'

'I don't know what to make of it really — other than to think that it'd be a wonderful opportunity — help us really get on our feet. It would solve a lot of problems. In fact, I can't think of any downsides to it, at all.'

'Downsides to what? — go on, Paudie, tell me more. What are you talking about? I don't really gather what you're getting at.'

'Well, here's the best bit, Ruth — they're going to convert the surgery for us!'

Now her attention is grabbed. She puts her knife and fork down, and looks at him squarely to fully read him. 'What — move the pharmacy into it — you mean? What's wrong with where it is? It's a bit small, I know, but it's in a better location than the surgery. Plus it's a shop as well. How would that work in a residential street? And — '

'No, no! You're missing the point, Ruth. Convert it for us!'

'What do you mean, "convert it for us"?'

'For us to move into! For us to live in, pet!'

Looking at his excited face in total disbelief, she frantically tries to comprehend who is going insane. Is it him, his parents or herself? Is this some kind of joke? It cannot possibly be a serious suggestion.

Two days later standing in the Waiting Room, it is all too real. She looks around the room properly for the first time. Vintage oak dining chairs are lined up along the walls. An oak dining table of the same era, with thick turned legs, stands in the centre stacked with dog-eared magazines. Cork noticeboards pinned with leaflets and notices hang on the walls. The chairs look as dejected as she feels. The polish is scuffed on the sturdy wooden legs and the drop-in seat pads sag in the middle. They are all covered in the same brown leatherette that is peeling, revealing dirty, greying linen cloth beneath. Along one wall is a Victorian mahogany side board with a mirrored top, speckled with age. It is so huge, she cannot imagine how it was brought into the room in the first place. It will no doubt have to stay there. Pondering if it was put there by Nora's parents, or maybe even her grandparents, she has heard that the house has been in Nora's family since being built. She thinks they may have commissioned it.

'Mrs O'Sullivan? Mrs O'Sullivan?'

She looks at the builder uncomprehending, then realises he is addressing her. She never considers herself to be Mrs O'Sullivan when the real Mrs O'Sullivan, Nora that is, is in the same room.

'Will we go into the Consulting Room and discuss what you'd like to do in there?' the builder heads towards another door leading into a different corridor.

Nora answers for her, 'yes, indeed, Maurice — a dining room, I think — and a kitchenette in the adjoining Examination Room. It's a tad small, but I'm sure you'll be able to fashion something out of it with your mastery. And the Patient Toilet in the hallway, here,' pointing, 'could be made more suitable for a family, don't you agree?' Nora has it all planned out.

Trudging behind them, she watches Maurice writing notes on a clipboard. She feels no sense of curiosity entering this unknown part of the house.

After assessing Brendan's office, Maurice turns and looking directly at her, 'Mrs O'Sullivan, do you have a particular style of kitchen in mind? Do you prefer modern minimalist, traditional large country house, country cottage, French farmhouse? —'

She tries to engage her brain and fails. Then summonsing some faint enthusiasm, 'hmm, I haven't really thought —'

Nora shakes her head and gesticulates emphatically, 'Maurice, no, no — certainly not modern — no, no, that wouldn't do — not in a period house such as this.'

'That's fine — it doesn't matter at this stage. It won't affect the price in the scheme of things. We'll be limited in what we can do with it space-wise — you can decide all that later,' still looking at her. 'I'll measure up the rooms and have a word with the decorator about calling in, if you ladies don't mind. Will I bring the estimate over to you in the shop, Mrs O'Sullivan?' continuing to talk to her.

Nora announces with a self satisfied smile, 'no, Maurice, I'm taking care of all that. Any matters of finance are to be brought to my attention, please.'

'If the price is agreeable to you both, I could be available to start at the beginning of next month. But I won't book you in until you're happy with the quote.'

Nora motions for him to follow her back to the Waiting Room, 'I'm sure your figures will be most acceptable as they always are, Maurice. But we can discuss them in due course. Can I just go over some of the detail for this room again? There's something I thought of in respect of the Secretary's office.'

Left behind in the Consulting Room while Nora and Maurice go back into what will become her sitting room, she decides that this is never going to be her place. Sure, she will live in it. She has no choice as everyone else has decided that for her. But it will NEVER be her HOME.

Chapter 10

Nurse Sonia puts her head around the door, 'can we shower you now please, Ruth. Both Mary O and I have some time...'

The two nurses are positioned either side supporting Ruth under her arms as she stands for the first time in weeks. Sonia reassures 'take it slowly — let's get you standing first — there — how do you feel? — any dizziness? — that's normal — right I have you this side and Mary the other — we'll head for the en-suite now.'

Sitting on a plastic chair placed within the walk-in showering area, she feels so alive under the warm water. Relieved that it is Sonia on duty, and not the sharply spoken, unsympathetic Nóirín, she feels relaxed, even possibly a little happy. Lifting her arms away from her body, she soaps under her armpits, glorying that she can rinse them clean with fresh, running water. Later tucked up in a newly changed bed, an unexpected wave of fatigue engulfs her, and she allows it to swallow her up.

The sound of his footsteps at last, she could hear his heavy boots. She had been listening out for that welcome sound all morning. He had returned. Calming her palpitating heart, and composing her face, she must not let him know....

'Ruthie, oh my, do I have a surprise for you?' trolley followed by Tilly coming through the door. 'You're normal now, girl! I've bacon, cabbage, croquettes and parsley sauce for you. And tonight, you can have a chicken vol-au-vent!'

'Thank God for small mercies!' pulling herself into a more upright position, 'I'm so delighted to see you, Tilly. Did you have a good day off? Get up to anything nice? See anyone in particular?' smiling cheekily.

Tilly lays the plates across the table deftly, 'ha, ha, ha! So it was you! Ha, ha, ha! You had Jimmy worked up, alright. He's worried about staff relationships — he's not sure it's allowed. I said to him, "hey man, what's wrong with you, it's only love. There's never anything ever wrong with love." ha, ha, ha!' Tilly scoots out to her next patient, still chuckling.

'Tilly has a point doesn't she?' her Friend pulling the armchair over. 'Is there ever anything wrong with loving someone? What are your thoughts on that, Ruth?'

That is a most difficult question.

It is a conundrum that has plagued her for years. It has caused her so much grief. And guilt. And pain, such pain she did not want to go on living at times. Love, a state of being that should be the simplest, purest emotion has been more troublesome than anger or hate ever were. Actually, she would rather not think about it.

Her Friend looks at her with compassion in his eyes, 'that's okay — you don't have to consider it now. Eat up. When you've finished, let's talk about something else.'

Later, he surveys the empty plates, laughs lightly and says, 'tell me, what was it like sharing the house with the O'Sullivans?'

Like many situations in her life, the reality was not as bad as she feared.

There were actually some good aspects to living there. They were effectively given a third of the house, equivalent in size to other properties that they would have considered large. The old Waiting Room made a spacious sitting room with bay windows to the front and side, making it bright for most of the day, even on the frequently overcast or rainy days of the West of Ireland. The builder opened up the ornate marble fireplace, but kept the radiators. This meant they had the option of lighting a cosy fire, or could rely on the central heating system if they did not want to go to the bother. The former Consultation Room became the dining room as dictated by Nora, which was practical as it adjoined the kitchen. It was large enough to be a living room with comfortable seating, and had plenty of floor space for the children to play too. The kitchen was tiny, but the builders designed it with a surprising amount of storage and food preparation surfaces. The "Patient Toilet" was transformed into a utility room for the washing machine and dryer. They did not need to use the main staircase because there was a second servants' stairwell through the "Practice Nurse" room. This was a relief as she was worried about the children clattering up and down the stairs, and disturbing the senior O'Sullivans. The nurse's room became a useful cloakroom for footwear, and the miscellaneous paraphernalia that all families and men collect.

The back stairs led to the bedrooms allocated to them by Nora. A separate bathroom for their exclusive use was converted from Vincent's old bedroom. A double bedroom for the girls to share was originally used by their aunts, and Paudie's old single room was passed on to Daithí. A large bedroom at the front of the house above their new parlour, and with similar double bays was designated for her and Paudie.

Exploring the room for the first time, she opened a massive three doored wardrobe veneered in flamed walnut, and had been entranced by the faint scent of old textiles. Although empty, she imagined silks, tweeds and furs hanging in there. Pulling out one of the top drawers in a complementary dressing table, she found a circle of pink powder that had been missed by one of the cleaners. Knowing this to have been Nora's mother's room, she imagined old Mrs Walsh dipping a down puff into a round box, and powdering her nose and cheeks whilst gazing into the tall mirror above. At the back of another drawer lined with green felt, she found a single clip-on earring fashioned into a bow and covered in marcasite. She clutched it tightly, planning to return it to its rightful heir. In a moment of poignancy, she hoped Nora had kept the other one.

The cottage had come fully furnished and due to its size, they never collected any furniture of their own. Nora arranged for the table in the Waiting Room to be restored. Ten of the chairs that matched and were in a better condition, were to be reupholstered. She intervened at this point, offering to get the material to recover them; something to her own taste from Hickeys in Dublin. With having a keen eye for all the decorative arts, she developed what was to become one of her favourite pastimes: a good rummage around antique and junk shops. There was a lot of space to fill, and after getting to know Nora's furniture restorer, she acquired an ability to see the potential in any battered piece of junk, confident that the skilled restorer would bring it back to its original condition. Nora was grudgingly impressed with the pieces she found, barely concealing her incredulity that she had the acumen to source them. Those small triumphs helped bolster her a little within the O'Sullivan dynasty.

Carmel had an apartment downstairs in the garden basement. The villa was built on the side of a hill, and although it appeared two storey at the front, at the rear it had three floors. French doors at the far side of another reception room in the "Private" part of the house opened onto a veranda. From that, a flight of stairs led down to a flagged terrace making up the top part of the garden. The rest of the extensive curtilage sloped gently down to the river. Carmel's rooms looked out on to this terrace. Her living quarters had only been one room deep because of the bedrock beneath, but extended across the width of the building, giving generous accommodation. Down on this level were various utility rooms such as a laundry; food and wine cellars, and the boiler room. These areas and the kitchen rooms at the top of her own flight of stairs were Carmel's domain. And she ruled her kingdom wisely. Carmel managed a team of daily helpers who did the laundry, and cleaned the surgery and all the living quarters. She also took care of the visiting gardener, Tom, feeding him well. Tom, in return, kept Carmel well supplied with fruit and vegetables from a kitchen garden tended to one side, and a glasshouse built along the South facing boundary wall. In there he produced apricots, peaches, figs and grapes. From the outside plots, he harvested berry fruits such as raspberries, currents and strawberries kept in large netted cages to protect them from the populous birdlife. The salads, summer and winter vegetables they consumed daily, arrived in the kitchen because of his knowledge and skill.

Carmel and Tom became her friends, their interactions mutually warm and respectful. Not wanting to burden either of them with the children, she insisted on keeping Irina employed as minder during the week. Nora and Paudie both challenged the point of paying fees, but she explained that it was important for consistency and for the children's sense of security. Privately she had other reasons. Irina's household was a normal one with Irina and Ingrida both being child centred. Marius was pleasant and playful with all the children, treating hers the same as his own. She also felt a loyalty towards Irina, and although she knew Irina would have no problem finding work, her long term plan was to leave Rath House. As far as she was concerned, Irina was going to remain her children's minder forever.

One reason she resolved to move on was Nora's edict to attend Sunday lunch each week. Much to her surprise, Paudie obeyed, relinquishing polo and selling the ponies. As he kept all the equipment, she wondered whether it was laziness in shifting it, or if he considered it a transitory hiatus. One or more of Paudie's siblings would occasionally be in attendance. Vincent, the surgeon, would invariably come alone. His wife, a consultant in the Accident and Emergency Department at St. James' Hospital in Dublin, always seemed to be on duty the particular Sundays he visited. They were a childless couple, and she wondered if this was intentional, but knew she would never be party to such personal information. Theresa, the GP, was married with four children and lived in Australia. She never got to return home, so when Brendan retired, he and Nora visited often, usually for six weeks at a time to make the journey worthwhile. Mairéad, the barrister, granted them her presence monthly. She was single, but referred to her friend, Loretta, often. It only dawned on her years later, that Mairéad was a lesbian such had been her ignorance about LGBTQ+ matters back then.

The lunches were a complete ordeal for her. The men talked incessantly about medical politics, complaining about the Health Service and the Minister for Health, and gossiping about professionals she had never met. Considerate by nature, Brendan tried to include her, but whenever she made a comment, usually from a pharmaceutical perspective, Vincent would immediately challenge her before she had even finished speaking. If Paudie made the same observation, the men nodded sagely, affirming its accuracy. Vincent remained aloof and dismissiveness of her. She often wondered why a man with such poor people skills ever chose to be a doctor. From the way he talked about his patients, and with a certainty of opinion that could only be described as arrogant, she realised he was emotionally distant from people. He could have been an engineer working with inanimate objects, except she had observed mechanics showing more care towards vehicles than Vincent had shown empathy towards humans. In short, she regarded him as a younger male version of his mother.

Whenever Mairéad joined the party, she remained an outsider. Nora and Mairéad talked about members of the extended family, or people who used to live in the town who had since died. That was when Mairéad was not talking about herself; or her large house in Ballsbridge, Dublin; or her current legal caseload; or her holidays in exciting and glamorous sounding places which always hit a tender spot. Mairéad specialised in Commercial Fraud, a complex area. She would have defied anyone understanding what Mairéad went on about most of the time, going into the intricacies of her clients' business activities. Nora, enraptured by her brilliant offspring, boasted about her successful, groundbreaking daughter to anyone who cared to listen.

The only way of coping was to let the children escape as soon as they finished dessert, and excuse herself on the pretext of settling them. Once released from the table, she helped Carmel clear away. Carmel had protested at first, but she had countered that as co-host, it was only proper she should help. Her argument was weak, but Carmel sympathetically indulged her all the same. And Nora never uttered a word of protest at her servitude….

The door opens tentatively and a woman peers around. It is Lisa, her deputy in the shop. Nervous, Lisa only partially enters, 'is it all right if I come in, Ruth?'

'Lisa! Please do! Come in, come in! What a pleasant surprise! How nice to see you! Pull up that chair,' waving her in with delight.

Lisa passes her a clear plastic food bag, 'I brought you some cherries — they looked so nice in the supermarket and I know you like them. I've already washed them and put them into a fresh bag. I know you're immune compromised.'

'Lisa! You're very good.' Unable to resist, she pops one into her mouth then offers the bag, but Lisa shakes her head. Spitting the stone into a tissue, 'it's so nice of you to call in on your day off — how are you? How's the shop?'

Lisa takes the opportunity to discuss some minor staffing issues about a new employee's timekeeping, looking to Ruth for some guidance. Then she talks through some ideas for reorganising the shop, '… I got them to move the W7 rack over towards the dispensary. Then reposition the Cocoa Brown more towards the window; I put the SoSu next to the Essence. Is that all okay, do you think?'

'Of course it is. It'd be what I'd have done myself. I've been meaning to talk to you about reorganising that area — try and increase the footfall — encourage the younger customers into looking at what we stock. So, tell me, how are you in yourself, Lisa?'

Lisa hesitates considering how direct she should be, then blurts out, 'to be perfectly truthful, it's been hard,' Lisa's expertly mascaraed eyes fill up with tears.

Spitting out another stone, she swallows the fruit and looks at Lisa with a slight frown. 'Is everything okay? Are you having difficulty with some of the other girls? I know one or two of them aren't as committed as you. Or is it Paudie? He can be such a lazy toad — just give him a prod, will you?'

'No, no, no — its nothing like that — everyone's pulling their weight in the circumstances. It's just…' Lisa dabs the corners of her eyes carefully with a tissue pulled into a point.

Looking at Lisa's perfectly made up face which only accentuates her beauty, she stares at her quizzically, 'yes, Lisa? — Go on — spill the beans — you can tell me, you know that.'

Letting out a sob, 'it's just — it's just — not the same.'

'What's not the same?' she wracks her brain over what else could be making Lisa's life difficult.

'It's just not the same — you not being there.'

'What, at the shop? But I haven't been at the shop regularly for months now. And all of you have coped really well, especially when Bernadette was taken on to do the paperwork and ordering.'

'Yes, I know that. But she's not you. Nobody could be you, I mean — replace you. Everyone's saying the same — Everyone — the other girls — the customers — especially Paudie — everyone is missing you. You ARE O'Sullivan's Pharmacy — nobody wants to talk to Paudie — everybody is looking for you to consult with — get your opinion on their illness, their medication. What colour foundation to get, what pearls to buy for a Confirmation. Every day it happens — nearly every customer. It's a reminder you're not there....'

Lisa leaves when she notices Ruth tiring, and promises to call in the following week.

Ruth tries to analyse the conversation and is relieved to see her Friend settling into the vacant chair as she needs to discuss her thoughts. To her mild frustration, he raises another topic.

'How did the children find moving in with their grandparents? And how did that affect you?' he asks smiling gently.

The children were mixed about it.

Daithí was delighted to be in his father's old room; with somewhere to have his own space, and not have to be with girls. Although he got on well with his sisters, she knew that he found it embarrassing to admit to his friends that he shared with girls. He could keep his Lego models safe from Sophie and turn his light out later, being older. Deidre was nonplussed at not having her own room like her brother because she found Sophie a nuisance too. Sophie tended to pick up and twiddle with other people's belongings, often breaking them despite having her own toys, chosen by herself. They were thrilled to have chests of drawers and hanging space for their clothes, and full sized beds to sleep in.

Downstairs was spacious to run around in during bad weather. The massive garden was magical with paved paths that wound in and out; and statuary and features arranged as focal points in surprising twists and turns. Mature shrubs crowded together making great places for dens and there were trees to climb to spy over the surroundings. Their Grandfather allowed them into his side of the building for games of Hide and Seek, and Tag. Carmel was like another grandparent giving them free rein too. And Tom was endlessly patient with their questions and noisy playing. He gave them ripe fruit to eat; showed them creepy crawlies, and taught them how to identify different birds. Nora was more rigid and demanded restrained levels of behaviour. In hindsight, it was a good move for the children.

'And Paudie? Was it a good move for him?' her Friend enquires, keeping a neutral expression.

Oh, yes indeed — very much so.

Paudie was the baby of the family, and in her opinion, over indulged. His parents always sorted out any difficult situations he got himself into, and as a result, she thinks he never developed strength of character, or "cop on" as Billy would have called it. By not completely facing up to the consequences of his behaviour when younger, he has an insufficient sense of adult responsibility, including at times, a duty of care towards others. He avoids hard decisions, veering towards the easiest option and resists making personal sacrifices. Raised by a mother who was difficult to please, he tends to yield easily. Except when it comes to herself — he ignores her needs if they conflict with his own. Or with his mother's when she was alive. Paudie's loyalty, first and foremost was always towards his parents.

This is fundamentally different to her own values. She believes that his new family of her and their children should have come first. That was how it was with Billy and Vera. Family lore was that when young people left home "they make their own bed, so they can lay in it". Her parents resisted interfering and rarely passed comment. They were happy enough to see her come home. But if she visited a little too often, particularly when she was unhappy with the marriage, they would gently nudge her back to Balnarath. Her parents took time to listen to her complaints, but rarely sided with her. Vera understood her well, yet would always present Paudie's and Nora's perspectives for her to consider. Overall, she thinks Billy and Vera were generous in their attitudes towards the O'Sullivan family, and held an ameliorating spirit that that was not reciprocated.

Paudie was very content back in his childhood home, availing freely of the ease and comforts provided. With the cleaners doing their side of the house on Nora's insistence, Paudie took it as an opportunity to increase her hours in the shop. Nora evidently agreed, saying it was a good business move. Remaining close to his parents, Paudie called into them every evening, leaving her to deal with the children.

'And what about you, Ruth? Apart from your strained relationship with Nora, was it a good decision for you? Did it strengthen the marriage for you to have more comfortable living conditions?'

Strengthen the marriage? Oh no, quite the opposite — it had a disastrous effect on their sex life.

The one satisfactory area in the marriage was the regular, good quality and imaginative sex. She always felt less annoyed with Paudie after they made love. His overt desire for her made her feel attractive and confident in her sexual allure, even though she was a mother of three children, and was often covered in baby sick, snot and dried food. When there was no time to sort out her hair, or she wore scruffy clothes and had not applied make up, he nonetheless, made her feel beautiful. He took care to please her in bed, not stopping until completely assured she had orgasmed, preferably several times. It seemed important to him that she viewed him a good lover. Most skilfully, he understood the need to ramp up sexual tension especially if she was not in the mood. Unlike some men who thought that libido in a woman could be controlled like a light switch, Paudie knew how to set a romantic scene. He flirted and caressed before moving on to the more blatant sexual moves. Seeming to enjoy affection too, he understood her need for cuddles and kisses.

The senior O'Sullivans and they, had the two main bedrooms at the front of the house. Separating the chambers was a smaller room above the hallway which had originally been a nursery. Nora had converted it into a dressing room, removing the door into her own room in the process. Paudie was convinced that he could hear Nora and Brendan talking in their room which to him demonstrated that noise travelled between the rooms. Paudie hushed her if he thought she was talking too loudly. But with the disruption of moving house, they were worn out for the first few days, and neither had the energy to make love, so privacy was not an issue.

After a few weeks, surprised that Paudie has not made a move on her, she decides to take the initiative; something rarely needed. After the drought, a rain dance is needed. Getting the children off to bed promptly one evening, she dons a purposely bought baby doll nightie and French knickers. Returning downstairs, she gives Paudie "a come hither" look, enticing him to come upstairs with her. He regards her blankly. Then forcing a laugh, says it is far too early. She sits close up to him on the sofa as they watch TV. After a while she caresses his thigh, gradually moving inwards and upwards. This normally kick starts him, but this time, he says he thinks his mother is calling him. Leaping to his feet, he promises to be back in a minute. Later, when the TV programme finishes, she goes into the hallway to look for him. The lights are off, signifying that Nora and Brendan have gone to bed.

In the twilight of her own bedroom, she disconcertedly finds Paudie's dozing under the covers. Undeterred, she pulls open the front ties on her nightie, and slips in besides him, pressing her breasts against him. No response. Disengaging a little, she strokes the broad back facing her, and gently kisses his shoulders. Sliding her hand over his waist, she runs her fingers through his pubic hair. Caressing him to an erection, she helps roll a condom onto his penis. He turns around, and climbs onto her assuming the missionary position. Holding her vulva apart with her fingers, she makes it easier for him to navigate her pubes and lips. He enters without any attempt at fingering her first. Thankfully, she is already in the mood, and sufficiently wet for lubrication. After a few thrusts, she gets into rhythm with him, and the springs in the old bedstead strum a musical accompaniment. Within a minute or two, she senses an absence in her vagina, and Paudie rolls off onto his back. His flaccid penis looks tiny in the orange streetlight, and the condom looks like a shrivelled party balloon much like her disappointment.

All future attempts at seduction failed in a similarly facile fashion. Paudie became so acutely embarrassed about his erection issues, she felt unable to do anything other than reassure him that she was not fazed by it. Telling him not to worry, she suggested it was a temporary problem caused by the stress of moving, or work. But equally alarming was his disinterest in her. He never offered cunnilingus or sex toys as an alternative. On rare occasions like her birthday, out of a sense of duty rather than desire, he manually stroked her to orgasm, but ordered her to quieten down when she climaxed.

Naturally, she questioned her part in Paudie's impotence. Early in the relationship, she had sensed Nora defining her as cheap. Being Protestant meant she was seen as English in Nora's eyes, and English equalled Easy. Although both sides of her family were fully Irish, with each grandfather fighting for Irish Independence, those facts did not alter Nora's view that she was likely to be promiscuous. Nora's Roman Catholicism would have had a lot to do with it — sex was seen as dirty and sinful unless within the sanctity of marriage. For her though, sex between two consenting adults who respect each other, married or not, is neither sinful in God's eyes nor dirty. In her opinion, the only time sex is dirty is when there is coercion and/or consent is not clearly given. Men who persist in unwelcome sexual attention are dirty. Men who prey on children are heinous. Men who take advantage when someone is drunk or incapacitated are despicable. She has only made love with a man she has liked. And she is NOT dirty. But Nora had the habit of looking her way if the subject of sexual activity outside of marriage came up. Matters were not helped by her youngest sister, Sam, having an unplanned pregnancy during her last year at school. Sam decided to keep the baby after contacting a charity for crisis pregnancies, and because

Billy and Vera pledged support. Sam remained a single parent until meeting her husband on the same Primary Teaching course. Pondering over this now, she wonders if Nora's attitude infiltrated Paudie's perception once he was back home, and under Nora's daily influence.

When the senior O'Sullivans went away to visit Theresa in Australia; or to the USA to visit other relatives; or on some long haul cruise, sexual relations would improve a week or so later. Normal Service resumed once they had the house to themselves for any substantial period. When Brendan and Nora returned, Paudie reverted to being their child again….

The arrival of the evening meal interrupts her musings.

Munching on the vol-au-vent, she thinks about Lisa's visit. It has never occurred to her that Lisa might miss her. She would gamble the price of an expensive hairdo on Lisa being happy with her absence. Lisa avoided getting close to her and she never understood why. It was as though Lisa mistrusted her, and never seemed entirely comfortable when they worked closely together. With an excellent work ethic, Lisa had proven herself to be consistently honest. Liam, the accountant, commented on how fortunate they were to never have a case of embezzlement from staff like his other clients. Reliable, biddable and excellent at staff training, Lisa prioritised customer confidentiality, and was clear with junior assistants about it. She knew she could leave Lisa in charge, and always assumed Lisa was relieved when she did. So why is Lisa missing her? It all seems very strange….

A cautious knock heralds Paudie entering. They swap notes on their respective days. Paudie, as usual, has had one full of stress and near crises, all of which were impossible to deal with. Ruth tells him about her meals and her visitors.

'… so, I was very surprised when she started to cry,' wiping her mouth of crumbs with a paper napkin. 'What would you make of it, Paudie? You're the one who sees her all the time.'

'Ruth, you just don't get it, do you?' shaking his head.

She tilts her head to one side, 'get what, Paudie?'

'That people like you — adore you, even.'

Waving her hand to disagree, 'no, no, very nice of you to say so, but no — Lisa has never liked me, I know so.'

'Ruth, listen to me — it's not that Lisa doesn't like you. It's because she's in AWE of you. She feels uncomfortable when she's with you because she feels nervous. Over the years, I've watched her with you so many times, Ruth. She aspires to be like you, but is worried she'll never make it. When you look at Lisa, I know you see a beautiful, immaculately kept and capable woman, which she is. But that's what you are too, Ruth. Except you have extra qualities. You have something else.' Looking for the right word, 'You have — charisma — and a fierce intelligence. Lisa knows she can never fill your shoes. But God above, would she like to be able to!'

Chapter 11

...the footsteps echoed; they were coming closer. She would see him....

'Ruth, sorry to wake you, I just need to do your obs,' with a ripping sound, Mary O pulls the velcro apart on the monitor cuff. 'Yes, that all looks normal. Ruth, would you like to start using the en-suite instead of the bedpan? Your blood pressure is good.'

'Thanks be to God! I would love to Mary. Can I really? Like, straight away?'

Back in bed, she positions herself high on the pillows and watches the small statured nursing assistant leave the room. Mary holds the door open so that Tilly can enter.

'Tilly, I hope you don't mind me asking, but —'

Tilly places a slice of toast onto a plate, 'butter? Go on, Ruthie, ask away.'

'Do you ever experience racism when you are out and about, especially when you're with Jimmy?'

Putting a heaped serving spoon of scrambled egg onto the toast, 'no — I have to say — in all honesty — thankfully — no, I don't.' Bringing the plate over and wheeling the table closer, 'we get looks, mind you — black woman, white man — you know yourself. But then people generally cop on to themselves and stop staring.'

'That's good — I mean nothing too ignorant — I'm glad to hear that. Although I'm sure you're made to feel uncomfortable at times. So overall, has Ireland been good to you, Tilly, would you say?'

'Ruth, coming to Ireland was the best thing that ever happened to me. I wake up in the morning and I know I'm going to be safe — no militia man is going to come — run me out of my house — take my stuff — maybe burn it down. Then come looking for me,' Tilly shudders, and stares at the wall behind the bedhead lost in thought. Then refocusing, 'anyway, Ruthie, you don't need to hear any of that. You've your own troubles, girl.'

After Tilly leaves, she carefully loads her fork with the crumbly egg. But the food does not settle in her stomach comfortably. She feels embarrassed about asking Tilly such personal questions. Knowing what it is like to be a stranger in town, she wanted to show understanding and offer solidarity. Mortified that she elicited what could only have been a painful disclosure from Tilly, it makes her cheeks burn with shame. Scolding herself, she instructs herself to apologise to Tilly when she comes back.

'Have you always tried to reach out to strangers, Ruth?' her Friend watching her closely.

Yes, she always tried to.

She was very much one herself when she moved to Balnarath. Strangers have been an important part of her life, and rather than viewing them as a threat, she tries to view them as an added extra. She believes they bring more than they ever take. The most obvious examples were in the business. The town grew commensurate with the waxing fortunes of local property developers. When construction started on a new housing estate, and the houses became occupied, a trickle of new customers would tentatively test the pharmacy services. There was also a surge of one-off houses built during the economic boom. Like mushrooms, they seemed to pop up overnight. One day a field would get cleared of crops or grass. The next time she went down the same road, a grey walled box would have appeared in the middle of the plot. A few weeks later, a skeleton of honey coloured rafters would sit on top of the box. It could remain like that for a while with the builders being occupied elsewhere. Then another flurry of activity, and a black hat would creep over the gables. The grey walls would acquire smooth undergarments in the same shade of prison grey. At some later date, they would be dressed in a coat of snow white, or occasionally yellow, and plastic windows would peer out like spectacles. Then after another period of time, the builders' white vans would be replaced with dark jeeps and bright coloured hatch-backs, parked on half-finished stony driveways.

Making sure to treat new customers with consideration, and trying not to pry, she would recall the florist who sold her the lilies all those years before. If she had felt more comfortable with the woman, she might have been more forthcoming, and probably avoided her faux-pas as the locals would have known all about Nora and her ways. But she also remembers her sense of infringement. If new faces returned to the shop, she acknowledged them in friendly tones, and worked on gradually developing a relationship of warm trust.

In her opinion, one of the best things that happened to the town was when the old Convent closed down after the last few elderly nuns were rehoused locally. The building stood empty for a year or two. Then without fanfare, it was taken over by the State, and reopened as a direct provision centre for asylum seekers. Black families were suddenly walking the streets and frequenting the shops. Coming from Dublin, she was familiar to a limited extent with other races, but not as much as her cousins over in London, Birmingham and Manchester. When she visited them as a child, she found people of colour unusual and a bit scary. But as her cousins had black friends coming over to play, she soon learned they were "just like us".

Observing how the locals coped with the changes sometimes amused her, but often times, saddened her. On the whole, people rubbed along together as they had little choice. For her, the best part was the children mixing together in school. That gave her hope for the future. She was quick to stamp out any racist talk amongst her own three, but fortunately that was never an issue. Daithí's future husband Ben is mixed African American and Hispanic, and Sophie once had a serious relationship with a boy of East Asian heritage.

She struck up a friendship with one woman customer from South Sudan, named Aamira, who had a small child. Whilst discussing some health issues, Aamira confided that the doctor thought she was lactose intolerant. Offering some dietary advice, she suggested that Aamira ask the Centre Manager to order in lactose free dairy products because she was concerned that Aamira might have bone health problems in the future.

Having black skin in the west of Ireland was not conducive to Vitamin D production, and avoiding products that had a high calcium content along with lactose, could lead to problems.

Following the matter up, it transpired that the Manager had refused, citing the Government Food Allowance not stretching to special foodstuffs — the Manager simply did not have the budget for it. So she sourced some products for Aamira herself, and would only accept a nominal payment for them, explaining she had got a good rate from the supplier. That was not wholly truthful because those foods were new to the country, and were ridiculously expensive back then. Conflicted, she did not want to charge at all because the woman's meagre spending money would barely cover it. But she did not want to embarrass her either by giving them for free. She guessed Aamira would never return to the shop out of a sense of pride. When her asylum application was approved, Aamira was offered a housing association house in Mullingar, and they lost touch. She often thinks about Aamira and her daughter, wondering how they got on in the end.

'That's interesting, Ruth,' her Friend interjects. 'It sounds like most of your life was dominated by business. How can I put it without seeming rude — that the way you approach most things — is with a business mindset?'

No, no she has to disagree — that is not the most important thing in her life. There are plenty more, like her family, her home, her art.

Paudie was the one who was all about the business. She wanted other things. When eventually the business reached break-even point; then grew to an in-profit status, and then healthy bank deposits built up, Liam advised them to reinvest the cash into the business. This was music to Paudie's ears, and to him meant enlarging the shop to offer more lines, attracting a larger footfall. For her, a greater priority was to get their own home. Paudie had always said they would. But of course, Paudie being Paudie, pulled that agreement. She had been livid, so he promised that when funds built up again after refurbishing the shop, she could look for a house. His arguments made good business sense, but it left her feeling disgruntled. After a few weeks of cold silence, she cheered up at the prospect of better working conditions especially when Paudie suggested an office, and a decent staff kitchen instead of a shelf in a corridor with an electric kettle filled from the toilet wash hand basin. Paudie wasted no time by approaching Maurice Hennessy for a site meeting.

Shaking her hand, Maurice holds it for longer than she is used to, 'is everything to your satisfaction at Rath House, Mrs O'Sullivan?'

'Yes, thank you, Maurice — you and the lads did an excellent job — completely transformed the place. You'd never know what it used to be like. Come to I think of it, there are a few repairs need doing — one of the small window panes at the top of the dining room bay has a crack from Daithí's football. It's not causing any problems, but I suppose it should be replaced. What do you think?'

'Definitely, Mrs O'Sullivan — all broken glass is dangerous. Anything else?'

'Hmm — Sophie was swinging on one of the kitchen cupboard doors and it snapped at the hinges.'

Maurice laughing, 'children! — they're all the same! Look, I could call around this evening, if it suits. Go through each room and draw up a list.'

As they inspected the shop, Maurice suggested using all the space in the yard behind the shop, bringing the building up to the service road at the rear of the terrace. By installing a full width roller door, delivery drivers could unload without causing the traffic holdups out the front which incensed the traffic warden. A large storage area for stock, staff facilities and the promised office could be created out of the extra space acquired. The existing dispensary would be moved back making a larger retail area. She could not help but be excited. Warning the staff and customers about a period of disruption, Maurice did his best to minimise it. Collecting a good team of tradesmen, they acted with respect and unexpected speed. It seemed unusual compared to the usual disaster stories that went around the town about building work. Another surprising aspect was Maurice himself….

'Ruth O'Sullivan?' a young woman about Sophie's age comes into the room, head wrapped in a navy coloured satin headscarf that matches her uniform.

She carries an aluminium walking frame, 'great, I'm glad to have come to the right person. Hello, I'm Kashaf Khan, Senior Physiotherapist, I'm pleased to meet you. I brought this for you to try — see if it helps. Can I ask you, please, to have a practice while I assist you — I particularly want to see how you negotiate the bathroom…'

They return to the room with Ruth pushing the frame on its front wheels, 'Ruth, that's excellent — I'll make a referral to Occupational Therapy for a raised toilet seat to make using the toilet easier. It's far too low with your leg muscles being so de-conditioned. But we'll do something about that. Get your strength back up — I'll come back later to go through a few simple bed exercises to start you off. I haven't time now as I'm running late for clinic. I didn't want to leave you without help getting to the toilet, or risk any falls while we build you up. Is that okay with you?'

'Hi, Kashaf,' Tilly passes the physiotherapist as she leaves the room, 'sorry, Ruthie, I've been so long coming to collect your dishes. It's a nightmare out — hey, girl, why are you crying? What's up, honey?' Tilly stops and looks at her slumped on the bed, with concern in her eyes.

'Tilly, I'm so sorry for asking you all those personal questions earlier,' she sniffs loudly.

Passing her a tissue, Tilly exclaims, 'you're crying about that! I thought something important had happened — that Kashaf had bad news for you, or something — hey, listen, Ruth, you'd never hurt me, I know that. I can sense what a good person you are. And so does The Lord.' Retrieving a twin packet of Twix bars from her box, 'now listen — take this — put it in your locker — No more nonsense now. See you later, girl,' and trundles out the door.

She tears the Twix packet vertically, and pushes up one of the chocolate covered finger biscuits. She is always ready for chocolate, any time of the day or night.

Her Friend watches with an amused look on his face while she finishes. Tracing a forefinger over the curved wooden end of the chair arm, 'the renovation of the shop was a good experience for you, Ruth? How did you find working with Maurice?'

It was different to her other professional relationships.

Maurice was not just her builder, he was her ally. Life was so busy, so consumed by work and family life, there was little time to make friends in Balnarath. Pals from school had dissipated with her moving West. Visits home were reserved for Billy and Vera, and sometimes her sisters. Because she left her Art degree early, she never got to forge lasting relationships with other students. And Bríd moved to Argentina with Ramón. Thinking about Bríd, she remembers how they swapped notes that Sunday night when Bríd returned from her first trip to Kilkenny.

Before she can get a word in about her and Paudie, Bríd gushes about her amazing weekend. Ramón collected her from MacDonagh Junction Station in Kilkenny City and drove south, close to the border with County Tipperary where the stud was located. It had guest accommodation provided for foreign buyers and trainee jockeys, so she was shown to a comfortable apartment in a converted stone farm building. Transfixed under an en-suite shower, she regales wallowing in the free heat. They could only have a quick hop in the bath in Stoneybatter because the bathroom was always freezing, even in the height of summer. Nestling down into a comfy bed, she resisted sleep because she wanted to review how relations were going with Ramón now they had met up again. She was contemplating whether he still liked her or not, when there was a frantic knocking on her door. Ramón was standing in the hallway wretched with worry. A mare was in a difficult labour, and the Vet could not be contacted. While the owner tried desperately to find an alternative, Ramón thought to come and get her. Pulling clothes on over her PJs, she followed him immediately down to the stables. Shown into the mare's stall, she got stuck in, and successfully delivered the foal with both mother and baby none the worst. Throughout the weekend, the owner was so impressed with her way with the horses, he offered to approach the vet about taking her on for her final placement, adding that she would be welcome to live at the stud. Better still, the vet only worked with horses and large agricultural animals.

Bríd brimming with glee '…it's just so unbelievable — I can't believe it — it's an unbelievable opportunity — like I might have said once or twice before —'
Predicting what Bríd is about to say, and chiming in unison, '— only the men get to work with the large animals!' they both burst out laughing.

A very real fear for Bríd was to never be taken seriously for equine and livestock work because of being a woman. Female vets were always consigned to the small animal clinics. As much as she loved cute furry guinea pigs and charming talkative parrots, horses, and cattle to some extent, would always be her true calling.

'That's a lovely anecdote, Ruth. But please, what about Maurice?' her Friend cocking his head to one side.

Okay, okay, back to Maurice.
While working on the shop, he made a point of engaging with her. Uncomfortable with stuffy formality as it reminded her of the O'Sullivans, she quickly corrected him to call her Ruth. He did not need to be told twice. When there was a query about some building detail, he always asked her rather than Paudie which intrigued her. She assumed men preferred to discuss such matters with other men. Back then, men were the more senior partners in a family business and the ones to be appeased. When he went to the deli to buy food, he never failed to offer to get her something. Most times she declined, but occasionally, having been too rushed to make a sandwich

before work, she would order something. Then there would be an argument over payment — him claiming it was his treat, and her refusing, threatening to never place an order with him again until he conceded. Paudie always went for a pub lunch, taking a full hour and a quarter. She never had that option needing to buy food for the evening meal, or run errands for the children. Eating something light in the small corridor behind the dispensary, she fitted her break time around the staff lunches, then prepared prescriptions for Paudie to sign off on his return.

With his keen eye for detail, Maurice missed little of what went on in the shop. She knew that he was privy to people's lives behind their front doors, but she never heard him pass comment on anyone. Instead, he showed sympathy and understanding when others gossiped unkindly. Paudie underestimated him, and gave patronising instructions about patient confidentiality, and how to treat the female staff. Maurice accepted them with gracious deference, promising to have a word with his men. She winced with embarrassment over Paudie's superior attitude. Maurice was quick to pick up her moods and would always enquire after her health. She suffered painful menstrual periods at that time, which took much of her strength. Paudie would dose her up with Ponstan and codeine. Seeking out a quiet corner to sit, she distracted herself with paperwork until the painkillers worked. During a long drawn out saga of GP appointments when she was largely fobbed off, she was eventually referred to Gynaecology. She was diagnosed with endometriosis along the Caesarian scar. Areas outside her womb had developed uterine cells that also bled whenever she had a period, and which caused debilitating pain and anaemia. There was no treatment other than a hysterectomy as working on the scar could worsen the problem. She was warned that the endometriosis could spring up elsewhere in the abdomen, too. Not knowing how she could possibly fit a hysterectomy into her life, and convincing herself that it was only for a few days in the month, she resigned herself to enduring the condition. Pain relief in all its forms were products she kept well stocked in the shop, offering sincere sympathy for anyone coming into the shop requiring it….

The door flies open and Deidre bounces in, 'oops, Mammy, I was supposed to knock, wasn't I?' giggling and pulling clean clothes, another box of Butlers chocolates from a tote bag, and heaping them on the bed. Then she throws her arms around her mother and hugs her for several moments. Unable to resist rearranging the top of the locker, she takes some flowers past their best over to the bin for dumping.

Ruth opens the chocolates and offers the box to Deidre. Mumbling through a rich truffle, 'how are you feeling, Dee Dee? Any morning sickness?'

'Funny you should mention that; I did feel a bit off this morning. But it's my boobies I've noticed the most — they've gotten huge and solid feeling — like rocks,' rolling her eyes.

'I know, I know — I remember that feeling well. You'll have to keep buying bigger and bigger bras,' nodding with sympathy. 'And look out for some front opening ones for breast feeding.'

They chat on about pregnancy symptoms and baby equipment.

'…wow! Is that the time?' Deidre glancing at the clock, 'I'd better let you rest now, Mammy. Thank you for all that really useful advice. I don't know what I would do without you!' Realising the implications of what she has said, wailing, 'oh Mammy what AM I going to do? Without you — if you — you know — if you —?'

'Ahh, now, pet! Maybe you won't have to do without me, after all.'

Deidre ceases her sobs abruptly, and looks at her mother, 'you mean, you feel that much better? — you might —?'

'I have to say, it has taken me by surprise, but yes — I do feel so much better.'

'Oh, Mammy!' Deidre, laughing and crying at the same time.

After Deidre leaves, she begins to feel a little nauseous, and looking at the empty spaces in the chocolate box, is not too puzzled as to why. She looks up at the sound of her Friend's voice.

'Were they nice?' coming over to peer in the box. 'Did you enjoy them?'

Nodding, without smiling, she feels guilty about her greediness.

'Ahh, there's no harm done. It's just what you need, girl,' sitting down. 'Did Maurice remain a friend after the shop conversion was completed?'

No.

She did not see him again for quite a few years. During the interim, her life was an incessant hamster wheel of days that ran into weeks. Before she realised it, years had passed. An unrelenting cycle of business development; growing children; school progression, and out of school activities. It was a constant darting from one task to another. Like she was encased in a rubber ball, she bounced and boinged off the inner walls while the ball was thrown back and forth between work and home.

Feeling it to be her duty, and an expression of love for her family, she contented herself with the knowledge that her time would come, remembering the words Vera had told her years before. One day she knew the children would be fully grown, the domestic pressures would ease, and she would be able to do all the things there was never time for. How foolish it was to assume all that. There was only a small chance of that happening now....

The door opens slowly and knowing instinctively who it is, she greets the emerging figure 'come in and sit down, Sophie. Have you finished work early today?'

Sophie closes the door behind her and walks over to sit down without kissing her mother. 'No, I didn't go in. I went to get a sick cert from the doc on account of my knee, and he said in the circumstances, he'd give me a full week off. And he'll renew it again next week, he said. By the way, he asked after you — how you were doing.'

'That was nice of him — to give you a sick note AND enquire after me. So how's your knee?…

… you're going to be an aunty? What do you think about that?…

…Sophie, before you leave, I want to talk to you. I've been thinking a lot about our conversation the other day.'

'No, it's ok, Mammy. Forget about it. I'm sorry I shouldn't have brought it up.'

'Why? Has your father said something?'

'Daddy? No — why do you ask?'

'Hmm — nothing, but I don't agree with you. I mean, I don't agree that you shouldn't have brought it up. I think you were right to. And I'm glad you did as now I have the chance to talk to you about it.'

Sophie shakes her head in protest.

Putting her forefinger to her lips, 'please, Sophie, let me speak. It's important for both you and me, that I do. I have to be perfectly straight with you, I found rearing the three of you, and helping to run the business at the same time, very hard. Most of the time, I thought I was a complete failure. I never felt I had the time and energy to do either job properly. If I focused on the business, it meant there wasn't enough for you three. And when I focused on you three, I felt I was letting your father down by leaving him to carry the full burden.' Rubbing her forehead to concentrate her thoughts. 'But all of that is only by way of explanation. It doesn't take away the fact that you felt you were being pushed out, and weren't given the attention you rightly deserved from your mother. I just want to say that I've always loved you, Sophie, and I am very sorry that I let you down, and hurt you over the years. I hope you can find it in your heart to forgive me. Please.'

Despite the stiffness in her leg, Sophie propels herself out of the chair like a jet pilot baling out, and hobbles as quickly as possible to the door.

'No! Sophie, please don't go! I didn't mean to upset you!'

Without turning around, 'I'll see you later, Mammy,' and quickly exits.

Her Friend reappears in Sophie's vacated chair, and leans forward earnestly, 'how has that made you feel, sweetheart?'

Terrible. That did not go down at all well.

It looks like she has made matters worse instead of better for Sophie. And now, she feels absolutely wretched. Only wanting to speak openly and with honesty, she made a complete mess of it. And she has no idea what to do next. Knowing Sophie as well as she does, how deeply she thinks about things. How she keeps things close to her chest, she knows she will be hurting inside. Maybe, she just needs time to think about what has been said. Anyway, it is too late now — it has been voiced, and it is out there in the open. Perhaps, the damage Sophie suffered happened at too important a phase of her life — went on for too long, and now can never be repaired. Despite what she said to Deidre earlier, she does not know if she will recover from her illness. If she will ever have the opportunity to put things right for Sophie. And that uncertainty is breaking her heart.

Chapter 12

'Mrs O'Sullivan, how gratifying to see you out of bed and sitting in a chair — such a marked improvement. However, would you mind getting back onto the bed so that Dr Geraghty can examine you?'

Ruth hoists herself with some difficulty out of the armchair.

Dr Geraghty rushes over to assist.

She has a strong sense of independence, but speaking with gratitude, 'no, it's okay — I'm fine Doctor G, honestly, I can manage.'

Lying back on the bed, her head raised by the pillows, she observes Dr Mulhall. Noticing that his eyes are not on his patient, she watches them follow Dr Geraghty's bottom as she moves around the bed as she gently presses anatomy, checks skin and shines a torch into orifices. Doctor Mulhall asks Dr Geraghty to give a presentation on the care of the patient, and summarise the drug trial for the benefit of the team. As she addresses her colleagues, his gaze wanders from the top of Dr Geraghty's head, down to her feet and back again. On the way, it lingers at areas of especial interest — her breasts, her waist, her hips, her legs, and singled out for particular attention, the mound of Venus outlined by the thin, clinging synthetic material of her trousers.

Dr Geraghty concentrates on her task, and turns and looks at her occasionally, as if to include her in the meeting. She senses the medic regards her more a person than just a patient. Engaging in individual eye contact with team members, she appears oblivious to her boss. Or is she refusing to look at him? That possibility is interesting. Dr Mulhall, engrossed with his quarry, does not notice that he too is being examined. After her lecture, the consultant thanks his junior, but she barely acknowledges his generous compliments and congratulations. She wonders why Dr G is not proud to be so raised up in the eyes of the team, and detects a slightly dismissive shrug of her shoulders. Then the doctor seems to acknowledge that she is in dangerous territory, and throws a brief smile at her boss; one that does not quite reach her eyes.

After the posse leaves her in peace, she feels drained and contemplates whether she should get out of bed after all the prodding. Lying still and musing, some of her former inner determination kicks in, and she decides to push herself. She resolves to be as active as possible. Fed up of being viewed as sick, it makes her feel somehow subhuman. She needs to pee anyway, so that concludes the matter.

Returning from the en-suite, her Friend is laying on the bed and with a cheeky grin, motions for her to take the chair. 'Come on then, when did you see Maurice again?'

At a funeral — it was Gearóid Hanley's funeral.

Standing outside the church after the Mass with mourners thronging around her, she spots a familiar head making its way towards her. Maurice is dressed in a black woollen lumber jacket with a corduroy lined collar. His hair seems dull with dust as though he has hastily left a site.

He beams at her, 'Ruth, wow, it's great to see you! You're looking well. Nice Mass wasn't it, considering the day that's in it?'

'Hello Maurice — how are you? Yes indeed, it was very fitting for Gearóid. By the way, the reading was excellent, well done — you seemed to have no nerves. How are you keeping? Are you busy these days?' taken aback by the pleasure she feels in seeing him.

'I am — very — why? Do you have something for me?'

'No, nothing in particular — I just know you lads seem to be in great demand these days. Building seems to be going on everywhere you look.'

Maeve Cullen appears at her elbow, 'Ruth, thank you so much for coming.' Kissing her on the cheek, 'you are coming for the meal, aren't you? I know you are, Maurice — you're to sit at the top table with me. But Ruth, you'll come too, won't you? Please do.'

Her intention is to leave as she does not like to impose on families in grief, and certainly never expects them to feed her.

But Maeve insists she go with them in the funeral cortége for the burial, and then walk back with them to the Hanrahan Hotel for the wake.

Inside the hotel dining room, Maeve ushers her to a place beside her at the immediate family members' table as the other chief mourner, her sister Róisín, is sitting with old school friends on another table. Gearóid, the local poet and playwright had been Maeve and Róisín's brother.

Curious about Maurice's connection to the family, 'were you a close friend of Gearóid's, Maurice?'

'Gearóid did more for me than any father would — 'a server interrupts him with an offer of vegetables.

Turning her attention to Maeve, she hesitantly asks, 'Maeve, if you don't mind me asking, what will happen to Gearóid's house? Will you or Róisín move in to it? It's your old family home, isn't it?'

'Good God, Ruth, are you joking? No, I'm perfectly happy with my comfortable, warm, clean bungalow out in Cappagh,' Maeve laughs. 'No, I'll put it on the market. Róisín and I have already talked about it. Róisín has no interest in leaving London.' Maeve looks at her quizzically, 'why, you're not interested in it, are you, Ruth? — Hey, I can tell by your face — you are, aren't you?'

'Possibly — I might be.'

'It's in a poor state, mind. I don't think Gearóid ever did anything to it after Daddy died. Is that right, Maurice?'

Maurice, his mouth full, nods emphatically and swallows, 'I tried my best over the years — tried to make it better for him. But he wasn't interested. As long as he wasn't getting wet from the roof leaking on top of him, and the lights worked so he could see to write, he was happy.'

Maeve turns back to her, 'but listen, Ruth, if you're interested, I'd be delighted to sell it to you. I can't think of a nicer person to take on my childhood home. But in its condition, it'd need a lot of work to make it anyway decent for a family to live in. But look, I'd reflect that in the asking price, of course. I'm sure we could come to some arrangement that suits us both.'

'Okay' deep in thought, 'that's very good of you, Maeve. When can I go and view it? And Maurice, would you come with me, please — for some technical advice?'….

The noise of the door opening pulls her out of the plush hotel back to the sparsely furnished hospital room.

'Hello, Mrs O'Sullivan — I'm Blessica, an Occupational Therapist,' a short woman carrying a large white plastic hoop walks in. 'I brought this for you — I'll go fit it on to your toilet and then I'll talk to you — it's not a particularly nice thing to be holding while we talk, is it?' she giggles. Returning, 'Ruth, can we test it out, please; to see if the height suits you?'

Returning to her armchair, 'Blessica? Is that your name, did you say? What a beautiful name. Where does it come from?'

Blessica answers cheerfully, 'The Philippines.'

'Oh that sounds interesting,' pausing, 'and rather exotic.'

'Ruth, can I ask you some other questions, please? About how you are managing to eat; washing yourself, that kind of thing? And how are you getting on with the walking aid?…'

Later returning to something far more glamorous, Ruth declares, 'The Philippines, yes, that does seem exotic. I think I might like to visit there.'

'If you do, be sure to let me know. I'll tell you the best places to go,' Blessica grins at her. She promises to come back another time, then departs.

She feels conflicted about being presented with a raised toilet seat. On the one hand it signifies progress — she can go to the toilet without having to wait for help; without needing a bedpan or commode; or deal with worse, as she did in Intensive Care. But a disabled person's toilet seat? She is not at all sure about that.

Her Friend peers into the en-suite out of interest and then sits on the edge of the bed, 'what happened when you went to view Gearóid's house?'

It felt really significant, like it was some kind of turning point.

A few days after the funeral, she met up with Maeve and Maurice at River House. Handing the key over to Maurice,

Maeve gave her apologies, saying she had to get back to the shop as a bad paying customer had made an appointment to settle a hefty bill, and she did not want to miss the opportunity.

Standing on the pavement, she looks up at the frontage of a tall Victorian building. The garden is a jumble of briars which obscure the view of the ground floor. A high sided tunnel had been hacked through to the front door.

Trying to dispel any negative first impressions, Maurice jokes, 'mind Gearóid's organic wild garden. He was forever getting into trouble with the neighbours over it. And his riposte was always "all of Earth's plants have an equal right to exist, as they are want.",' chuckling. 'He was such an old rogue — idle as Hell, but with such a mind — he'd argue any point, and would always win with some piece of logic that made sense at the time, but you could never quite remember afterwards,' laughing to himself, lost in memory. The key turns smoothly in the lock, 'I see a squirt of WD40 has worked.' Maurice indicates for her to go in ahead.

Crouching down to gather up post scattered across the hallway, she inhales stale pipe tobacco smoke, damp plaster and domestic grime. She walks to the bottom of the stairs and piles the post under the monkey tail of a mahogany hand rail atop a decorative cast iron newel post. She pauses, feeling overwhelmed that she has reached an important fulcrum; the possibility of purchasing a property. One where she might spend the rest of her life. It feels as significant as marriage.

Maurice observes her closely and offers, 'Ruth, will I show you around? I know this house as well as my own. I've imagined time and again how I'd restore it. Builders' bad habit, I'm afraid,' he smiles at her.

Indicating her assent, Maurice leads her to the top floor first.

'You see this big landing here and that trap door above,' pointing. 'I've been up there in the attic and I know for certain it has great potential for conversion. A proper staircase could go up here,' moving his two hands upwards. 'I could make a big master bedroom with a vaulted ceiling right up to the rafters with automated roof windows and blinds. It would be romantic to lie in bed and look up at the stars on a clear night; or watch the snow falling, or even the rain. I could fit you out a big walk-in wardrobe and dressing room, and a big bathroom with twin sinks and a freestanding bath.'

Mesmerised by his excited gesticulations, she is caught up in his vision of a fantasy bedroom. They turn into a room, 'this currently is the master bedroom — look, it's the full width of the house. I would have to take a look at those sashes.' Stepping out again, 'then this room behind overlooks the side return courtyard at the back; follow me down, please.' He agilely descends a half flight of stairs leading to a short hallway. 'This is an original back extension, that is, the house was built with it from the beginning; not as a later add-on,' mansplaining. 'This bedroom on the left is a good size, and the one at the end even bigger.' Opening the left hand door, 'this could be made into another bathroom. And the big one remain a bedroom. That way, the lads could have a room each, and have their own bathroom to share.'

'Maurice, these rooms would be perfect — and your ideas for the attic, brilliant!' her excitement is building.

'Wait until you see downstairs. Come on,' waving her down.

The front room has all the original plaster and wood work; all the period details are intact. Walking over to a polished black stone fire surround and hearth, she traces a finger along embedded white fossils in the cool surface. A wooden overmantel made up of sections of bevelled mirrors, and small shelves supported by delicately turned posts, is inlaid with coloured marquetry. She thinks it exquisite.

'The fireplace is Kilkenny marble. Quite rare nowadays. And the overmantel, rosewood. Come on, let's go into Gearóid's study.'

The room behind has french doors with steps leading down into the courtyard. It is lined with antique oak panelling and bookcases filled with Gearóid's library.

'I think it would be a mistake to rip this lot out, but that would be up to yourselves. This was Gearóid's favourite room and the one place he was careful in. His books were like his children.'

Another three stairs lead down into the back extension with a guest toilet on the left. They enter a dining room with a side bay looking across the courtyard. The kitchen has an old stained table in the centre piled with rusting equipment and utensils, and separate scullery and larder off. The scullery has the original white stone Belfast sink, and more stained wooden draining boards. The larder is fitted out with white marble slabbed counters, and paper lined wooden shelving. She notices a mousetrap on one of the shelves.

Completely enchanted, this is the kind of house she has dreamed of owning all her life. Like the period buildings she knew so well as a child in Dublin, and where she had so envied the occupants. For her, big old houses are posh, and although it seems such a middle class aspiration to live in one, she cannot help herself. She knows there and then, she HAS to have the house. A small problem though, is going to be convincing Paudie….

Kashaf puts her head around the door, 'Ruth, do you feel up to talking again?'

Kashaf goes through some exercises she can practise in bed and some for trying in the chair.

'I'll leave these sheets here,' placing some papers on the table. 'Try to do each exercise in ten repetitions, three times a day. I normally suggest after breakfast, mid afternoon and early evening. I'll call back in a few days and see how you are getting on. We must try and keep your lungs clear and build your muscle strength up, Ruth. That'll help prevent falls. Any questions before I leave you in peace?'

After Kashaf departs, she feels jelly legged with the effort and plonks down onto the bed for a nap. Certain she'll doze off in no time, she finds sleep elusive. Her mind is overstimulated by the steroids.

'Did you have any difficulty persuading Paudie to buy the house?' her eyes fly open with her Friend's question.

Difficulty? — that's an understatement.

It was a huge battlefield. More than a battlefield — a whole war. On one side was her with reserves in the form of Maeve,

Róisín, Irina and Maurice. The opposing army was Paudie with the senior O'Sullivans making up his battalion.

She knew that Paudie had little motivation to move. Why would he, she had reasoned? He lived mortgage free in the well appointed house he grew up in, with his elderly parents in easy reach. Not having to worry about their wellbeing, the different generations of his family could enjoy each others' company. Like any miser, he gained great satisfaction from watching his bank figures grow. His favourite pastime in the evenings continued to be counting the day's takings. His best buddy, Liam, egged him on, as far as she was concerned. Why would he want to make a big hole in their savings for a deposit and finance the restorations? Why lose money paying interest fees on a mortgage? She understood his position only too well.

As for the in-laws, she knew Brendan loved having them around the place, and it had helped him adjust to retirement after being such a popular and busy GP. It had been Nora's idea principally for them to move in, so there was no way she was going to be co-operative.

She, however, was determined to have her way; for once.

Fortunately, Maeve was in no rush to sell, being well off financially, as was Róisín. Maeve reassured her that if Gearóid had still been alive, they would not have even thought about selling the house. They viewed it more a medium term investment, something with a future return. Both sisters said she could take as long as was needed to win Paudie over — they would rather have her and her tribe live in the family home than strangers.

Maurice did his bit too by offering to work on a daily rate as work arose, rather than giving an inflated estimate based on all eventualities in advance. Being in high demand during those Celtic Tiger years, she thought that most generous of him. It also meant she could employ him on a piecemeal basis, spreading the cost over a longer period of time. He suggested doing enough essential work to get them into the house and then work around them while they lived there. He was helpful beyond what could be expected, and she was appreciative of that. Irina was a wonderful support in general, propping her up whenever she was about to collapse under the combined weight of O'Sullivan attrition.

Nora tried every ploy she could think of to scupper the plan. Working her way around the family members in turn, Nora charmed and cajoled in equal measure. With the children, she suddenly became an interested, doting grandmother overnight, telling them what fine children they were and how proud she was of their achievements. She hinted at future privileges like reallocating their bedrooms so that Daithí could have a bigger room, and the girls their own room each. However, not quite yet — when they were older — maybe. With Paudie, Nora implied that the house could remain his home after she and Brendan passed away. But even Paudie had to admit scepticism with that idea as he was neither an only child, nor the eldest son. His siblings may have agreed to him staying on in the house in the event, but he knew them well enough to know they would want their shares bought out by him. And it would be full market value — there would be no financial favours for their younger brother.

In respect of Brendan, Nora played the role of emotionally distraught and victimised mother-in-law. Brendan understood people, and his own wife in particular, and was not taken in by her histrionics. But that did not mean he was going to be disloyal and leave Nora unsupported.

When it had come to her, Nora had to be a bit more subtle as she was made battle hardy from years of relentless passive aggression. Nora started out by feigning empathy. Saying to Paudie, that of course she understood Ruth's position of wanting her own home, but declared it neither wise nor practical, knowing full well that he would use that as ammunition for himself. Dodging a direct confrontation, Nora dropped pieces of information, from sources in the "know" that implied legal complications with River House and Gearóid's Probate onto Carmel, confidant that Carmel's genuine concern would compel her to pass the "rumours" on.

Nora guessed correctly that any coldness would only serve to harden her resolve. Nora took care to be polite, accommodating and unusually generous. Paying her compliments regarding her outfits, Nora offered to loan the exact piece of jewellery that would match the ensemble. She even mentioned that her daughters probably would not miss an item or two from her collection, if she was to hang on to something indefinitely. Adding brightly, besides which, if she was to give something as a gift while alive, her heirs would have no redress anyway. Playing the game, she would borrow the item for the day, but always took the precaution of returning it to Nora with a witness present. Sometimes there would be the pretence of Nora insisting she keep it, but she would equally insist that she could not possibly do so, thanking her for her generosity all the same.

Her Friend fascinated, 'how was it resolved in the end? How was Paudie finally persuaded?'

It became an impasse, one she thought impossible to resolve.

Increasingly more desperate, she felt destined to be unhappy whatever the outcome. If she relented and stayed at Rath House, she would never have the pleasure, freedom and fulfilment of her own home. She would have to endure the tensions of living with her controlling in-laws for probably decades as both Bendan and Nora were in stubbornly good health. Plus there was the added insecurity of not owning her own home, and living somewhere the O'Sullivan clan controlled. She knew that she would have few rights or legal claims over it. Any day, with the right set of unfortunate events, she could be made homeless with no capital behind her. It did not just happen to refugees and asylum seekers — it happened to established women in Ireland too.

If, on the other hand, she forced Paudie to buy River House against his wishes, he would never be happy, and forever hold it against her. Ultimately that would have been the wrong decision for her too, as she loved and wanted the best for him deep down.

One day, feeling particularly despondent, she went for a walk along the river to cheer herself up. Aware that her head was slumped downwards looking at the path, she forced it up to pay attention to the trees and bushes, and distract herself from brooding. The leaves were unfurling into a luminous springtime, lime colouring. Listening to the chattering songbirds with their courting small talk, and inhaling the miasma of alluvial mud, she wondered if she could ever have a life not dictated by others. Passing the bottom of the garden of Rath House, she caught glimpses of Tom through the foliage, working up on the flowerbeds; but she had no inclination to shout up to him in greeting. Examining her emotional needs as she plodded along, she did not consider them to be extraordinary. Attempting her best with regards to other people, she did recognise her shortcomings. But really, she asked herself, what was the purpose of it all? Slaving in the shop and rearing children who would ultimately leave her? Then what? More work until retirement? Then remain living alongside, not with, a man who had become remote, only ever pandering to his insatiable parents? What good things were there to look forward to? As she rounded a meander in the river, she noticed an incongruous thicket of unruly willow sandwiched between neatly kept gardens and realised with a jolt that it was the garden of River House. The sadness that she would never get to dig up that jungle, and create her own little Garden of Eden broke her heart. Feeling utterly hopeless, she silently pleaded for God to help her….

Coming through the door, the trolley of food arrives followed by the young woman who has served her before. The woman quietly rolls the trolley back and forth across the room according to some coordinates known only to herself.

Unable to tolerate the silence, Ruth blurts out, 'hello, how are you? Just remind me of your name again — ah, Naomi, that's it — I remembered that you were a nice person, but I just couldn't think of your name for a second, please forgive me.'

Naomi looks bashful, 'em, Mrs O'Sullivan, would you take a cheese salad for your supper?' bringing over a small plate of glossy, cold pasta speckled with green; half a tomato sitting on top of a single baby gem lettuce leaf, and a rectangle of yellow cheese sealed in plastic. 'You're allowed a yoghurt too,' packing her wares quietly before exiting, leaving the door wide open, swung back on its hinges, tight against the wall.

Finding the packaging on the cheese impossible to open, she flings her legs over the side of the bed and walks over to the wash bag balanced on the basin. Finding the effort easier than expected, she considers the earlier exercise most effective. She rummages around the bottom of the bag looking for nail scissors.

Paudie comes into the room, 'Good God, Ruth! You're up and about!'

In a flash, 'Excuse me? And where was the knock?'

Thumbing at the wide open doorway, he ignores her, 'will I help you back to bed?'

'No, thank you, Paudie, I can manage,' a curt edge to her voice. Wheeling the table towards the armchair, and dropping it low, making clear her intention to eat there.

Watching and daring not to interfere, Paudie offers, 'I'll go and grab another chair from somewhere….'

Paudie returns, pushes the door closed and sets up a folding chair next to Ruth. Ruth is aware that she still holds some of the anger from trying to get River House, but realises it is inappropriate and unjust.

She decides to talk about her visitors, '…anyway, Sophie leapt out of the room — well, not exactly leapt, on account of her leg. I think I might have made things worse, Paudie,' groaning and looking at him beseechingly.

Paudie leaning over to clasp her shoulder and sooth her, 'look, Ruth, you've been a fantastic mother to those kids. I couldn't have hoped for a better mother for my three children.'

Pausing and searching his face for any inconsistencies, 'really? Do you really mean that?'

'Yes, Ruth, I really mean it.'

'Sophie doesn't seem to think so.'

'Look, Sophie's just panicking over you — you know — you not being around for her. I KNOW you were always there for ALL three of them. As I said, I couldn't fault you. You were fantastic to all of them.'

Unconvinced, she asks provocatively, 'and wife? Have I been a fantastic wife to you, Paudie?'

The door opens and Jimmy pushes in a barrow laden with another armchair, 'I brought you this, Mr — er — oh, yeh —

em, Mr O'Sullivan. Sit yerselves down on this, sir. I brought another fold-up chair as well. I'll lean that one aginst this wall, in case you has another visitor, missus.'

Chapter 13

The next morning, Ruth lounges in bed allowing her breakfast to digest. The plates have been cleared away by the ever cheerful Tilly. Her Friend stands by the window looking out. A screech of brakes pierces the air, 'wow! That was close! A young fella had a lucky miss there. He came tearing around the corner and nearly took out a dog. He's mounted the footpath to avoid it and narrowly missed an elderly woman, and a young girl with a buggy.'

Ruth eases herself out of bed and goes over to see.

Her Friend pointing, 'they're pouring out of the shops to take a look. People have got out their phones and are taking videos. Cars are backed up the road now. Great, The Gards have arrived. They'll deal with it.'

'Young drivers — their confidence is always bigger than their sense. It used to terrify me witless when mine first started to drive, particularly Dee. Daithí was a typical boy — driving came so naturally to him. And Sophie, well she's just so competent at everything she does. But Deidre, my God, she'd be so busy chatting, driving with only one hand on the wheel, off in another world. And as for her sense of direction — '

'Ruth, do you want to get a shower before they all start arriving,' nodding towards the corridor.

Returning refreshed from her ablutions, her Friend sits in the new armchair and beckons her to join him in the other.

'Were your prayers about getting River House ever answered?' her Friend wants to know.

Yes, they were, and in a most unexpected way. It all happened one wet and windy Sunday afternoon.

They are lounging around the sitting room as it is too inclement to go out. Daithí is playing with his toy cars on the floor. Deidre is sitting next to her mother on the sofa reading a book. Sophie is behind them practising pirouettes. Paudie has his feet up on a recliner and is hiding behind a large broadsheet. She is thumbing through the Travel supplement from the same newspaper.

Daithí lines up in pole position, 'when are we going to move into the new house, Daddy?'

Her motor splutters and stalls, shaking the magazine onto the floor.

Paudie primes his engine, 'what new house? I don't know what you are talking about, Daithí,' lowering his newspaper visor.

Daithí revving, 'yes you do, Daddy — you know — the one you and Mammy keep arguing about.'

Paudie revving louder, 'Daithí, your mother and I do not argue — we discuss,' pompously.

'Yes, you do, Daddy,' Deidre coming from behind the book and positioning herself at the starting line. 'You DO argue. I've heard you shouting at Mammy.'

'Yes, you DO, Daddy — and I've seen Mammy crying afterwards,' Sophie comes from behind the couch, ready for the starting flag.

'So? WHEN can we move, then?', Daithí shoots off, tyres screaming.

Paudie's engine misses and backfires, 'ahem. Why? Do you WANT to move from here?'

The three children in unison and level pegging, 'YES, PLEASE, DADDY!'.

Paudie looks at her, the admonishing eyebrow cocked. Then at the children and then back at her, suspicious she has thrown in a spanner. Pressing the pedal down hard, 'but why? Granny and Grandad's house is great. Come on — you're all happy here,' then not so confident, he lifts his foot a tad, 'aren't you?'

Daithí takes over the lead, 'I'll get a much bigger room in the new house. I can't set up my race track properly in my bedroom here — it's too small.'

'But your grandmother has said she'll reorganise your rooms, hasn't she?' Paudie trying to keep up.

'Yeh, but that's a BIG FAT LIE! There's no other rooms here!', Daithí pulls ahead.

Feeling compelled to marshal, she scolds 'Daithí! That's very bold! Please don't talk like that!'

Daithí pouting defiantly, puts his foot down some more, 'but it's true — Grandad has all his doctoring stuff in the other room.'

Sophie hits the pedal to the metal, 'yeh! Grandad's got a skeleton in there!'

Deidre overtaking, 'yeh! And I'll have my own room all to myself,' looking sideways at Sophie as she passes.

Sophie screws her nose up and pokes her tongue out at Deidre as she overtakes, 'yeh! And I'll get a room all to myself, too,' taking the lead.

She makes a ruling, 'Sophie, please don't do that. It's not nice.'

Deidre closes the gap, 'yeh! And we can have a trampoline in the garden! All my friends have trampolines!'

Paudie trailing behind, 'but you can have one here.'

The children levelling with one another, 'NO WE CAN'T!!!'

Daithí edges ahead, 'we already asked Granny and she just said,' in a mimicking voice, ' "Most certainly not — there's insufficient room — the garden is fully accounted for.".'

Going behind the pit wall of her magazine to smile discreetly.

Sophie speeding ahead, 'I want a trampoline!'

Coming out from the pitstop to marshal, 'Sophie! "I want, doesn't get" and Daithí, don't be rude about your grandmother — please, lads.'

Deidre sees the chequered flag ahead, 'Pleeease, Daddy, can we have a new house? Pleeease?'

The final lap.

'And we won't have to stay quiet when Granny and Grandad are resting.'

'And I can have my friends over to play on Sundays.'

'And we won't ever have to have dinner with Uncle Vincent, ever again.'

'Or Aunty Mairéad, YAY!.'

Looking across at Paudie as the children trounce him, she sympathises with his bewilderment. So self absorbed, he has failed to keep up with his own children. Knowing he will need time to think about it, she decides to not make reference to it. But inside, a bottle of winner's champagne has popped.

A week or so later, Paudie raised a few tentative queries about River House.

The two of them are sitting at the dining table, the children already excused to go play before bedtime.

Paudie has finished his meal and tops up a wineglass, 'so tell me, how would Maurice proceed with the work? Has he suggested a plan of action to you?'

She is still eating and finishes a mouthful while she gathers her wits, 'yes, if we were to buy the house, Maurice has proposed the most sensible thing would be to start with the loft conversion because it involves carrying materials up through the house. He'd erect scaffolding; build the dormer at the back and install the roof lights. And then, while he's at it, replace the other slates because the roof's starting to leak. That's if we were to buy it, of course.'

'Hmm, hmm — sounds very expensive,' twiddling with some long hairs on his eyebrow.

'It would be costly, yes. But once the roof's done, it can be forgotten about. It's unlikely that we — that is — if we were to buy it, that is — would ever have to do it again.'

'Hmm, hmm — then what?' twisting the bushy brow into a corkscrew shape.

Speaking quickly, this probably being her only chance, 'well, Maurice suggests — if you were in agreement to buying the house, that is — rewiring the whole place. At the same time, inject a chemical damp course and do some dry rot treatment on the bottom floor because there's no damp course membrane in the old brickwork. Then the first fix plumbing for the central heating and the new bathrooms. That's because that work's disruptive and's best done before we move in — that's if you were in agreement to buying it, of course,' now breathless with anxiety.

'Move in? You expect to move in before the house is finished?' his hand dropping, the corkscrew unravelling and the eyebrow rising.

Taking a chance, 'I thought we might. The whole thing could take quite a while. And I was thinking that if we were to do it gradually, we wouldn't have to take such a big chunk out of our saving, all in one go, like.'

Folding his arms resolutely, 'I couldn't possibly live in a building site, Ruth! Absolutely not! How would that work with the children?' Throwing his arms wide apart emphatically, 'the safety issues? The dirt? I have to be presentable for work, you know! No, absolutely, not! I need to go tally up.' And closes down the discussion.

On a later occasion in the living room.

Throwing his arm over the back of the sofa in an expansive gesture, 'Ruth, I've been thinking and I've been talking with Liam. He thinks it's a good idea to invest in property. It's giving the best and most reliable return at the moment.'

She thinks Hallelujah, 'oh really, Paudie? That's interesting. What do you have in mind?'

'Well, Liam thinks the old Hanley house would increase substantially in value if it was to be renovated. I think it would be a good investment for us.'

'Really? I hadn't thought of that,' lying as it was one of her strongest arguments.

'Yes, I've rung Maeve Cullen and I'm meeting with her for lunch tomorrow…'

Smiling to herself later, she recalls Vera's wise counsel, 'always let a man think it's his idea in the first place'. If Liam advised Paudie to do it, it is a damned certainty now.

Chapter 14

I'm sure we had dinner earlier, a bottle
of decent wine, I gave you flowers
and a small gift, everyone smiled at us,
treated us as friends and not tourists.

Waking, she is not sure why the Brian Docherty poem resounds in her head. Around in a circle, the verse swam in that theta wave sea between sleep and consciousness. It is something she has not thought about for a long time. But then she has not thought about Maurice for a long time, not until her Friend raised the spectre. The room is dimly lit from the corridor lights shining through the glass panel above the door. For a change, she is not sweating as she rolls over onto her side. She notices her Friend's shadow cast against the curtains.

'Ruth, can't you sleep? Would you like to reflect some more, or would you rather doze?'

The steroids are making her too jittery to sleep for long.

'Good, there's something I want to ask you — how did the extended O'Sullivan family take the news of the impending move?'

Very well, considering what they were like as people.

The announcement was made during the next family lunch. Vincent and Mairéad could not have been more enthusiastic. Vincent stood up, walked around the table and thumping Paudie on the back, declared it the best decision Paudie had made in a long while. Then he went around the other side to shake her hand. She was unable to recall any occasion when Vincent had touched her before. Mairéad, following Vincent's initiative, hugged Paudie and kissed both his cheeks. Then she came over to her to repeat the gesture. A cloud of Madame Rochas perfume enrobed them and she had to surreptitiously wipe off the greasy residue left by Mairéad's lips. Observing her parents in-law, Brendan remained deadpan, experienced in not showing emotion in stressful situations. Nora chomped on a mouthful of roast chicken like it was a wasp.

The children jumped up and down excitedly in their seats, and she asked them to calm down so as to not add to Brendan and Nora's discomfort. Thinking about it afterwards, she wondered if Paudie's siblings were relieved that the family of cuckoos was about to leave the ancestral nest. It would prevent a whole heap of problems after their parents' demises. She did feel guilty about leaving the elderly people to live on their own, but that dilemma was quickly resolved. Shortly afterwards, Mairéad was appointed to the judiciary and was despatched to the Western Circuit Court. Although keen to keep her apartment in Dublin, Mairéad felt it too far to commute on a daily basis. She commandeered the old surgery rooms, taking over her old grandmother's bedroom. This helped Nora to cope with the change, and relieved her of any sense of duty and obligation. This absolutely suited her down to the ground.

Carmel and Tom were touching in their display of regret at the family leaving. Both assured her it was for the best, openly expressing delight for her. Giving them open invitations to visit her at River House, they both agreed enthusiastically. Tom took up the offer readily and called over often to check on the building progress, bringing plants for the new garden. Carmel never quite made it. However, the older woman's face would light up whenever she revisited Rath House, either with the children, or sometimes on her own. Carmel would press baking, jam and chutney on her to take home, and small gifts that she had found in the local shops for the children.

Paudie remained a dutiful son and dined with his parents at least once a week. She took it as an opportunity to give the children pizzas for dinner. Paudie considered them glorified sandwiches and not a proper meal at all. As soon as she sliced them, the children would tear the sections apart like rapacious lions while she had her favourite soup and salad....

Her Friend remarks, 'that all went well for you, for a change. And the building work? How did that go?'

Like it generally did, nothing unusual there.

Being involved in any kind of construction work is highly stressful. Although it is usually an elective decision, regarded as something that will improve quality of life in the long run, she believes people have to be in a happy place in their mind and feel strong physically to consider embarking on it. The most stable of us can be reduced to hysterical children during the process. Working with the public and being privy to the ups and downs in their lives, she has heard all the horror stories about bad builders; shoddy workmanship; unforeseen disasters and sheer exhaustion caused by the experience.

Back then, The Celtic Tiger was a rapidly growing cub and was voracious in appetite. The country seemed obsessed with property acquisition. Apart from their ailments, all her customers were interested in was gossiping about who was building and buying what; how it was to be financed and where it was sited. Any farmer having a field with road frontage was considered to be sitting on a gold mine.

It had its advantages because specialist bath and kitchen showrooms appeared in every town, including Balnarath, and the builders' providers carried a wide variety of materials and premium ranges. She rarely needed to travel to Dublin to get anything of top quality. Once a decision was made, it could be ordered in. Her computer skills developed as IT systems were instituted in the Pharmacy trade, and she thoroughly enjoyed browsing the internet for ideas. She once found a great website for wallpaper....

Her Friend interrupting her thoughts, 'so the timing was right. But how did you find the experience?'

She was like a cocked gun in the interim between finding River House and Paudie finally agreeing to buy it.

Once she had the 'go ahead' from Paudie, she embraced the whole project with immense enthusiasm. Sensing freedom ahead, she could not be fired out of the restricting barrel of

Rath House fast enough. Willing to endure any amount of hard work; any disruption; any financial cost; any privation — anything to get her own home. She was committed to providing a less stressful environment for the children; and one for herself too. There was even a small notion of matters improving between her and Paudie. That fanciful idea floated around like water lilies in bud on some sentimental pond deep within her.

Having a builder whose work she knew, and whose judgement she trusted, helped immensely. She knew from the outset how fortunate it was that Maurice had accepted the job. Taking on a house in that state could not be contemplated without him.

She feels sleepy now….

The door creaked open slowly. The lump in her throat must surely be her heart. Knowing herself to be completely subsumed, with her appetite stolen, her sleep robbed, this man had taken full control of her mind and body. He had reduced her….

'Ruth? Can I take your obs before we do the staff handover? Apologies for turning on the light, I know its earlier than normal. We had some new admissions in the night and I have a lot to get done before I go off duty. I hope you don't mind.'

Fully awake, she decides to go shower and brush her teeth despite the early start. The day ahead is going to drag, she just knows. Under the stream of warm water, she thinks back to the saga of moving into River House.

The building work was not the most challenging aspect. It was trying to get Paudie to move in. Once the attic conversion had been completed, and the rewiring and central heating system installed, she prioritised getting the children rooms and their shared bathroom finished. She thought at that stage, they could all move in.

In the sitting room at Rath House with the children in bed, she puts the suggestion to Paudie.

Paudie, his eyebrow peaked, 'why, for the love of God, would you want to move in now? Surely, you'll want to wait until the new kitchen's in. Women always say it's the heart of the home. And with your love of cooking, Ruth —'

Interrupting him, 'no — it's ok, Paudie — I can make do with the set up as it is. It won't be for long. Maurice says he'll get straight on with it. Besides which, every other woman, and man for that matter, has managed well enough with it in its current state; so I'm sure I can do the same.'

'Well, if Maurice says he's going to get on with it, why not wait a few more months while he does. Then none of us will be in his way.'

'But it's not just the kitchen, Paudie — there's other work to be done, you know that. If we wait until everything's done, we'll never get into the place. You know yourself what old buildings are like. They always need something doing to them.'

'Ruth, it doesn't make sense. What's the hurry? It's not like we have to leave here. It's not being sold, or knocked down to make way for the new road, or anything.'

'Paudie, the children want to move into their new rooms. They've been involved in their design and they're mad for them.'

'That's not important, Ruth, they can wait. I still think it'd be better if the kitchen's in first — all the rooms completed — everything fully decorated — the house professionally cleaned like we did with the pharmacy. And the landscaping out the back too, as that'll be disruptive. In other words, Maurice and the builders completely off site before we move in. Being at my parents is fine. We're in no hurry.'

'For fuck's sake, Paudie, no it's NOT fine! Yeh, maybe you're in no hurry. But I'm telling you straight, I AM! And so are the children! I tell you what, YOU stay at your parents until the house is up to your fucking precious standards. But I'm moving in to River House and if they want, the children can come too!'

And that is exactly what she did....

Drying herself with a soft clean towel that Deidre has brought in for her and deciding to rub on a bit of body lotion, she thinks back to that joyous day she fled from Castle O'Sullivan. First thing after breakfast the following Sunday, she bundled clothing into the roomy estate car used for transporting stock, making several trips to collect toys the children still wanted. By evening time, the children and her sat on builders' crates eating Burger Macs in the new dining room.

Deidre with a mouthful of fries, 'Mammy, when will we be able to sit at a table?'

'Possibly tomorrow, or the day after, sweetheart. I've one bought already. I'll ring the shop and ask them to deliver it.'

Daithí joins in, 'when Irina picks us up from school tomorrow, will she bring us back here, or will we go to hers?'

'No, back to hers, love. We'll leave the builders be. I'll collect you after work and then we'll all come back here. Is that okay?'

Sophie looks concerned, 'but when's Daddy going to live with us again?'

A tall figure appears in the doorway, 'from now on, Sophie — if your mother will have me.'…

She finishes in the shower room and feeling a little light headed, she flops onto the bed. A sharp rap on the door and without missing a beat, it swings open.

Mairéad strides across the room, 'Ruth! I've come to visit you. I heard you'd been readmitted, and as I've no hearings today, I thought I'd come and visit. I brought you this to read,' placing a magazine right next to her on the bed. 'It's last week's Sunday Times Supplement. If you look at Page 21 — I've highlighted the relevant page in the Contents, should you forget — and I've tagged it with a paper clip, just in case — it's a travel article I wrote about my latest trip to Peru. I know one of the editors and he commissioned me to do it.' Removing a dressing gown from the preferred armchair, she tosses it onto the other one and sits down. 'So, how are you?' Not waiting for an answer, 'Pádraic told me about the drug trial. He said you're doing well enough on it. You certainly look better than I expected. I'd even go so far to say, better than the last time I saw you.' Tapping her forefinger on her chin, 'I think that was before my trip to Peru. Did I tell you that I was booked to go then? I can't remember if I did or not. Anyway, the trip was SUPERB! I couldn't recommend it highly enough. I have to say, Maeve Cullen did an excellent job with the itinerary. The hotels were so-so, but that's only to be expected…'

Her eyes soften and relaxing into the bed, she knows there is no need to speak until Mairéad is ready to leave. Her Friend stands next to Mairéad, leaning against the curtain drawn to one side of the window, and gazes out as Mairéad lectures. He turns to look at her, 'what was it like having your own home, Ruth?'

It was utter heaven.

There was building work to cope with, but the finished areas filled her with joy. Every time she went into one of the children's rooms, she felt thrilled with the result. The children were equally as enthusiastic. Daithí was allocated the original master bedroom on account of being the eldest. Maurice fitted white wardrobes and a large shelved unit along one wall, with random cubby holes, comprising blond wood cupboards and drawers. Daithí's belongings were stashed away with plenty of space for the future. Buying him a double bed and Lexington preppy bedding from Arnotts, she let him chose a large woollen rug from the same department store. The floorboards had been sanded and stained a pale, limed oak colour. Daithí immediately set up his extensive Hot Rod tracking, and associated garages and buildings, all over the rug. The room resembled a small village.

In Sophie's room, next door to her brother, Maurice fixed a princess coronet over the bed. He provided more wardrobe and drawer space, reasoning that being female, her shoe and clothing collection would end up being far bigger than Daithí's. Sophie was into ballet at the time, so opted for the full stage look with plenty of pink. Tuile curtains like tutu material were custom made. Furnishings for her Barbies were illuminated with theatrically placed lighting.

In the rear extension, the children's bathroom was adjacent to Deidre's room at the back, making it like her own en-suite, which delighted her. Her room had two windows which she thought was really cool. One overlooked the courtyard subsequently filled with lush evergreens in large pots. A larger window on the back wall viewed the garden down to the river. In the distance was a vista of open countryside and mountains. Deidre was most particular about having a desk with lots of small drawers for her writing materials. Being an avid reader, she also needed plenty of shelving for her growing collection of Young Person novels.

As for her attic suite, it was transformed into somewhere she could never have imagined. A newly purchased super kingsize bed seemed lost in its vastness. The dressing area was fitted out like a celebrity's. Even Paudie admitted to being impressed. There were racks and racks of hanging space for all his shirts and work pants, and she could have cleared out one of her favourite boutiques in town and relocated the entire stock in there. The twin basins in the en-suite were a welcome convenience when Paudie shaved and she wanted to brush her teeth. Soaking in the bath in soothing candlelight, she adored looking out of the dormer window at whatever the weather was doing — that idea put into her head by Maurice. It became her Sunday night treat….

'Heavens, is that the time?', Mairéad glancing at the wall clock. 'Ruth, I'll have to dash. I've another appointment arranged. Between you and me, I've to get the gruaige done, the state of my roots.' Mairéad goes over to the mirror above the hand basin, and tilts her head to inspect. Baring her teeth to check for food scraps between them, she finally finishes with posing. 'It's been great talking with you, Ruth. Take care now. I've instructed Pádraic to keep me posted,' she sweeps out of the room.

Her Friend slides into the vacated chair, 'Did the house bring you happiness, darling?'

In many ways, yes, it did.

While ever the building work was in progress, she employed her creative design skills and had a sense of fulfilment. This later extended to the garden with Maurice doing the hard landscaping and Tom advising her on planting. She opted for just one area of lawn at the bottom of the garden for ball games and a trampoline. This was where the bouncy castle was inflated for birthdays, First Holy Communions and Confirmations. She also asked Maurice to build her a summer house down there, for somewhere to sit quietly regardless of the weather. Between that area and the house was a series of paved and gravelled terraces created out of the slope; these were divided and edged with shrub and flower borders. Not bothering with fruit or vegetable gardening, she knew she would never have the time to maintain them. Surveying the colourful floral scene from the house was a pleasure that even Paudie remarked upon.

Dissatisfaction set in when all the projects were completed. Then she felt she had nothing to plan or look forward to. Back to rebounding inside the rubber ball, Paudie continued to deny her holidays. The children only got to travel abroad by going on school trips. Whenever she felt fanciful, she went into Maeve's shop and wasted her time talking about possible trips that she knew were never going to happen. Maeve was a good enough friend to indulge her, and because Maeve had known Paudie since childhood, she would berate him for not taking his hard working wife away on holidays. It had no effect on him. His skin was as thick as the real rhinos she knew she would never get to see on safari. Dublin Zoo would have to do.

'That house was big,' her Friend commenting, 'and you've already described the time and energy it took to clean it. Did you ever consider employing cleaners like the O'Sullivans had?'

Oh yes; frequently; in fact, nearly every time she had to clean the bloody place.

It was a topic she raised with Paudie on numerous occasions. But he always refused. Because it would cost money automatically put her at a disadvantage. Paudie returned to his default position of either declaring insufficient funds; or the business being the priority; or all surplus monies being ring fenced for investment.

There was a tacit lack of sympathy from him. A kind of schadenfreude, she thought. An underlying current of having pushed him to move, she could now singlehandedly deal with the implications. It became evident though, that there was more to it than just that. This tussle was connected to a deeper issue for Paudie.

One Sunday evening, Paudie has returned from polo and the children are in bed.

She is watching a period drama on TV. Paudie sidles up on the sofa and puts his arm casually around her shoulder. A minute or two passes and while she remains fixated to the screen, he slides his hand onto her upper arm and pulls her closer. Repositioning herself to see the picture more clearly, he starts to nuzzle at her neck while she strains to see over his head. His other hand arrives on her thigh and wheedling upwards, ferrets its way into the gap between her tracksuit pants and sweatshirt. Now inside, it shoots up, deftly lifting the underwire of her bra and clamps itself firmly onto a breast. His fingertips find the target nipple and twiddle like he is tuning a retro transistor radio.

Grabbing the forearm attached to the errant hand, she yanks it down firmly, 'I'm in no humour for any of that, Paudie — I've been cleaning and ironing all day. I haven't stopped.' Readjusting her bra, she reasons, 'look-it, it's impossible for me to keep this up, Paudie. I can't work six days a week and do all the housework on my only day off. And be a sex pot — I'm not Superwoman.' She pauses to let that take root in Paudie's mind. Then starts up a familiar argument, 'Paudie, please, let me get a cleaner — we can afford it — you know that — for just one day a week — at the very least, — please,' beseeching.

He withdraws, sits upright and crosses his arms in determination, 'no, Ruth, no! I can't be having strangers in the house.'

'But they wouldn't be strangers for long. Besides, we're both experienced employers. We know what to look for when taking someone on — what the pitfalls are and how to climb back out. Please — Paudie — please!' begging.

Turning to look at her and acknowledging her distress, 'look, I'm not being a bollocks about this, Ruth. I just don't want people in the house, is all,' his voice softening.

'What are you talking about, Paudie! You were brought up in a house full of people!' too uptight to pick up the subtle change.

'Exactly! That's the problem! Don't you see? I've had enough of it! — Look!' Then quietening his angry tone, 'look — since moving into this house, I'd never realised how important privacy is to me. And it's been one of the best things about living here. When I was a child, there was always someone invading my space. I'd walk downstairs in the morning and there'd always be someone coming in and out the door — patients, Dad's colleagues, couriers. It was like Grafton Street on the last Saturday before Christmas. I could never come down in my pyjamas like our lads do — or relax. I always felt on show. That I was being watched — everything I did, noted and judged by people in town. It was like living in a public building like a library, not a home. Even my own room was never a safe place because some cleaning lady, or other, would be in and out, at all times to suit themselves.' Running his fingers through his hair in agitation, 'when I went off to boarding school, it was the same. Sharing a dorm with boys who weren't family. The Brothers roaming around trying to catch you out and have an excuse to punish you.' His eyes glaze over briefly, then continuing, 'Domestic staff complaining if you left a sock on the floor. And The Halls at Trinity were no better.' His shoulders slumping, 'I couldn't face that again, Ruth. Jumping every time someone comes into the room. Having to remove myself when I'm settled doing something.' His face brightens a little, 'but look, I'll help out a bit more. I know I'm not great when it comes to that kind of thing — but I'll try, I promise.'

Hearing this, she feels such sympathy for him and guilty that she rejected his advances so snappily. Clicking the switch on the remote, she cuddles up and caresses his inner thigh. He grins at her. Then he gets his ride up in the attic.

Paudie's intentions to help around the house never materialised in practice. He would help to clear the table and load the dishwasher for a few days. Then the pattern would be broken by him having to work late, or by some other interruption. She wondered if Paudie had any inkling of what housework entailed. The dreary, monotonous grind. The thankless lack of acknowledgment. The dispiriting way all the hard work could be undone within minutes by some careless or thoughtless action.

Unfortunately matters worsened. Without warning, Billy had a major and completely debilitating stroke. It came as a great shock to her, Vera and her sisters. Billy had always been a strong, reliable and safe male in the family. Although a powerful figure towards outsiders, who demanded no nonsense and respect at all times, within the family, he was gentle and kind. Protective of his female household, all of them relied on him for practical and emotional support. The sisters had to rally around and she decided to relinquish her Sundays at home to visit her parents; to do whatever she could to help. In no time, River House became increasingly grubby and the growing ironing mountain avalanched. Standards were reduced to the basic minimum, and depressingly so. Complaints about unlaundered clothing; missing foodstuffs in the fridge; stained toilet pans; gritty floors and scary cobwebs came flying at her from all directions. The house became a place of angst and no longer solace.

One evening, in dire need of some time for herself, she went for a walk alongside the river. It was summertime and the weather was surprising hot and dry. The air down by the water had a still balminess to it. The water fowl were active with broods of chicks paddling behind them in arrow straight V formations. The willow leaves had darkened to their deepest shade of midsummer green, and cow parsley spired into fluffy white clouds despatching a musky perfume. Part of her noticed the bucolic loveliness, but feeling so troubled, she was unable to appreciate it. Pulled in so many ways by work, each of the children, Paudie, the house, and now her parents, she thought she might splinter into shards — then, at least, she could offer a piece to each.

Looking into the smooth water drifting by, she pondered how peaceful it might be to wade into it. Keep on walking towards the centre; on and on into deeper waters until they reached her shoulders; crept up her face; crowned her head and flowed through her hair. When fully submerged, she would inhale deeply and fill her lungs with calm water. Then she could sink into painless oblivion. Brought out her reverie with a jolt, fearful of where her thoughts were taking her, she fought to gain control. Focusing intently on a blackbird nest in a white blossoming buckthorn tree, she thought of the new life residing there, dependent entirely on their parents for food and protection from predators. In desperation, she pleaded with God to help her — to please rescue her….

'Hey Ruthie! Have I got a treat for you today! Roast chicken breast!' Tilly bounds in full of good humour and singing joyfully before speeding out again.

Chomping on bland, sawdust dry meat, she recalls how she avoids roast chicken since leaving Nora's. Admonishing her flippancy over its relative cheapness and availability, she has to remind herself that roast chicken for Sunday lunch was a luxury for Nora and Brendan, and all their generation.

She notices her Friend's eyes burning with passion. He takes the opportunity, 'do tell me, were your prayers answered, Ruth?'

They were. But in a way she could never have anticipated.

Sitting across a desk in a recently constructed modern clinic, a newly appointed, middle-aged, female doctor looks at a computer screen. 'I've found your notes, Ruth. Let's have a look at the results of your latest bloods. Hmm — from these

levels, Ruth, I can see you have entered the peri-menopause.'
Leaning back in her chair and addressing her directly, 'let me
explain. This is the time leading up to your eventual
menopause, the time when your menstrual cycle will cease
completely and you'll no longer be fertile. The average age for
that would be 52. From now onwards, you can expect your
hormone cycle to become erratic — your periods and their
flow more likely to be unpredictable. The fluctuations in
hormones can adversely affect a number of other body
systems.' The doctor takes her glasses off and rests them on the
blotter. 'Experience has taught me that it can be a challenging
time for a woman — fatigue is a common symptom for every
woman. In your case however, you are already suffering from
severe exhaustion. If you're going to get through the next few
years, you need to have a radical reassessment of your lifestyle
and current commitments — see where areas of stress can be
alleviated.' Wheeling her office chair to the end of the table so
there is no longer a barrier between them. 'Now, let's explore
what can be done in your particular circumstances. I find it
useful to do this exercise with women otherwise they just let
matters drift. Working six days a week is far too much for
anyone on a regular basis. I strongly recommend that you build
in at least one extra day off per week.' The doctor grabs a pen
and notebook to jot down bullet points. 'What about childcare?
There's probably not much wriggle room there, I would
imagine. But could you share the burden a bit more — reduce
the running around after them — the Mam's Taxis? You also
have the added commitment of your parents — again a
difficult situation to manage especially with the distances
involved.' Continuing to write then looking up. 'Domestic
responsibilities? Can you increase the amount of help you're
buying in?' The doctor studies her face, 'you are delegating the
household duties aren't you? Using a laundry and ironing
service — getting groceries delivered — employing cleaning
contractors, that kind of thing?'

Feeling intimidated by the proactive doctor, she is unable to
admit the truth, and stares back like a terrified rabbit.

The doctor pauses, looks at her keenly, then pulls out
another pad from a drawer in her desk, 'I'm writing you a sick

note for two weeks. You're to give this to Mr O'Sullivan. Technically, if you enter the pharmacy to work during this time, the business insurance cover will be invalidated. And your husband will be breaching Health and Safety Regulations that could initiate a full inspection and result in a hefty fine. Please explain this to him.' Tearing the sheet from the wad and handing it to her, 'tell Mr O'Sullivan to ring me for further clarification, if necessary. During the next two weeks, I want you to rest first and foremost. I would recommend getting away for a few days on your own, or with a friend; to do something lighthearted and have some fun. When you return more refreshed, you can work out how to eliminate some of these responsibilities.' Handing her the notes, 'if you don't take this seriously, Ruth, I guarantee you'll be back in this surgery with some form of illness. Come back and see me in two weeks and I will write another note, if deemed necessary.'

Returning to the pharmacy later that morning, Paudie's face is a picture when she hands him the sickness certificate and explains quickly why he has to honour it.

'But how will I cope?' he wails. 'How will I manage without you? You run this place, Ruth. If I have to do all you do, I'll never get the scripts out of the door.'

Turning away with a soft sigh, she admits defeat. She knows it is futile arguing with him, 'I'll go get cracking with the backlog, so —'

Grabbing her arm and turning her around to face him, 'no leave them, Ruth. You'd better start your sick leave now. Gather up what you need and go home. But don't take any files or anything — just your personal things.'

Feeling drained, she does not stop to explain to Lisa on her way out.

Chapter 15

You knew the constellations, pointed out
the Pole Star, 'Ah yes, the sailors' friend';
we agreed our ancestors were mariners
who would take their bearings by that star.

Woken by her own gentle snoring, she wonders for a few
moments why the poem has come back to her again.
Repositioning herself in the plastic, easy wipe chair, a sickly
odour arises from its warmed surface. Her heightened
sensitivity to smells has returned; another unwelcome legacy
of chemo.

The slow opening of the door pre-warns of Sophie's arrival.
'Hi, Mammy, I thought I'd call in and see how you are…'

'… and so, your Aunt Mairéad evidently enjoyed her trip to
Peru. Have you thought much about traveling yourself,
Sophie?'

'No money for that, Mammy,' shaking her head. 'I've
plenty of other priorities before I get around to that one.'

Looking at the young woman, she thinks how like her
father and his family she is, and always has been. 'Listen,
child, don't focus on work all the time. It's important to do
other things too — have a bit of balance. I know you've the
camogie — that's important for exercise and the social side.
But you should try to find some other interests, too. Get some
variety in your life. That was a mistake I made, Sophs. And I
do regret it, especially now.'

Nodding in agreement, Sophie calmly, 'I know what you're
saying Mammy — I do understand.' Leaning over the chair
side, 'look, I brought these for you,' retrieving a paper
shopping bag and handing it over to her mother.

'What's all this, love?' opening the bag, then tipping the
contents onto her lap. Picking her way through, there is a a box
of graded pencils; an eraser and sharpener; a travel set of

watercolour paints; pastels in different colours, charcoals and a thick pad of good quality drawing paper. 'Sophie! I don't know what to say. It's been ages — I don't know how you even remembered — I couldn't think of a better thing to bring me — I don't know if I'll manage — be any good at it — it's been so long. Thank you; thanks a million, Sophie, that's so thoughtful. Here let me give you a hug, come here, darling.'

Her enthusiastic reaction pleases Sophie. Ruth thinks she has not seen her daughter look so happy in a long while.

After Sophie leaves, she decides to give her gifts a trial run. Debating what she can portray, she concludes she has no other choice than to emulate Van Gogh and draw her sick room. Selecting different pencils, she reminds herself of their relative degrees of hardness on the cover of the pad, then resharpens a chosen one. Having fashioned an impression of the room on the first page, she examines it critically. She is about to tear it up and start again, when she stops. Warning herself to be less hasty and not so hard on herself, she puts off a final verdict until later. Putting the materials away, she hears a light knock on the door and stops rustling the paper bag.

Calling out brightly, 'come in, come in whoever you are!'

Irina enters looking around the room, unsure about the unfamiliar surroundings, then homes in on Ruth, 'Ruth, I allowed come in? Yes? No doctor, no nurse?'

'Irina! Come in here right now, girl! How delighted I'm to see you — of all people! — such a welcome sight'

Irina breaks into a grin and walks over to hug Ruth. 'I bring fruit — here in bag. And look, have good plate — I know you like this one — you loove fruit. How you been? How you feeling, girl?'

The friends chat about life in hospital as Irina rinses the fruit under the running tap, dries it with the paper hand towels and arranges it in a favourite bowl of Ruth's. Then taking it over to the locker. 'You look good, Ruth — much, much better now. You get better? Yes? Please — I need my friend back home,' clasping her chest at heart level.

'Ahh, thank you, Irina, you're so good to me — I can't wait to get back home to you all, myself. But tell me, how are you getting on with Paudie? No, don't say!' waving her hands. 'Let me guess — he's driving you up the wall? Yeh?'

'Oh my Gott, Ruth! He drive me crazy,' Irina throwing up her hands and rolling her eyes dramatically. 'He keep leaving little yellow sticky paper, what you call it? Post ups?'

' "Post-its", you mean?'

'Yeees, he put them everywhere — on everything. He write: "clean me please"; "polish me please". I want shove them in he's mouth,' rolling her eyes again and gritting her teeth in frustration.

'What's he putting them on, for God's sake?'

'On his fucking metal — what you call it? These ugly, yellow metal thing?'

'You mean, his horse brasses? All the brass he has collected over the years?'

'Yeees! Those metals, Ruth — you know that house too big to have time to clean those fucking things. He love them, he clean them — yeah?'

'Absolutely, Irina — you're so right, girl. Take no notice of him. You carry on with what you normally do. If he wants them polishing, he can pay you extra time to do it — but only if you want to, mind — they take forever to do. Leave it with me — I'll have a word with him.'

Nurse Nóirín enters the room and Irina leaps up from her chair. Distrustful of authority figures, she makes rapid excuses to leave.

Later on, she contemplates how Irina always has the ability to cheer her up, chuckling to herself about Irina's often unique perspective on life in Balnarath.

'So, you did get a cleaner in the end,' her Friend laughing.

Amazingly enough, yes she had. But it was only fair as Paudie got outside help too.

Once she got over the initial shock of being sent home by the GP, she warmed to the idea of being off work immensely. Even more surprisingly, she did not feel the tiniest twinge of guilt. The doctor had done her job excellently. The timing worked out well in terms of the weather. After a wet, cold early August, the rain cleared that first afternoon and stayed good.

She thought about going away like the doctor suggested, but dismissed it, thinking it would give her an opportunity to visit her parents an extra time or two. What appealed more was the prospect of enjoying her house and garden, something she rarely got to do. Planning to do a cleaning blitz for the first few days, she could then relax and wallow in her clean, cosy nest. The physical activity and seeing the efforts of her labours were therapeutic in a way. Having had a break from the chores, they did not seem as tedious. And the family noticed the improvement, appreciating her efforts for once. That job done, she turned to other neglected matters, particularly the garden.

The responsibility of tending the garden troubled her before she moved in. She sought Tom's advice, emphasising the need for low maintenance. He assured her that everything would work out fine and to stop worrying about it. Towards the end of the landscaping project, there was one area left to plant up. Tom came over one evening with some Penstemons in different shades of red, purple and white that he had grown.

Tom and her walk down to the freshly dug flower bed. 'Listen, Ruth, if you want a hand maintaining the garden after the work's done, I can help, you know.'

Straightening up from positioning some plant pots ready for digging in, she looks at him with interest, 'why, do you know someone suitable; who's reliable and available?'

'Yes and no — what I mean is — me — I'm all those things — I could do it if you like. I've been talking with Carmel and we've decided to scale down the fruit and veg, particularly the veg. I'm producing way too much — far more than they need up at the house and most of it's being wasted ending up rotten and being composted. Mr and Mrs O'Sullivan don't have the appetites they once had, and Miss O'Sullivan always dines out.'

She could have guessed that Carmel's plain, old fashioned cooking would be far too unsophisticated for Mairéad.

'That'll easily free me up one day a week, if not more, and I could give it to you — only if it suited, mind.'

'Wow, that'd be great, Tom — I'd really like that!' A snag occurs to her, 'but what about herself? Nora?'

'With all due respect, Mrs O'Sullivan wouldn't even notice. She's never shown any interest in the garden, nor with what goes on out there.'

She has to agree with that point. Nora, being accustomed to domestic staff since birth, never gave much thought to the practical workings of a household. As long as everything was done smoothly to her satisfaction, she never paid much attention to how it all materialised.

'Yes, I have to say, I'd be delighted if you would — I'd pay you a full day, every week of the year. I know there wouldn't be much to do in the winter, but knowing you, you'd more than make up for it in the summer. And if you needed extra days then, that'd be no problem at all.'

'That's very decent of you, Ruth — I wouldn't let you down,' looking bashful.

'I know that, Tom — you don't need to tell me.' Then tapping her cheek in thought, 'problem is, how am I going to convince Paudie?'

Later, pouring tea for Paudie, she broaches the subject, '… and so it would appear Tom's available. But you probably don't like the idea, Paudie, do you? You probably want to get your own mower — some ride-on machine — all men love those. You'll probably want to potter around in the garden on Sundays. Dig the land — Irish men have a real love of the land — a real grá for it. Probably get yourself a shed like Billy's — you know — like a man cave — choose lots of tools like hedge cutters, strimmers — men love gadgets —'

Paudie looking at her aghast, cuts in before she gets too carried away, 'oh no, I wouldn't say that, Ruth. I think it's a very generous offer of Tom's.'

'Really!?' she looks at him quizzically. 'But I thought you said we can't afford help in the house. And you don't want strangers in?'.

'Well — hmm, sure, it would be difficult enough to find the money,' unwilling to make it seem too easy. 'But in the scheme of things, I think I could just about stretch to paying Tom. Tom isn't a stranger — and he can get in and out using the side gate. He wouldn't have to be in the house necessarily. Anyway, you have enough to do already, Ruth,' implying that the lawn clipping and garden maintenance would be her responsibility.

'You're so right Paudie, I never thought of that'.

Laughing to herself afterwards, Paudie cutting the lawn every Sunday was never going to happen — tending grass was something groundsmen did.

The unexpected time off from work meant she could chat with Tom about some new ideas, and have a drive over to a garden centre for a browse. She also wanted to try out some new recipes; meet up with Maeve for lunch. Have a day or two clothes shopping to refresh her wardrobe; and ditch some tired outfits. Analysing what could be jettisoned from her life, the only agreeable and realistic responsibilities were the household duties. During the following fortnight, she tried discussing it with Paudie, but he skilfully dodged her until the last evening.

'Paudie, I go to see Dr Jones tomorrow about being signed off from being sick.'

His attention alerted, 'what do you mean — "see about being signed off from being sick" — I thought you were back at work tomorrow — the two weeks are up, aren't they?', looking stricken.

'It depends — Dr Jones has to agree to me going back to work. She said she has to be satisfied that "suitable arrangements" have been made.'

'What do you mean — "suitable arrangements"?'

'My apologies, Paudie — I probably used the wrong phrase — I should have said, changes to my circumstances.'

'"Changes to your circumstances"?' his errant eyebrow lifting to its fullest height.

'You know, permanent changes to relieve stress and keep my fatigue levels manageable. Now, I've been thinking, I can't really do anything about the children, or my parents. You don't want a cleaner in the house, so that only leaves the option of reducing work down to part-time. Say, to 4 days. And in special circumstances, like Christmas, maybe 5 days at an absolute max —'

Interrupting, 'only work for 5 days?' explicitly ignoring the 4 day suggestion. 'No, no, absolutely not, Ruth! Under no circumstances! You need to be there whenever I'm there — this last fortnight has proven that,' frowning and shaking his head sternly, his mouth a hard, unhappy line.

'Okay, Paudie. So what should I say to Dr Jones?'

Paudie lost for words, pauses for a minute; opens his mouth to speak, then stops. He knows there is only one acceptable option available to him.

At last, she wins — she can have her cleaner.

The next day, wasting no time when collecting the children, she asks if Irina knows of anyone commendable.

Irina answers instantly, 'I know perfect woman for you, Ruth.' Smiling with excitement and thumbing her breastbone, 'me! Irina.'

Wide eyed, 'you? But why? How?'

'I very bored at home — Children at school — I clean this house in one hour. What I do for rest of day?' Shrugging her shoulders, 'I come look after you — collect children from school — bring them home to your house. My grandkids very big now, don't need Babcia anymore. Good? Yes?'

'Good? Oh yes — very, very good, Irina!' she hugs her friend in glee.

Paudie, as she had half expected, does not think it so "Good? Yes?"

'Oh, Ruth, for God's sake, can't you find anyone better?' he sighs in exasperation.

'Better? No, Paudie, Irina's perfect. We both know the standard of her work — she keeps her own place spotless. She won't be a stranger in the house as we've known her for years — we know she's completely trustworthy and the children love her. She's like family.'

Attempting some resistance, Paudie slips in, 'I don't think Sophie likes her.'

'Don't be ridiculous. Sophie sulks because she has to be pulled up more often than the other two. But Irina never singles her out. She's always fair — the punishment always fits the crime. Besides which, Irina's meticulous in letting us know when something's happened.'

Trying again, 'Irina might not be as good in other people's places — she might have one standard for herself and another for others. What if she doesn't do things how you want them? How would you ever get rid of her if she wasn't up to scratch? You'd lose your childminder as well, then.' He folds his arms, nodding knowingly.

'Paudie! Will you stop nitpicking — and give the woman — and me — a break, for God's sake! Okay, I'll get contract cleaners in then, and they'll cost twice as much!'

Battle won, Irina started the next day.

Her Friend guffaws. Then more seriously, 'tell me, Ruth, was there anything else that happened during that fortnight off from work? Anything or anyone that was pivotal?'

Hesitating, something comes to the forefront of her mind. But she pushes it away back into the dusty archives. There is something else she wants to add, though — she learned the importance of making time for herself.

Doctor Jones, as an objective observer, noticed her being drained physically and emotionally. Unable to get help elsewhere, there was no use turning to Paudie, or her parents to shore her up against the perpetual demands. They had their own preoccupations and she was not their dependent. She had to face the responsibility of her own self-care. Unwilling to ignore the needs of others, she had not realised up until then, that to keep on giving, she needed to give to herself too. It was imperative to keep her personal resources topped up ready for redistribution to others.

Only partially satisfied, her Friend insists, 'yes, okay, I get that. But apart from Dr Jones, did anything, or anyone else help you come to that conclusion?'

It was a time of flux, but she eventually worked it all out.

Once the children became independent and she learned to delegate better, she portioned out some time for herself which, she has to admit, Paudie largely tolerated. She was subtle about it though; did not push for so much personal freedom that would alarm him. Especially as she had to temper his overarching ambition.

Her Friend tilting his head to one side, 'oh? What do you mean by "tempering his overarching ambition"?'

Paudie is driven — he needs to succeed in business, almost to the point of self harm. And generally ignores the effect this has on everyone else. She thinks that Paudie needs to prove himself endlessly. It is not that hard to understand having a mother who was hard to please; a well regarded professional father and siblings who are all high achievers. There is nothing warm or nurturing about that family. On the contrary, she observes a mien of competitiveness. Personally, she feels totally inadequate in their company.

Paudie never achieved the academic success his brother and sisters did. But then again, he never fully applied himself to his studies either. Why was that, she wonders? Maybe it was easier to not bother rather than risk failure. It is easier to explain it away to yourself as not really trying, rather than not being good enough. Failure was never acceptable in that family. Brendan and Nora got him through his Pharmacology course, and provided the means for the business. Although they disapproved of her, she had provided him with an unpaid worker. It begins to occur to her that maybe it was something to do with his parents.

Brendan came from an ordinary farming background with parents who rented a smallholding, eking out a modest living. He was exceptionally bright at school and the principal, Brother Ignatius, encouraged him to apply for medical school. Brother Ignatius organised financial support for him from the local GAA club as Brendan was a gifted hurler and a significant player who helped them win the county championship final repeatedly during the years he played. The rest of the finance had come from credit union loans. Once Brendan qualified, he was in substantial debt. He always wanted to work in the community and the only option was to join a GP practice as a junior with a small income, making it difficult to both live, and clear his debts. Meeting Nora was a godsend. She often wondered what Brendan saw in Nora as she was plain looking, bereft of any sexual allure that she could detect and had an abrasive personality. The woman was indulged by her wealthy parents and spoiled by a privileged background, resulting in a self-absorbed, demanding sense of entitlement. She wondered how Brendan coped with being Nora's financial inferior and living with the Walshes in their home — she knows men often rail against being beholden. Had some of that lowered self-esteem been passed on to Paudie, she ponders. Vincent is an alpha male, but Paudie as the pampered baby of the family, seems to lack the same resilience. And there is that need to continually prove himself against his siblings. The problem for her is that he does not know when to stop.

One example was when Paudie unilaterally decided to expand the business.

One evening in the dining room of River House, Paudie and Ruth are alone.

Paudie pushes his empty plate away, 'Liam told me something very interesting today — Bolger Construction have put in for Planning Permission for a new shopping centre on the Old Mill site.'

She half listens, walking into, and out of the kitchen, with dirty tableware to load into the dishwasher, 'hmm? Really?'

Leaning back to stretch and create room for his expanded stomach, 'apparently, they're looking to put in a large unit for a supermarket. Liam reckons Patsy Hanratty might relocate Supervalu there. There's plenty of space for a large carpark, and if they've any sense, they won't charge parking for it. You know as well as I do, parking fees kill town centres. The times I've had this out with the Town Council — so often I've argued…'

Zoning out in boredom, this being a favourite political issue of Paudie's, one she has heard so many times before.

Paudie continues oblivious to his absent audience, '…Liam reckons as well as a hairdresser, barbershop, a florist, the usual mobile phone shops etc etc, he's certain they'll want a pharmacy.'

'Hmm? — really? Well, the town could easily stand another one. I don't think it would make much of an impact on us, Paudie, there's plenty of custom to go around. We're out the door with people most of the time, you know that.'

'I don't think we would need to share any custom, Ruth.'

Bringing him over a cup of coffee and sitting at the table, 'how d'you mean, Paudie?'

'I think we should take up the pharmacy unit — move into the new centre.'

'Whatever for? The business is thriving where it is — and we own the building outright. Leases, rents, whatever — those shopping centres are notoriously expensive. Higher Rates, Management Charges — all that means is we'd have to have a huge turnover before we could start to break even.'

'I don't mean give up the current shop — I mean expand the business. In other words, run both.'

Flabbergasted, 'but, Paudie, why? We have an arrangement that works — we're well off. Why on earth would we want to take on all that hassle at this stage in our lives?'

'Ruth, it'd be great. Listen, I have to hurry now — remember I've a Lions Meeting to go to. Don't wait up — I'll talk to you in the morning when you're rested, and are more reasonable.'

Her jaw drops in disbelief at his arrogance, but he flies out of the room before she can retaliate.

The prospect was impossible to contemplate. Factoring in salaries for several qualified pharmacists to cover the extended hours a premises in a shopping mall would need; additional shop assistant wages and the fees attached to the unit itself, there would not be enough left over to employ a manager. Two shops was an awkward number. It had to be a chain of three or four shops to cover the salary of a manager. That would mean HER running two shops, effectively doubling her workload. And for what purpose exactly? What would it gain them in the long run? A bit more in the already substantial pension pot?

And at what personal cost? She thought Paudie naïve to not consider the impact on his own health….

Paudie's polite knock on the door breaks her thoughts. He walks over smiling to embrace her, but he seems flat in mood.

After general chit-chat about their respective days, she remarks, 'you look tired Paudie,' scanning his grey, drawn looking face.

'I am, to be honest, pet — I've had a few late nights this week,' rubbing his eyes, making them bloodshot.

'Don't do that Paudie, you'll damage your corneas. Late nights? Partying, is it then? Taken up some new, or maybe not so new, habits — like loose women?' joshing him to liven him up.

Picking up the cue, 'bollocks! You've caught me out!' bantering back.'If only!' rolling his eyes. Then in a more serious tone, 'no, I've been getting the accounts up to date for Liam.'

'The accounts? Whatever for? The November deadline's not for ages.'

'Oh, it's just Liam, you know how particular he is — I don't mind, I'll catch up on my sleep on Sunday. Now tell me more about your day? Any visitors?…'

Nattering on about her various callers, she watches Paudie's eyes gradually closing until his head nods in irresistible slumber. Ceasing her chatter, she picks up the bag of art materials from beside her chair. An hour or so later, Paudie wakes with a jolt. Taken by surprise, she scrambles to get her things back into the bag before Paudie notices.

'Ruth, sorry about — hey! Is that the kit Sophie brought you? Have you been working on something? Let me see.'

'No, Paudie!' trying to stuff the drawing pad into the bag.

Too late, he gently puts his hand over hers, 'please, Ruth, show me your drawings — I want to see them.'

She hesitates, not sure that he is really that interested as he is usually dismissive of her art. Deciding to give him a chance to redeem himself, she releases her grip.

Paudie takes the pad and sits back.

She tenses, fearing his scorn.

He turns the cover over to her depiction of the room. After a while, 'that's very good, Ruth — you haven't lost any of your talent.'

She exhales with relief.

Moving on to her second piece, he stares at the image for an age. Passing the pad back over to her. 'Ruth, sign that now — then give it back to me.'

She studies his face trying to read his thoughts. He is inscrutable. Deciding to capitulate, at the bottom of the page she jots, "To Pádraic, with all my love, Ruth x," then hands it over.

Looking at what she has written for a long minute, he then stares up at her, 'do you mean that, Ruth?'

She is unwilling to answer audibly as it makes it too real, so she swallows nervously and nods.

'That's one of the nicest things you've ever done for me, Ruth. I love you so much.'

He embraces and kisses her; then says it is late and he has to go.

Tucked under his arm whilst leaving, is a portrait of a distinguished looking man asleep in a chair.

Chapter 16

Nurse Nóirín wheels in a drip stand and carries a bag of turquoise liquid in the other hand. 'We've a few changes regarding your treatment, Ruth. I'll administer the drip today as you've had no adverse reactions. Dr Ghebremariam will pop in later to see you.'

'Dr Ghebre — um — not Dr Geraghty?'

'No, Dr Geraghty doesn't work at the hospital anymore, Ruth.'

'What? — Oh no! That's a bit sudden, isn't it? I really liked her! I never got to say thank you and wish her luck. Where's she gone?'

'I don't know any details, Ruth. SHOs, junior doctors, medics come and go all the time in hospital — that's normal.'

'But she said she would oversee the trial until it finishes. That's certainly the impression she gave me. I'd have considered her the kind of woman to come and explain any changes in person.'

Ignoring her comments, Nurse Nóirín carries on meticulously as if nothing has happened, 'now, I'll prepare your port, Ruth, and get the infusion set up.'

Sensing she will get no more information from Nóirín, she gives up asking any more questions. Instinctively she knows that whatever happened to Dr Geraghty is not normal, either for Dr Geraghty, or how hospital postings work in general. Working a period of formal notice is normal in any job. No, she decides, this is not normal; and she feels concern for the woman. A gut instinct tells her that Dr Mulhall might be behind it. This leaves her feeling uneasy.

While Nurse Nóirín silently adds notes to her chart, her Friend speaks up from his armchair, 'so tell me, Ruth, what happened about the new pharmacy?'

It became another issue of contention between them — yet another difficult period in their marriage.

Paudie was obsessed with the prospect of a brand new, shiny shop. Walking around their premises, he commented on flaws he had never noticed before. As though wearing Inspector Clouseau spectacles, he reassessed all aspects with what he considered clinical objectivity. To her, it seemed more like ineptitude. Lisa and other staff members were interrogated on why they did things the way they did which either rattled, or irritated them, depending upon the confidence of the worker. The systems and protocols in the smoothly running shop had been developed with precision over the years by her and the staff. His interference was NOT appreciated.

A trait of Paudie's that had increasingly annoyed her over the years was his attitude towards women. It was as though he considered them to be his hand servants. Only ever managing a female staff team, he could order women about without compunction, and with little nicety. He was the same at home with Sophie, Deidre and herself. If any female friend offered to buy, or do something for him out of good heartedness, such as giving him a lift; or carry something heavy; or help him with one of his own tasks, he would instantly take them up on it. She often considered it impolite, or inappropriate for him to accept. And he rarely expressed gratitude as though he expected that women should pander to him. Little was ever given back in reciprocation.

She knew that this was one of the factors that encouraged Deidre especially, and Sophie to some extent, to leave home. While ever he was with them, they later complained that he would not let them get on with their own activities. There would be constant requests to leave whatever they were doing to go help, or wait on him. Oftentimes, he seemed like a needy, attention seeking toddler. This was one of the reasons, she reckoned, that Irina had not taken to him.

With men however, she noticed him to be completely different. He would never order, but would request politely, even deferentially. Daithí was rarely called upon to assist, and when he was, Paudie would go to efforts to check that Daithí was really okay about doing it. At those times, she gritted her teeth to stop yelling out that of course Daithí would do it. He needs to pull his weight like all of us. He doesn't need plámásing, Paudie!

Back to the shop, Paudie made comments about the age of the building saying it was old fashioned, and not fit for purpose, it not being built to modern design standards. This was all nonsense as far as she was concerned. The traditional style had given the shop its charm and people loved it like that. Ordinarily, Paudie would be as pleased as a dog with two tails at the compliments. Then he started to dismiss them with smart ripostes about medical practices being better sited within appropriate buildings.

Every time the shopping mall moved onto the next stage of development, a renewed fervour in Paudie, and a renewed resistance in her, was resurrected; becoming a hot issue for a while. Then with their busy lives, the matter would lose intensity. But it remained an underlying threat, poised to envelop her in fresh panic....

'That's all finished now, Ruth,' Nurse Nóirín carefully detaches the line. 'Doctor Ghebremariam will come down to you presently. I will be ending my shift shortly — good day to you.'

'Have a nice evening,' she calls to the nurse's back as she briskly exits.

Her Friend waves his hand to attract her attention, 'go on — what happened next?'

Gradually the shopping centre units became reserved as the project neared completion. Paudie had registered his interest with Bolger early on, and the developer became increasingly insistent that Paudie make a firm commitment by putting down a hefty deposit. "In confidence" and emphasising the need for "discretion", Bolger hinted that negotiations were being made with Boots, The Chemist. Not at all convinced, she did not believe the centre prestigious or big enough for such a major chain. To her, it was a rather unsubtle manipulation, a typical tactic used by businessmen witnessed many times before. The Celtic Tiger had sharp claws. It had however, fed Paudie's anxiety, as intended. He in turn, passed the pressure on to her. It got to the stage where every conversation they had was steered towards the subject.

Paudie enters the kitchen with a mobile phone to his ear, 'yes, Joe — of course — leave it with me, will you? I promise, I'll get back to you first thing in the morning — yes, that's right — Yes, okay, by 9am. Yes, the money's definitely available — it's on short notice — I'll be able to transfer the deposit straight away. Yes — you'd have it the same day, yes. Yes — yes — okay? —'bye, Joe, 'bye, 'bye, 'bye.'

Putting the phone away in a pocket and addressing her, 'look, Ruth, we have to make a decision on this now. — it's make or break time. Can I ring Joe Bolger in the morning? Please? With an affirmative?'

'Paudie, you know how unhappy I am about this. I've said I can't see how I can possibly run two shops — I've told you that over and over.' She goes into the dining room and slumps onto a dining chair, holding her head in her hands, elbows on the table.

Paudie stands in the kitchen doorway, figuring out what to say to convince her.

She lifts her head and with resignation, 'but look-it, Paudie, I don't want to stop you doing what you really want either.' Looking him in the eyes, 'It's just —,'

Daithí runs down the three steps into the room and thrusts the landline phone towards her, 'Mammy! Granny Vera's on the phone, she sounds upset.'

Taking the phone quickly, 'Mammy? — of course — I'll drive straight over — I'll meet you at The Mater — don't worry, I'll find you. Will I bring anything over for you? Yes, you're right, we can sort it out later. I'll get there as soon as I can — try not to worry. 'Bye, now,' clicking the red button.

'Paudie, I'm sorry — I have to go. Daddy's taken a turn for the worse — another stroke they think — it doesn't sound good.'

'Will I come with you?'

'No, it's okay. You stay here. I'll find out what's going on and I'll let you know as soon as I can.'

186

Talking with Irina later, Irina expressed disgust that Paudie had not insisted on driving her down to Dublin while she was distracted with worry, and provided her with some support. Irina said she would have come over to mind the children. They concluded that would mean Paudie making an effort; offer some personal sacrifice and demonstrate empathy, none of which was typical of Paudie.

Chapter 17

A tall, slim man enters the room, 'Mrs O'Sullivan how nice to meet you properly; we haven't had the chance to talk before. Please allow me to introduce myself — I'm Gabriel Ghebremariam, the Oncology Registrar.'

With an artist's eye, she studies the man's face as he talks about supervising the drug trial. Surveying his bone structure, she notes a combination of high cheekbones and bridged, narrow nose; perfectly proportioned forehead, mid section and jaw. Large dark eyes; flawless dark brown skin; neat, close cropped black beard and hair. She concludes that he has a most beautiful aesthetic. She itches to sketch him.

'Do you have any questions, Ruth? By the way, thank-you for permitting me to address you by that name.'

'Yes I do, Doctor Ghebre — Doctor Ghebre —.'

'Dr Ghebremariam,' smiling at her.

'Ghebre — mariam. Mariam — as in Mary?'

'That's correct, Ruth — Mariam or Mary, our Saviour's Mother.'

'You're a registrar so that means you're training to be a consultant, is that right? Will you apply for a post here or back in — um?'

'Ethiopia — I'm from Tigray, northern Ethiopia.'

'That sounds interesting. I've seen pictures of priests with colourful umbrellas. Is that the right place? I think I would like to go there.'

Smiling wistfully, 'yes, that's right — Ethiopia is a beautiful country — very different, very unique. You must travel there some time, if you get the chance. There's much to see — the rock churches, Queen Sheba's palace, the Stelae at Axum, the Simian Mountains. There's so much to experience.'

She gazes at him enthralled, 'yes, I'd definitely like to do all that.' And with you by my side, doctor, she thinks naughtily.

The Registrar leaves and her Friend continues their earlier conversation, 'did you get the second pharmacy?'

Arriving at The Mater Hospital, she located her parents in the Stroke Unit and stayed with them through the night. Billy was allocated a side room and fold-up beds were provided for her and Vera. She was surprised that Billy was not in ICU and surmised that he was either not as critical as they thought, or more disconcertingly, he was on a terminal pathway. Early the next morning, the staff urged Vera and her to go home to eat, shower, rest and return later, as there would be challenges ahead. Once it became evident that Billy would remain in hospital for the foreseeable future, Vera told her return to Balnarath to mind her family and business.

Her mother holding her by both arms, 'please don't worry about us, Ruth. We'll manage — your father's in the best place. He's stable and nothing's going to change for some time — they've told us that. You visit when you're able, love.'

'Mammy, before I go — tell me, are you feeling well in yourself? I noticed you being a bit stiff and slower than normal when you move about the place.'

Answering evasively, 'don't you be worrying about me, Ruth. What do you expect at my age? I'm no spring chicken,' laughing lightly.

'Mammy, don't be ridiculous, you're still young! What you're displaying is not right. Will you go see a doctor, please?'

'I'm just worn out, pet, — it's been tough going nursing a man, especially one the size of your father. Now stop fretting and get on the road, will you? You've a long journey ahead. I promise, I'll ring with any news.'

Travelling along a quiet, late morning motorway, she had chance to think. Firstly she focused on her parents and their situation. Matters had deteriorated, and with Billy's abilities reduced even further, she thought he might never get to go home. Her mother had barely managed before and with this decline, she could envision her father going into a nursing home; that's if he survived the latest infarction. The changes she had witnessed in her mother concerned her. Enough people with Parkinson's Disease had been customers over the years and she had an ominous feeling.

As she neared the West that particular feeling of dread was replaced with the one she faced at home. Paudie had been sensitive enough to not put pressure on her while she had been away, but she knew she could not delay the inevitable any longer. Resigning herself to accepting the new shop, she decided there was no other choice. Paudie had agreed to River House so she felt it only fair to let him have his way this time. She was determined to accept defeat with grace. Yet, she had no idea how she was going to cope with the extra responsibility; and all the work in setting up a new shop. Clenching the steering wheel hard in desperation, she prayed to God to help her….

The boots tip-tapped down the wooden floor. The hypnotic percussion stopped outside the door. 'He's back! He's back!' her heart shouted. Awake since early morning, she had been anticipating this moment….

Reverend Barbara places a calling card on the table, then notices her eyes open, 'I'm sorry to have woken you, Ruth. I should have visited another time — a lot of patients nap after lunch.'

'No, no, Barbara, please don't apologise. I'm delighted to see you. Can you stay awhile, or do you need to go?'

The cleric offers her a service of Holy Communion and Ruth welcomes it. They go on to recite the private version of the liturgy together.

Watching the priest as she tidies the remains of the Eucharist away, 'Barbara, can I ask you something? Does God always forgive people? I mean, if they break one of His Ten Commandments? I know all the priests say He does. But what about people who know the rules, but decide to defy them anyway — knowingly do it. Do you really think God forgives them? Is He really able for that? What's the point of having laws if you're going to let people get away with breaking them?'

Barbara looks at her directly, 'yes, Ruth, the Lord always forgives. But with some caveats — most importantly they have to acknowledge what they have done, in other words, own up and admit they are wrong. Then He'll forgive them; I have absolutely no doubt about that. And His mercy is instantaneous. I personally think though, that when He forgives people, they often don't or can't forgive themselves. And that's such a pity — people carry around a burden of guilt that binds them up in psychological knots.'

'So how does that work with repeat offenders? Can you just keep doing wrong and get away with it just by asking for forgiveness every time you do it?'

Laughing gently, 'good question, Ruth. The Lord will look for some attempt at repentance which is just another way of saying to retrace your steps — you know — try to return to the better behaviour we all know we should be doing. If we don't make that effort and keep on purposefully repeating what we know we shouldn't do, then there will be consequences.'

She thinks about this for a while. 'By consequences, do you mean like getting caught and being prosecuted. Or experiencing violence yourself if you keep dishing it out — living and dying by the sword, and all that? Or losing the person you keep wronging? Or having no peace of mind even if you don't get caught — that kind of consequence?'

'Precisely, Ruth — I couldn't have put it better myself.' The rector waits allowing time for Ruth to disclose any other issues.

'That's very interesting, Barbara — it's something I wanted to ask a priest for years, but never had the courage too. Some of them would look awful bad at you if you question anything.

'I know they are intimidating concepts — I can understand your reticence in discussing them. But that's what I am here for, Ruth. Come, let's pray together.'

Ruth closes her eyes while Barbara continues, 'Lord God, please look favourably upon your faithful servant, Ruth, and help her in this special time of need. Please assist the drug trial and bring healing, comfort and hope to her and her family.

Please bring strength to Paudie; and look over Deidre during her pregnancy and delivery. Bless Daithí's union with Benjamin and help them face the bigotry of others. Help Sophie to reconcile with her mother and grow in maturity. In all the ways you would wish; Amen.'

'Amen.'

Barbara leaves and her Friend sits in the warm chair. He thumbs through her sketch book, 'you've been busy, Ruth. Considering you're confined to this room, you've found plenty of material. All these hospital workers and drawings from looking out of the window — you've some talent there.'

She blushes at the praise, 'thank you. I've been finding it therapeutic. It's funny, my art has happened at different stages in my life with gaps in between. I must be in an "on" mode at the moment —,'

Interrupting her, 'I'd like to come back to that at another time, but now — you were telling me about the second pharmacy. What happened after you returned from that trip to your parents?'

After arriving home, she had to run around catching up with tasks. Paudie returned home from work, but they had no chance to talk privately until the children excused themselves from the dinner table.

Touching his arm to get his attention, 'Paudie, I'm sorry I haven't got back to you about the new shop — I just didn't get a minute while I was over there. But look-it, I've been thinking about it, just listen, go ahead. Let's just do it and I'll try my very best to make it work. Ring Joe Bolger and tell him yes, and send him the money he wants.'

'It's too late for that now, Ruth,' looking at her with a rueful twist to his mouth.

'Oh sweet Jesus! I'm so sorry Paudie. Is it my fault? Has someone pipped you to the post — got in first and reserved the pharmacy before I gave you the nod? I'm so sorry! Look, could we —?'

Interrupting her, 'no, nothing like that, Ruth. I found out this afternoon — I'm a bit shocked myself, really.' Looking at

192

her confused face with wide eyes, 'The Mall — it's all locked up.'

'All locked up? What? For the night?'

'No, indefinitely — Joe's gone bang — he's gone bust. The Official Receiver has moved in today and boarded the place up.'

'What?' she pauses to understand. 'Oh no! That's terrible! Terrible for him — and for all those businesses who —,' she stops, realising something.

Reading her mind, 'yep, I know. Thank God, we didn't commit to it after all. If I'd sent over the deposit that next morning after you'd left, we'd have lost it all. It would've been snapped up by the Receiver and put straight into the creditor fund. And as you well know, we'd have been way down the food chain for getting anything out of that — probably never seen our money again. The Receiver, lawyers, accountants, banks would have all taken their dues first, leaving very little for us small guys. No, Ruth, we've had a very lucky escape, thanks be to God!'….

The mobile phone rings on the bedside locker. Getting out of the chair and shuffling over, she sits on the side of the bed while she receives a FaceTime video call.

'Bríd! Bríd! Is that really you? I can't believe it's really you! What a sight for sore eyes! How are you, girl?'

'I know! I know!' the image on the screen giggling. 'How are you, Ruth?…'

They catch up like they only saw each other a few days previously.

'…tell me, what's that on the side of your nose? It looks like a dressing.' She as usual, misses no detail.

Bríd putting her hand up to her face, 'oh that — I keep forgetting about it — it's nothing — just something they cut out. It's my fair cailín skin, you know,' laughing. 'Cursed with freckles all my life, ha, ha. I keep forgetting to put sunscreen on in the morning. You know what I'm like, Ruth.'

Nodding and frowning in concern, 'only too well, Bríd!'

'And riding hats don't really shade my face.'

'Bríd, now listen to me — you can't be too careful. Don't take any risks — look what happened to me —,'

Bríd interrupting her, 'I know, I know, Mammy…'

'…so Daithí's going to marry Benjamin…

…Deidre's expecting her first, we don't know when yet — she's waiting for her dating scan…

…Sophie's bought a house…

…Paudie's the same he always is…'

'…Ramón Junior looks like he's going to get sponsorship so he can turn professional…

…Maria's in her final year at veterinary college…

…Mateo's progressing at Law School…

…Lucia's doing voice at the Music Conservatory and hopes to be a professional soprano — don't know where she gets that from. Certainly not from me or her father, ha, ha…

…Juan's a fresher and funnily enough, like you, he's an artist…

…Tadgh's preparing for his entrance exam for the University of Buenos Aires…

…Róisín's mad clever at school and mad into the ponies, like the rest of us…

…and Donncha's a real home bird — says he's never going to leave, like some old bachelor farmer back home — reckons he's going to run the stud when his father and I are too old, ha, ha…'

'…oh, Bríd, it's so good talking to you — I wish I could come and visit you and Ramón. Meet your children and see where you live — it'd be SO unreal….'

After the exciting call from Bríd, she feels exhausted and climbs into bed to rest.

Her Friend however, is having none of it and wants her to reflect some more. 'You were happy with Paudie in those early days when Bríd and Ramón were your friends. Have you ever felt that kind of romantic love since?'

With Paudie? Are you joking? — what are the chances of that?

There was never the time or energy to work on their relationship, she can see that now. It helped briefly when they got their own space moving into River House. Paudie got his libido back big time, but hers had migrated in the meantime. Sex was another chore to be added to the list. Duty put a dampener on pleasure. Conversely, anger was stoked. She has to admit, she had gone around like a seething ball of Furies much of the time. Frustrated with Paudie over his entrenched attitudes and ways; resentful of being responsible for everything; emotionally taciturn because her physical health was never taken seriously. Battling to make a life that suited her as much as him. A perpetual cycle of bickering that waxed to loud arguments and waned to silent sulks. That was the dominant up and down tune in her life — an ear worm that could not be purged.

On top of that was the individual needs and demands of the children. Wanting to do the best for them, she facilitated whatever hobbies, interests, sporting activities each of them had taken a notion for. There were years of her being sole proprietor of Ruth's Chauffeuring Services spending countless hours waiting in the car for lessons / sessions / matches / practices to finish. Keeping consistent pressure on them to do their homework, music practise and projects made her feel like a warden in a workhouse. Even Paudie relied on her to prompt him to do the tasks he was supposed to be responsible for. Her love life had sunk as murky dregs to the bottom of the barrel that was family life.

Her parents' increasing infirmity became another burden. The nurturing she had relied on all her life became inverted. She was the carer and they the cared for, whether either side liked the role reversal or not. To be fair, the burdensome task was shared with her sisters. Sam, living in Lucan was relatively nearby and as a national school teacher, had school holidays available to help Vera with Billy. Rachel had relocated to London so was limited in what she could offer. Ronnie was resident in Lusk with a family of four children. But she had always been a dreamer and badly organised. Billy often declared 'that gal's away with the fairies.' The effort involved in reining Ronnie in to help and keep her to allocated tasks would not be worth it. It was more productive to relieve her of specific duties and let her waft in and out of the situation as she pleased.

The second youngest sister, Susie, was the most help. Her marriage had broken up around the time of Billy's second admission into hospital and Vera let her move back home. Susie was a hairstylist at an upmarket salon in Dublin City centre and worked long hours with an oversubscribed client list. She worked Saturdays and took Tuesdays off in lieu.

As she feared, Vera was soon diagnosed with Parkinson's Disease and Billy never did recover enough to return home. Surviving his stay in hospital, he was discharged from the Stroke Unit into a nursing home; but the move was too much for him and he passed away soon after. Vera's grief at losing the most significant person in her life accelerated the progression of her own illness. Billy and Vera had met as young teenagers, being each others' first and only love. They had melded together as a single unit over their many happy years together and for one to flourish without the other had been inconceivable.

Despite the warnings that her father was in fragile health and would probably not be around for long, she experienced a surprising level of shock at his death. For her it was like a stable rock she had always rested on suddenly crumbled away to sand and dust. But her mother's vulnerability meant she had to remain upright and cope.

Susie became increasingly concerned about leaving Vera for extended periods while she went to work. Although family friends called in to check on her and Sam called over whenever she could, it was obvious that Susie needed help. She decided the most useful thing was to have Vera over in Balnarath at the weekends. As Irina had recently taken on the housework, her Sundays were free. Susie and Sam believed it too onerous for both her and Vera to travel every week so alternate weekends were agreed. Sam could take over on the other Saturdays and Susie did not work on Sundays. This seemed an equitable arrangement for everyone.

Needing to alter the household routine, she gathers her four together to organise the practicalities. It is evening and they are all lounging in the front room.

'Now Paudie, could you collect a takeaway on the Friday evenings I drive over to collect Vera as I won't have time to cook?'

Paudie staring at her like a hare caught in lamplight, 'umm — possibly. It would depend.'

Staring right back at him feeling unamused, she says nothing and turns to the others. 'Now, I need the three of you to be on hand on Saturday while I'm at work — are you listening? Hey, Daithí! Deidre! You too, Sophie! Are you all listening?'

Daithí drags his eyes away from the TV. Deidre peers over the top of her latest Jacqueline Wilson novel and Sophie, ignoring her mother, taps away like a court stenographer on her phone. 'Sophie! Put down your phone, please! I'm trying to talk to you!'

Four pairs of sullen eyes fix on her.

'Thank you — I have your attention. Now!', brandishing a refill pad. 'I want to draw up a rota of times that each of you will be responsible for minding Granny Vera. You won't have to do much. Just give her a cup of tea and a piece of cake every few hours. She can have whatever breakfast and lunch you're having — the usual stuff in the fridge. I'll cook later when I get home from work. If there are any problems, ring me and I'll call back home at lunchtime.' Getting into her stride, 'The important thing is that you help her when she wants to go to the toilet. You don't need to stay in there with her, just wait outside the door in case she needs help. And chat with her every now and again so that she doesn't feel lonely.' Opening the pad, folding the front cover back and clicking a ballpoint. 'You can either do a whole Saturday on your own which means you'll only have to do it once every six weeks. Or you can break each Saturday up into 3 shifts where you do a few hours each. I'll be leaving at my normal time of 7.30, but I'll have Granny up and dressed before I go. Whoever's on first starts at that time. I'll be home again at 6, or thereabouts, depending upon your father,' throwing him an accusatory look. Paudie deflects it away with a shoulder shrug.

Daithí jumps in, 'hey, what about my piano lessons?'

Deidre joining him, 'and, I always meet up with Molly and Sarah on Saturdays, you know that, Mammy.'

Sophie wails, 'and Granny's so slooow!'.

Daithí adds, 'and my run? When am I supposed to get that done? Huh?'

Deidre continues, 'I can't let them go into town without me, I'll get left out.'

Sophie whines, 'and she takes ages to eat.'

Daithí wants to know, 'and my Camera Club? You know that's my favourite. And Simon is going to teach me —'

Deidre fretting, interrupts, 'I'll get left out and I'll be all on my own.'

Sophie whinging, 'and she takes forever in the bathroom!'

Daithí up on his feet, 'what about my Camera Club field trips? Eh?' dramatically thumping his chest 'Who's thought about those?'

Their objections and resistance rise to a crescendo, and her anger matches it, notch for notch; meanwhile her patience plummets, level by level.

'For fuck's sake, she's your Granny and she's not well! Here!' hurling the writing refill onto the sofa, 'sort the fucking rota out for yourselves!' she storms out of the room.

She charged down through soft rain to the wooden summer house at the bottom of the garden and burst into tears; tears she had not shed since Billy died. Lying on the padded bench, she bawled and bawled until no more tears came. Calmer now, other feelings invaded the void — guilt and shame. Climbing up to the house, she decided to go to each of the children, and apologise for losing her temper and using bad language.

Daithí reassuring her, 'it's okay, Mammy — you were right — of course we have to help mind Granny. And as you said, it won't be every week.' She gives him a loving hug and goes down to Dee's room.

Deidre oblivious, 'oh, we just drew up a rota like you said to. I'm going to do the early session because Sarah and Molly are never ready to go into town until lunchtime. They might come here first and do their make-up.'

Back up the stairs to the room she least wants to enter.

Sophie, being more difficult to placate, 'I didn't like you shouting, Mammy — and you never curse,' pouting her lips. 'Daddy said you were very bold to do it and he's going to have a word with you about it!'

'Oh, is he now?' bristling. 'So, what's the verdict then, Sophs? Are you going to help out or not?'

'S'pose so,' then turning to her with a sneaky smile, 'will you pay me for doing it?'

Finding Paudie in the sitting room, 'go on then — I know you want to give out to me.'

'I have to say, it wasn't very nice to witness, Ruth — most unpleasant — tut, tut,' chastising pompously. 'And another thing, I don't think it's right that the children should have to care for an elderly person.'

'Really, Paudie? Really?' ready for him. 'What do you suggest then? That I miss work and drive over to mind my mother instead? Or that WE — because my sisters can't afford to — that WE pay for her to go into respite care? And as for caring for an elderly person — my mother is not elderly, she's still a relatively young woman — she just has an awful neurological illness that I'm surprised that, you of all people, seem to have little empathy for. And it won't do the children any harm to learn some compassion for — and patience with — people worse off than themselves.'…

Her thoughts are interrupted by the door opening.

Kashaf puts her head around the door jamb, 'Ruth, is it okay for me to come in for a while?'

'Of course, of course — um?'

'Kashaf. How have you been getting on with the exercises?' the physiotherapist comes over to her chair, 'not too taxing, I hope?'

'No, in fact, I've been feeling much better since doing them. A bit more lively — in better spirits — you know — like you do after a good workout.'

'That's excellent news, Ruth,' looking surprised. 'In that case, I think we can move you up a stage. Stand up for me, please, and let me watch you walk across the room. Are you using the frame?'

'No, I haven't been for a day or two. I'm only going as far as the bathroom, but I'm doing it without any assistance.'

'Great! Now walk over to the window, take your time, please — now back towards me.

You're remarkably steady. I want to show you some new exercises — we'll do them together…

…Right, these sheets I brought are no good to you now, Ruth — you're way beyond them. I need to print some new ones off with today's exercises. I'll bring them up to you later. Any questions?'

'Yes, I do Kashaf, if you don't mind me asking? It's just I'm interested in other cultures — can I ask you where you are from?'

'Me? Bradford.'

'Bradford?'

'Yes, Bradford in England — oh you mean my grandparents,' laughing. 'They were originally from Uganda, but were forced to leave by the dictator Idi Amin. As Commonwealth citizens, they decided to settle in Bradford.'

She remembers vaguely her cousins talking about the event. 'I know Birmingham and London — Bradford is where, exactly?'

With patience, Kashaf answers, 'Bradford's in West Yorkshire, Ruth — that's north of Birmingham — Birmingham's in the West Midlands.'

'Sorry, Kashaf, my geography's terrible — I should do something about it. So tell me, what brought you to the West of Ireland? Do you like it here?'

'My husband's job, Ruth — he's head of the Pathology Department here in the hospital. Yes, we're happy here. Beautiful, peaceful place. A good country to raise a family. I'll call back later with those exercise sheets,' smiling genially and heading out of the door.

Her Friend sitting on the bed, 'poor Kashaf, I wonder how many times she has to explain her heritage to people. But moving on, I want to ask you something. When Vera was ill, you had alternate Sundays free, is that right?'

Yes — correct.

For the first time ever she had a regular day off. Paudie was back involved in polo; not so much competing, more consulting and refereeing. When he was not away with the children doing that, they would spend time with their horses. The children were keen equestrians which left the house quiet on Sundays.

When Vera stayed, the two of them spent the day going for Sunday lunch then driving to some scenic spot to drink tea from a flask and reminisce. Or if the weather was bad, mooch around a shopping centre slowly, or go to the cinema. Initially, Vera had been thrilled to go to places she considered upmarket, viewing it as a treat. But as her illness progressed, she became embarrassed about being seen in public. She was self conscious about her laboured movements and difficulties with eating. The disease affected her jaw and throat, and she developed swallowing issues. When she drank, liquid would spill down her chin, and saliva dribbled from her lax mouth in a constant stream. Despite reassuring her mother that people were too polite to stare, Vera claimed the stress of going out no longer made it enjoyable. Sadly her decline was rapid and she succumbed to a chest infection that quickly turned to pneumonia. Vera died within hours of being admitted to hospital, leaving her distraught.

She was filled with competing feelings at her mother's death. There was a strong sense of relief that she no longer witnessed her mother in distress, and that the woman was released from her misery. She was angry and felt guilty about Vera being subjected to pointless medical procedures towards the end — it would have been kinder to let her slip away peacefully in her own bed. And she felt great sadness as she missed her mother so much. Vera was her only confidante apart from Irina, and a marvellous role model of goodness. But she had many happy memories and she loved those times on her own with her mother. She was so glad she had made the effort to bring her over.

Back to the original question, as for the other Sundays, she could do whatever she pleased. At first it felt strange, almost to the point of panic. Questioning what she could do with her time, she feared being bored, or lonely being so used to the company of others. Nonetheless, she soon found ways to occupy herself.

Probing some more, her Friend enquires, 'did you meet up with any friends on those Sundays?'

Not that she can remember — they would have been doing things with their own families. Feeling dozy now — enough of all that stuff — the exercises must have been more strenuous than she realised.

Last night you graced one of my dreams,
and we were happy together,
lying on a beach holding hands in the dusk,
using our free hand to count the stars above us.

Opening her eyes, she discerns Paudie silhouetted against the fading light from the window. His eyes screwed up, he tries to scan some papers in the twilight. He becomes aware he is being watched.

Shifting his gaze towards her, 'darling, you've woken up. I hope I didn't disturb you,' putting the documents away into his briefcase.

'What's that you're doing, Paudie?'

'Just multitasking — I must have learnt something from being around you women all these years,' teasing her. 'Using time efficiently as you always do, Ruth. You haven't eaten your supper. Are you not hungry?'

'Is it here? Good! I'm famished. I hope that's a cheese sandwich — I'm craving cheese since I went on these steroids.'

'That reminds me,' he picks up a cloth shopping bag lying next to the briefcase. 'I brought you this,' producing a packet of Rambol French cheese covered in walnuts. 'I know you're partial to a piece of this.'

'Paudie, you're brilliant! I do love you!'

Fixing her with a wry expression, 'now it's my turn to ask — do you, Ruth? Do you love me?'

'Of course I do,' doing a rapid sweep of the room to find some way of changing the subject. She spies something on the window cill, 'what's that over there? Have you brought me something to read? I feel up to a bit of light reading.'

'What's what?' Paudie turns to look where she is pointing. He retrieves it, 'a world atlas? I wonder what that's doing here?' He passes it to her.

Opening the book to check the flyleaf, she finds the hospital library stamp. 'Is there anything else there, a note or anything?'

'Just some papers — hang on, they look like exercises. Yeah, they're exercise sheets.'

God Bless Kashaf, she thinks to herself, and then out loud. 'The physio came today and we talked about where places are, and I told her my geography's a disgrace. She must have got this for me and dropped it in when I was snoozing. Good woman herself! Would you do me a favour, Paudie? Would you get my pocket Filofax out of the bureau and bring it in tomorrow? I want to look up some old addresses — get a better understanding of where people live.'

Chapter 18

'Here's your pain relief patch, Ruth. You're happy to put it on yourself after your shower? Just put the old one in the medical waste bin. Sorry, Ruth, I don't need to tell you that — you're an old hand at this. We've so many new patients on the ward, I tend to repeat the same things out of habit.'

'There's no need to apologise, Sonia. It's much better to remind people than have something go wrong. I've learnt that one over the years. Tell me, Sonia, is there any news on Dr Geraghty?'

Sonia's cheerful expression drops then turns neutral, 'news? How do you mean, Ruth?'

'Has anyone heard from her, I mean?'

'No — but we wouldn't expect to. Staff, particularly the medics, come and go all the time. The interns are only ever with us for 12 weeks.'

'But Dr Geraghty was in a permanent post, wasn't she? I've met Dr Gabriel, and I think he's gorgeous. But I liked Dr Geraghty. Dr Mulhall must be very sorry to see her go.'

'Dr Mulhall isn't here, Ruth — he's on longterm sick leave. Didn't Dr Gabriel explain? Dr Gabriel is Acting Consultant during Dr Mulhall's absence.'

'No, he introduced himself as Registrar.'

'Oh, that's Gabriel being self-effacing — he's a brilliant doctor and he's so modest about it. Anyone having him look after them is in the best of hands. I'm sure you'll get on with him really well, Ruth. So you can take care of yourself this morning? I'll dispose of that empty pill cup on my way out.'

Digesting this latest news, she has lived long enough to know that the expression long term sick leave can be a euphemism, She recalls a number of people in positions of authority who have avoided scrutiny by pulling out the medically ill card. Alternatively it is used as a more discreet term than suspended, pending investigation. Trying to resist thinking along those lines as she hates people being judgemental, she decides that it is probably all innocent: Dr Geraghty has moved on to a fabulous new job after being made an offer she could not refuse. And poor Dr Mulhall has been overdoing things and is genuinely ill — not too seriously, she hopes. That'd be ironic. Yet she can't help feeling curious all the same. There was definitely something bothering Dr G. She often seemed unhappy if you caught her unawares. And he never struck her as being full of the milk of human kindness despite his chosen profession; a bit too much like Vincent.

'Have you ever felt judged by other people, Ruth? Apart from Nora, that is?' her Friend queries.

Always.

Holding a prominent role in the community, she is careful to act with probity at all times. Although the town has grown in size and with it a certain level of anonymity, key figures will always be under public scrutiny. Dispensing medication carries risk, and running any kind of business providing goods and services is a legal minefield. People would not hesitate to sue especially as the compensation levels awarded by the Irish courts are, in her opinion, obscenely lucrative.

Paudie had some close misses over the years. But thankfully she, and sometimes Lisa, spotted when something did not seem quite right — all due to their own diligence. Paudie would blanch whenever they raised a query, quickly correcting his error, but never openly admitted he had messed up. Lisa would always disclose to her what happened on the quiet, but she would keep any mistakes she intercepted to herself. As much as she trusted her staff, she felt it wise to keep her own counsel.

When it came to children, they could always be relied upon to let their parents down.

One such occasion was Sophie getting into trouble at school. A girl in her class had become a school refuser and on further probing, bullying was uncovered.

Paudie and her are invited to the school to meet with the Principal and Sophie required to join them.

'…Jessica Milne has suffered badly as a result of this,' the Principal explains. 'She has missed a lot of this important First Year at secondary school and as I'm sure you can appreciate, will need counselling and support to overcome the reprehensible behaviour experienced at the hands of the culprits,' shuffling papers on the large boardroom table. 'Sophie is extremely fortunate to have not been suspended like the other perpetrators. Jessica has said, to Sophie's credit, that she did not believe that Sophie was as involved and was more on the periphery. She believes that Sophie was largely going along with it because she felt coerced by the ringleaders. I think that is a very generous interpretation by Ms Milne.' Tapping the edges of the paperwork into a neat pile, 'after careful consideration of all the facts, I am prepared to deal with this matter in respect of Sophie by suggesting that you, Mr and Mrs O'Sullivan, discuss with Sophie some means of reparation. But let me make it clear, I do NOT mean financial. In these prosperous times that can be a little too easy. If Sophie suggests something that is acceptable to both Jessica and the Board of Management which includes myself, I am prepared to recommend to the BOM that nothing be entered on Sophie's permanent record. That would then be the end of the matter.'

Rarely feeling so mortified in her life, she trailed out of the Principal's office like she was the guilty miscreant. Sophie with a red, swollen face from crying was asked to freshen up in the girls' bathrooms and return to class. Paudie stayed completely silent and stony faced while they drove back to the Pharmacy. A waiting pile of prescriptions meant she could not speak with him until later.

While on her own in the stock room stacking a new delivery, an idea formulated in her mind. Whatever problem the family encountered, she always felt responsible for sorting it out. Sophie would want the easiest way out of the situation — that was human nature. But she thought it morally correct that Sophie should not get away with bad behaviour; that it was only right for her to pay some personal price and then hopefully learn from the experience.

Back home that evening when the others had finished their food, she asked Paudie and Sophie to stay back at the table. Her proposal was going to meet with resistance, but she was prepared. Paudie was good at vetoing ideas, but not so good at suggesting positive alternatives, particularly if it involved himself, or he had not come up with them first.

Sophie was distraught. But because nobody came up with anything better, her proposition was presented to Jessica; then the BOM and was duly accepted. The agreed plan was for Sophie and Paudie to take Jessica with them to the riding stables for six weeks, enabling Jessica to learn the basics of riding Sophie's horse. To her fervent relief, the stratagem worked. Sophie and Jessica gelled over the experience becoming close friends. Thankfully, the accusation of bullying was never raised with her outside of the family. She hated to think her children might be regarded badly in the town.

Her Friend remarks, 'that was a clever way to handle the situation. Looking back now, why do you think Sophie got involved in the bullying? Have you any thoughts on that.'

At one time bullying was kind of accepted as part of normal life, especially at school. But now people are much more aware of the harm it causes, often in the long term. Why someone does it must be because of something amiss in their own lives, she believes. Being bullied at home, for example, might make a child bully others at school.

'Good point, Ruth — well argued. What about Sophie?' her Friend fixes her with a stare. She knows he is not going to let it drop.

Maybe Sophie was reacting to stuff in her life too. Looking at it another way, children who have been shown unconditional love and kindness at home probably do not feel the need to exert power over others. Sophie was always unhappy so unlike Deidre. Did she act out her dissatisfaction by allowing someone else like Jessica, get a hard time, too? Did it somehow make her feel better that she was not the only one? She does not really understand her daughter. All she knows is that she cannot relate to her in the same way as the other two.

'Okay, let's move on to Daithí. Did he ever let you down? Disappoint you as a parent?'

Not so much disappoint, more expose the family to gossip. It was when Daithí made his sexual orientation known. Noticing that Daithí had not been his usual laconic self for a while, she also watched him being irritable and snappy with his sisters over insignificant issues, ones that would have normally passed him by. He was eighteen at the time and in Sixth Year at school. She considers it a pressurised year for anyone. In a short six month period, Daithí had to finish the syllabuses for seven Leaving Certification subjects. He needed to make far reaching decisions on a potential career and select appropriate Third level courses to further those aims. He had to complete a Central Applications Office (CAO) form, applying for up to ten different courses at various colleges around the country. Whether to stay local, or move to another part of the country had to be decided upon. He had also been contemplating getting a part-time job to help finance himself through college. Although being involved with a girl long term at the time, that had stopped abruptly. When she enquired about Amie, he said he thought she was well, but had not spoken to her for a while. She was aware he wanted to do a media course that could lead to a career in film production. Paudie was not impressed — he preferred the mainstream and traditional. As an artist, she was fully able to relate to Daithí's desire to be creative. Paudie pushed more for a solid, professional career that would be reliably profitable. Daithí, she recognised, was under a lot of pressure and his mood would understandably be affected. Concerned about him coping, she wanted to know if anything was worrying him….

Tilly clatters through the door bringing refreshments, 'Well, girl, I mean, Ruthie! I have to say you look fabulous! What brand of face cream are you using?' Tilly laughing 'I want some of it too!' giggling some more at her own joke. 'See you later, hon,' clattering back out.

She drinks her milky tea. When she is finished, her Friend resumes conversation, 'go on, what happened with Daithí?'

Wanting to talk privately, she persuades Daithí to go for a walk along the river.

'… I've noticed you don't seem so happy these days, Daithí. What's wrong? Do you feel able to tell me? Or would you prefer to talk to someone outside the family?'

'I've done that already, Mammy.'

'Oh! You mean you've already spoken to someone at school? The Student Guidance Counsellor, you mean?'

'No, not with her — someone more relevant — someone who understands exactly what I'm going through — how I feel — help me plan what I want to do.'

'You mean work out your career path? I can pay for you to see a career guidance counsellor privately. I've heard of a good one —,'

He interrupts her, 'no, Mammy — not that. Look, I may as well tell you, I'm going to have to tell you some time. My head is wrecked feeling like I'm lying — but look — please understand — I'm only telling you. Only you at first, right? I need to tread through this carefully — as and when I feel ready. I've been advised to go at my own pace — nobody else's, right? No telling Daddy, or anyone, okay? Is that clear? Do you promise?'

Completely bewildered, 'of course, Daithí. Tell me what's troubling you, son and I'll try my best to understand.'

'Look,' staring off into the distance. Then looking at her face to watch her reaction, 'I don't know how to tell you this, or what you are going to think, but — Mammy, I'm Gay.'

'Gay? Gay?' she pauses. 'Do you mean homosexual, Daithí?'

'We prefer the word Gay — but yes, homosexual if you like — if it helps you understand.'

'We? But I DON'T understand, Daithí — who's we? You're a normal boy — you do normal things — you have normal boys' interests. You have girlfriends. How can you possibly be Gay? How can you possibly even know? You're far too young. It's normal to experiment at your age — it's just a passing phase. You'll get over it. You're just going through a difficult patch with the Leaving Cert and all.'

'Look, Mammy, I know it's difficult for you to comprehend. I was warned that I'd have to be patient with you. But you have to believe me when I say it's not a passing phase. I'm not going to get over it. It's who I truly am and it's who I'm always going to be. And I hope we can still be friends, like we've always been. You've always been there for me, Mammy, and I need you more than ever now. I need you to understand,' his voice breaking into sobs.

'Oh, Daithí,' throwing her arms around him just above the waist. 'You're my little boy,' pulling her head back to peek up to his face. 'And I'll always love you no matter what. I'll try my very best to understand. I might not always get it right, but you can help me, teach me. We can go through this together. I just want you to be happy.'…

Tilly comes back into the room, 'Have you finished, darling? Can I take your cup please, Ruthie?'

Passing it over to her, 'do you have a family, Tilly?'

'What children, you mean? No, I've never been blessed that way. But I've a good life and I'm grateful for that. A house to live in — this job — my church community. And now Jimmy. I help out with the children at our events in church, Bible classes and so on — I enjoy their company. I like their take on the World — they can be so funny sometimes,' chuckling.

'They're a mixed blessing, I can tell you, Tilly. They say they break your arms when they're little, and break your heart when they're big.'

'Hey, Ruth — that's very good — I've never heard that said before,' she breaks into a Gospel hymn on her way out.

Her Friend picks up the threads of the story, 'how did Paudie take the news?'

How do you think?

She mulled over Daithí's revelation, but got used to the idea relatively quickly knowing it did not alter how she felt about him. Nothing could change her deep love and protectiveness towards him. If anything she felt closer to him, empathising with his angst and flattered by his trust in her. But aspects worried her. Whenever they were alone for a few minutes, she would ask Daithí about implications that troubled her.

'What about a permanent relationship, Daithí? Will you be able to find someone to love — someone to settle down with?'

'The Gay community is much bigger than you think, Mammy. We've dating agencies — support groups — pubs and clubs where Gay men like to meet up. I hope to connect with someone special in time — when I'm ready for commitment. The same as it was for you or any straight person.'

Another time, raising the subject of children, 'Daithí, won't you miss being able to father your own children and be a parent?'

'Mammy, I can still be a father. Some women are happy to be surrogates. Some Lesbian women approach Gay men to father their children. In some countries there's even talk of Gay couples adopting. I can also be a favourite uncle to Deidre's and Sophie's,' smiling at his own presumption.

Regarding his safety, 'what about diseases, you know, HIV and AIDS?'

'Mammy, all people involved in sexual activity, regardless of sexual orientation, are at risk of sexually transmitted diseases. Sensible people practice safe sex. I do know how to use a condom.'

On another occasion, 'Daithí, I've heard there's a lot of violence in Gay lifestyles. I don't want you to get hurt either physically or emotionally. I worry about you.'

'We prefer to use the term Gay lives not lifestyles, Mammy. It's not a lifestyle choice, it's who we are intrinsically. And yes, there may be violent relationships. But there's a lot of violence in heterosexual relationships too, Mammy — usually against women who come off worse. As you well know, they've less physical strength than men.'

In respect of Daithí's perception of women, 'but I thought you liked women. You've always been so good to your sisters. And you've had girlfriends.'

'Being Gay doesn't make me a misogynist, Mammy. I still love you and Dee Dee and Sophie to bits; and all my women friends. I deeply respect, even honour you all. I just don't find I'm sexually attracted to women which is a good thing. I can have great friendships with women and sexual feelings don't muddy my attitude towards them. But that can be different for some Gay men. Some are happier being Bi — they marry women, have families, but have male relationships too.'

'Really? Are you sure?'

'Mammy, there are a number of men in this town who appear respectably married with families who had Gay relationships before they married; and some who continue to have Gay affairs while remaining married and often very happily.'

That one had really given her something to think about afterwards. But she was not allowed to talk any of it through with Paudie, or anyone else. They both knew that Daithí would have to talk to his father eventually. Wanting to get the Leaving Certificate exams out of the way before the sky fell in, as Daithí put it, she agreed with him wholeheartedly. But she cringed thinking about the impact it would have on Paudie.

After Daithí bravely broke the news, Paudie was stunned, unable to articulate thoughts, or express his feelings for some time. Retreating to the Dispensary, he only engaged briefly when spoken to. When he eventually disclosed his thoughts and feelings, in much the same way she had, he comforted himself by labelling it a temporary phase; a fad that Daithí latched on to because other lads were doing it.

Soon though, he became angry. Loving his son, he could not allow himself to become directly angry with Daithí;

instead he turned it on himself and somewhat towards her. He ranted that they had failed as parents, frantically reviewing his behaviour to identify where he might have damaged his son. Then a sense of helplessness descended over him.

Reaching that stage, he did what he always did when faced with major trouble. He sought help from his parents.

Yanking the pull bell at Rath House, Paudie's face is grim. 'I don't know how my parents are going to cope with this — especially at their age — it's really unfair on them.'

Her countering, 'this is not about your parents, Paudie. Daithí is entitled to be himself.'

Carmel's face lights up when she sees it is them. After waving them towards the sitting room, she bustles off to prepare tea and sandwiches. Brendan with a delighted smile on his face, rises stiffly from his chair and walks over to shake their hands in greeting. She walks over to kiss Nora's powdered cheek and catches a musky whiff of Tweed perfume escaping from the fully buttoned up, brushed cotton blouse. 'Hello Nora — I trust you are keeping well.'

Brendan with forced jollity, 'good to see you both! Is Carmel providing tea? How is everyone?' surmising something is amiss for them to both turn up unexpectedly.

Paudie launches straight in, 'we've had some very bad news, Father, Mother.'

'Not some very bad news, Paudie,' her correcting him, 'some unexpected news, is all.'

Brendan looks at her then at Paudie, but says nothing.

'I really don't know how to break this to you both,' Paudie running his hands through his thick hair, seeming at a loss. 'It's Daithí — he's turned homosexual.'

Her quickly interjecting, 'no, Paudie, Daithí hasn't turned homosexual. Daithí is just Gay.'

Brendan continues to listen, Nora sits as if made of marble.

'And I don't know what we can do about it,' Paudie, with anguish in his voice.

Her interposing, 'nothing, Paudie — we don't do anything other than love and support our son.'

Being posited an active question, Brendan takes the cue to respond with clinical objectivity, focusing on the practicalities from a medical perspective. Dipping into his memory bank of similar family situations, he explains that there is no scientific evidence of pathological disease in homosexuality. There are certain safety concerns to be addressed vis-a-vis HIV and AIDS. Societal prejudice leading to mental health problems could be a serious issue going forward. There are advocates of Conversion Therapy, but he is not convinced of the efficacy and therefore cannot recommend it.

Paudie sits silently nodding, having the greatest respect for his father's opinion.

Meanwhile, she observes Nora. The cup of tea and plate of cakes placed unobtrusively by Carmel onto the Birds Eye yew side table remain untouched.

As the men pontificate, Nora suddenly wakes from her state of petrification and takes command. Projecting a clear authoritative voice across the room towards the men engrossed in their own arrogant certainty, 'Brendan! Please! Stop this immediately! Daithí is not a case history. He is a decent loving man who has a great deal to offer the world. His sexual orientation is completely irrelevant!' Turning her attention towards her youngest son, 'And Pádraic! Just pull yourself together, man! This is not about you!' strangely echoing what she had said. 'You should be proud of the young person your son has turned out to be. He is the same loveable, admirable boy he has always been. This changes absolutely nothing — and frankly, it is none of your business! Go home and treat your son with the decency and respect that he deserves!'

Thereafter, Paudie's perspective's changed completely and he was able to accept, and support Daithí with some pride.

'Deidre, then — What about her? What has she been like to parent?'

She always felt close to Deidre like she did with Daithí, but in a different way.

With Deirdre, she felt she could understand the way the child, and later young person thought. She could empathise with her emotions; in short, see herself in her. There are differences, of course. Deirdre is much more academic than her and she probably has more common sense than her daughter. Deidre followed a more traditional route than her siblings. She worked hard; attained much at school; did well in her exams, and decided on a career from an early age which she carried through to fruition. With Dee doing her degree in Galway, she never had to leave home as it was easy to commute. That meant she did not have to go through empty nest syndrome until Deirdre married and bought a house with Marcus. A big issue for Deidre is her over sensitivity. She is upset and hurt by others easily. But the remarkable thing is she is able to get over it quickly and forgives people easily.

The main area of difficulty is her relationship with her father. Dee always felt Paudie favoured Sophie over her and her brother although in reality, Paudie did spoil his son. But she has to agree, there is a special bond, a closeness between Paudie and Sophie. Dee gets annoyed with her father in a way she never does with other people. It is as though she does not respect him which is unusual for her. She prickles against any orders he gives her, resenting anything she does to oblige him. Maybe it is out of loyalty to her. Perhaps she can sense her mother's anger and out of love, takes her part. Sometimes it feels like the family is split into two alliances. A triad of her, Daithí and Deirdre versus a duo of Paudie and Sophie — families are just too complicated.

'And your own siblings, Ruth. None of your sisters have been to visit you. Can we expect them at all?'

Sadly, no.
When Susie's marriage broke up, she was living in a rented flat which she let her husband keep on as she just needed to get away from his violent temper. Not wanting the indignity of using a Women's Aid hostel, Vera let her come home. As she effectively became Vera's carer, it was not possible for her to move on. During the later months of her life, Vera said she wanted Susie to consider the house her permanent home and was to stay living there after her death. By that time, her

parents had bought the house from Dublin Corporation in a Right To Buy scheme. With Vera deceased, the other sisters, all of whom incidentally are well off, understandably want their share of the house although she herself said she does not want or need a share. All she asked for was a few pieces of her mother's jewellery to pass down to her own girls. Located near the city centre in Crumlin, and on the Dart line, it is a valuable property especially as Billy and Vera spent money keeping it updated and comfortable. Susie wants to buy her sisters out, but cannot raise a big enough mortgage on her hairdressing wages to cover its full market value. Susie has offered them what she can afford, but the others have refused. They want to sell it, split the proceeds four ways, suggesting Susie get herself a cheap apartment with her share. But this will mean her moving out to the suburbs. And she does not drive, nor wants a long commute by public transport especially after a late night in the salon. It has led to terrible arguments.

She understands everyone's point of view and each of the sisters have tried to pull her into their camp against the others. When she refused to do this, they got angry with her. The situation became so toxic, she had to withdraw and avoided taking phone calls from any of them. She has given Paudie strict instructions to not let any of them know about her illness as she could not cope with their reactions. She is not sure if it was the right thing to do, or not. Perhaps they have a right to know. It's something to think about, maybe. Should she reach out to them — but what will be the cost? Getting dragged into that poison pit again? Sometimes you just have to let people go whether they are kin or not….

A knock on the door precedes a familiar friendly face looking in. 'Oh good, they haven't let you go yet,' a woman grinning broadly.

'Maeve Cullen, get yourself in here right now, girl! Thanks so much for coming in to visit! Pull that chair over here so we can have a good auld natter — how are you keeping? How's the business?'

Maeve enters and places a vivid dark mauve flowered Cineraria plant with daisy-like petals edged in pure white onto

216

the table. Then slides the spare armchair across the polished lino. She grins at Ruth, 'how are you, is more to the point? You're looking well, Ruth. Been having a nice little holiday, have you?' teasing her.

'Stop! Stop! Will you?' laughing back.

'What's this?' Maeve picks up the world atlas, 'planning a quick getaway, are you?

'I wish! I wish! But I'm promising you now, the minute I get out of this place, I'll be down to you haunt you about some big trip. I've already promised Daíthí…'

They discuss some other suitable destinations that would be relaxing, post treatment.

Moving onto local affairs, Maeve fills her in on local gossip,'… they asked me where they might find the cemetery and the Parish Priest to look up the Church Records.' Maeve regales her about some American visitors who called into her shop trying to trace Irish relatives. 'Turns out the man was a cousin of Maura Delaney's and was wanting to find her grave for his research.'

Interrupting, 'Maura Delaney? Did I know her?'

'Of course you did, Ruth — everyone knew Maura. You know, Maura Mahoney. She was Delaney before got married.'

'Of course. I didn't know she was originally a Delaney. There's quite a clan of them. Poor Maura — she drove everyone mad with her busy-bodying.'

'I know; she'd come in looking for travel brochures. There was never a hope of her going anywhere. I think she just liked to pretend she could. She liked the photos in them, God Bless her.'

'A bit like me then,' ruefully.

'Ah now, Ruth! You carry on improving like you clearly are — Good God, the last time I saw you, I thought it might be the last. But look at you now. We'll get you booked on that same half world cruise that Brendan and Nora went on. You know, the P and O one from Southampton to Australia. You could visit Paudie's Theresa. Remembering Maura, you know, got me thinking about Nora too. Poor women, the both of them didn't stand a chance back then.'

'How do you mean? What had Nora got to do with Maura Mahony, of all people?'

'You know — you must do — come on, you must have heard the talk. I used to listen in on my mother and aunties gassing about it — oh, of course you're not local, I always forget that — you're so one of us. Listen, I'll fill you in…

…they were found naked down in the tall grass at the far boundary of the convent grounds — the Mother Superior sent Nora home immediately. But Maura, poor Maura,' shaking her head and looking sad. 'That wicked witch of a nun took all her perversion out on the poor girl by stripping and beating her. She wouldn't dare touch Nora, of course, on account of her being a Walsh, and her mother being a Butler, and coming from big money, as she did. You might have heard that the Butlers were the principal sponsors of building the main church in town after Catholic Emancipation. No, Nora got off lightly. But Maura, she was only from poor farming stock. She was an easy target for that sadistic, whore of a nun. It was said that some of the other novices would spy on the women while they made love. Then one of them had a row with Nora and out of spite, snitched on them. To make matters even worse for Maura, the old c —, I won't say the word in polite company, handed her over to the Priest, to be "corrected back onto the right path" — and we all know what his "correction" would have entailed, dirty old bastard. There was plenty of talk about him too, but of course he always got away with it. Good God, it gives me the heebie-jeebies to even think about it.' Studying her friend, 'you okay, Ruth? You look like you've seen a ghost. I'm sorry I shouldn't be talking about all these old stories. They're unpleasant, I know. Please forgive me.'

'No, no, you're grand, Maeve, I'm not that easily shocked. With all the horrors that have come out about the Catholic Church over the years, it's no surprise. It's just, I never knew about Nora, is all — but then I never really did get to know her.'

'She was a difficult woman, alright — no getting away from it. She must have been Hell as a mother in-law, I do sympathise. I remember the things you used to tell me when you were buying Gearóid's house. But the funny thing is, whenever she came in to book one of her trips, she would always talk so highly of you, something she only ever did about her own family.'

'What? About me? Talk highly about me? Nooo.'

'Yes, she did! Especially after you had moved out. I should have told you before, really. Nora used to say that you were the best thing that ever happened to Paudie. That she used to have serious doubts about what would become of him before he met you and that you were the making of him. She used to talk about how hard you worked and that the success of the business was largely down to you. But then everyone in town thinks that. She also said what a marvellous mother you were and how the children were a delight to be with, and that was all down to how you had reared them to be so polite and respectful. Yes, Nora was your biggest fan — amongst many of us, of course,' Maeve smiling at her sweetly.

Chapter 19

We were glad there was no light pollution,
no-one else near us, no chatter or music
from a restaurant, we needed no soundtrack
for this moment in our perfect bubble.

A snort shakes her awake; gulping to tighten her throat tissues, she reaches for some water.

Leaning against the wall, her Friend sees her stir and walks over to sit in the other chair. 'We were talking about being judged by other people. Maeve seemed to be saying that people view you very positively. Does that surprise you, Ruth?'

It most certainly had. In fact, she still finds it hard to believe.

People were generally mannerly around her such as thanking her for her help. But all that praise from Nora? That was truly revelatory. Not feeling at all worthy of it, she feels guilty about her misconceptions and misunderstanding of both Nora and Maura Mahoney. Realising she has misjudged both of the women, she could have been kinder and more patient with them. It was wrong of her to have not looked beyond their behaviour; seen that they were real people and not just caricatures to dump ridicule and disrespect upon. They were women who had been deeply hurt inside. Particularly with her own journey of discovery with Daithí, she has some idea of what personal torture both women must have gone through. Forced to conform to a rigid societal norm and act in opposition to their true selves. No wonder Nora seemed so humourless. Maybe it had been much the same for that dreadful Mother Superior.

With regard to Maura, it was understandable why she would seek out the approval of others and look with distain at other people who broke the social mores. Maura had been badly punished for actions that were neither evil nor hurtful. Maura had probably been in love with Nora and that could never have been a bad thing, at least according to her values.

It also opens up some more insight into the relationship between Nora and Brendan. Brendan must have known about Nora's past — people would have fallen over themselves in that narrow minded community to make sure he knew before marrying her. The men in particular, would have at best, seen it as their duty to a fellow man and at worse, used it as a way to get one better over him. Yet despite it, he had made an "honest" woman of her and taken on her notoriety. Maybe it was the trade-off he accepted for being set up in his own practise and provided with a comfortable standard of living at Rath House. This gave him the means to allow his children to pursue their ambitions. Maybe it was not that difficult a life for him if he could keep any masculine pride suppressed. But then again, she had always considered him a decent, very nice man.

'You said that love is always a good thing, Ruth. Do you believe that to be the case in every instance?' her Friend stroking his beard thoughtfully.

That is a questionable statement, she agrees.
It has not always been a good thing for her.

'Go on, Ruth, it's okay to tell all — it's safe enough to face it now.'

Okay.
Sometimes love leads to pain — deep hurtful pain. Like it did for Nora and Maura.

'And for you? Has love hurt you too, Ruth?'

Yes, she has to be honest. It did once.
She has never spoken about it. In a way, it would be good to deal with it. Finally admit the truth.
Once, she fell in love with someone other than Paudie.

221

When she was young, she had been smitten with Paudie. But the depth of passion she felt for the true love of her life was completely different. Thinking back, she remembers the first time it occurred to her that she could love someone other than Paudie.

There was a glass partitioned office in the old Waiting Room. It allowed the receptionist to gate-keep the door into the corridor leading to Brendan's consulting room and the Practice Nurse. The glazing provided some phone confidentiality and private conversation while people waited to be seen. Maurice asked her to call in to discuss dismantling the office and see how best to restore the room.

Maurice sits at the secretary's desk fiddling with a faulty power drill. Seeing her come into the Waiting Room, he propels himself out on the wheeled office chair into the main room to greet her then continues whizzing around like a child on a toy, pushing against the floor with his thick soled boots. 'Here, Ruth, this is so much fun — you should try it.'

'No, Maurice, you're fine,' laughing nervously at this somewhat bizarre behaviour, 'but you carry on, so.'

Thrusting a little faster, 'ah, go on, Ruth — you have to try it — it's great craic!'

'No, it's okay, Maurice. Really — I'm fine as I am,' giggling politely as he glides back and forth across the shiny floor.

Emboldened by her amusement, 'watch this!' he pushes off from a far corner, feet held high, scooting diagonally across the room. 'Yee-hah!!' and just in time, spins around before hitting the far corner.

The door from the main hallway flies open and Nora stands in the doorway looking thunderous.

Maurice brakes hard by stomping his boots to the floor, leaps up and doffs his wooly hat.

'Maurice! I was wondering what that horrendous noise was! I could not believe it was the sound of construction work and now I know for certain it was not!'

'My sincere apologies to you, Mrs O'Sullivan — I'm sorry to have disturbed you. I was testing the chair to see if it was worth salvaging.'

'It might well have been if you hadn't destroyed its castors across the floor! Enough now, please! This is not a kindergarten. Ruth, kindly pop into my sitting room before you leave. I would like to discuss the bedrooms arrangements with you,' Nora closes the door swiftly.

Maurice waits, his ear towards the door to listen that Nora has retreated. Exhaling deeply, 'Jeez, what a woman! Does she ever have a face like a bagful of chisels.'

The description instantly paints an image in her mind. As she substitutes Nora's features with workman's chisels, she has to laugh. The pointed nose, the piercing eyes, the thin lips like sharpened edges; all give her the urge to giggle. The more she thinks about it, the more she finds it funny. She begins to guffaw so uncontrollable, she thinks she might pee her pants. Years of pent up tension are released in seconds, in a most unexpected eruption of hilarity.

Afterwards, she was unable to remember the last time she had howled so much and her ribs ached for days. Whenever she felt a twinge, it reminded her, making her snigger again. She recalled Maurice stood watching her as she convulsed, his eyes shining with pleasure. And she thought she perceived admiration in them too….

Naomi comes quietly into the room carrying a plate, 'Mrs O'Sullivan, I've egg mayo and crackers.' Placing the food on to the table, shoulders and head down, she slopes out of the door.

'Thank you, Naomi!' calling after the young woman. She realises she was over familiar the previous time and the girl is probably painfully shy.

Opening the foil wrapped butter, she cuts the hard yellow pat in half. Attempting to spread it, the cracker breaks into pieces. Alternating spoonfuls of creamy egg with shards of cracker, she disinters long suppressed memories as her Friend sits calm and attentive.

During the time that Maurice restored the old surgery, she found her attitude towards the project changing. Initially there was disinterest as she loved the little cottage and could have happily lived there forever. And she had major misgivings about living with Nora. As the work progressed, she could see liveable rooms emerge from the spartan clinical ones. Maurice was instrumental in that. He ensured that she, rather than Nora, was completely happy with the work, taking pains to make it homely and family friendly. As the weeks progressed, she increased the frequency of her site visits to three times a day, calling in when she dropped off and collected the children, and popping in at lunchtime.

Maurice had a knack of drawing her into his vision and his positivity gradually made her excited about living there. Colour was always her forté and Maurice seemed genuinely impressed with her ideas as they were bolder and different to the safe, neutral colours chosen by his other clients. As each room was finished, he admitted to having doubted her, but upon seeing the results, considered her most talented at interior design. These acknowledgements struck her because Paudie found it difficult to concede to anyone having a better idea than himself, particularly her. Maurice validated her in a way that Paudie rarely did.

Since discovering her wicked sense of humour, he seemed intent on making her laugh. Through the trade, he picked up jokes and funny stories and would regale her with the less salacious ones. Billy had had a great sense of humour and she was used to a house full of teasing and joking. Dubliners were known for their dry wit and she had encountered it as part of daily life. Since moving to the West, she found people to be softer, more gentle in their approach to one another and she missed the opportunity to have a good belly laugh, even if it was at someone else's expense. Life was serious in the shop with sick and anxious people, and others in pain. And she had to keep a level of propriety with the staff. Time with Maurice became a pleasurable relief.

With his practical approach, Maurice was reassuring when unforeseen problems arose and she felt grateful for that. Having to fire fight in all areas of her life when Paudie would flap around aimlessly, it was nice to rely on a capable man. Making sure to express her appreciation, he reciprocated by claiming she was his easiest and nicest client to work with….

A quick rap, followed by an even quicker opening of the door and Paudie strides in, frowning and looking concerned. He turns to close the door.

'Paudie! Are you okay? You seem under pressure.'

'Yes — no — I'm fine — It's you, I'm —,'

Naomi reopens the door and silently gathers the dirty crockery before leaving the door wide open on departure.

Paudie walks back to the door huffing, closes it firmly until the latch clicks. Looking grave, he sits down. 'Ruth, are you okay?' his eyebrow up.

'Yes, perfectly okay. Why, did you think I wouldn't be? What's up with you?'

Faltering, 'are — you sure? —You haven't been upset by anything while you've been here? — Nobody's done anything untoward —?'

With impatience, 'Paudie, what are you talking about?'

Paudie looks towards the door as if to check they are still alone. 'Listen, I've heard some shocking news. It's only a rumour, mind. But you know how there's generally a grain of truth — no smoke without fire etc, etc. I don't want to be guilty of casting aspersions, but — I'm not sure how —,'

'Paudie! For God's sake, will you just spit it out —please! The suspense is killing me!'

'Okay, okay — now you're quite sure nobody's done anything to upset you? You know? — anything inappropriate? Any doctors — done anything to you, you didn't like — anything like that?'

'Yes, Paudie, all the time,' folding her arms across her chest defensively.

'No, I don't mean your treatment, woman,' getting exasperated with her. 'Non-medical, I mean! You know — inappropriate —' his face twitching.

Finally realising what kind of behaviour he is hinting at, 'no!! Don't you think I'd have said? For Heaven's sake,

Paudie, will you just tell me what you're going on about! Please!'

'Okay, okay,' readjusting himself on the seat, 'I've just heard at the Golf Club —,'

Interrupting him, 'Golf Club? But you don't play golf, Paudie.'

'Yes, I know — but I do now — a bit anyway, just —,'

'Since when?' her antennae on alert.

'Just for the last week or two — but never mind that. Do you want to hear what I have to say, or not?' his eyebrow rising again.

Picking up the warning, 'sorry, I was just surprised about the golf, is all — no, please — do go on.'

'Your Doctor —you know — Doctor Mulhall — he's been suspended!'

'Nooo!! Why? Whatever for?'

'One of his female subordinates has made an allegation against him. Now it's all hush, hush, but the word's out, all the same.'

'Oh?' pausing, 'what kind of allegation?'

'The details are unclear at this stage, but it's something sexual, it's being said. Some kind of inappropriate behaviour — someone alleged "coercion"; one woman at the club suggested "misuse of power by a person in a position of authority". I don't know any more than that. Just that the "victim",' making imaginary speech marks. 'His target, if you like, has had to leave and work at another hospital. Now, are you sure you haven't been troubled by anything of that nature? You're very vulnerable here —'

Interrupting, 'and what do you know of the victim?'

'Oh, she's that doctor who used to come in and do your chemo — what's her name?'

'Dr Geraldine Geraghty.'

'Yes, that's the one....'

Later as he arranges to leave, 'oh, I nearly forgot with all the drama.' Reaching into his jacket pocket, 'here's your Filofax, Ruth.'

Paudie gone, she sits deep in thought. There had been something in her hunch about the two doctors, after all. She analyses the relationship between them. She has lived long enough in a white, patriarchal society to know how women get preyed upon. A young, intellectual and attractive woman will always present a challenge to a certain type of domineering male. It is not always about sexual attraction or lust. Often it is about power. Some internal drive in a man to control a woman. Reduce the threat she poses with her superiority of personality, looks and intelligence. It seems almost impossible for some men to resist reducing a woman to some level way below themselves. Is it about their own low self esteem, she wonders. Have they suffered at the hands of women as children, in some way — had emotionally neglectful mothers; subject to abusive female teachers; had sisters and girls around them who mocked their vulnerabilities? Or is Dr Mulhall just plain greedy. He probably has a wife who meets most of his needs, she guesses, but maybe he just wants some extra excitement on the side. Unable to come up with any more fanciful permutations, she tires of it. The diary catches her eye.

Flicking through the pages, she finds her personal details at the front. Medical appointments fill the diary section. The address and phone number part is largely a collection of local people with some more interesting ones from the Town Festivals. Thumbing back to the personal information sheet, she turns the page to finds her Visa card details; all the relevant numbers listed in the event of losing the card. An idea or two pop into her head. She will have some fun, she decides.

Her Friend is looking out of the window, 'Paudie's just come out of the mini-mart on the corner. I wonder how he's feeding himself these days?'

A surge of guilt balloons up inside her. During her entire stay in hospital, she has not considered how Paudie might be fending for himself, nor how he might be coping without her. Perhaps that is why he has been going to the golf club. The nineteenth hole there has a reputation for good bar food. She makes a mental note to enquire after his health.

Changing the subject, her Friend asks, 'what do you make of Paudie's news, Ruth?'

Her intuition had been correct.

There was something amiss between Dr Geraghty and Dr Mulhall, she just knew it. She could be jumping to conclusions as Paudie is a terrible gossip and quick to judge. For someone who is hardly faultless himself, she thinks him overly harsh towards others. Not that startling though, having being raised by the hypercritical Nora. Although now, of course, she realises where some of that came from. It seems to her that whenever people get hurt, they often deal with the pain by passing it on to others; the infliction of damage moving around in interconnected circles. Who knows what has been going on for Dr Mulhall? Maybe he is in love with Dr Geraghty? His unprofessional attention as her boss had been unwelcome and Dr Geraghty quite rightly took protective and corrective action. The big problem with love and sexual desire is when it is not mutual.

'That's an interesting take on the situation, Ruth. What about you — have you ever experienced unwelcome sexual attention or coercion? Have all your expressions of love been mutual ones?'

In answer to the last question, largely yes, apart from some unrequited crushes when she was younger which were painful enough to deal with at the time.

Regarding the first, thankfully no, she has never experienced any form of abuse or inappropriate behaviour beyond the usual catcalls and some rather lame, fairly harmless passes. Her affair with Paudie led to marriage and her flirtations with Maurice were only too welcome.

Once the old surgery was finished, her attraction towards Maurice in the absence of further contact remained a passing fancy. Then Paudie decided that the shop should be renovated.

He arranged that preliminary site meeting and instructed her to attend. She was determined to get what would suit her and the staff best. Paudie had denied her a home, but she was damned intent on getting a decent workplace out of him. Despite this clear focus, she found her mind wandering during the meeting. Watching Maurice lithely climb the step ladder, inspecting and measuring, she closely followed his movements. His slim muscular physique and absence of a paunch contrasted with Paudie who had lost firmness since giving up polo and partaking unreservedly of Carmel's baking. Working outside had given Maurice a suntan whereas Paudie was pasty from Sundays spent indoors with his parents. The dark skin tone accentuated the whiteness of Maurice's teeth and being a humorous sort, he flashed them often. Wishing to appear professional, Maurice had made an effort to wear clean, smart-casual clothing. He looked good in chinos and a checked shirt, and wore a new pair of modern boots. Paudie's Farah trousers and sweaters bought from local menswear shops that catered for elderly farmers seemed dated and ageing by comparison. And as for his shoes, they were old fashioned leather brogues, fastidiously polished every Sunday evening. Although Maurice was the older of the two men, she thought Paudie looked considerably older than him. Overall Maurice looked far more attractive. And sexy. She felt a tingling in her vulva that had not been initiated in a long time. Relieved that neither man could read her thoughts and without any sense of guilt, her mischievous side gained satisfaction from finding another man more desirable than Paudie. It assuaged some of her chronic resentment.

The two men conducted the meeting principally between themselves. But the subtle interplay between the three of them was interesting. Paudie clearly considered himself the client and therefore the most important person in the building. He showed little interest in her opinions, largely ignoring her comments. Maurice, as he had with Nora, brought her into the conversation to confirm Paudie's decisions. She liked that. Back then, building work was seen as a man's domain, particularly in commercial settings. A woman might have more say with home improvements, but as the man usually financed it, he would take charge. Maurice to her delight, seemed a more enlightened man.

When Maurice called around to Rath House later that day to look at the minor repairs, Paudie viewing them as insignificant, left her to deal with him while he went in to see his parents. Because Maurice had come straight from work, she made him soup and a sandwich, and provided some scones. While in the kitchen, she heard him talking to the children in the dining room. He asked about their toys and they responded eagerly to his interest. Afterwards when she showed him the broken items, Maurice joshed with Daithí about the window and with Sophie about the kitchen cupboard door. This further warmed her feelings towards him as she considered him a nice man with children. Paudie only showed a fleeting attention towards them.

Maurice walks through the sitting room to get to the front door and she jokes, 'I hope I haven't spoilt your appetite. Mrs Hennessy will be gunning for me over a ruined dinner.'

'There's no fear of that, Ruth,' his face suddenly serious. 'I'll be doing the cooking when I get back. Thanks for the food, anyway — I was well ready for it.'

Closing the front door, she marvels at how uplifted she feels. Later in bed with Paudie snoring next to her, she feels a twinge of guilt for fancying Maurice. But not so much to disturb her sleep….

Mary O comes into the room, 'just checking you're okay for the night, Ruth. Is there anything you need before you settle down? You're able to get yourself ready for bed, aren't you?'

'Oh hello, Mary — I didn't realise you did nights.'

'Yes, sometimes — not as much as days — we have less staff on at night so my turn for the night shift comes round less often. If you need anything, just use the buzzer.'

'Thanks, Mary. Hopefully I won't need you until morning.'

Climbing into bed, she takes the Filofax with her. Turning to the back cover, she unzips a pocket concealed there and looks inside. It is still there; untouched for years. She goes to pull it out, but changes her mind. Zipping up the pocket, she closes the diary and carefully places it on to her bedside locker. She clicks the light switch and snuggles down into bed.

The boots pounded down the hallway, much like her heart; he had arrived. The wait had seemed interminable. At last, she would see him. Yearning to touch him, to…

Footsteps and barely lowered voices in the corridor have broken into her dreams. Tossing about with irritability, she complains inwardly about night staff who should show more consideration. How is a sick person supposed to get better when their sleep is constantly disturbed? Awake, she is now aware that her bladder is full. Returning from the en-suite, her Friend has pulled a chair up to her bed and is waiting for her.

'Shall we return to the subject of Maurice? Are you too awake to sleep now?'

It is a bit late to check now he has put the idea into her head.

Comfortably back in bed, she allows herself to think about Maurice. When he was working on the shop, she got to see him most days, even Saturdays, as he prioritised their job. Despite this preferential treatment, Paudie huffed and puffed while ever the builders were in although in reality he was the least inconvenienced. Maurice and his men were well behaved and the female staff did not mind them being around. The workmen moved the stands and stock around for them; and set up temporary counters, all conducted with good humour. They soon learned to avoid Paudie's moods and came to her for direction with her acting as a buffer when Paudie was being unreasonable. A challenging, exhausting experience was made fun because of his Maurice's wisecracks. Acutely observant, he made candid observations about the shop team. But most of his attention was discreetly on her. He had an uncanny ability to pick up on any insecurity she had and ameliorate it. If she was too busy to get to the hairdressers, he would say that longer hair suited her. If she was premenstrual and feeling fat, he would say how nice she looked. If the children, including Paudie, had been driving her mad, he would say how difficult it must be for working mothers.

Yes, Maurice was a joy to have around, smiling as she drifts off to sleep.

Chapter 20

Perfect, the exact thing, as she taps on the screen. A new Dries Van Noten velour tracksuit from Brown Thomas with delivery promised for Monday. The website photo shows a soft blush pink with dark salmon coloured panels on the sides creating an illusion of slenderness. The range includes some matching T shirts and she decides to add them to the order. With only wearing night clothes all the time, she plans to don these new items during the day. She makes a mental note to get Deidre to bring in some bras for her. Wearing a bra will make her feel more human.

Her Friend seemingly bored with her shopping, strikes up conversation. 'What happened when the shop renovations came to an end — I mean, with Maurice in particular?'

Nothing much — he came back to do the snagging, but that was it. The next encounter was Gearóid's funeral. With no interaction in between, any feelings she may have had, had subsided in the meantime.

Then during the subsequent house viewing when she watched him talk animatedly about the potential of the house, she was reminded of qualities she found attractive in him; both physically and emotionally. Feeling some connection as they agreed on so many things, she classed him as a friend, and a supportive one at that.

As the negotiations between her and Paudie over buying the house dragged on, she began disclosing her frustrations to Maurice. She suspected that he and Maeve compared notes. Maurice's flexibility over the proposed works went beyond what was normal for a builder. This hinted that Maurice viewed her differently from other clients. But nothing overt was ever shared between them and all discussions were kept totally professional. She wondered if he did see her differently to his other clients from some of the nice things he said about her. But she thought it best and safest to assume he did not. Her self confidence, especially about her sexual allure, was not good at that time.

When Paudie finally agreed to buy the house, she was aching to tell Maurice.

She visits him on the quay, at an old warehouse that he is converting into apartments.

He welcomes her with a warm smile, quickly followed by a frown of concern and slides ear defenders down around his neck, 'Ruth, great to see you! Is everything okay?'

Ecstatically bursting out, 'he's said yes! Paudie has agreed to buying the house!' fighting an urge to throw her arms around him.

He holds her eye and remains rooted to the spot. Pauses for a long moment then offers, 'Congratulations! You must be delighted. It's been a long haul — but that's normal for around here.'

Not expecting his hesitation, she feels her elation subsiding.

'Come, look at what I'm working on,' he wants her to see the Show Apartment.

Walking into a minimalist styled kitchen, she is compelled to ask, 'Maurice, would you still be able to do the work on River House, or does it not suit you anymore? Are you too busy with this place?'

His eyes locking on to hers, 'I wouldn't pass it up for the world, girl.'…

A knock and the door is slowly pushed open by Sophie using her crutch. Hopping into the room, she heads for the vacant chair.

'… he sent me for an x-ray to make sure nothing's fractured. I'm just after coming from there now. Sorry I didn't bring anything. I went to Radiology straight from the surgery and I didn't have time to call into a shop. Plus it's hard carrying anything with these,' indicating the walking aids. 'If it comes back clear, but doesn't improve in a week or two, he wants to refer me to Orthopaedics.'

233

'That's so inconvenient for you, Sophie,' pulling a commiserating face.

'It's okay, Mammy — he's given me another week off work so I'm having an unexpected holiday,' baring her teeth into a smile.

'I hope you're resting, Sophie — giving that leg chance to heal.'

'Weeell, kind of — I discovered that I can sand, and paint skirtings if I lie straight alongside them on the floor.'

'Sophie! What if you have a fracture or something?'

Sophie changing the subject, 'in other news, I got the results for the second last module,' then faltering.

'And?', her mother prompting.

'I got another Distinction,' a serious expression on her face.

'Sophie, that's unreal! Well done!' throwing her hands up theatrically to compensate for her daughter's lack of enthusiasm. 'I always knew you took after me,' jesting to lighten the atmosphere.

'You always say I'm more like Daddy,' Sophie remarks quietly.

'Well, yes you are that too — you just have the best of both of us,' smiling back, resisting Sophie's flat mood.

'Mammy? Tell me! Do you love Daddy?'

Momentarily taken aback, she allows automatic pilot to take control, 'yes, Sophie, I do,' but needs more information, 'why do you ask, pet?'

Sophie rubs her thighs in anguish, 'it's just something I sense between you. I've been thinking about it a lot lately — while I've been laid up with this knee. You never seem happy with Daddy like the way I feel with Seánie. Do you wish you'd never married him?'

Taking a few moments to carefully formulate her words, 'Sophie, I was madly in love with your father when I married him — I had no doubts about him at all. But marriage needs a lot of working at — on both sides — especially when you have other demands like work, money worries, children. All those things have a major impact, you know.' Then adds quickly, 'but having you three was a wonderful blessing. Your arrival made us a unit. It brought out sides in your father and myself that I didn't know we had. Having children often pushes you into maturity and provides a sense of security even for the parents. Anyway thankfully, I'd say it did for your father and I.'

'Okay, I get all that. But having us three? Did that create a gap between you both? I mean, did we get in between you?'

'Sophie, why are you asking all these questions? Is there something bothering you?'

'It's nothing. I'm fine. Forget I said anything. Look, I have to go. I'll come and see you over the weekend sometime.'

'You only just got here! But look, I won't hold you up if you want to get going, darling.'

Sophie nodding and grasping the crutches, pulls herself into a standing position.

Reaching out her hand to Sophie, trying to connect with her, 'are you sure you're happy? Are you okay? Do you want to talk some more?'

Ignoring the hand, 'No, I really have to go,' then taking pity, 'but I will come back on Saturday.'

'Okay, my love. But come on your own again, please and we'll talk some more.'

Sophie looks quizzical, but declines to speak. She turns towards the door.

'By the way, watch out for a phone call or an email in about six weeks or so.'

Sophie, turns her head sideways to hear, but does not turn around, or ask why.

'That corner sofa set you plan to buy from Harvey Norman when you can afford to — it's on its way to you.'

Turning then, 'what do you mean, Mammy?'

'I ordered it for you. If it's the wrong one, let them know straight away and change the order. It's all paid for,' she smiles at her daughter.

After Sophie's departure, despite observing the interchange between them, her Friend does not comment on what has happened. Jumping into Sophie's seat, he is keen to get back to Maurice, 'what happened when Maurice worked on River House?'

235

It was an incredibly stimulating time.

Exhausting, yet it made her feel alive and that her life was taking a turn for the better with an imminent escape from Rath House. Watching the house transform into a home for the children, and herself, was such a positive experience. Paudie showed little interest despite her repeated attempts to engage him. Conversely, this gave her freedom to design the interiors and with Maurice's attitude of anything was possible, she felt uninhibited in her creativity.

Extracting agreement to expenditure from Paudie was the biggest challenge. With full access to their bank balances, she knew there was plenty of money available. But she needed a few contrivances during their heated negotiations. The additional expense, she argued, was a good investment because it would add value to the house. As remedial work, it would prevent further costly repairs. She posited it was in the best interests of the children to have a good quality living environment, pointing out that his own parents never stinted on spending on their family home. But the one that always hit a raw nerve then and even now, is when she describes Paudie as hard working and deserving of a prestigious house, one of a higher standard than others. Paudie has an inferiority complex when comparing himself to other professionals. He can never quite place himself at the same level as lawyers and doctors. Dare anyone suggest it, pharmacy is more — ahem — commerce. That one generally worked.

Maurice and his subcontractors were paid in cash for labour and she settled up directly with Cuddihy's builders' providers for materials. They were both committed to preserving as much of the original of the house as practicable. He requested daily site meetings for direction which she was more than happy to oblige. It gave her a good excuse to leave the shop and indulge in her new favourite passion of interior design. And of increasing significance, it was an opportunity to spend time, often alone, with Maurice.

On a site visit, only the plumber is in the house as Maurice has gone to Cuddihys. She wanders downstairs to the dining room to wait. Closing the door when the plumber starts drilling a wall, she starts working out the floor plan of the adjoining kitchen — sink under the window overlooking the garden; range cooker set into the chimney breast. Then she hears a noise that quickens her heart — the front door slamming and Maurice thumping down the bare boarded hallway.

Spinning around as he rattles the old brass knob of the dining room door, she composes her face. 'Hello, Maurice,' she greets him brightly.

'I'm glad you're here, Ruth — I need to show you some dry rot I discovered in the press under the stairs. I can treat it, but we need new stair parts. We'll not get them local. They're only available in salvage yards as nobody makes them quite the same anymore. You up for a trip to the Midlands?'

Her mind whirs, 'yes, I think I could get away from the shop,' she squeaks.

'It'll take a full day, mind — can you manage that?'

'Yes, I think so.'

She made damn sure to.

Early one morning a few days later, she climbs into the passenger side of Maurice's van full of giddy excitement. It feels like going on holiday. Maurice had warned her to not wear good clothes as it will be dirty work and his van will be dusty. But as they plan to call into places for lunch, she has dressed respectably in newish jeans, a striped Breton sweater from Pamela Scott and Dubarry deck shoes.

He remarks, 'you're looking well, Ruth.' He adds, 'those jeans make you look like a teenager.'

Does he say that kind of thing to every female client, she wonders. Laughing at his preposterous suggestion, she feels flattered all the same. She sits high up next to him enjoying the scenery. She cannot believe her festive mood. It is a rare treat to get away, even for only a day. Glancing at his muscular thighs, she has an urge to place her hand on the closest one, but restrains herself.

Arriving at a large village, Maurice suggests, 'let's call in somewhere for breakfast.'

Sitting in a plain looking cafe, they order coffee and breakfast rolls. While they wait, she asks something she has been wondering about for a while. 'Maurice, I hope you don't mind me asking, at the funeral you said Gearóid Hanley was like a father to you. Was he an old friend of yours?'

The server brings over the food and drinks on a tray.

Maurice rearranges the plates, passing the correct one over to her side. 'Yes he was both of those, friend and father figure. In fact, I would regard him as my saviour.' He pours a sachet of sugar into his coffee, deep in thought. Then looking up at her, 'I don't tell many people this, but as a lad, I was a bit of a gurrier. My father died when I was a youngster and that left my mother with five children to rear on her own,' taking a slurp. 'She tried her best for us — worked hard — picked up jobs where she could. But money and food were always short. When I went to Secondary School, I hated it. I had a stammer and The Brothers — the teachers — were hard on me about it. They said I wasn't trying enough to control it which only made it worse,' taking another sip. 'But I was hardy and they detected a defiance in me that they thought it their duty to break. One day, I decided I'd had enough of their beatings so I gave up school to help Ma out instead — be the man of the house, if you like.' Adding some more milk to the cup, 'much to my shame, and I'm not proud admitting it, I turned to thieving — mainly from houses as it was so easy. Everyone kept their houses unlocked back then, so it was too easy getting in to look for cash stashed away. People didn't use banks, so it was very rewarding' Taking a bite out of his roll, chewing and swallowing, 'I'd have been around twelve when I chanced across Gearóid. I didn't know him as he lived in the posh end of town. When nobody answered the front door, I thought it safe to go round the back — that was how I normally operated. The rear door, as usual, was unlocked. So I goes into the larder, as he always called it, to pilfer through any tea pots, storage jars — places where people usually hid cash,' tearing another mouthful. 'Then absolute disaster, Gearóid comes down into the kitchen and catches me rotten. He demanded to know my name. Like a lot of people who stutter, I couldn't say words beginning with the first letter of my own name,' biting into the food. 'As I tried, and failed, Gearóid stopped me. He ordered me do some breathing exercises with him. I was so young, I just did as I was told,' a final mouthful. 'When I'd calmed down, he began talking to me like I was a person, not the obnoxious miscreant I was. He put it to me that he wouldn't report me to the Gards if I came to him for the next eight Sundays to have voice lessons. He threatened to report me if I didn't turn up every time. As you probably know, Gearóid was involved in dramatics and wrote and directed plays — he understood all about articulation.' Picking up fallen pieces of bread from the plate, 'anyway, for the next eight Sundays, he had me doing breathing exercises and got me to read lines from plays. My reading wasn't so good, so he worked on that too. I got to enjoy going there so much that the eight Sundays just ran on and on. I ended up going every week until I was 16. He'd get me to read loud whatever he'd written that week so that he could hear how it sounded. It could be poetry, prose, a new play — Gearóid introduced me to the world of literature. He basically completed my education and I owe him so much.'…

Jimmy pushes the door open with the trolley, 'how'ya, missus — em — Ruth? I've a nice bit of fried fish for ya and some of that martyr sauce — and — er — something — with custard. Will you have a glass of water? That jug's empty — give me two secs while I get more for ya….

…now, here's a clean jug instead of that mouldy auld yoke. Have you some minerals, hon?'

'You're very good, Jimmy. No, plain water's grand. No Tilly today?'

'She's a bit of a throat. I told her to stay home — mind herself and not spread it about.'

'I'm sorry to hear that. She has a beautiful voice — I heard her singing. Yes, she should mind herself. Please give her my regards and tell her I was asking after her when you go home.'

'I will of course, M — Ruth, thank you. I'll bring ya some tea later,' pushing his trolley back out.

Opening the sachet of tartare sauce and squeezing it onto the plate next to the breaded fillet reminds her of the pub lunch she had with Maurice that day.

He orders fish and chips and she requests the daily roast which is beef. The server brings a ramekin of condiments and one with tartare sauce for the fish.

Going back to their earlier conversation, 'you've no trace of a stammer now, Maurice. No one would ever know.'

'No, I know — thank you for saying so. That's down to Gearóid's skill and him building up my confidence especially in public speaking.'

'Do you still read?'

'Yes, I love it when I've the time — anything and everything. Fiction, nonfiction, plays and particularly poetry. Gearóid introduced me to that too — the old classics, Irish and modern poets. My favourite at the moment is Brian Docherty.'

'Brian Docherty? Never heard of him — but then I don't read poetry,' laughing.

'Brian's a Scotsman who has a doctorate in Irish poetry, and lives in England.'

'Umm — that sounds? What? I don't know really,' flummoxed at finding the appropriate adjective.

'Cool, Ruth — that's the word you're looking for — cool,' laughing with her.

Yes, it had been cool and she allows her memories to flood back, delicious ones she has suppressed for years….

Jimmy comes back in with the tea trolley, 'I'm to give you this — it's from Herself and you're not to tell anyone, mind,' passing her something hidden by the back of his hand. 'Eat it with your tea now, missus.' Scooping the dirty dishes, 'I'll take that now you're finished. You've a great appetite, I'll say that much, hon,' and hurries out.

Opening a foil covered parcel, she finds a thick slice of what she surmises to be homemade chocolate biscuit cake. Sending silent thanks to Tilly, she savours every mouthful, picking up every last crumb with a moistened finger. Scrunching up the wrapping and disposing of the evidence in the bin, she turns back to her Friend seated in the other chair.

'How did the rest of the day out with Maurice go?' inviting her to continue.

The reclamation yard turned out to be simply fascinating.
Somewhere she had never been to before, but wished she had.

It is a huge warehouse and vast yard crammed with quirky
architectural items. They rummage together for hours.
Eventually they find the right staircase components with the
correct details and collect some period doors to match the
originals in the house for the attic conversion. She likes the
look of some pieces of carved stone thinking they will provide
interest in the garden for when she gets around to it.

'What's that you've found, Maurice?' watching him connect
together some long black metal parts.

'It's an old system for suspending cooking pots over a fire.
I've been looking out for one in good condition for ages.
They're usually eaten through with rust — but this one's the
job.'

By the time they load up the van, it is late afternoon. On the
journey home, she is curious to hear the rest of Maurice's
story.

'You said you used to visit Gearóid until you were sixteen.
What happened then?'

'Part of Gearóid's rehab plan for me was to get me back
into school and he took it upon himself to intercede for me
with the Brothers. They all respected him so they became
encouraging rather than destructive. I went on to sit my Inter
Cert and did surprisingly well, all down to Gearóid of course.
But despite Gearóid and the school begging me to stay on to
do my Leaving Cert, there was no way I was going to remain a
day longer than I had to. All I wanted was to earn money. I'd
given up the burglary on meeting Gearóid, but Ma had still
needed help. So I worked Saturdays and evenings filling
petrol, doing my study between customers. But going full time
at the petrol pump was never going to pay enough. I'd shown
an aptitude for woodwork at school and I'd thought about
becoming a carpenter or a joiner.' Turning on to a main road,
'Gearóid and Maeve's sister, Róisín, was a nurse over in
London and had recently married a surveyor. They'd just taken
on a house with a huge mortgage so it was arranged for me to

move in with them as a lodger. Róisín's husband, Andy, helped me get an apprenticeship with one of the big building contractors he worked with.' Overtaking a slow moving tractor, 'their house was a kip and I helped them renovate it. The firm I worked for had high standards and we had a lot of top quality, prestigious jobs. Between the foremen at work and Andy's technical knowledge, I learnt a massive amount. With nixers at the weekends and evenings, I was able to send money home to Ma and save up enough to buy a wreck of my own. When I did that one up, I sold it on for a good profit and moved onto a bigger one — then another — and that's how I went on.'

'What brought you back home to Ireland?'

'I loved London and I got a lot out of living there. But I'm a country boy at heart. I sold up, made a killing on my last London house with enough to buy a site, build a house and set up business back here. Money was coming into the country from the EC and I was set up ready for the beginning of The Boom.'

'How did Nora get to hear about you?'

Laughing, 'Nora had steadily worked her way through the local lads and had fallen out with all of them. I think she had no other choice when she asked me. I repaired the veranda and the stairs down to the garden. Happy enough with that, she allowed me inside to do a whole rake of other jobs. Over the years working, I'd learnt manners and I think she liked my approach. And I'm clean and tidy in my work. I'm used to working with clients with big luxury houses and I know how to behave in other people's homes. I show some respect for other people's property. Funny thing is, I often find that the clients who have the most money or the highest status, are the easiest and most pleasant to work with.'

Joking with him, 'good Lord, I must be terrible to work with then, as I only have modest money and certainly no status,' laughing depreciatively.

With sincerity, 'no, Ruth, I wouldn't say that at all — you're a delight to work with. And to be around too.'

Feeling bashful, she turns to look out of the window, not sure how to respond….

Noticing the time on the wall clock, she remembers something pressing.

Picking up her mobile, '… you've set a date, Ben? That's great! Listen, the reason I'm ringing you, apart from wanting to know how you are of course, is to ask if you and Daithí have bought the wedding outfits yet? — No? — that's great — right, as mother of the groom, would you please allow me the honour of paying for them both? — Yes, you've got that right. And shoes too — Thank you, Benjamin. I really appreciate that — Let me know how much and your bank details, and I'll transfer the money straight over. No, on second thoughts, text me on your details via WhatsApp today and I'll send over some money, and you can spend it how you wish.'

Her Friend smiles and nods his approval. 'What were Maurice's personal circumstances at the time? Did he ever disclose them to you?'

As they near home, Maurice asks her, 'are you in a rush to get back? Would you like to call in and get some dinner at Kinsella's?'

Having relished the day so much, she is in no hurry to end it and readily agrees. Still sated by the heavy meal earlier, she opts for a light seafood salad. Maurice orders a bacon cheese burger with yet more chips. Marvelling at how men can get away with eating so many carbs, she decides to go mad and order a dessert too. The day has been a treat after all; she may as well have the whole hog while she's on the pig's back.

With laser like curiosity, 'Em — Maurice, do you have a family?'

'No, Gwen and I haven't been that fortunate,' taking a bite from his burger.

'Gwen? That's a lovely name — unusual.'

Swallowing, 'it's Welsh — Gwen's from Wales.'

'Wales? So — em, did you go to Wales?'

Shaking his head, chewing another mouthful, 'in London, I met her in London. How's your salad? Is it nice?'

Nodding, 'so —?'

'What the holy bejaysus? Maurice? It IS you. I thought I saw you across the bar,' a red faced man with a girth looking like a giant pillow squeezed in the middle by a leather belt, stands at the end of the table. Addressing Maurice, but staring at her, 'Maurice, I'm glad I seen you — that estimate you sent me a while back, I'd —,' then to her directly, 'don't I know you?'

Used to being recognised, she answers nonchalantly, 'O'Sullivan's Pharmacy,' accepting there is little chance of anonymity.

Maurice interjecting, 'Cathal, Mrs O'Sullivan is a client of mine. We're having a planning meeting over a bite to eat. There're still a number of items I need to go over with Mrs O'Sullivan before we finish up. Can I get back to you tomorrow?'

The man grunts a reluctant assent and sidles away.

'Nosy fucker — he's no intention paying for any work. I know his type — sussed him out from the start. Time wasting messer. Now he's just wanting to see something that's none of his business and spread malicious gossip,' Maurice scowling.

Not knowing how to get Maurice back on to the subject of his wife without seeming nosy herself, she considers the moment lost. Maurice never makes any reference to his home life and she is not sure if it is because he is a private person, or whether it is a difficult subject best avoided. Occasionally when she fancies her chances with him, she thinks he might be in self-denial about being attached. Then she tells herself to be realistic; however much her fondness for him has grown, there is nothing to be done about it.

When the van parks up outside Rath House, her mood nose dives. Sad that her day with Maurice has ended, she feels apprehensive about being with Paudie too. After Maurice's disclosures, she understands him better and feels some intimacy has developed between them. Admiring what she has heard, she likes him all the more....

A light knock on the door foretells Reverend Barbara's arrival, 'Ruth, I'm glad I haven't woken you up this time. Would it be agreeable to sit with you for a while?'

After sharing Holy Communion, she asks, 'Ruth, tell me, how do you feel your treatment is going? Only if you would like to talk about it, of course.'

'To be truthful, Barbara, way beyond my wildest expectations — when I first came into hospital, I thought it was for palliative care — you know — to see me to my end. But now —,' smiling joyfully, 'I feel so well — almost back to my normal self. I have real hope of walking out of here. I don't know if the treatment will be permanent, but it would be lovely to have a few more years. Be there for Deidre — meet my first grandchild — hold him or her. I was so glad to have my mother around when I had my first when its all strange and scary. I'd love to see Daithí settled — get his US citizenship — produce his film successfully. And as for my other daughter — I just feel she needs me around a bit longer — help her grow up some more.'

'Yes, I have to agree — I've noticed big improvements in you too. God willing, let us pray with hope that all of those things will happen for you and your family, Ruth.'

'Barbara, you say: God willing. It's something I hear people often say. Do you really think it is up to God if we live or die?'

'I do, Ruth — yes, I really do. It's the Holy Spirit that gives us life, and it's the Holy Spirit that takes it away.'

'The Holy Spirit? Where does God fit in with that? I've never really understood that one.'

'Ah, yes — a difficult concept to comprehend, indeed. All about The Holy Trinity, Ruth — God comprises God the Father, God the Son and God the Holy Spirit. Different Christian theologians have different definitions — different explanations about what it means. Remember St Patrick, he used a three leaf clover to try and explain it. For me personally, I don't think that the human brain has the capacity to fully understand. It's like when my scientist son tries to explain the latest research in Quantum Physics to me. I think my brain's going to explode trying to make sense of the contradictions scientists observe.'

'What about people taking control of life and death, though? People who kill others — people who take their own lives? Surely that's them and not some other-worldly power doing it?'

'People don't always succeed in trying to kill themselves. People don't always die after acts of violence — sometimes other events intervene. But I do take your point.

Again personally for me, I believe that God is Light, a good force. But with light, there is an opposite, an absence of light or darkness. And darkness can take different forms and there is evil.'

'What happens when we die?'

'I believe that we are more than just a bunch of cleverly grouped cells. We contain a soul, a spiritual aspect, as well as a physical one. Our collection of body cells will inevitably expire in some fatal event and return to the Earth. Yet our souls cannot die as they have no physical presence.'

'And that's when our souls go to Heaven? But what exactly is that?'

'For me, Heaven is where God exists — His residence if you like. So for me, dying will be like going home to His place. But as I think I've said before, He's also with us, always and everywhere while we're here on Earth. It's that concept of an all encompassing powerful entity that we struggle to comprehend.'

'It's a lot to take in,' sighing. 'Like you with your son, my brain is hurting trying to think about it. Thank you for your wise thoughts and explanations, Barbara.'

Chapter 21

'Are you feeling up to some more reflection after Barbara's visit' her Friend enquires.

Go on so.

Her Friend looks pleased, 'did your relationship with Maurice deepen at all during the restoration of River House?'

No, nothing beyond a friendship — a mutual liking and respect.
Maurice remained completely professional and nothing beyond that was made available, whether she would have welcomed it or not. In reality, the pleasure of seeing the house take shape and being creative ameliorated tensions in her marriage. After she moved in, Maurice had to finished the project. But with Paudie and the children around, there was little more than building talk between them. Handing over the final payment, she felt sad to see him go and he said she must never hesitate to contact him. After that, life moved on.
The next time she saw him was when she was signed off work by the GP. Having the opportunity to catch up with neglected chores, she contacted him. Paudie was never one to do DIY so there was a list of small jobs to do. She rang Maurice the first weekend of her sick leave and he promised to call around early Monday morning.

Maurice arrives at the gate and lets Paudie out first, who mutters a clipped greeting as he passes. Maurice walks up the path smiling broadly at Ruth who is standing at the open door, 'it's good to see you again, Ruth,' studying her face. 'How have you been?'
Feeling emotionally distant from him, she answers with an anodyne response.

She spends the day popping in and out of the rooms he works in bringing food and drinks to him. Her initial reserve dissipates quickly as Maurice jokes and banters with her. Laughter comes easily as though they have only seen each other the day before. In the interregnum when they had journeyed separately, she had jettisoned any feelings of attraction allowing them to cool in her wake. But seeing him now, and his warm interest in her, recaptures them.

Maurice has not completed the tasks by the time Paudie comes home. Gathering his tools, 'I want to bring some different drill bits and specialist fixings for the jobs I haven't finished. Will I call back in the morning, Ruth?'

The next day he is finished by mid morning and asks how the garden is coming along. Taking him outside, she demonstrates how the planting complements his landscaping. She outlines her future plans.

'Ruth, you always did have great ideas. I've never known anyone with such an ability to visualise. That's one of the biggest problems I have with clients — getting them to understand what I am proposing — getting them to imagine what it will look like when I've finished. That's why they often change their minds in the middle of a project which makes my life difficult. Are you doing anything nice for the rest of the day?'

'No, nothing in particular — I wasn't sure how long you'd need so I haven't booked anything for after lunch. I might go to that new garden centre and see what they have in.'

'Instead of that, what would you think to a spin out with me? There's somewhere I'd like to show you. We could pick up some lunch from a shop on the way, if you like.'

Jumping at the chance to do something spontaneous, she grabs a Jack Murphy jacket in case of rain and puts on comfortable walking shoes as advised by Maurice.

Driving south along the coast road, Maurice asks about each of the children; enquires after her parents; questions how the shop is faring and then gently probes the circumstances of her sick leave. It is nice having someone show interest in her and her life; a rare occurrence. After about 40 minutes, they turn off the main road into a minor one heading towards the sea. Partway along, they drive off on to a rough farm track. Traversing fields dotted with grazing sheep, Maurice pulls up alongside a small cottage hidden by a hedge of native trees.

Inviting her to get out of the van, he escorts her to the entrance of a whitewashed building, unlocks the red painted door and pushes it open.

'You go on in, Ruth — I'll get the food from the van.'

Entering a long vaulted almost ecclesiastical porch, she opens a waxed wooden door at the end and finds a large living room. To the right is an inglenook fireplace with cut turf stacked ready for burning. Strong sunlight from two windows illuminates the wall to her left which is entirely covered, floor to ceiling with groaning book shelves. In the centre of the room is a table with dining chairs and beyond these, two more internal doors. Two Art Deco leather club armchairs sit by the fire and a vintage floral sofa with a standard reading lamp positioned overhead stands adjacent to the book lined wall. The stone flagged floor is almost entirely carpeted with richly coloured Kilim rugs in a variety of traditional and muted coloured patterns.

Walking over to the books, she plucks one at random. Written in fountain pen on the first page is the name, Gearóid Hanley. Another book selected has the same, and the next.

'You're interested in my book collection, Ruth,' Maurice placing food items on the table.

'Are these all Gearóid's books?'

'Yep, most of them — Maeve gave me first refusal when I helped clear the house. I ended up keeping all of them. Many of them are ones that Gearóid used to help me with my studies and I couldn't bear parting with them. There's some real gems — he acquired some valuable editions over the years. He was always combing the charity and second hand bookshops. I had to extend the shelving to accommodate them all.'

Wandering over to the fireplace, she recognises a metal contraption with an old, cast iron cooking cauldron hanging from it. 'Hey, Maurice, that's the thing you bought at the reclamation yard!'

'Well spotted, Ruth,' laughing, 'of course you'd remember. Go on through the doors. You can take a look at the rest of the place.'

Incurably inquisitive about other people's houses, she needs no further prompting. One door leads into a small kitchen with a copper sink and blue gingham curtaining hiding the shelves beneath. The room is fitted out with an eclectic mix of cupboards and open shelving made from recycled timber. On one side there is a bright blue vintage larder dresser, very like the one she had in the Stoneybatter house. At the top are the same sliding doors in reeded glass with white plastic finger inserts. Pulling down the drop leaf, she finds a work surface covered in Formica. Inside is a selection of earthenware storage jars. Maurice clearly has the same magpie tendencies as herself.

Turning a noisy brass knob on the other door, she finds a bedroom with a double bed.

She notices something familiar, 'em — Maurice? — that bedding?' calling back into the main room.

Looking mildly uncomfortable, he joins her, 'yeah, I confess — that IS your old stuff. It was too good to throw away, Ruth — and I needed some,' grinning, suggestive of the mischievous boy he must have once been.

Buying new bedlinen for the super king sized bed in the attic, she had no use for the duvet covers and sheets from the old double bed at Nora's. She had offered them to Maurice to use as rags. Maurice reusing them for his own bed did not offend her. She was pleased that they have been recycled as they were in good condition; but of more significance was that they were now an intimate part of Maurice's life....

The door opens, shooing away her thoughts. She is glad that it is the porter, 'Jimmy, tell Tilly her baking was delicious and most welcome. But she's not to go to that trouble again.'

Jimmy laughing, 'you may tell the birds to stop flying, miss. Here's some fry. I like a fry on a Friday evening, meself,'

Jimmy puts down a plate holding one thin rasher medallion, a cocktail sausage and a single slice of black pudding. 'Oh, and you get a yogurt for after,' plonking a tub and teaspoon next to the plate. 'I'll be seeing you next week, God willing,' and rushes off.

Seconds later, Jimmy runs back in, 'your drink! I forgot your drink. Here, you get this orange juice with your fry. Like a Full Irish hotel breakfast, isn't it?' departing before she can agree.

She thinks how nice it is to have a fry and tackles the food with relish. In no time she has the small meal polished off. She wheels the table away towards the door to make collecting the plates easier.

Her Friend comes to sit in the other chair. With a twinkle in his eye, 'I can see you enjoyed that. So tell me, what was that place?'

It was Maurice's bolthole.

A derelict farm or smallholding that he had come across with about ten acres of land. He had bought it as an investment property with the intention of restoring and selling it on. Coming to appreciate its charm, he decided to keep it for himself and it became his private sanctuary.

During the visit, she is eager to know more, 'is this your house? Where you and Gwen live? Is she at work?'

'Yes, no and no — I own it, but Gwen doesn't come here. Our house is in Toormore. Gwen isn't able to work,' setting their lunch out on the table. 'Will you have tea or coffee? If you're feeling adventurous, I've a set with Earl Grey, Assam, Peppermint and Lemon and Ginger teas — that one's good for sore throats especially if you put in a teaspoon of honey. Or I can grind some coffee beans — I've some premium Ethiopian Arabica. I used to have a client who was a coffee importer and he said that was the best.'

After lunch, they walk over his land down to a cove only accessible by hiking across the fields. It is a typically breezy day with strong westerly winds pushing back the hair from her invigorated face.

'I love it down here!' shouting to her over the noise of shingle being shoved up and down the beach by big surfs.

She moves closer to him so he can hear her softer voice, 'I can understand why. It'd be great to sketch or paint those low cliffs receding into the distance. The large, open skies you can see in all directions and the changing moods of the water. Those wild flowers in close up — look at that pink sea thrift and the yellow vetches — and the white Queen Anne's Lace over there —,' pointing.

Maurice moves in closer still. Stopping her in mid flow, he pulls her into his arms and kisses her mouth with lips slightly parted. Unable to stop herself, she kisses him back and relaxes into his arms. And they kiss and kiss. Clinging on to one another as though each is a life raft for the other. She is lost at sea, perhaps in peril. Carried by strong currents through the riptides of life, she is caught in an eddy that swirls her around and around; in danger of drowning in circumstance.

Disengaging, Maurice takes her hand and leads her back to the air dried grass fringing the beach. Sinking down, he drags her with him. She hears the sheep bleating as he runs his hands over her clothing, feeling the fleshy contours of her body beneath. And her body, now reawaken, responds. A waft of bruised, lemon perfumed, maritime thyme mingles with Maurice's seductive scent, an odour so subliminally familiar, her body opens up like an orchid attracting a pollinating bee.

Stopping abruptly, Maurice pulls her to her feet, 'please forgive me, Ruth, I shouldn't have done that — I don't know what came over me. I apologise. I'd better take you home before I do anything else mad. Come on, we'll go lock up the cottage.'

Walking back in silence, she is aware of the enormity of what happened, but has little time to process it before reaching the door. Entering the cottage to collect her coat, she feels an overwhelming reluctance to return home. Maurice follows her in to collect the milk. Now it is her turn to take his hand and she leads him into the bedroom where the soft cotton bedding beckons….

The door swings open and Deidre enters, laden with several paper shopping bags in each hand.

'Deidre! Are you sure you should be carrying those?'

'Mammy, how are you? I couldn't resist — I had to bring them in to show you,' putting the bags down and coming over to kiss her.

Deidre wastes no time in pulling item after item from the bags.

'…and this top, I got this one from Penneys — it'll fit better after the baby's born. I'm going to have to forget about slim fit blouses with buttons for now — I'm just busting out of them.' Giggling, 'did you hear what I said? — busting out — I sure am, Mammy. I've never had such large boobies in my life,' laughing at her own joke. 'And I just couldn't leave these behind — aren't they so cute?!' holding up a pack of newborn sleep suits.

'I can't wait to go shopping with you, Dee Dee — they're going to be the most spoilt grandchild ever.'

'And these heels — I've been looking for some like these at a price I can afford, for ages.'

'You won't be able to wear them for much longer — but once baby's born —'

Paudie appears in the open doorway, 'girls! Some load of noise you're making — I could hear you both as soon as I walked into the ward. Are you having a party? Can I join in?' The phone rings in his jacket pocket, 'sorry, ladies, I'll just step out again — I have to take this call.'

How she loves spending time with her daughter, she thinks, as Deidre talks excitedly about the baby's new bedroom. Deidre takes out her phone to show her decorating ideas she has found on different websites.

Paudie reenters the room and she asks, 'was it a call out — have you to go back to the dispensary, Paudie?'

'No, nothing like that, Ruth. I've sorted it all out.'

'Sorted what out?'

Paudie changing the subject, 'now, Deidre, how are you getting on? Any problems?'

'No, I'm all good, thank you,' a little tersely. Then excitedly, 'guess what? Mammy's an absolute legend! She's after ordering me a Bugaboo Fox travel system for the baby. I can't believe it! Marcus and I would never be able to afford that!'

'Really?', Paudie's eyebrow lifting, 'by travel system, do you mean a pram, by any chance?'

'Dee Dee,' she interrupts, recognising the expression on Paudie's face, 'if you and Marcus are short on nursery furniture or any equipment, anything, just let us know. Daddy and I would be delighted to help you,' looking over at Paudie's dropping face. 'We struggled when you were small so we know what it's like. But we're in a much better position now.' Savouring Paudie's discomfort, 'we will, won't we, Paudie, dear?' giving him a feline smile.

'Harrumph — come on, let's leave your mother in peace now. I'll carry those bags to the car for you, Deidre. I have to get going' Paudie walks over to kiss her goodbye.

'Paudie, that was a short visit. Do you have to go so soon?'

He pauses to think, then, 'yes, there's something I think I forgot to put away in the fridge in the dispensary. I need to run over and check if I did.'

She looks at him not sure she believes him, but lets it drop, 'while I remember, there are going to be some parcels delivered to the shop on Monday. Will you bring them in when you visit, please?'

'What?! More spending?! I thought I was safe with you being tucked up in here.'

Tutting, 'for Heaven's sake, Paudie — money's for enjoying — you can't take it with you, you know,' rolling her eyes at Deidre.

After they leave, she continues with her new routine of demarcating day from night by changing into fresh pyjamas. After her evening wash, she climbs into bed and turns the bedside light off. Although she does not feel particularly sleepy, she knows the hospital day will start early. She muses about the Prednisolone keeping her awake which is a nuisance, but marvels at how it is doing wonders for her general health. Everyone has commented on it. One unwelcome side effect though is weight gain and she is anxious she has gained too much. She hopes she will not look like a little pudding in her new tracksuit. Still she reasons, that would be a very small price to pay for good health.

Her Friend stands in the shadows, 'Ruth, tell me, did you go on to have an affair with Maurice?'

To her shame, she had.

At the time, she was unable to restrain herself. Neither the willingness nor the willpower was there. Also there was opportunity. During her fortnight off work sick, she met up with Maurice at the cottage most days. Alone together, they talked, shared meals and made love with the frequency and fervency of a long gone youth. When she returned to work, Irina's arrival into the household freed up more time and energy. Her refreshed personal resources were then diverted towards Maurice.

Looking back, the children were really good kids — they gave Paudie and her few problems. As Irina continued to keep an eye on them, it was a responsibility shared. She was able to relax about them and the house; and could focus on her own needs for once.

Thinking about Irina, she remembers how efficient, energetic and emotionally supportive she was. Never missing any occasion when Paudie was either bombastic, or thoughtless, Irina's body language indicated her contempt for him. But Irina was careful to conceal it from him, keeping her sour facial expressions out of his eyeshot. Getting to know her over the years, Irina disclosed some difficult experiences with men. She fell pregnant with Ingrida when she was sixteen and the father abandoned her and the baby. Marrying another man soon after delivering her child, her husband turned out to be verbally aggressive and physically violent towards her, and unkind to Ingrida. He left them behind in Poland when he decided to relocate to the UK and never arranged for them to join him. Irina considered it a welcome release and one that eventually allowed her to follow Ingrida and Marius to Ireland. Irina loyally took her side even when she knew she had been in the wrong. Whenever she was bad-tempered with Paudie, or impatient with the children, Irina always soothed her afterwards and affirmed her actions. She could rely on Irina interceding with the children on her behalf. But never with Paudie — Paudie would be cold shouldered and made to feel a complete reprobate.

But back to the question, when she took on the weekend care of Vera, that left a whole Sunday free on alternate weeks. Meeting up with Maurice during those days was her special treat; a kind of reward for all her hard work and heavy responsibilities. It was a time she lived for during the rest of the fortnight. Daydreaming about Maurice distracted her from her unhappiness.

Maurice's cottage provided a safe venue where they would not be discovered. But it became more than just somewhere to have sex, although their lovemaking was blissful. When visiting, she became the woman she truly felt herself to be. She took up sketching and painting again; the deep emotions unleashed pushed her to a new level of expression. On wet days, Maurice introduced her to books and read poems to her in his husky, velvet toned voice. He had an extensive knowledge of music and a large collection of CDs, playing genres of music to her that she would never have tried without being coaxed. With plenty of life experience and being widely read, he proved to be a deeper thinker than she had credited him for. He had a way of making her consider topics and issues that she had never given much thought to. Comparing Maurice with Paudie, Paudie seemed poorly educated, although in reality he was the opposite. It occurred to her that Paudie was lazy minded whereas Maurice inspired and excited her, stretching her intellect. Life with Paudie had been under-stimulating; plain boring to put it candidly.

Regarding her emotional needs, Maurice acted like a good best friend consistently displaying empathy and a high emotional IQ. He never took her for granted, nor seemed to lose respect for her simply because he had won her over. With Paudie, she often felt he needed a good shaking to see the obvious and considered him emotionally needy, tending towards self-centredness. Maurice, in comparison, was more mature, selfless and generous in spirit. It was like Maurice had a female psyche within a male body.

Physically, she had not felt as sexually gratified since the early days with Paudie. Maurice was sexually experienced and took care to understand her body. He appeared to get as much enjoyment out of pleasing her sexually as she did herself; all ways Paudie had once been, but no longer bothered with. It was like releasing a bottleneck of sexual affection — physical actions of love she had withheld from Paudie, and was now willingly offering to Maurice. But as is life, there was a downside to this self indulgence: the burden of guilt; they were both married people. As they became more intimate, Maurice slowly divulged details about his marriage to Gwen.

Gwen was the PA for one of the clients he worked for in London. Stunning in looks, he described how all the workmen drooled whenever she was around. Outside of work, she performed as a singer, mainly in casual venues like pubs and clubs. She had a musical partner, Iestyn, who played keyboard and guitar. Iestyn was Gay, and their relationship was amicably professional. Not only beautiful, Gwen was savvy and well able to handle attention from men, but Iestyn acted as her minder, dealing with any drunks chancing their arm with her. Maurice admitted to stealthily and carefully courting her until she succumbed to him.

Gwen and Maurice had much in common. They both loved live music, theatre and visiting cultural buildings like galleries and museums. They quickly fell in love; agreed to co-habit for a while and then confirmed their commitment by marrying quietly at the local Registry Office. Gwen was born and raised in Swansea, and although she appreciated the countryside, was very happy living over in London, enjoying the city lifestyle. Maurice though, had only seen his time in England as something temporary — a place to learn a trade and make better money than in Ireland. He became increasingly unsettled, wanting deeply to return home. Gwen however, was reluctant and unsure about relocating to Ireland. She had visited, but never loved the place like other people seemed to. But she finally agreed for Maurice's sake. Maurice confessed to convincing Gwen that it would be a better environment to raise a family, and that their money would stretch further, providing them with a better standard of living.

In hindsight, Maurice realised it was wrong to have manipulated her. Gwen sank into a depression shortly after they moved over and never recovered. Despite strong medication, Gwen merely existed rather than lived. Unable to work because of her mental health disabilities, and having lost all interest in music and singing, she spent her days watching UK television via satellite as though in need of reliving a familiar existence. Maurice ran the household, including cooking the meals and doing the housework as Gwen had no motivation to do so. Additionally, Gwen was emotionally withdrawn, unable to engage with Maurice on any personal level. She refused to go with him to the cottage as she preferred the known security of her own home. Maurice believed that some of Gwen's depression had come from grief over their childlessness. Fertility tests had revealed Maurice's infecundity possibly from a bout of mumps as a child. He had recollections of swollen testicles along with a painful jaw when he had been a toddler.

Piecing Maurice's story together with its paucity of marital fulfilment, her heart went out to him. It seemed paradoxical that Maurice with all his wonderful qualities should be married to a woman inured from appreciating them….

We were the only people truly awake,
our love an energy field to sustain us,
and we agreed the number of stars
was always one less than infinity.

It is inevitable she should remember those Brian Docherty lines — all those memories of Maurice pushed to the forefront of her sleep scape.

'Good morning, Ruth,' Nurse Nóirín wheels a blood pressure monitor up to her. The nurse goes through her check list of tests then takes the opportunity to bring bad news. The ward is full, but there is a prospective patient needing to be admitted. For medical reasons, they need a room alone. 'As a result, we may have to move you out of here and put you in one of the six bed bays. We'll see what happens — the new patient might be admitted over the weekend, or it might not happen until early next week. I just wanted to give you prior warning so you can get prepared.'

Keeping her disappointment hidden, she mumbles agreeable comments about understanding the staff's position on this. When the nurse leaves, she lets out a big sigh. This is something she has not anticipated. The privacy and exclusive use of a single room with an en-suite has made her stay in hospital somewhat bearable. Private health cover in Ireland does not always ensure private accommodation; it depends on availability and she knows this. While she grapples with her anxiety and discombobulation, her Friend makes a gesture catching her eye.

He does not seem to think it important enough to discuss and wants to return to their previous conversation. 'Before you fell back asleep last night, you were remembering feeling guilty about you and Maurice.'

Indeed — that was one of the worse aspects to it.

The other was the insatiable yearning for him between their assignations — that was hard to contain. They agreed to have no communication between trysts as it was too risky. Maurice gave her a key to the cottage with the ongoing promise of meeting up on her free Sundays. As the affair progressed, she knew deep down that the situation was unsustainable. Suspended between two existences, she was not fully committed to either. Unable to be a wife emotionally to Paudie because of loving another, she, nonetheless, respected him enough to hate the deceit. She was certain that her love for Maurice was sincere, steadfast and pure in form, and not some transitory lust. Given a free choice without consequences, she would have chosen Maurice over Paudie in a heartbeat. Maurice met her needs in ways Paudie was incapable of; not out of any spitefulness, she acknowledged; simply ineptitude.

Enough of all that — she cannot think about it anymore — it is all too disturbing. Swinging her legs out of the bed, she decides to have a shower and brush her teeth while she still has the facilities. Returning to the room, she finds a bowl of cooling porridge and even colder tea. With a rabid appetite, she devours them.

Her Friend is keen to get back to work, 'how did your relationship with Maurice move on?'

It moved on because she made it.

Several events changed her outlook on life.

One was Vera's death. Her mother's funeral so relatively soon after Billy's brought the fragility of existence uppermost in her thoughts. The realisation that no amount of prudent planning could prepare her for the unexpected turns of life became clear. With both her parents dead, she was no longer able to describe herself as someone's child. She was a senior member of the family now and this led to thinking about her future. Vera's experience demonstrated that youth was no guarantee of good health. Questioning whether she had attained her life goals, she doubted that she had lived the life she had imagined for herself. Had the anticipated privileges of adulthood turned out to be as good as she had hoped? Had she really made best use of her resources and life opportunities?

The other major life event had been Daithí coming out as Gay. Respecting his desire for confidentiality, she had to come to terms with his disclosure on her own. Quizzing herself on how she had raised him before she understood better, she gained some self-knowledge. Daithí reinforced her belief that life was too short to live as a lie. To not be true to oneself was a terrible waste of a life. After careful thought, she knew she had to initiate decisive action.

She is walking the cliff tops with Maurice by her side and feels contented being in the presence of her greatest love within a beautiful setting. A gentle breeze skips towards them over the sea and the warm sun plays hide and seek with the clouds. Luxuriating in the moment, she feels life could not get much better. Then a jolting shove from her conscience pushes her from her idyll. The dark realities lurking in the wings of her mind fill front of stage. The brightly illuminated facts stare out at her and she is the captive audience.

Stopping abruptly on the path, she turns to face him, 'Maurice, I can't go on like this — I'm completely tormented. I don't know which way to turn — I don't want to be with Paudie, I want to be with you. But you're married — I'm married — and I have kids. It's an impossible situation and it's half destroying me. I want to be with you all the time. I feel I only half exist when I'm not with you. I just don't know what to do,' tears of desperation fill her eyes.

Gripping her shoulders and looking into her eyes earnestly, 'Ruth, I do understand what you're saying and I agree with you — it's the same for me. I don't love Gwen; I only pity her. My life only has meaning when I'm with you, too.' Pulling her towards him, 'from the moment I first set eyes on you at Nora's, I knew that you were the woman I should have married. I want to spend the rest of my life with you. I want some happiness,' despair in his voice.

The threatening tears spill down her cheeks, 'oh Maurice, what can we —?'

Interrupting her, 'listen to me, this is important — would you ever leave Paudie, Ruth? Leave him for me?'

Pulling away slightly to read his face and without hesitation, 'yes, I would leave Paudie for you. But I couldn't leave my children — not 'til they've finished school and flown the nest.'

'I know that — I know you well enough. But what if we were to set up a home together, one that included them? Would you do it then?'

Reacting instantly as though her unconscious mind has already thought about this possibility and made a decision, 'yes — yes, I would; but only if they were happy to leave their father and join us.' Pausing to think, 'or we could share custody like other separated couples.'

'Good!' with relief, 'you agree in principle. But would you be prepared to do it in stages? What I'm driving at is, could you move in here with me straight away and leave the children at River House for a few months? Let me explain — that three bedroom house I'm doing up as an investment property, the one I'm planning to rent out, could we all move into that? When its finished? The children could live with us there until they leave home. Then we could move away, set up a new life somewhere else, if that's what we wanted.'

'But what about Gwen?'

'It would release her. It would allow her to go back to London — to where she'd be happier. Or perhaps Swansea, even — it'd be up to her. She's not happy here with me — I know that much.'

Needing to confirm, 'Maurice, are you saying to leave on my own — move in with you now? Into the cottage — leave the children at River House?' unable to mention Paudie's name.

'Yes, that's exactly what I'm saying. As soon as you can.'

'But what would we do for money? I'd have to give up the pharmacy — I wouldn't be able to work there anymore.'

'You don't have to worry about that, Ruth. I've more than enough — I've enough to give Gwen a good settlement. And as to us, I've been thinking that we could set up a joint venture. An interior design and building company using your artistic flair and my practical knowledge. I think we could make a real go of it. But if you didn't want to do that, it wouldn't matter — I can earn more than enough for all of us.'….

A polite knock followed by a slow opening of the door and Paudie enters the room.

Shaken from her reverie, she is startled that it is him, of all people, especially at that time of the day. Sharply, 'Paudie! Why aren't you at the shop?'

'Don't worry, darling, Lisa's covering for me. I've done all the morning scripts and the Saturday afternoon Caredoc clinic isn't open until after lunch. How are you?'

She tells him the news of her imminent move to the shared ward.

Paudie is indignant, 'that's terrible — I'm going to get straight on to the VHI first thing Monday morning. We've paid a king's ransom in premiums over the years. The least you should have is a private room.'

'It doesn't matter, Paudie — really, I don't mind. If some unfortunate person needs the room more than me, it's only fair. Anyway, you shouldn't be leaving Lisa on her own, you know she's not covered by insurance when you're off the premises.'

'Look, she's not going to issue any new ones until I get back, she knows the craic. You shouldn't be worrying about the shop anyway.'

'Of course I worry about the shop. I'm still a partner in the business, you know!'

'Yes, Ruth, I am aware of that — but not for much longer.'

Sinking her eyes into a deep frown, 'excuse me? Say that again. What do you mean by that exactly, Pádraic O'Sullivan?'

'That's why I'm in early today — to see you on your own before the girls and their other halves start traipsing in. Ruth, I've great news for you. I'm so excited. That's why I've been going to the golf club — it's been to negotiate with a prospective buyer. That call that came in last night, it was for a meeting to discuss the sale. I didn't want to say anything in front of Deidre as I wanted to tell you first. But I had to hurry off to meet with them and receive their offer in person — shake hands on it.'

Snapping closed her dropped jaw, then waving a hand, 'Paudie, you've lost me. What exactly are you talking about?'

With glee on his face, 'I've sold the shop!'

Shaking her head with disbelief, 'No, no — I don't understand, Paudie. Why on earth would you want to sell the shop? You're not due to retire, yet? What are you talking about, Paudie? You haven't even discussed it with me!'

'I don't want to work in the pharmacy anymore, Ruth. I've been thinking about it a lot lately. I want to spend as much time as I can with you. I wouldn't let you come back to the shop even if you were well enough to — it wouldn't be right after all you've been through. And because I only want to be with you, it means I have to leave the shop too. I can only ever function when you're close by. It's always been that way for me. I only want to do whatever you want to do — whatever makes you happy. I don't want to be taken away from you by

263

other things; distracted from you by business and work. I want us to enjoy our time together — forever, with whatever time we both have left.'

'Hmm — I think that's a bit rash,' not at all sure about this turn of events.

'No, it's not. I've been thinking about it long and hard since your relapse. Life's too short, it's a cliché I know. But it's also a truism for good reason. You need to start doing some of the things you've always wanted to do. And selling the business means we can do them together,' beaming at her.

Chapter 22

After Paudie leaves, her Friend and her look at each other in silence while the dust from the exploding bombshell settles.

'Hmm, that's a most interesting development — so, what are your thoughts on that one, Ruth?'

Complete and utter shock.

The last thing she ever expected Paudie to do, is give up his main source of income. The business is the most significant part of his life. He has the ponies, but she has always thought it was work that kept him going. It is what gives him a function, a role in life; provides him with status. And with her uncertain health, it seems folly to give up the one thing that gives him structure and a routine to his life. But it is not too late. The papers still have to be co-signed by her. Thankfully, there is still time to talk sense into him. Nonetheless, it is nice to think that he would give it all up for her and do the things she has always wanted. The fact that he has offered is a nice, selfless gesture. She has to credit him with that.

'Let's go back to that other time when you seriously considered doing something you really wanted.'

Oh yes, THAT occasion.

That time when she was prepared to give up her marriage; her established business and reliable income; even her children, possibly; her good reputation; everything of importance to be with the man who was making her, frankly ecstatic! The discussion on the walk concluded with an agreed date for four weeks later. On that day, they would leave their spouses, and move into the cottage together.

In the meantime, fired with a sense of urgency, she went through all her possessions and culled them to an absolute minimum. Needing to travel light with several relocations planned for the near future, she also wanted to leave no painful reminders for Paudie. The local charity shops benefitted greatly from her largesse and the busyness kept her from dwelling on the outrageousness of her intentions. Like her, Maurice launched into making preparations. He tidied up his home with Gwen doing outstanding repairs and giving it a thorough clean. He bought in plenty of provisions and batch cooked lots of dinners, putting them in the freezer for her. Over at the house they would later move into, he worked late into the night to speed up the process. During their interim Sunday together, they excitedly finalised the plans in more detail. They talked and planned their future with great optimism, and she had rarely felt so happy….

The trolley comes into the room with Naomi trailing behind. In silence, she takes the cover off a plate and places it on the table along with other courses, then rearranges dishes on the trolley, seemingly in no hurry to finish her round.

Hesitating, she asks 'Naomi, can I ask you something personal?' Then without waiting for permission, 'do you like working here? I mean do you enjoy it? Is it a nice job?'

Without emotion, 'yes, Mrs O'Sullivan, it is,' Naomi follows the trolley back out the door again.

Pulling some roast chicken apart, she recalls the last few days leading up to her departure. Like Maurice, she made sure everything was up to date with nothing left for her spouse to do for a while. She predicted Paudie's reaction would be fairly limited based on how far they had grown apart; the fact their sex life was non existent, and the incessant low level sniping and bickering that constituted conversation between them. He would be largely unaffected by her departure. Convincing herself further, she thought he would probably be relieved she had made the first move; to end a marriage reduced to a sham. She realises now how much this echoed Maurice's rhetoric about his marriage to Gwen. How much had Maurice and her developed the same narrative to suit their own selfish ends?

With regards the children, she planned to meet them the following day after her departure. Wanting to talk with them on neutral ground, she decided to do it at Irina's after school.

She needed to explain to them that she was not leaving them, just their father, and that there would be a home for them with her shortly. Prepared that one, or more of them might opt to live with Paudie, she was willing to make the sacrifice if absolutely necessary.

When The Day arrived, she cooked the usual Sunday fry. As soon as the other four left for the stables, she raced upstairs and threw her slimmed down wardrobe into some large new cases she had kept concealed in the back of the estate car. On the way out, she propped an envelope addressed to Paudie on the dining table and left her home for the last time. All the years of yearning and the final acquisition of her dream home no longer seemed important. If she ever returned, she accepted it would no longer be hers….

Naomi returns for the plates and places a cup of tea on the table. She leaves again without uttering a word.

Her Friend looking agog wants to know more, 'what was in the envelope, Ruth?'

Dear Pádraic,
I'm writing to let you know I'm leaving you.
This marriage isn't working for either of us.
I know you're not happy and I'm not either.
I'm going to live somewhere near but not local.
I won't be coming to the shop anymore.
I don't want to embarrass you.
We can sort out the details later.
I won't be taking the children with me.
The place I am going to is not big enough.
I'm going to move somewhere else soon.
Then they can join me only if they want to.
I am sure we can work out a custody arrangement.
Please don't try to contact me.
I will meet with you to finalise things when you
have time to get used to everything.
I hope we can keep things friendly.
I wish you all the best, Ruth

Looking backing, she cannot believe how inadequately written, how cold and callous that letter must have seemed; how stupid and naive she was. Her cheeks flare up in shame and she wipes a tear with a tissue.

Driving out of town, she remembers the overwhelming sense of relief from what was being left behind. Balnarath had been her home for a long time, but she was ready to live somewhere new. Only its shortcomings were uppermost in her mind. The petty parochial politics; the more unpleasant characters; only ever considering it a place to do business and not actually enjoy. Pulling up at the cottage, Maurice had not arrived yet so this gave her time to take in her cases and start unpacking….

The door shoots open and in come Deidre and Marcus followed by a hobbling Sophie. At the rear, Seánie carries Sophie's handbag. After kissing her on the cheek, Seánie makes his excuses to go off to hurling training. Originally intending to tell the children Paudie's news, now faced with them, she decides against it. Envisioning Deidre's excessive emotiveness and Sophie's flaw finding, she feels incapable of containing their neediness. Requiring more time, she views it more Paudie's plan and not hers. She is not committed to it. For once, he can take on the responsibility of dealing with his own children's reactions. She lets them lead the discussions and enjoys listening to the minutiae of their week thus far.

Noticing that Marcus has retreated from the female dominated conversation, 'so Marcus, tell me, how do you feel about being a daddy?'

Looking caught out, Marcus mutters, 'umm — yeh — should be good.'

Knowing the reticence of Irish men only too well, she probes further, 'ready to take on the challenge, so?'

'Umm — yeh — it'll be grand, I'd say.' Grand being a word frequently used to cover all eventualities from nirvana to devastation, she knows it is meaningless in this context.

Trying to empathise with his position, 'it'll be a massive change, mind. In any relationship, it's very easy to pull apart in times of stress. Try and pull together instead, would you both?

When you get through the child rearing stage, you'll get your lives back, I promise.'

'Yeh — right — umm, thanks, Ruth,' looking at the clock. 'Dee, we'd better get going. Can we give you a lift, Sophie? Save Seánie a trip?'

'Thanks, Marcus — but no. Seánie's helping me with the supermarket shop — with the leg and all.'

Marcus and Deidre leave with promises to return the next day.

Noticing that Sophie looks uncomfortable, 'do you want to see if Seánie can come for you now? He might just be chatting with his friends.'

'No, I'll wait until he's ready. I like to give him his space.'

'You're a wise woman, Sophie. It's important to not lose your sense of self in a relationship. Make sure you mind yourself and don't give everything to your partner and children. It's not sustainable otherwise.'

'Is that what you did, Mammy?' twiddling with the toggles on the cords of her hoodie. 'Did you sacrifice yourself to Daddy and us?' a look of anguish suddenly filling her face.

'Look, Sophie, I know there's something on your mind — do you want to tell me about it?'

Seánie's large frame fills the doorway. 'Well? I'm back. You ready Sophs?'

'Sophie, come back and see me early tomorrow — before the others. Please,' imploring her daughter with her eyes not wanting to disclose too much in front of Seánie.

Sophie understands her mother's non-verbals, nods and shuffles to the front of the seat. Seánie walks over to give her a hand up and passes the crutches to her with his other broad hand. With brief adieus, they both leave.

Her Friend taking the vacated armchair is determined to press on, 'what happened when Maurice arrived at the cottage?'

Oh. That. Well, if you insist.

After checking what closet space is available, she stacks piles of clothing on the bed in readiness. Beginning to feel concerned about his delay, she is relieved to hear Maurice's van pull up. She rushes into the main room full of joyous anticipation. Through the wide open door at the far side, she watches him plod heavily up the vestibule. She sees his face and knows something is wrong; something terribly wrong.

Her stomach sinks in dread and her voice box constricts. In a tone, high pitched with anxiety, 'Maurice?'

'I'm sorry, Ruth,' shaking his head. 'I'm so, so sorry,' he comes over and clasps her upper arms. 'I can't do it — I just can't do it. Look, come over here — let's sit down,' leading her to the sofa. 'I can't abandon Gwen — she's just too vulnerable. And I don't want to be responsible for breaking your family up either — I couldn't live with myself. I'm so sorry.'

'But, but — I love you, Maurice.'

'Yes, darling — yes, I know. I'm so sorry to do this to you — please, can you —?', shaking his head and looking down, then up again. 'No, I can't ask that of you. But — one day — I hope you'll find it in you to understand and forgive me.'

All she can remember is flashbacks of Maurice loading her things into her car. Somehow she got back to River House. She must have driven herself as she arrived alone. Thankfully, she knew the house was empty — she desperately needed space alone. Like a wounded animal, she staggered through the front door. Walking through the house in a daze, she knew she needed water for her parched throat and went down to the dining room.

Paudie was there. Slumped in an armchair with one long leg bent, the other stretched out in front, his arms dangled over the chair sides. Her letter lay opened on his lap. His ashen face and hollow eyes stared at her. She froze, not quite sure what she was seeing.

His voice crackles, 'you've come back. Thank God, you changed your mind, Ruth. You've come back home.'…

Her pain is broken by a soundless figure entering the room.

'Some birthday cake for you, Mrs O'Sullivan, from Mrs Cleary', Naomi brings over a piece of sponge cake with a cream and jam filling, covered in sticky white icing. Distracted, a new image emerges — one of a vacant *Marie Celeste* floating in a dense sea fog. She watches Naomi drift silently out again. Absentmindedly forking up the cake, she has no appetite, but the soft, sweet mush assuages her sadness. She understands all about comfort eating.

'Comfort eating? Was that how you got over your broken heart, my love?', her Friend looks at her with eyes full of compassion.

No, on the contrary, she lost an excessive amount of weight.

Partly it was the grief of losing her parents and Maurice. But mainly it was the overwhelming sense of guilt. She caused so much pain for Paudie, she believed that she did not deserve to live. It was a form of self punishment to deny herself food for both nourishment and enjoyment. Feeling unworthy of existence, her subconscious aim was to fade away to nothing; not even leave behind a shadow.

Along with intense shame, she felt deeply humiliated. In a cruel act of irony, Maurice had an envelope for her too. He put it in her handbag before closing the passenger door whilst seeing her off the premises. Opening it later, she found a poem copied from one his favourite Brian Docherty books. She surmised it was his way of expressing his feelings. In addition, there was a cheque for a substantial amount of money with a note clipped to it, saying it was to cover any expenses she may have incurred. The cheque was immediately ripped up in indignant anger. She felt he regarded her as little more than a concubine at best and at worst, a casual sex worker. Now she wonders if it was him atoning for his actions.

For the next year or so, she went through a period of what could be classed as reactive depression. Barely operating above automaton level, the restrictive and reliable routine of work and family life was good for her. It kept her mind and body fully occupied; giving the emotional pain time to subside. Sundays were the most difficult days. To Paudie's credit, he recognised her sadness and loneliness, perhaps presuming it to be over the loss of her mother. He began to deal with the horses promptly while she dragged herself out of bed, subsumed in the black cloud enveloping her. Then he would take them all out for Sunday lunch, afterwards going for a drive into the mountains for a short hike, or off to the beach. He made few demands of her.

Her Friend strokes his beard thoughtfully, 'how else did Paudie react?'

He had not reacted in any obvious way at all.

He never once asked her anything about that Sunday, nor what the letter was about. The state of their marriage was never referred to. Doubts about her fidelity were never alluded to either. It was as though it had never happened. She is not sure if he ever suspected her having an affair and if so, with whom. In fact he continued to call upon Maurice to do repairs so she could only assume he did not know. Obviously she avoided Maurice at those times and went directly to tradesmen like plumbers and electricians whenever possible.

Maurice made no attempt to contact her which helped greatly for her to recover from the debacle. As far as she knows, he remained with Gwen until she took her own life a year or so before she herself, became ill. Feigning sickness, how prescient she now realises, she sent Paudie to represent the family at the funeral. Her feelings by that time were fully resolved and she only felt sympathy for Maurice over his loss.

Contemplating her life with Paudie now, she acknowledges that he has changed over the intervening years. There is a maturity to him now and he is a little less self centred. After their minuscule separation and she had passed through her depressive illness, he encouraged her to do things for herself, like the Festival Committee, and resume her health and exercise routines. Truth be told, there was some sort of coming together between them. Maybe relinquishing the business would be beneficial. Give them the opportunity to spend more quality time together. Perhaps rekindle that flame of love from their earlier years. She knows she is capable of great passion. Could Paudie become the recipient? Who knows? Maybe their marriage might strengthen….

A familiar knock and Paudie appears for his usual evening visit. He comes over to her chair to kiss her on the cheek as normal, offering greetings as he walks.

To his surprise, Ruth stands as he approaches and when close enough, she puts her arms around his neck and kisses him fully on the mouth. He is startled, momentarily pulls back, but then relaxes with delight, taking the opportunity to give a long kiss back. He pulls her closer so that their bodies can embrace each other; rediscover territory they have not explored for a long while. He nibbles her earlobe and moves down to kiss her neck. She finds her nipples tightening and her vulva waking up from a long sleep. Although realistic about where they are, to her amazement, she feels reluctant to pull away. The adult in her knows she has to.

'Good Lord, Mrs O'Sullivan, you haven't forgotten how to turn a man on, have you? Aren't I, the lucky one? Maybe I should have sold up years ago. If only I had known,' twinkling his eyes at her. Then motioning for them to sit down next to each other on the bed, 'look, I know you're not really convinced about my intentions to give up the business, Ruth. And I don't blame you. If it had even been hinted at a few months ago, I would have laughed at the idea myself.' Opening his blazer jacket, he pulls out a wad of folded sheets from the inside pocket. 'I called in to Maeve after I left you earlier to pick these up as proof that I really mean it,' unfolding and smoothing the papers, then giving them to her.

'What are these, Paudie?'

'Look at them and see — they're an itinerary and travel documents. Maeve has sorted it all out — booked everything for us.'

'Booked what? Itinerary for what?'

'Go on, take a look, will you? It's a trip for next month. It's all arranged — I've spoken to everyone including the doctors. We're going to Argentina! We're going to stay with Ramón and Bríd, among other things. Maeve's sorted out the best places to visit, hotels, connecting travel, the whole works.'

Looking at Paudie stupefied. After a moment or two, she begins to laugh. She tries to contain herself but cannot and has to laugh some more.

Paudie is taken aback, 'what's so funny about that, Ruth? I thought you'd be absolutely delighted. Instead you sound — I don't know — like you're not taking it seriously. You always wanted holidays — to travel abroad — didn't you?'

'Paudie, I do, I do,' trying to rein in her mirth. 'Of course, I'm delighted — I am, of course.' Trying to appease him, 'I really am so grateful you've done this. I think I'm just blowing off a safety valve, you know — after everything.' Her face falls into a more solemn expression. 'But, I have to say, the first holiday you've picked for us,' starting to giggle again. 'Just happens to involve polo and horses — ha, ha, ha!'

Looking sheepish, Paudie clears his throat, and has to laugh too. 'well, I'm not really used to traveling, you see. I just thought it might be safer the first time to stay with people we already know.'

Then the realisation hits her. Why has she never seen it before? Finally, she understands a crucial missing piece about the inner workings of her husband. God love him, he is afraid. He has never had the courage to leave the safety of Ireland. Taking his hands in hers, 'Paudie, it's okay — it's okay — there's no need to apologise. I LOVE the idea —it's just what I'd have chosen myself.'

Later on her own, she closes the Atlas satisfied that she understands exactly where Argentina is. Leaning over, she opens the locker drawer and retrieves the Filofax. Flipping to the back, she unzips the secret pocket and pulls out the sheet of paper folded into a small rectangle. Opening it, she reads it again for the first time in years.

ALMOST VALENTINE'S DAY AGAIN
by Brian Docherty

Last night you graced one of my dreams,
and we were happy together, lying on a
beach holding hands in the dusk, using
our free hand to count the stars above us.

You knew the constellations, pointed out
the Pole Star, 'ah yes, the sailor's friend';
we agreed our ancestors were mariners
who would take their bearings by that star.

We were glad there was no light pollution,
no-one else near us, no chatter or music
from a restaurant, we needed no soundtrack
for this moment in our perfect bubble.

I'm sure we had dinner earlier, a bottle
of decent wine, I gave you flowers
and a small gift, everyone smiled at us,
treated us as friends and not tourists.

Wherever we were, it wasn't British
or February, perhaps Lesbos or Milos,
the end of a special day together, the air
warm around us, even the birds asleep,

we were the only people truly awake,
our love an energy field to sustain us,
and we agreed the number of stars
was always one less than infinity.

Folding the paper carefully along its original creases, she then screws it up tight. Going over to the bin, she puts her foot on the pedal. The lid pops up and she drops the small ball. With a sigh of satisfaction, she lets the lid fall down with a loud bang.

'That was an unusual display of affection towards Paudie, Ruth. Have your feelings towards him changed, would you say?' As she has come to expect, her Friend has missed nothing and wants explanations.

Easing herself into the chair next to him, she leans back feeling relaxed.

It is no big deal really.

Yes, Paudie has been a horse's arse for most of their marriage, but he is basically a decent fella. She could have done a lot worse. Maybe her life would have been more fulfilled with someone like Maurice, but look what a disappointment he turned out to be. He led her along in some fantasy world that almost destroyed her family and even possibly herself. Never brave enough to sort out things with Gwen on his own, he was going to use her as a parachute to get out of his unsatisfactory situation. Jump from one desirable woman to another. She can class herself as that now. And Gwen had been one before Maurice had got hold of her; and then forced her to do what he wanted. He never did the one thing that could have made Gwen happy — let her have a choice between going home, or staying with him. Maybe they could have had a long distance relationship; air travel between Ireland and the UK had become easy and cheap as chips by that time; who knows? Or split his time between two locations, working different projects, one at a time. Or had extensive holidays back in Ireland. Lots of couples do it. But did he ever explore the options?

Back to Paudie, yes he has been a lazy feck a lot of the time, but he has always carried on providing for them. And he is a product of his upbringing. Now he wants to make amends. She can forgive him. And feeling at peace about it, she does believe it is a genuine forgiveness. She has been no angel herself, but somehow she feels forgiven; and she wants to pass that pardon onto him, too. The marriage has survived her bad behaviour and his.

The next morning, Naomi comes in to collect her empty breakfast dishes and almost collides with Dr Ghebremariam entering on her way out. He apologises, but Naomi barely registers him.

Smiling shyly as he renegotiates his entry into the room, she puts him at ease, 'hi, Dr Gabriel — that was close — I could almost see you two needing beds here yourselves,' jesting. 'How nice to see you — I didn't realise consultants worked weekends.'

'We have to in Oncology, Mrs O'Sullivan — but we rotate with other teams. It's my turn this weekend. Do you mind if I examine you?'

'Not at all, doctor, work away. And please, do call me Ruth.'

The doctor gently and solicitously checks her over thoroughly, and asks an extensive range of questions. She considers it the most thorough check up she has ever had. 'Your bloods are very good,' looking at her chart. 'And all your other signs have been improving steadily. 'Shall I show you these graphs?'

'No, you're fine, doctor — I believe you. I was never one for maths and figures.'

Gabriel smiles at her protestations. 'Okay, I have one final question for you, Ruth — how would you feel about going home? Let's say, all being well, after your infusion tomorrow morning. You can then return as a day patient for the subsequent ones. I don't think you need to be in here any longer, do you?'

She is shocked, 'if you think it would be alright, doctor?'

No sooner has the doctor walked out, Sophie and Seánie appear. Making his excuses, Seánie says he will go to the carwash, get diesel and call back afterwards.

'Mammy, what's the matter? You're being very quiet. Are you annoyed with Seánie for going off?'

In a stupor, she fills Sophie in on her unexpected discharge home, '…I really can't believe it.'

'That's amazing news, Mammy! Will I text Daddy and get him to bring in some clothes for you for the morning?'

'No thank you, pet — I better tell him myself.' Giving herself a good shake internally, she needs to focus on other important business. 'Now, before anyone else turns up, let's talk. Come on, what's been at you? I know it's something to do with me and your father. Please tell me, will you?'

'Oh — I don't know Mammy,' sliding the zip on her fleece top up and down. 'I don't know if I should — it's probably not that important now — maybe I should let it drop — it was such a long time ago — I don't know really, Mammy.'

'Sophie for God's sake, just TELL me — go on, go for it, girl.'

'Okay, maybe I will. It was just that day — you know the one, when Daddy, Daithí, Dee Dee and me had been at the stables and we came home early. Daddy said he was worried about you. He thought you might be sick as you hadn't looked right that morning — that we should go home straight away and mind you.' Sophie starts to look stricken, but carries on. 'But you weren't at home when we got back. Daddy was worried when he saw the car gone. I thought you'd gone shopping. Then you came home soon after. I was in the front room and I saw you walk past and go down into the dining room. I got up to follow because I wanted to ask you something. I heard Daddy say that you had decided to come back, to come back home. And I thought that was a weird thing to say because you'd only been out for some shopping, or something. I didn't go in straight away, I went into the study because Flossie was scraubing at the wood on the wall and I knew you'd go apeshit if you knew. When you and Daddy weren't in the dining room anymore, I went on down and I saw a sheet of paper lying on the floor. So I picked it up and read it. And in it, you said you were leaving Daddy but you wouldn't be taking us three. Is that true, Mammy, were you going to leave us?' staring at her mother intensely.

Astounded, she does not know what to say; how honest she should be. How to explain the misunderstanding Sophie has carried for all these years. If it was Daithí, she would feel safe enough to disclose the whole story. He would not judge her, she is certain. Dee Dee would see her point of view as she knows how intolerable her father can be. But Sophie? There is a brittleness to Sophie, an emotional fragility. Cogitating the dilemma rapidly, she decides it will serve no purpose for Sophie to know all the sordid details.

'Sophie, I went through an unhappy period in my marriage with your father. Yes, I did decide to leave him, but I returned again after a few hours. I think you misread the letter. In it I wrote I couldn't bring you three with me that day as the place I was going to live in temporarily was too small. But I was going to move into a bigger place soon after and the plan was for you to join me then. I was going to tell you in person the next day after school. It had all been arranged.' Pausing to observe Sophie's reaction, 'I am so sorry you've been carrying this burden around with you all these years. Did you never talk to anyone about it?'

Sophie shakes her head.

Elaborating some more, 'it was a mistake I made and one I bitterly regret. I don't know what more I can say, really. People do stupid things. I was unhappy and I thought it was the solution. But it didn't work out that way. I realised, eventually, it wouldn't have been the right thing to do.'

'Did Daddy get over it?'

'To be perfectly honest, I don't know. We've never talked about it. But we're still together, aren't we?'

Seánie reappears at the door, 'hi folks, everywhere was dead so it's been quicker than I expected. You ready now Soph's?' Looking at Sophie and then at her, 'hey, am I disturbing you? Will I go away and leave you two to talk?'

'No, Seánie, I'm coming now. Just give me a hand up, will you?'

Hobbling over, Sophie kisses her on the cheek, her eyes shining with tears. 'Thanks, Mammy — thanks for that.'

After Sophie departs, emotions wash over her body; a melange of enlightenment, release and a strange sense of freedom. Intense, but draining, her eyes feel heavy and she needs to sleep.

The boots reverberated down the hall. His imminent arrival expanded her heart, reducing her capacity for breath. Light-headed, she watched the door handle turn. In moments, she would be in his arms again. The rattling handle released the sticky catch and the door swung open. And there, stood in the doorway, was her greatest love. Shod in shiny black riding boots was Paudie.

Startled awake by voices in the corridor, she plumps up her hair and adjusts her dressing gown. In file, Deidre carrying a large white cake box, followed by Marcus carrying bags and then Paudie last.

She smiles broadly at her family and excitedly bids them find seats. After much ohing and ahhing at a buttercream cake in the box, Paudie goes to find a knife, plates and forks. After they each have a generous slice, Paudie suggests, 'so we'll ask the nurses if you can keep the rest of the cake in their fridge — then you can eat it during the week.'

'There's no need for that.'

'You're hardly going to eat it all today, Ruth? Or are you?' his eyebrow raised.

'No, I can take my time sharing it with you all at home.'

Deidre cuts in, 'at home? How are you going to manage that, Mammy?'

'After my treatment in the morning, I've decided I'm outta here!' thumbing over her shoulder. 'Sick of the place, I am.'

Deidre looks horrified, Marcus straightens up enthralled by this act of rebellion and Paudie jumps in, 'absolutely not, Ruth. That would be extreme folly. I cannot possibly allow it —.'

Ruth feels her temper rising, 'sorry to inform you of this, Paudie, but it isn't actually up to you,' and glares at him. Then relents as she knows he has her best interests at heart. Looking at him with a softer expression, 'they are letting me go.'

Deidre in a panic, 'it's not because the treatment isn't working, is it , Mammy? They're not saying it's too late or anything?'

Realising she has to come clean, 'no, no, pet. Nothing like that. On the contrary, its because I'm so well — I don't need to be in hospital.'

A moment of silence while everyone digests this information, then Paudie jumps up, 'what?! — that's incredible news, darling! What time will I collect you tomorrow? I won't bother bringing you any clothes — I'd only bring the wrong outfit — don't bother getting dressed — come home as you are. And while we're talking about good news, I have more to tell you both,' sitting and turning to Deidre and Marcus. 'Your mother and I,' looking over at her, she nods an assent. 'Your mother and I have sold the shop.'

Deidre shouts, 'no way!! Daddy, you're not — that's BRILLIANT news, it's about time you and Mammy retired.'

'And to celebrate, we are going on a trip to South America like your Aunt Mairéad,' looking triumphant.

'What!! That's an AMAZING thing to do, Daddy, Mammy! What date do you fly out? Will you need jabs? Will you have enough time?…'

After despatching Deidre with the remains of the cake to give to the ward staff and Marcus likewise with bags of chocolate and fruit from her locker, she turns to Paudie. 'Mr O'Sullivan, we're going to have a splendid retirement, you and I. Don't be thinking there's going to be any scrimping, mind — money WILL be spent — we're going to really enjoy ourselves.'

Grinning boyishly, 'I know that. And funnily enough, I'm really looking forward to it.'

Later she sorts through the room to gather her belongings ready for the next day. She has no intention of delaying a minute longer than necessary. Refolding spare sets of pyjamas, she reflects on her stay in hospital and decides it has not been bad at all. But the most importantly thing, apart from getting better, has been the time and opportunity to think about her life. It has been a most surprising journey and it has enabled her to change perspective and make amends.

Once in bed, she texts all the important people: Daithí, Irina and Maeve about her impending return home. Sighing with contentment, she turns off the bedside light and nestles into the rustling pillows for the last time. In no time at all, she is in a deep sleep.

'Ruth, wake up, please,' her Friend is gently rubbing her cheek. 'You have to get up now.'

Still dozy, she sits up in bed and lifts her legs over the side.

'Here give me your hand, I'll help you up.' Still holding her hand, 'come, come with me now, please.'

Standing by the bed, she looks down at her sleeping form, 'I don't understand. Where are we going?'

'I'm taking you home with me.'

'But it's too early — it's still dark outside — it's not morning yet.'

'I know that — but I am taking you with me to my home, sweetheart,' her Friend smiles at her kindly.

'But, I don't understand. I'm still lying down there on the bed, yet I'm up high — with you —has something happened to me?'

'Yes, Ruth — now is the time for you to come home with me.'

'But I'm well — I've been getting better — I've my own home —'

'No, Ruth, you were very sick.'

'No, no — you don't understand — the treatment. It's working — I'm getting better.'

'What treatment, Ruth?'

'The immunotherapy — you know — the drug trial.'

'No, Ruth, you weren't on any immunotherapy.'

'You mean —?' her voice trails away.

'Yes,' nodding at her, 'you were in the Control Group — the infusions were simply coloured saline.'

'But, what about the Prednisolone? The steroids?'

He shakes his head.

'What? I was in the Control Group for those, too?'

'Yes, my dearest — they were just sugar pills.'

'But I can't go yet — I haven't given Paudie his gold Rolex. It isn't being delivered until tomorrow.'

'That's okay, Ruth — he'll get it soon. When he feels able to open your post. He'll know you bought it for him — that you gave him a gift as a representation of your love.'

'Oh my Lord — so I really have to come with you — now?'

'Yes, my sweetheart, you do. But don't worry, there're lots of people I want you to meet and things I want to show you when we get there.'

'But what about everyone there?' turning away slightly and gesturing towards the room that is diminishing.

'Don't worry — they'll all come and join us in due course. The time will pass very quickly, I promise. You will be reunited again. Come on, Ruth, we have to go now.'

Epilogue

15th April, 2043
Sotherby's Auction Rooms,
London,
England.

'Bidders, we now move on to the Premium Lots; those significant items that generate additional interest amongst collectors of fine art and have extraordinary investment value. I see from my screen that a number of additional registered bidders have logged on.

As usual, bidding will be conducted in the international currency of the latest, or final country of residence for the artist. Please note the Currency Converter button at the bottom left hand corner of your screens. If you click on that, the last bid offered can be converted to your chosen Dealing Currency which, may I remind you, includes all international currencies, and all certified cryptocurrencies, including, iCash, GlobeEx and SoftTran. The rates are in real time and are generated by the International Monetary Exchange, regulated by the International Currency Regulatory Authority…

… and now Bidders, we move on to Premium Lot number 3: 'Sketch of a Sleeping Man', graphite on bleached paper by Ruth Wilton. Complete with a signed inscription by the artist. Provenance authenticated. Subject: a line drawing of the artist's husband, Pádraic O'Sullivan, completed shortly before her death. I can disclose that the lot is being sold by the estate of Pádraic O'Sullivan, late husband of Ruth Wilton and has remained in the possession of the said Pádraic O'Sullivan. A rare opportunity to acquire a piece by this sought after artist…

…The sale will be conducted in Euro as Ruth Wilton was a resident of the Republic of Ireland…

…Please locate the Paddle button on the centre, right of your screens. For this item, bids will increase in increments of 50,000 Euros…

…I will begin with an opening bid of 500,000 Euros — do I have any takers? Thank you. 550,000, any offers — thank you…

…One million Euros. I have an offer for one million Euros. Do I have a further bid….'

Extract from the online version, The Sunday Times Culture supplement, dated July 2043.

" …with all the excitement generated at the Auction I wanted to find out more about this enigmatic artist. Looking at her portfolio Ruth Wilton's output ebbed and flowed throughout her lifetime. Periods of prodigious work are interspersed with more fallow periods. It must be assumed that other demands made upon her such as family responsibilities and business account for some of the paucity. But I was left wondering why there were other times of furious activity. Did The Muse come and go for this outstanding creative?…

…Much of Ruth's work has been collected by her son, the multiple Oscar winning Hollywood film producer, Daithí O'Sullivan. When interviewing his representative for the purposes of this article, they explained that items of Wilton's work have turned up regularly over the years in house clearances, charity shops and local auction houses, mainly within Ireland. This must have elicited much delight for owners learning their true value. The producer has gathered them together for public display by The Wilton Foundation, that prestigious organisation co-founded with his husband, Benjamin. They created the Earthsphere Museum and Gallery situated in los Angeles which houses permanent collections of modern and historic art. Wilton's renown 'Hospital Collection' is kept there — sketches of people the artist drew from her hospital bed. Requests for loan of Ruth's work for temporary exhibitions by principal galleries around the world come in frequently. When I asked if the Foundation had been the successful buyer of the latest sketch I was told no comment was being made at the present time…

…there has been much speculation over the drawing. Was it originally part of the 'Hospital' series? Dating seems to place it at that time. Why was it the only example of Ruth's work left in her husband's possession and why was it not passed on to his son for expert preservation upon his death? In an attempt to get answers to these questions and other puzzling aspects I sought a meeting with the second Mrs O'Sullivan. After some difficult and protracted negotiations I was granted an interview with Pádraic's widow Lisa. Although guarded in her responses she did disclose finding the portrait of her husband tucked between the pages of an old atlas. The atlas had originally belonged to the now demolished hospital where the artist spent her final days and somehow ended up in the O'Sullivan household library. The interview was ended abruptly when I brought up the subject of Daithí's curation. I was left with the distinct impression that relations are rather strained between Ruth's son and his father's second wife…"

Printed in Great Britain
by Amazon